THE WANDERER
AND THE
NEW WEST

ISBN: 978-0-9924629-5-6

Edited by Rachel Gluckstern and Jim Spivey

Cover design by Ben Mcleod

Interior formatting: Mark Thomas / Coverness.com

THE WANDERER
AND THE
NEW WEST

Adam Bender

~

Dedicated to Gary Zingher for igniting my fervor for action-adventures stories and for encouraging me to spin exciting tales of my own.

Special thanks to my spectacular wife Mallika, who happily reads my unpublished manuscripts and always gives her most honest opinions.

~

Table of Contents

A MISSION STATEMENT FOR THE NEW WEST

By New West Reporter

We live in a time of great individual freedoms. No government can tell us how to live our lives because we are free. In America, we are above the law.

We live in a time of great violence. Rob a bank, steal from a neighbor, murder a man who looks at you funny ... but do it at your own peril. The people are watching, and we know the difference between right and wrong. Stand your ground, but beware: in America, we make our own justice.

This is THE NEW WEST.

These pages chronicle a people unbound by law — their actions and the consequences. We print only the wildest truth.

CHAPTER ONE

The Parishioners Are Packin'!

The gazes of eighty-three Catholics swung from the priest to the back of the church, where a tall man in a cowboy hat stood with ready hands by his hips. He had dark brown hair and a stubbly chin speckled with salt, but he wore his wide-brimmed hat low and it was hard to make out his features.

Father James Hopkins broke from his sermon and gave the stranger a cold stare. The unknown man gasped somewhat sarcastically and stuck up his palms over the gray Stetson. The motion of his arms lifted his leather jacket high enough to reveal two handguns holstered around his waist — a Lassiter six-shooter on the left and a semiautomatic Breck 17 on the right.

Somewhere in the pews, a small child began to cry.

"I don't mean any trouble," the gunman said. There was a twang to his voice reminiscent of old Western movies.

Father James stole a glance at Ben Martin, who was twisted around like everyone else for a view of the stranger. The back of the sheriff's neck looked nearly as red as his plaid shirt, contrasting strongly with the gray sticking out the back of his Army hat.

"Truly," the gunman continued as he strode down the aisle,

"I am sorry to interrupt the solemnity of this fine house of God. However, there's a man I am looking for, and I believe he is here."

Martin bolted upright from his pew. "Who do you think you are, coming in here and making demands?"

Father James motioned for Martin to take his seat, then held out a welcoming hand to the gunman. "My son, why don't you join us? We can sort out whatever this is about after Mass."

The priest could feel the sheriff's burning glare. He tried to ignore it, tried to keep his eye contact firmly on the man with the guns.

The stranger dropped his hands and shook his head. "I ain't your son, Father. And I'm afraid this is something that just can't wait. See, I'm after a monster who done near took a girl's life. Goes by the name of Tom Jenkins."

Father James tried hard not to look at the teenager sitting in the front row, thinking it might give away the boy's location. "Now, listen here, stranger, I won't stand by while you make accusations against a member of our community! If he has done something wrong, by God we — and only we — will be the ones to cast judgment!"

"Beg your pardon, but I don't trust you will." The gunslinger leaned back on one leg and cast his smile like a dare. His right eye gleamed crimson. For an instant, Father James thought Satan himself might be in the church. Then he noticed the edge of a thin lens above the stranger's cheek and saw what had made the red glare — an augmented-reality display.

Martin snarled, "I believe I know you, *Wanderer*."

The suddenness of the conviction left Father James mute.

He wasn't the only one. The townsfolk, whose heads had been bouncing about like bobble-headed baseball stars, zeroed in on the sheriff's lips. Over the past year, they'd all heard tales of a vigilante called the Wanderer popping up in various places around the West, performing various good deeds such as stopping robberies and dueling with members of the Red Stripe Gang. Father James had thought the Wanderer was just a legend made up to make people feel a little safer.

However, this was almost certainly not the effect the Wanderer was having on Ben Martin. The sheriff pointed accusingly at the gunslinger and sneered. "You go from town to town startin' trouble. I heard you even set a man afire! Now you mean to start trouble right here in this holy place." Martin stood up again, jabbing his finger harder toward the Wanderer. "Well, if it's trouble you want, it's trouble you'll get."

*

The Wanderer stroked the warm ebony handle of his Lassiter revolver as the fat man with the rusty sheriff's badge pulled a double-barrel shotgun out from his seat. It appeared to be a six-year-old Pilgrim of the pump-action variety. Presumably, it had been kept tucked away in the back of a pew, right next to the *Book of Psalms*.

Neither man budged. A hushed silence filled the church. Then, one by one, the men and women around the church rose to their feet with guns of their own. The majority brandished Breck 17s.

The sudden rise to arms didn't surprise the Wanderer in the least. He had made Liberty his home for the past week. That was long by the standards of a man who felt most comfortable when he rode the train, but the dusty hamlet had deceived him with its fresh-swept streets and baked bread aromas. Yesterday afternoon, the thought had occurred that here might be a town he could stay for good — a place to stick the screaming past in a coffin and bury it alive. But violence caught up to him, like it always did, and now he knew that the white paint on Liberty's wooden porches merely disguised the same rot infecting the rest of America.

Leaving his own guns in their holsters, the Wanderer mocked, "Well, look at that! The parishioners are packin'!"

His cool disdain elicited more than a few confused looks. Finally, the sheriff stepped out into the aisle and stuck his Pilgrim smack in the Wanderer's face. "Now, look here! The name's Ben Martin. I've lived in this town for more than fifty years, been sheriff for nearly twenty, and I'll be *damned* if some outsider thinks he can just come in and shoot up the church! You must be some crazy —"

The Wanderer snatched the end of the shotgun and pushed it straight up to the ceiling. "No," he growled, "starting a gunfight in a church is crazy. In fact, if you ask your preacher, I'm sure he'd tell you it's a downright sin."

Taking advantage of the momentary attention, the priest called, "Everyone put down your guns! The Lord can stand his own ground!"

Martin looked as if he'd just been slapped across the face with a cold fish.

"Better do as your preacher says," smirked the Wanderer, releasing the tip of the shotgun.

Flushing an even deeper red, the sheriff let the Pilgrim drop to the floor. With frowns of great futility, most of the other armed men and women followed — all but one shaking teenager in the front row. The Wanderer spoke a single word under his breath: "Recognize."

Through his glass eyepiece, an electric green oval closed around the boy's face. A few seconds later, the message *ID CONFIRMED* flashed onto the screen.

"So, there you are, Jenkins," the Wanderer called, adding a friendly wave. "What say we avoid the Lord's wrath and take this disagreement outside?"

"According to you," said the teen, shakily raising his semiautomatic, "I'm goin' to Hell already."

A great boom echoed through the sanctuary, but the Wanderer slid neatly into cover behind a pew. Two more errant shots from the boy's Breck 17 whistled in ricochet off a column behind him.

A bubble of stunned silence burst into a dissonant roar of bellows and shrieks. The Wanderer pushed aside the bottom flap of his jacket with his left hand and took out the Lassiter, but a stampede of panicked churchgoers surging up the aisle blocked his aim. Ben Martin reached down to the sacred floor for his Pilgrim, but another parishioner's foot collided with the shotgun and sent it clattering away. The crowd pushed the whining sheriff up the aisle and out the door.

"Map," directed the Wanderer, and a diagram of the building layout appeared in his view. He saw two exits from the sanctuary — the main entrance behind him and a fire door located near the altar, close to where Jenkins had been sitting. They were connected by a hallway forming the perimeter of the sanctuary. With the crowd surging up the aisle, the main entrance seemed the safer bet, but he still had to find a way to squeeze into the herd.

He was just about to force his way when a big man with a ponytail stopped short and used his broad shoulders to hold back the crowd. People bounced against his back and fell off like a bunch of bowling pins. With a grateful tip of the hat, the Wanderer made his escape. He ran hard down the hallway but couldn't locate his quarry inside the church. Taking a hard right, he burst through a fire exit into white daylight.

The Wanderer caught just a glimpse of his prey shuffling toward the parking lot, but the sky burned so bright that he had to lower his hat for shade. When the sunspots finally faded, he saw Jenkins spinning around with his gun. In one swift circular motion, the Wanderer brought the silver Lassiter from his hip to point at Jenkins's chest.

*

A flagpole hoisted Old Glory between the two red-roofed bell towers of the Church of Santa Maria. Martin was catching his breath in front of the former mission's blue gates when two shots rang out. He waddled quickly toward the parking lot, passing Gerard Breck's smirking headshot on a banner announcing the Breck Ammunition traveling gun show. The congregation followed closely behind.

The sheriff found the Wanderer kneeling by a red pickup truck, head down as if he was in prayer. Tom Jenkins lay dead at the gunslinger's feet, surprise plastered on his young face.

"Everyone get back!" called Father James, circling around the herd.

Ben Martin stepped up to the preacher and pointed accusingly at the Wanderer. "He killed him! Just like that, he killed him!"

The gunman snatched the young corpse by the collar and folded him over the side of the truck's flatbed. Martin yelled, "How can you do this? He was just a boy!"

The Wanderer didn't even look up. "A piglet's still a damned *pig*, isn't he?"

"You're ... you're under arrest!"

"Heh. Under whose authority?"

Martin hesitated. He didn't have the fitness to take down a man like the Wanderer by himself. Turning around, he could see he didn't have support from the townsfolk, either. It was like there was an electric fence preventing them from getting anywhere close to the rogue.

"It was self-defense!" shouted one of the parishioners — Martin traced the voice to Jackson Veras. "Tom shot first!"

Martin got up so close in Jackson's face, actual droplets of spit materialized on the man's glasses when the sheriff yelled. "Who are you? His lawyer?"

"Don't start with me, Martin," sneered Jackson, stabbing the sheriff with his finger. "I've never seen this man before, either. But you know what I did see?"

"What?"

"A cowardly sheriff pointing a shotgun, and an honorable man protecting himself."

"An honorable man?" Martin pointed at the gunman. "Him?"

The Wanderer pushed the corpse of Tom Jenkins the rest of the way into the truck and, with the slightest of smiles, wiped the blood off his hands using a piece of the dead boy's shirt. It was all Martin could take. The sheriff charged, but Jackson got a grip around his waist and held him back, strong and tightly.

"Come, sheriff," wheedled Father James, approaching with one hand extended. "Come back into the church so we may finish the Mass. Let the bounty hunter finish what he —"

"Hey!" snapped the Wanderer. "I ain't no bounty hunter!"

Everyone shut up. A hot breeze sent a cloud of dust crackling into the bumper of the parked cars.

"There's a girl in the hospital named Sara Heller," he continued. "She was near death last night on account of this pig Jenkins, and if she remembers anything about last night, she just might wish she *was* dead. Sara's got a sister named Sharon keeping vigil by her bedside. You can ask her what Jenkins did, if you don't believe me, but don't forget to tell her what I done to that hog."

He spat into the flatbed, adding a wet exclamation point to the speech. The Wanderer turned his back on the parishioners and walked toward the sun.

"Hey!" called Martin, making a renewed push against the arms of Jackson Veras. "Where do you think you're going?"

The Wanderer took a few more steps and called back, without turning, "Wherever the track leads."

CHAPTER TWO

Was He Justified?

Rosa hovered over the keyboard with the intensity of a bull getting ready to charge. She was working on an infographic, a map of the state of Arizona. She had geographically plotted different-sized circles to represent the number of gun deaths in the past year. They had ballooned in the two cities in the lower half of the state, which was understandable given that they were population centers. In small towns, however, the number of town deaths didn't proportionally follow population. That was because the small towns with the biggest circles had experienced mass shootings in the last year. All involved the Yossarian assault rifle, a fully automatic weapon that could wipe out a crowd of people in under a minute. The one outlier seemed to be Union — a lot of deaths this year, but Rosa didn't remember any major shootings reported.

She scrunched her eyes and, after a moment, snapped her fingers. Of course! The Red Stripe Gang had taken Union. It might as well be a black hole now, at least where any news was concerned.

The Gang had taken over several towns around the country,

using them as bases after committing robberies and other crimes. The Red Stripers were named for their flag: an American flag without the blue square of stars — just thirteen red-and-white stripes. The Gang had started as a giant coalition of America's most dangerous motorcycle gangs, loosely held together by a belief in organized greed and debauchery. They had a predilection for drugs, gambling, violence, and motorcycles. The members were predominately white men — though there were some women, too — and many had ties to the neo-Nazis and the Ku Klux Klan. The Gang also attracted closet psychopaths who'd never done a bad thing when there'd been adequate law enforcement, but who now felt free to act their true selves. The Gang was large, organized, and attracted the worst elements of America — and no one seemed to have the cojones to do anything about them.

The reporter felt least confident about her data for the mountainous regions in northern Arizona, which showed very few gun deaths. Lower population, of course, but the numbers still seemed small. She wondered if it might come down to a limitation with her data — the fact that she only had information on *reported* gun deaths. With fewer witnesses and a wide-open wilderness for killers to hide bodies, perhaps many casualties went unreported.

In the end, though, it didn't really matter if she counted every single fatal shooting in the state. She had another map, exactly the same, but it was for the full year before Congress overturned the National Firearms Act and legalized sale of fully automatic rifles such as the Yossarian to consumers. There were still plenty of gun deaths, of course, but the circles looked like dots by comparison.

That was the real story right there — all the deaths skyrocketing after the legalization of the fully automatic rifle.

The doorbell chimed. Rosa cursed. The real world had once more invaded her solitude. She was sitting in her home office, originally the second bedroom. It was a one-story rancher, which meant that she could get to the door in seconds, but she didn't want to get up. Instead, she held her typing position, willing whoever was at the door to go away.

The visitor pounded. The reporter glanced at a small pot of dying basil on the windowsill. She visualized the words she'd spent hours cultivating wither away like the brown leaves of the herb.

"Hey, c'mon, Rosie! Open up!"

It was Jackson. Still, she hesitated …

"It's for *The New West!*"

That got her. She popped up from her chair and sprinted to the door. "What do you have?" she asked her brother, adding a hug as if an afterthought.

With a sly smile, he bounced past her into the ranch house and onto her sofa. He was still wearing his church clothes: a short-sleeved button-down and an ill-fitting pair of blue slacks. Even though he was now a father in his thirties — not to mention a lawyer, for God's sake — Jackson still looked as uncomfortable in nice clothes as he had when he'd been younger. Then there was his black mane. Even tied back into a ponytail, it was longer than her own shoulder-length haircut. Combined with the round glasses on his face, he was starting to look a lot like a hippy.

"How comes the writing of the great journalist, Rosa Veras?" he asked.

He was the only other person who knew about *The New West*. For some reason, she was deathly afraid of people finding out she was writing it, so she had been posting anonymously. It wasn't that she feared controversy. The whole point was to get away from the cut-and-paste journalism of her peers. But there was her day job to think about. She worked remotely for *Our Times*, the national newspaper based in Vegas. It was owned by Breck Ammunition, and as a result didn't actually publish much in the way of real news, at least not the kind of hard-hitting stuff that she wanted to write. But while she might not enjoy producing fluff pieces, that's where the money was, and she had to make a living somehow.

"I was on a roll until you showed up," she told Jack. "You shouldn't lie about having a lead —"

"There was a shooting at church!" he blurted.

Rosa stared wide-eyed at her brother. He looked okay — almost pleased. Sweeping a stack of takeout menus off the wooden coffee table by his knees, she picked up her tablet and created a new page in her notebook. "Are you all right? Tell me everything."

As he told her about the Wanderer and the confrontation with Tom Jenkins, Rosa began to picture a tall drink of water with a sombrero, stirrups, and a big silver gun. She checked the description with her brother.

"Not a sombrero," Jack corrected. "What's the hat the white cowboys always wear in the movies?"

"A Stetson?"

"Isn't that like a shoe?"

"No, stupid, that's a stiletto."

He seemed to think on that. "Stetson. Sure, maybe. Oh, and he had a glass over one eye — might've been AR!"

She raised her eyebrows. Augmented reality seemed like pretty expensive tech for your average gunman. Clearly, this Wanderer guy had found his way into some money. Maybe he'd held up a stagecoach.

"What's so funny?"

"Nothing," she said. "Wait, hold on, Jack. How were you close enough to see his eyes?"

Her brother eyed his shoes. It was an expression of guilt that he used to wear for their parents after forgetting to do his chores. "When everybody started running out of the building, the Wanderer was trapped. So, I ... stopped to let him out."

Rosa blinked in disbelief. "Wait, you helped the *gunman*? After what happened to —?" She covered her mouth, but the wounded look on his face showed the damage had been done. She rushed forward to hug him. "I'm sorry, Jack, but ... that was dangerous! I just ... don't want to lose you, too."

He smiled weakly. "I know. It was just ... there was something different about the Wanderer. He didn't just burst into the church shooting. He told everyone why he was there, who he had come for, and he didn't even take out his gun until Jenkins started firing. He held steady even after Ben Martin got all riled up! I mean, Jesus, anyone else would have shot that fat bastard."

She breathed thoughtfully. "Ben means well."

Jack rolled his eyes. He'd had a grudge against Ben Martin since they were kids and the sheriff came to arrest their father. Dad went to state prison with a life sentence, and they hadn't seen him in years. Their father was a passionate sports gambler who'd lost his head after losing a bet on the Super Bowl. A fistfight ended in a gun duel. He'd won the standoff, but lost everything else.

Rosa had come to believe her dad deserved the sentence, but Jack never doubted his innocence, always insisting that there had to be more to the story. She guessed that was a big reason that her brother began to practice law. The irony, of course, was that the very crime their father was imprisoned for had become commonplace in America. It just wasn't the kind of thing for which people got in trouble anymore. At the same time, there was no movement to retroactively exonerate the incarcerated.

After Dad went to prison, their mom tried to raise them on her own. But she soon turned to the bottle for company. Ben Martin began stopping by every few days to check in on them, usually with a greasy bag full of hamburgers and fries clutched between his fingers. He wasn't very good with kids, and Rosa assumed he was coming by mostly out of guilt. Jack resented him, but she'd always given him credit for trying.

"Look, Jack, I know how you feel about Martin, but why would you take the side of a lawless man? Aren't you supposed to be an attorney?"

The glass of Jack's circular frames magnified his eyes. "Yeah, that's right. A *defense* attorney."

She raised her eyebrows. "And here I thought Jenkins was the accused."

A little red entered his cheeks as he grinned. "Hey, can't a lawyer choose his cases?"

She laughed and turned to her tablet, tapping the stylus against the glass of the device as she read her notes. Rosa could swear she had talked to Tom Jenkins once for a story in *Our Times*, but for the life of her couldn't remember what it was about. Baseball, maybe? She knew he was still in high school. Rosa recalled slightly more about the Hellers, having written a piece earlier in the year about student council elections. Sharon was class president. Sara was popular, too, but only because she was blonde and bland.

Rosa asked, "So did this Wanderer say where he planned to wander next?"

"No, but if he's smart, he'll leave Liberty. Didn't see a car …"

She bit her lip to keep from laughing. "Maybe he had a horse?"

"Steady!" he replied with a grin. "Seriously, though, I bet he was headed for the train. But that was an hour ago — he's probably long gone."

*

The doorbell of the mayor's mansion responded to Martin's touch with the opening notes to "You're a Grand Old Flag." After a few thumps of his foot against the floorboards of the great white porch, he paced away from the west-facing entrance and looked out at the desert. The arid view offered a harsh contrast to Mayor Alex White's lush lawn.

The door clicked open — Martin swiveled around to face a butler in a dark brown suit. He had an arch to his gray eyebrows that gave him a look of permanent surprise. "Sheriff? To what do we owe the pleasure?"

"I need to see the mayor. Now."

"The mayor is engaged in a state legislature meeting, but if you don't mind waiting—"

"No, now. Tell him it's important."

Martin remembered a time when a mayor would have nothing to do with the state legislature. But that was before White and his ilk got voted into local, state, and federal offices around the country. The Born-Again Patriots' platforms against Big Government had turned into a large-scale consolidation making many traditional political positions redundant. In White's home state of Arizona, the group had eliminated traditional state lawmakers, giving mayors the additional responsibility of casting votes on the legislature.

The butler beckoned the sheriff inside and went to inquire after his employer. Martin removed his Army hat and tapped it against his thigh. His matted gray hair glistened with sweat as he gaped at the large entrance area. The floor was pure white tile with a crystal chandelier hanging from the ceiling. Thomas Jefferson hung smugly on one wall, while a war scene with muskets was carried out on the other.

"Nice foy-er," muttered Martin, pronouncing the word like a true American. He pulled a flask from inside his police jacket and had a quick swig of whiskey.

The butler called from upstairs, "The mayor will see you now."

At first, Martin took the steps two at a time, but soon, he began to wheeze and had to slow down. After a long slog, he made it to the top and followed the butler into a large study.

"Sheriff!" exclaimed Mayor White with a youthful enthusiasm that belied his shiny bald head. Congenially, he slapped the policeman on the back.

Martin looked past the mayor to a webcam and large TV on

the opposite wall. The screen displayed a woman in a suit giving a speech, bordered by a rectangle of interested faces — other members of the state legislature, he assumed. Martin watched the bright red lips of the lady rep move but couldn't hear what she was saying. A bright green *MUTE* in the bottom-right corner explained why.

"I didn't mean to interrupt," apologized the sheriff, shuffling sideways to avoid the webcam's blank gaze.

Apparently befuddled by this behavior, White turned to see what Martin was looking at. "Oh! Don't worry about that gal. I have the microphone off. I don't have to speak for another thirty minutes or so."

"But can't they see … ?"

The politician grinned broadly. "That's the clever part! Keep this under your hat, but a few weeks ago I recorded a video of myself listening attentively. It loops every five minutes. You know, these meetings are such a bore — I just had to do it."

Martin wasn't sure how to respond.

"What? I'm not the only one, believe you me!" White pointed to one of the static faces on the border of the screen and began to circle his finger around the screen. "Fake … fake … fake … mmm, not sure, but probably fake … fake …"

Martin did believe him. Ignorance and arrogance seemed to be the way of all these Born-Again Patriots who'd let the law slip away in America. All talk and no listening — not even to each other. When they'd finished overhauling states and localities, the Born-Again Patriots had eliminated the entire national government, including the president, congress, and federal court system. All power moved to the states, and, for the most part, they now acted independently from one another. To maintain some small level of coordination, governors occasionally held conferences in the neutral territory of Washington, D.C., but this was mostly for appearances. It had been a long time since anyone referred to America as the United States.

Mayor White fell back into his chair and waved the sheriff to sit down on the other side of the desk. "So, what's new? Oh! Actually, I'm glad you're here. You see, I've been meaning to have a word with you. A few of the constituents have reported seeing you going in and out of the old police station. You're not still living there, are you?"

Martin gaped in response. He had explained this to the mayor several times before, but it was like talking to a brick wall. After White slashed the law enforcement budget five years ago, Martin had been forced to close the station and lay off his entire police force. Ben held on to his title of sheriff — someone had to — but they expected him to work from home with a reduced salary. The problem was he didn't have a home anymore, not since the missus had kicked him out.

Not that he really expected White to understand. These damn Born-Again Patriots had come almost entirely from the private sector — guns, oil, telecommunications, and so on — and once they took over the government, the first thing the businessmen did was lay off everyone. All of a sudden, there didn't seem to be any public money left for anything, even law enforcement. The new politicians argued that the private sector could provide security. If you couldn't afford to hire someone, you could get a gun and protect yourself.

Martin felt a catch in his throat as he replied. "The station is all I have left."

The mayor's bald head twisted reproachfully. The movement reminded Martin of a vulture. "Now, Ben, you're a town hero and everyone appreciates what you did at that Walmart, but you can't just —"

"Mayor, another lunatic showed up at my church today! He shot a boy!"

White sarcastically gasped, "Good God! Was he *justified*?"

Martin scowled. "Justified? That's not the point!"

"I don't follow."

"We can't have this kind of lawlessness! I'm supposed to be sheriff, but things have gotten to the point where I can't do anything about vigilante craziness like this."

The confusion on the mayor's face remained. "Why bring this to me?"

Martin could feel his temperature rising. "Because men like you *make* the laws."

The politician hooted. "Ben, Ben, Ben … the government hasn't made laws for years! Now, if there's some sort of burdensome regulation getting in the way of what you're trying to do, maybe I can help, but —"

"Goddammit! I'm supposed to be enforcing the laws! I *am* enforcing the laws, except there's barely any goddamned laws to enforce anymore! Well, I'll tell you this, Mayor, I am not going to be reduced to just another vigilante! You hear me? I am the sheriff of the *fucking* police!"

The mayor turned the color of his name. "There's ... there's no need for profanity. I think you should leave. You need to cool off for a while. Have a few more beers, perhaps."

Martin ignored the dig at his drinking and persisted. "But this man, the Wanderer ... he's still out there, probably killing more innocents!"

"Is he still in Liberty?"

"Well, no, I don't think so, but ..."

"Well, then, he's not your problem, is he?"

Martin looked past him to one of the room's east-facing windows. The blinds were closed, but the sheriff knew it was the town of Liberty upon which the mayor had turned his back.

White exhaled with resignation. "Look, if you really want him dead, put a prize on his head. I know a guy."

"You mean a bounty hunter," he growled. "You're asking the sheriff of police to hire a bounty hunter."

The politician walked to his desk and scrawled a phone number on a yellow Post-it. When Martin rejected it, White insisted. "If you want this Wanderer gone, it's the best way. Trust me."

Ben Martin snatched the piece of paper and stormed off.

*

Rosa's Ford pickup kicked up a cloud of red dust as it stammered into the parking lot of Liberty Station. The door squealed in agony when she pushed it open, but she ignored it. She had bought the truck fresh-rusted from Jack years ago. The train station wasn't much to look at, either — just a trailer with white siding and a permanent boot over one wheel. Red sand stained the group of plastic chairs scattered around front. They looked relieved to be empty.

She cursed. There was no sign of the Wanderer. Trains didn't come through Liberty many times each day, and she'd hoped against hope he'd still be waiting.

Rosa jogged up to the trailer window used for ticket sales. Steve, the old station manager, continued to work on a crossword puzzle as she read a flyer taped up to the glass. It featured the boy half of a young couple's selfie, and there were tear-offs at the bottom with phone numbers.

Wanted, preferably dead:
John Hanson
$5,000 award! Call Jessica for more info.

Rosa groaned at the misuse of the word *award*. It should have said *reward*.

"How long ago did the train leave?" she asked Steve.

"Where did you come from?" gasped the station manager, noticing her for the first time.

She laughed. "Sorry, Steve."

He closed his eyes. At first, it seemed like he was in deep thought, but Rosa soon began to worry the old man had fallen asleep. She was about to wake him when his eyes snapped back open. "I'd say the train left at about quarter of eleven."

It was almost noon according to her watch, a cheap plastic number in hot pink. Jack had given it to her as a gag gift a few months ago after she declared her intention to become a "real reporter" and write *The New West*. He'd joked real reporters wore watches to secretly record conversations for investigative pieces. But rather than pay for an expensive model, he'd bought her a kid's toy — something that cheap parents could give to children who wanted the real thing but didn't know any better. It had a flimsy band and told the time on a standard gray LCD screen. The watch's only "smart" feature was a built-in digital recorder, which she'd never bothered to use since her tablet had one and recorded higher quality audio. Jack had never really intended for her to wear it, and, in fact, he'd begged her to take it off. So she wore it anyway, out of spite.

"Sorry, Steve — I have something to ask you."

Steve had been working at the station ever since he retired from his old job as a train conductor. She didn't really understand it. Why would someone who had been on the move his entire life choose to stop at Liberty of all places?

"Where you headed today, my dear?" he asked, turning to his monitor.

"What? Oh, nowhere."

Steve laughed. "You're the second person to ask for a ticket there. Let's see, maybe I can give you a few options?"

Rosa waved at the ticket seller to get his attention away from the screen. "No, I don't want a ticket at all. I'm actually writing an article and was hoping to, um, to ask you a few questions."

Steve's eyes brightened. "I'm going to be in *Our Times*? Fantastic! How can I help?"

Steve was too sweet for lies. "Oh, well, it's not actually for *Our Times*, but it's still important. I just need to know if you sold a

23

ticket, maybe about an hour or two ago, to a man that looked a bit like a cowboy from the movies? You know … Stetson hat, couple of guns, that kind of thing?"

Steve looked down at his desk and scrunched his eyes in deep concentration. After a few seconds of this, his head lifted with elation. "Come to think of it, that funny man going nowhere may have been the one you're looking for! In fact, given he was the only man who came by to ride the train today, I reckon I'm sure of it!"

With a grin, Rosa pulled a stylus out of her pocket and started writing on her tablet. "What did you make of him?"

"Well, you know, I see a lot of people here. Some come to the train with a lot of baggage. Others come with just their person. This man didn't have much of anything, but I'll be gosh-darned if he didn't look like he was carrying the weight of the world!"

He was dramatic. She liked that. "Steve, I have to say, you make a gold interview! Where was he headed?"

"That's what I was telling you before — he didn't know."

She narrowed her eyes. "What do you mean?"

"He just wanted to go somewhere, anywhere, and he wanted to leave straight away. The next train due out was headed southeast, so he bought a ticket to the end of the line and said he'd figure out where to get off when he got there."

CHAPTER THREE

What's the Angle?

Rosa found a packed parking lot and a buzz of activity at the big white shoe box the town called Liberty Hospital. She had plans to do a story about this place one day. It would be a report on the ever-increasing number of gunshot victims, the strain this put on the nurses and doctors, and the resulting long waiting lines in the ER.

After many minutes of circling the lot, Rosa spied a crying family walking toward an SUV. She cornered the space and pushed her way in before another truck she'd seen could make a play.

At the front entrance, a pair of automatic doors spat an icy breath, making her cover her arms. She made a beeline for the reception and asked to see Sara Heller.

"Oh, you're Rosa Veras, aren't you?" chirped the middle-aged lady at the desk. "We haven't seen you in a while."

She swallowed hard. "Yeah, I know."

"Heller, did you say? Will you be seeing your nephew as well?"

"Not today."

They left it at that. Not wanting anyone else to recognize her,

Rosa kept her eyes glued to her tablet all the way to Sara's room. She found the door ajar and Sharon Heller gabbing about some inane topic — Easter displays? A syrupy man's voice responded, and Rosa froze. Father James was here. She hadn't wanted to see the priest. She knew she'd have to talk to him for the story, but she had wanted to do it by telephone so she could quickly end the conversation if things got awkward.

Gathering her courage, Rosa pushed through the door and stepped inside. She could just make out Sara's supine hand in the metal-framed hospital bed. Sharon looked at her like an uninvited stranger, but Father James came to her rescue. "Rosie?" he asked with disbelief. "It's been a long time. Sharon, do you know Rosa Veras?"

Recognition materialized in Sharon's eyes. "The reporter from *Our Times*."

Father James continued to beam. "What are you doing here, Rosie?"

She might be able to stand it if the priest was an old man — the stereotypical minister in black with white hair. But this was *Jim*, the cute boy from her high school days. He was her first, and they had gone out together until that mortifying moment when he announced his decision to swear off women.

"I …" She stumbled for the words. "I just wanted to ask Sharon and Sara a few questions about what happened today."

Sharon arched her eyebrows and patronizingly intoned, "I didn't realize you covered this kind of thing."

Rosa took the barb with a smile. It was a fair concern. The reporter's most recent interview with the eighteen-year-old student council president had been about decorations for the prom. "I guess I'm trying to expand. How is she?"

Sharon turned to her younger sister. "Alive, but she's not going to be able to talk to you. She's been sleeping … a lot."

Rosa approached the bed. Sara was tucked tightly in a white blanket and hooked to a web of plastic tubes. Her sixteen-year-old face looked chalky. "Do you know what happened?"

"I don't want to talk about it. *Especially* not to some reporter."

So the interview was going to shit before it had even started. Recalling a tactic that she had once seen in a film about investigative journalists, she tried a different approach. "You don't have to talk about Sara, but I was hoping you could at least tell me more about this bounty hunter who shot Tom Jenkins."

Sharon glared. "I didn't pay him to do it, if that's what you're implying. That man is a hero!"

Rosa scribbled that down in her tablet. "What do you mean?"

Sharon recounted how she and Sara had been out at the Coyote Tavern, flirting with some local boys, when Tom showed up high on cocaine. Tom and Sara had been on a few dates, so when he saw the other men, he went ballistic. Finally, Sara calmed him down by convincing him to go outside with her to talk.

"Where was the Wanderer during all this?"

"He was at the bar, too. I guess he saw the whole fight."

After Sara and Tom left, the Wanderer had come over to Sharon. "I was worrying," she said. "He made a lot of dad jokes to cheer me up."

This detail brought a smile to Rosa's lips. So the gunslinger had a bad sense of humor — he just kept getting more and more interesting. "I'm trying to form a picture of him. Can you tell me what he looked like?"

"Well, he was pretty old."

Rosa wrote that down, but then crossed it out when Sharon added, "Like, even older than you."

Father James smiled sympathetically. "I'd say late thirties," he said. "Maybe early forties."

"*Old*," stressed Sharon. "But he had kind eyes. I could tell he was good."

Sharon said she had talked to him for another ten minutes or so. When Sara still hadn't returned, the Wanderer had volunteered to go outside and check if everything was all right. Sharon said she heard a gunshot not long after he'd gone.

"I found the Wanderer holding Sara in an alley … there was blood everywhere. I didn't know what to do. The Wanderer took my hand and swore he would find Tom and make him pay."

*

She noticed Father James following her out of the hospital room and turned around to face him.

"You're quite good at that, you know," he said. "I couldn't figure out for the life of me how to get that girl to open up, and part of my job is taking confessions."

She tried to laugh, but it sounded forced. She still found it a little strange seeing him in the garb of a priest. He was always a good kid growing up, never got into trouble. Overall, he'd seemed normal.

"Have you spoken with Sheriff Martin yet?" he asked.

"He's my next stop."

"Be careful, Rosie. I've never seen that man so fired up."

Ben Martin had been sheriff of Liberty for as long as Rosa could remember. As the laws gently crumbled and his authority ebbed, he had taken to drinking. The liquor made him angry.

"Jack told me the two of you had to hold him back," she said.

Father James sighed. "I know there's still a good man inside him. But today he wanted blood, Rosie. I could see it in his eyes. I just thought there had been enough of that for one day."

She nodded solemnly. "So what do *you* think about this Wanderer guy?"

"I don't know. He shot one of my people. But ... well, that's why I went to see Sara for myself. It's terrible what happened. Still, I just want to believe there could have been another way to deal with that kid Tom than —"

"— with a gun. I know."

His hazel eyes looked through her. "Are you planning to visit Pablo while you're here?"

"I ..."

The ringing cell phone saved her, but Rosa cursed when she saw who it was: Rebecca Song, managing editor of *Our Times*.

"Work?" asked Father James.

"Sorry, I have to take this." She gave him a short wave good-bye, took a few steps down the hallway, and answered the call.

"You took a long time to pick up," came the editor's nasal-inflected voice.

"Yeah, sorry, Rebecca, I was in the middle of —"

"I sent you an e-mail yesterday. You haven't responded."

"I don't always check my mail on the *weekend*," she said, barely concealing her irritation. At the last second, she added, "Sorry I missed it."

Rebecca sighed audibly. "Stephen's not able to cover the Breck Ammo news conference at the gun show. It's your town this year. You can cover for him, right?"

Under normal circumstances, Stephen Jones would travel from the *Our Times* headquarters in Vegas to cover the Breck Ammo news conference. He had the guns beat and wrote breathless reports about new killing machines coming to the market.

"Yeah," Rosa replied without enthusiasm. She didn't want to do it, but a fight with Rebecca was never worth it. She asked when the gun show was happening, receiving a deeply meaningful silence in response. "Oh," Rosa added quickly, "the Fourth, right?"

"Yes, Rosa. It's *always* on the Fourth."

She resisted the temptation to hang up. "Okay. Well, e-mail me the details and …"

"I sent them yesterday. Okay? Good!"

The phone beeped as Rebecca hung up. Rosa took a deep breath as she put away the handset.

She had been dreading the gun show. It was a big carnival designed to sell the latest Breck products to the gun-hungry masses, and it moved from town to town across the west over the length of each summer. The schedule changed each year, but July Fourth was always the most important day on the tour because it was when Breck Ammo announced its latest products. This year, the dubious honor had come to Liberty.

"Everything all right?"

It was Father James returning.

"Uh-huh!" Rosa put on a smile. "I was just going."

*

Rosa found Ben Martin just where she'd thought he'd be — Betsy's Diner, stuffing his face with pie in a corner booth. There were morsels of crust spread across the table and cherry stains down his shirt, but at least he looked sober. It was a few hours past lunch, so the place was mostly empty. The only waitress she had seen so far was busy smoking and texting outside.

"Rosie!" exclaimed the sheriff. Crumbs dribbled down his chin as he spoke. "It's been so long since I've seen you. Heard from your old man lately?"

"Nope."

He always asked her that, knowing full well that her dad was in the state prison and who'd put him there. Given the state of the law nowadays, it didn't seem likely he'd ever get an opportunity to appeal for release. Rosa figured that Martin knew this, too, and maybe that was why he always acted so soft around her. To be honest, she was over being mad at the sheriff for arresting her dad, even if Martin had never managed to overcome his own guilt.

She sat down across from him in the booth with her back to the wall. "I'm here to talk about what happened today at church."

He scowled. "Why?"

She took out her tablet. "I'm writing an article."

Martin idly fingered a yellow Post-it note a few inches from his plate. It looked as though it had been crumpled up and flattened out again. "What's the angle? I hope you're not trying to make that vigilante into some kind of hero."

"Isn't he one?"

"Ha! I looked into that man's eyes and I tell you they were completely devoid of any soul." He pointed to her notes. "Write that down."

"What Sharon Heller told me was that he saved her sister's life from a monster and got revenge."

Martin scowled. "No man has a right to take the law into his own hands. I tried to stop him, but that damn preacher … you know, this kind of thing wouldn't happen if there was still adequate law enforcement."

"What kind of thing? You mean Tom Jenkins shooting a girl in the stomach?"

Ben Martin grinned broadly so that Rosa could see the red mash between his teeth. "You know I meant that goddamned Wanderer. It's people like *him* destroying America. Those among us who still remember the law need to stand up before this country sinks into even deeper shit."

Rosa smiled slightly as she jotted this latest gem into her notes. Could she print profanity? Well, it was her blog, wasn't it? When she looked up again, the end of Ben Martin's shotgun was inches from her face. The world blurred around the dark double-barrel, and she could feel her heart pounding.

"On the wall behind you," he whispered, "there's a roach. Quietly … slide out of the booth …" He kept the Pilgrim trained on the armored brown insect while she scooted out of her seat. "Lawlessness like that? It's got to be exterminated."

When Rosa was out of the way, she realized how angry she

was. She took a napkin from another table, crumpled it into a ball and tossed it at the cockroach. The bug scurried safely behind the red seat.

"What do you think you're doing?" he yelled.

"Thanks for your time, *Sheriff*," she said, spitting out the policeman's title sarcastically. The bells on the door jingled violently as she slammed it closed behind her.

CHAPTER FOUR

Not that Nice a Train, Darling.

Saguaro cacti danced across the copper landscape, arms raised in celebration of the great fireball descending into the mountains. The last rays of sunlight shone through the scratched train window and into the Wanderer's lonesome gaze. He was sitting by himself on the right side of the car. There was a worn denim knapsack on the aisle seat containing all his belongings. All the ones he needed anyway.

For the first few hours of the journey, he had tried not to think about Jenkins and Sara Heller, but now the bloody affair consumed his mind. Jenkins was just a piglet, and the Wanderer did feel a bit sorry about that. But young or old, he'd tried to kill an innocent girl. The Wanderer reckoned that when Jenkins shot Sara Heller in the stomach, he gave up his right to live. Well, he lived no more.

Riding the rails suited the Wanderer. Out west, the towns and cities were pretty well spread out and the trains took their sweet old time. It took hours to get from place to place. That was fine by him. He liked that feeling of knowing he was moving but not having to think too much about where he was going.

There were more passenger lines than there used to be, but they still shared the tracks with freighters, so it was slow going. The passenger trains had made a comeback in large part because the highways had become so dangerous. For one thing, the highways were covered with trash and roadkill, and no one ever seemed to repair potholes anymore. But the bigger problem was the Red Stripe Gang. The outlaws patrolled those roads on their motorcycles, and they seemed to have a passion for causing trouble.

"Coo-ool!" came a small voice from his left.

Turning from the window, he saw a boy gaping across the aisle at the Wanderer's silver revolver. The Lassiter was held securely in the leather holster on his left hip. The child appeared to be about ten years old.

"What are you staring at?" the Wanderer asked. He said it like a cowboy from the movies — tough but playful.

The boy looked him square in the eyes. "What are *you* staring at?"

They locked eyes for many seconds. Then the Wanderer faked a tackle and the boy jumped back with laughter. He fell into his snoozing mother, who awoke briefly to mutter, "Please, Andy, just let me … a little longer …"

When both man and boy were sure she had fallen back asleep, the Wanderer chuckled and pointed to his six-shooter. "Want a closer look?"

The gunman moved his knapsack off the seat next to him so Andy could sit closer. He lifted the revolver from the holster with the twirl of a showman and held it out with the smooth ebony grip facing the boy. She was his good gun and she was a beaut. Just the right weight and her aim was true.

The boy moved his hand forward, but the Wanderer pulled the weapon away.

"You can look, but don't touch. Dangerous."

Andy dropped his hands back down to his sides, and the Wanderer brought the Lassiter back for him to admire further.

"Have you shot anyone?" the boy asked excitedly.

"Yes."

Andy shrunk back. "But they were all bad guys?"

The Wanderer blinked. In the split-second of black, he saw the bad gun, his Breck 17, fire at a figure standing in the dark. The air smelled like gunpowder and leftover lasagna. "This one," he answered, pointing at the Lassiter, "has only vanquished evil."

"What's that say?" asked Andy, pointing at the initials engraved in script on the handle. "E ... B?"

"That's ..." The Wanderer eyed the letters carefully. "That's the brand."

Something outside the window distracted the boy. The gunman turned and saw that the scenery had turned residential.

Andy asked, "What's this town?"

The Wanderer turned and spat. "It don't matter no more. See that flag on top of town hall?"

He pointed to a building towering over the rest. On top of a dome that looked burned and partially caved in was a long steel pole and a banner with thirteen red-and-white stripes, but no stars. "That means it's a Red Stripe town. The Gang runs it."

Andy watched out the window with fear in his eyes. "Is

everybody who lives there bad?"

"No, not everybody."

He looked confused. "Why would you live there if you were good?"

The Wanderer liked this kid. Everything in black-and-white. "Sometimes, it's not so easy to leave."

The boy appeared to concentrate real hard, as if trying to get his mind around a new concept. When the train stopped and opened its doors, the smell of smoke rushed in from the Red Stripe town. The boy looked worriedly at his sleeping mother. "I ... I better go sit with her, just in case."

The boy's courage struck the Wanderer as funny. He laughed warmly. "Sure, you go sit with your ma. You keep her safe."

*

Now this was the kind of job that Charlie Johnson liked.

He was sitting on a park bench, watching the status bar on his wrist-worn computer slide right, one percentage point a second. The wide glass wristband had a big digital screen that always faced up no matter how much it was twisted, while a small pad extended out into his palm, allowing for one-handed typing. He could enter keys by tapping his fingers on his palm; a camera in the device scanned the movements and turned them into letters.

He glanced up to the third floor of the university's science building and looked into the only room with the lights still on. He could see just the pudgy back of his target, a professor of some sort — alternative energy, someone might have said. Sixty-four years old and too many donuts to count. A year ago, he'd suffered a heart attack, so the doctors installed a fancy new pacemaker. Charlie didn't know the professor's name, and didn't want to, either.

A girl in a short jean jacket and an even shorter skirt approached. She gave Charlie the eye, and he winked back. He was used to this kind of attention. He might be skinny and slightly shorter than average, but he had firm arms and a tight abdomen, which he liked to show off via tight T-shirts. Softly, the girl bit her lip and turned, sashaying a healthy bottom as she walked away.

He shook his head and chuckled. Man, oh, man! Maybe he *had* missed out by not going to college. Then again, it didn't matter. He was the right age, and that girl didn't seem to think he was out of place. Maybe after this job, he'd stick around and sneak into a party or three, find himself a girl for the night. He'd be off again before anyone questioned whether he even went to school here.

The status bar hit 100 percent. Charlie grinned. No one would ever suspect this was a hit. Just another sad case of an unhealthy man working too hard and paying the price. The best part was that Charlie didn't even have to be inside the lab, just in range of the pacemaker. The device was equipped with a wireless chip that let it sync up with computers such as the scientist's PC or his doctor's medical equipment. A beautiful piece of e-health, but it came with one big security flaw.

Charlie hit the kill switch, shutting down the pacemaker. The fat scientist stumbled backward into the window and sank slowly to the floor.

"Too many donuts!" the bounty hunter laughed. "Too many donuts!"

And that was ten thousand bucks for Charlie. Strutting over to the parking lot, he rang up the boss to report the job done.

"We are pleased," said the voice on the other line. It wasn't El Tiburón himself. It never was. This was the crime lord's right-hand man, Cochise.

"Piece of cake," replied Charlie. "Next time, I want a challenge."

There was a pause on the other end of the line. "We might have one for you."

"Well, don't be all mysterious, my man! Who's the target?"

"They call him the Wanderer. He was seen in Liberty earlier today — shot up a church."

"A church?" he exclaimed. He had to admit he was impressed. "Let me guess. Someone wants revenge."

"Didn't say, but they're putting up a hell of a lot of money."

"Dead or alive?"

"There's more in it for you if he's alive, but we'll leave that to your discretion. You should know he has a reputation as a marksman."

"Hey, chill. I'm not so bad with a gun myself."

*

The train rattled hard along a rough section of the tracks, and the Wanderer, walking down the aisle, had to use his strong hands to brace himself against the backs of the seats. He still hadn't the foggiest idea as to where to get off and find a hotel for the night, but he hoped a drink in the café car might provide some inspiration.

He passed a harried businesswoman with a black-slab smartphone pressed against her cheek.

"I'm not sure about the potato salad," she said. "Not after last time."

He was still chuckling over that when he pushed through the pair of greasy doors that led into the café car. It was a small cabin with about four tables and a snack counter. There wasn't a seat to be had, but that didn't matter. He was sick of sitting. The other customers turned warily as he made his way to the bar to order, and he felt the heat of their eyes on his guns. The woman at the counter had leathery skin and a lot of freckles, as if she spent most of her off-hours sleeping on a rock absorbing the desert sun. A lizard woman. The Wanderer threw a few crisp green bills on the bar, asking her if she had any dark beers available.

"Not that nice a train, darling."

"Shit," he returned. "Your best ale, then."

The lizard woman gave him a brown bottle, and he gulped down half of it in one shot.

She grinned victoriously. "Like that one, huh?"

He drank the rest and slapped the glass container down on the counter. "Not so much. But I better have one more, just in case."

She procured another beer from under the counter and popped off the lid with a twist of her wrist.

"I'd offer you a seat, hon, but we seem to be full up."

"That's all right. You work here long?"

"Last ten years."

"This line?"

She nodded. "And I'm real tired of it, too."

He took a long swig of the beer. "Of the next several stops, what's your favorite?"

The lizard woman cackled. "They're *all* shit. Why?"

The Wanderer grinned widely. "If you had to pick one to stay tonight, where would you get off?"

She laughed. "If I had to pick one? Freetown, I s'pose. Well, at least if I was planning on spending a little while. It's not for another week, but they'll have a nice fireworks display for the Fourth."

The gunslinger nodded appreciatively. He had almost forgotten about the coming holiday. "I reckon I do have a little while."

The doors to the café car slid open. A bearded man in a green flannel shirt rumbled toward the bar. "Whiskey," he growled.

The lizard woman smiled politely at the Wanderer and turned to take care of her well-muscled new customer. She brought out a short glass and poured it halfway full with brown liquid.

"More, dammit," said the bearded man. "All the way."

She did as she was told. "That's fifteen dollars."

He guzzled the drink in about five seconds. "Another."

The bartender narrowed her eyes. "Why don't you pay for that one first? Then we'll see."

The man flashed a couple rows of yellow teeth. Then he brought out his gun, a semiautomatic Breck 17. "Get me another, and we'll see."

There was a smattering of gasps as the other people in the car cleared out from their tables and made for the exit.

The Wanderer sipped his beer thoughtfully. "Why don't you put the gun away," he commanded in a voice that was quiet but firm.

The bearded man turned wide-eyed in his direction, as if

noticing him for the first time. "You want to speak up, stranger? I don't think I caught that!"

The Wanderer smiled. A few seconds later, he had the asshole choked by the neck and was pushing him out of the café. In the space between the two train cars, he pulled an emergency lever to open the exit door and dangled the bearded man over the fast-moving brush.

"Don't worry," the Wanderer said with a friendly sneer. "You'll probably survive this."

He then tossed the fool like he was a rag doll.

*

Charlie took a seat at a cubicle desk in the university library and woke up his smart wristband. He scanned the wire for anything about the incident at Liberty — status updates, candid photos. He was surprised to find a full-length blog post about the incident and the small town's reaction. It was titled *WHO IS THE WANDERER?* The piece was written in the succinct, objective style of an old-fashioned newspaper article — the kind of story no one wrote anymore.

When he was finished reading, he rubbed a finger against his glass bangle to scroll back up to the top of the page. The blog was called *The New West*, and the poster appeared to be anonymous — at least, he couldn't find the writer's name anywhere. Something to check into later, maybe.

The bounty hunter gazed blankly at the cubicle wall — chipboard with a wooden laminate, based on the warping. Someone had carved a crude image of a penis into it. So far, he hadn't heard much commotion related to his completed kill. He wondered how long it would take until someone found the body.

Just in case, he took his gun out of his bag and placed it gently on the table. It was a smart pistol he'd picked up in Canada a couple of years back. Breck Ammunition didn't make anything like it. Canadians called it the Separatist, while most Americans just called it the Canadian. It was black and boxy like a Breck 17, but it had one key feature that the other semiautomatic lacked: a sensor on the handle that could read the user's handprint. The gun would only fire for its owner.

Charlie pulled up a rail map on his wrist device and determined which train line went through Liberty. He grabbed the geographic coordinates of each stop, matched them to a train timetable, then entered all the data into a social media search. Immediately, a list of every public social media message made on the train that left Liberty at 11:00 a.m. appeared on the screen. For the first several hours, he found nothing of interest. But recently, very recently, there had been a surge of social activity.

JohnTheFifth:
Some whack job holding up cafe car on my train.

PilgrimFan1:
Guy in cowboy hat just grabbed perp and threw him off train. So awesome!

A different one was accompanied by a picture showing the back of a man wearing a leather coat and a gray Stetson hat. He was pushing another man through the door of the train cabin. To their left was a panicked-looking bartender. She had her phone out and appeared to be typing something.

Charlie scrolled down the social feed a few more inches.

GreenAngel92:
Just got held up over a whiskey. FML

He clicked this last message and hit *REPLY*. Smirking, he typed a message under the name *Darwinning*, one of his many handles.

Darwinning:
@GreenAngel92 omg r u ok?

After a minute, he got a reply:

GreenAngel92:
@Darwinning I'm ok, someone saved me.

The Internet stepped in before he could respond.

TaterSaladLife:
@GreenAngel92 @Darwinning Who?

GreenAngel92:
@TaterSaladLife @Darwinning Didn't tell me name. Bought beer and asked my favorite stop on the line.

"Too easy, this is just too easy!" chuckled Charlie, winding up his fingers.

Darwinning:
@GreenAngel92 @TaterSaladLife Wow! What did you tell him?

CHAPTER FIVE

Gonna Get You Good.

Stepping off the bus in Freetown, Charlie had to squint to see the screen on his arm under the bright sun. The wristband showed an inexpensive motor lodge on State Street that didn't look far and seemed fairly anonymous. It only had a 5.5 out of 10 average customer rating, but that was okay since he didn't plan to stay long. He adjusted the straps of his hiker's backpack and set off on his way.

He looked up from the wristband only once, when the wireless signal abruptly cut out, and he couldn't access anything on his device. He was annoyed but not surprised. This kind of thing happened often in rural areas. The telecom oligopoly had never found much of a business case in small towns like this to keep the network humming. No one was on their backs to fix things, either.

The wireless came back on when Charlie arrived at the motel, and he showed the manager his wrist to get access to his room. The manager transferred a key to the wristband and told him he had room number three. It was located in the middle of a long row of doors facing State Street. Charlie tapped his wrist against the lock and it clicked open.

The room wasn't much — just a double bed, pinewood desk, and florescent overhead lighting — but it would do. With a grunt, he lifted the pack off his back and placed it gently on the floor. The bag contained all his things — his pistol, tablet, sniper rifle, and several days' worth of clothing.

Charlie checked himself out in the mirror. His hair was starting to show again. Better shave it tonight or it would start looking like a 'fro, and no one wanted that!

The first order of business was to confirm that the Wanderer had arrived and find out where he was staying. Charlie checked for any social buzz in the area but it proved to be a dead end. Apparently his target had managed to keep himself out of trouble.

The saloon maybe. Based on the reports from the train, the Wanderer had a taste for beer. Besides, Charlie was *hungry*. It had been a long-ass bus ride with nothing but crackers and a bottle of water.

He strutted down State Street until he found a bar called the Happy Gunfighter. The place had one of those "ye olde west" themes that were so popular these days. Charlie slapped open the double doors and stepped inside. It took forever for his eyes to adjust to the dark. Except for the bored-looking barkeep, the saloon was quiet and empty. Charlie pulled up a stool and took a menu.

"Sorry about the lights," apologized the bartender, wiping his black-rimmed glasses with a bar cloth. "The owner doesn't like us to put them on during the day. Says it doesn't make any sense when it's so damn bright outside. I've tried telling her the sun don't come in here — windows are too damn small and facing the wrong way — but she don't ever believe me. I reckon it's because she only ever comes in at night."

"Uh-huh. So, how's the BLT?"

He shrugged. "It's got bacon on it."

"Sold."

As the bartender went to the kitchen to inform the chef about Charlie's high-cholesterol meal, the young bounty hunter got a sudden image of the university professor suffering a heart attack. He cursed himself for thinking about that. It was just a job. They were all just jobs.

Charlie ordered a Coke when the bartender returned. "Diet," he added.

The bartender lifted a hose and shot the brown, fizzy liquid into a glass. "Don't think I've seen you in here before. Here for the fireworks?"

"Something like that."

"Well, you're a week early. And I hate to be the bearer of bad news," he said with a wave around the empty saloon, "but most of the year, Freetown ain't all that exciting."

"That's okay. I make my own excitement. You feel me?"

The bartender shrugged.

"Hey, I think a friend of mine's in town. Maybe you seen him? Dresses like a cowboy and likes his beer dark."

The barman made a little hum. "I reckon there was a fellow like that last night ... Does he wear a glass over one eye?"

Charlie grinned. "That's him all right. Hey, don't tell him I was here? I wanna surprise him."

*

Charlie spent all of the next day observing the Wanderer and getting a feel for his daily movements. Mostly, he watched him eat and drink. For a guy who'd shot up a church, the Wanderer didn't do anything very exciting.

They made eye contact once while devouring tacos at separate tables in a Mexican place. It was the kind of throwaway exchange that any two strangers might have in a restaurant. Even so, the look sent a chill through Charlie's spine. Something haunted the Wanderer's weary eyes.

Charlie wondered who he was. It probably wouldn't be too difficult to figure out — just use facial recognition software and match the man to an ID. But the bounty hunter quickly dismissed the idea. He didn't like to know anything more about his targets than he needed to. Knowing too much about them only ever made the job more of a bitch to complete.

It was cool knowing he could do it, though. The good think about working for El Tiburón was the access to gear. Years ago, Charlie had first impressed the crime lord by using a stolen laptop to shut down the security system in a bank and rob the place blind. But that computer hadn't been all that powerful compared to the stuff he got from El Tiburón. The glass wristband, for example, had more than ten times the capability of that laptop despite being a fraction of the size and weight.

The funny thing about technology was how vulnerable it made everything. With nearly everything connected to the Internet, there was no limit to what a good hacker could exploit. Sure, people were always patching the holes to increase security, but the hacks evolved just as fast as the defenses. Cybersecurity was an impossible battle. Given enough time, Charlie could always find a new backdoor.

A buzz brought Charlie's eyes to the screen on his wrist. The hack was complete. He now had access to the location chip built into the Wanderer's eyeglass. Now he could track him wherever he went. Charlie finished his Coke and asked for the bill.

Tomorrow night he'd make his move.

*

Charlie looked through the scope of his rifle to make sure it was still pointed at the entrance of the Happy Gunfighter. He was getting restless. Two hours so far of waiting on top of this building. It was getting late. The Wanderer hadn't stayed out this late last night. Charlie had hoped to be done the job in time for a drink, but that plan was looking increasingly unlikely. The Wanderer was apparently going to stay at the bar until closing time.

Charlie still thought he'd found a great perch — a bank with a flat roof located directly across from the saloon. He had his Montag sniper rifle set up on a black stand, placing it as close to the edge as he could get. It was a perfect view, but he was getting sick of it.

Two gunshots rang out from the far edge of town. Charlie looked but didn't see anything. Probably came from one of the houses out that way. He couldn't be sure.

A squeak of hinges brought his attention back to the double doors of the saloon. He pulled in close to the scope and wrapped his finger around the trigger. The Wanderer came out propping up an old timer. The drunkard was raving wildly about something, but Charlie couldn't tell what.

"Hey," he heard the Wanderer say. "Let's just get you home, all right? You can tell me all about it tomorrow."

The bartender came out next. "He just lives a mile down the road. He'll show you. Thanks a lot, man."

"It ain't nothing."

"You're right, it *ain't* nothing!" the bartender said. "So your next beer is on the house, all right?"

"Make it two," the Wanderer replied with a gravelly laugh.

Charlie pulled away from his rifle and slapped himself on the cheek like a wrestler before the match. "Fuck! What's wrong with me? Fuck!"

He looked back in the scope and watched the Wanderer and the old man hobble off down the road. No, he couldn't do it. Not tonight.

Tomorrow.

*

Charlie was back in position on Thursday night.

"Gonna get you, Wanderer," he sang to himself. "Gonna get you good."

This time the gunman came stumbling out of the bar by himself.

Charlie laughed. "A few too many drinks on the house, maybe?"

The scope's crosshairs dropped over the Wanderer's heart. The bounty hunter wrapped his finger around the trigger and — a ferocious bark gave Charlie such a start that he knocked hard against the rifle, tipping it forward. He groped for the butt of the Montag, but gravity moved faster and took it straight over the edge of the roof. For a breathless eternity, the gun fell. Then the clatter of metal against concrete jolted time back to its normal tempo. The Wanderer looked hard at the long, scoped rifle and began to retrace its fall up the side of the bank.

Charlie instinctively fell flat against the roof to hide. "Oh no, oh no, oh no," he muttered incoherently. He was frantic. Had he been seen? The Wanderer had looked up, seen where the rifle had come from. Even if he hadn't seen Charlie, he would definitely come up for a look. He could be up here any minute!

Heart thumping, Charlie crawled away from the roof's edge. When he was sure he was far enough away not to be seen, he jumped onto his feet and bolted for the fire stairs. "Oh no, oh no, oh no …"

Was that a dog? It had sounded so close. Must have been in the window of one of the other buildings. Of all the damn luck!

The black metal steps didn't go down all the way to the street, so Charlie had to jump the last ten feet. He dropped into a narrow alley and felt his full weight shudder into his knees. As he bolted away from State Street, he heard the mutt again — only now it was far behind him, yipping with glee.

*

In the morning, the motel room stank of old scrambled eggs. There was a cart by the door holding a tray of crumb-covered plates and tin covers.

The room's scratchy tan curtains kept Charlie cloaked in shadow. He was crouched on the floor staring at a red dot on his wristband. The Wanderer had just walked into a gun shop. Oh no, the Wanderer had just walked into a gun shop!

Charlie checked the coordinates and learned it was a place called Joe's. He looked up the name and address on his favorite hacking website and quickly found keys to get into the shop's CCTV network. Within minutes, he had a behind-the-counter view of the Wanderer perusing the store.

It was odd the way the Wanderer browsed. Most people who went into a gun store either knew what they wanted already or asked the shopkeeper for help. The Wanderer browsed the place like Charlie might have browsed an electronics store. He took a slow circle of the place, occasionally putting his hand on display items or reading the backs of boxes, really taking the time to appreciate everything.

It was almost lunchtime when the cowboy finished, but all he ended up buying was a few boxes of ammo. The video feed wasn't good enough to see what kind, though Charlie assumed they were for the Lassiter and the Breck 17. The Wanderer left and began to walk down State Street … in the direction of the motel.

Charlie considered getting out. He'd already packed his things. His cover was blown, wasn't it? What if the Wanderer had followed him last night? What if he knew about the motel?

He felt his arm buzz. There was a new message from Cochise.

It's been a week. Status?

"Shit!"

He quickly replied:

It's been four and a half days. I'll get him — just taking more time than expected.

He pulled up the map again. The Wanderer was no longer moving toward the motel. He had gone back into the Happy Gunfighter — maybe to prepare.

Shaking his head, the bounty hunter told himself, "You're not going anywhere until the job is done." Saying it out loud somehow gave the statement more finality. "You just need a new plan is all."

Charlie crawled into bed and gave the matter a good think.

*

It was the next day by the time he decided. He'd always wanted to do something with self-driving cars. The last time he'd tried, he couldn't find one with old enough firmware to hack. But in Freetown he got lucky. He found an ancient SUV, one of the earliest models to feature an autonomous pilot mode, parked at his motel.

The red dot representing the Wanderer slid onto the sidewalk. It was time for his morning stroll down State Street. Charlie switched apps and tapped a button. The engine of the SUV roared to life. He set the destination as the Wanderer's eyeglass and overrode the vehicle's safety sensors. Then he pulled up a first-person view of the action.

The driverless SUV pulled hard out of the parking lot and

accelerated down State Street. The Wanderer didn't seem to notice until the truck was about a block away and traveling at more than a hundred miles per hour.

Charlie got a good look at the whites of his target's eyes and smirked. "Good-bye, Wanderer."

An alert popped up on the screen: *Connection Lost.* Freetown's wireless signal had just cut out again.

"No, no, no!" He grabbed a spare scope and burst out of the motel room to get a look. He got outside just in time to hear a loud crash.

A lot of other people filtered out onto State Street to see what had happened, too. Charlie peered through his scope and saw the SUV had slammed into a light post. The Wanderer was standing nearby the smoking truck, stunned, but still very much alive.

Charlie decided to try again the next day.

*

Okay, enough theatrics. Time to get the job done.

On Sunday night around 7:00 p.m., Charlie walked into the Happy Gunfighter with nothing but his pistol. He took a seat at the bar and kept an eye on the Wanderer, who was sitting at his usual table drinking a Sierra Nevada Porter.

After polishing off his dinner, the Wanderer got up and addressed the bartender. "There's something I gotta do. I'll be back, though."

Charlie waited a minute before following the Wanderer out the door. He kept about a block behind him, tailing his target to a 7-Eleven. Soon, the Wanderer came out holding a bag of groceries and resumed his walk up State Street. After a few more blocks, he turned down an alley.

Charlie took his Separatist out of its holster and followed. As he held up the smart pistol, a light on Charlie's wristband turned green to indicate that he could fire when ready.

The lane was dark and long, perfect for making the kill. But as the alley turned, it brightened, and Charlie found his target joining three homeless men around a campfire. From the grocery bag the Wanderer brought out a loaf of bread and a few cans of beef chili.

Charlie remembered nights back home in Vegas sitting around street fires just like that, eating cooked rat or whatever else his family had managed to catch that day … if they managed to catch anything at all.

With a sigh, the bounty hunter sheathed his pistol and turned back. The green light on his wrist turned red and then went out completely.

*

The next morning, Charlie received another message from Cochise.

We're waiting.

"Well, you're going to have to wait a little longer," Charlie said. But he didn't actually reply to the message.

He was at the gym and it felt good. He'd just gotten on the treadmill and was feeling the tension drip away with each bead of sweat.

He wasn't sure why he couldn't kill the Wanderer. Yeah, he'd had some bad luck, but he'd had plenty of chances. Why couldn't he pull the trigger?

The job had to be finished, of course. He needed the money to send back to his family. And El Tiburón was not one to fuck over. If Charlie didn't complete this job, at best he wouldn't see any more jobs. At worst, well …

A young woman in tight shorts began to do squats in front of his running machine. Marveling at the rise and fall of her fine ass, Charlie pledged to enjoy his day off. He'd get the Wanderer tomorrow.

BRECK AMMO EXPECTED TO REVEAL NEW GUN

By New West Reporter

Tomorrow, America will celebrate its independence with hot dogs, fireworks, and a big announcement from Breck Ammunition.

Rather than take the path of other blogs and speculate on what will be announced, we at *The New West* think it's important to reflect on how America's gun company shaped the country we know today.

It began with the rise of a startup company nearly fifty years ago. At the time, America got its guns from a variety of brands, and the most popular originated overseas — the superstars Glock, Zeller, and Kalashnikov. That all changed when a young entrepreneur from rural Nevada developed a plastic semiautomatic handgun in his garage.

The gun that Albert Breck created wasn't anything special. It was really just a clone of the current top-selling handgun out of Europe. But Breck was a true-blue American, and he timed the release of his gun with the rise of the Born-Again Patriot movement. Among other things, these politicians advocated for a boycott on all foreign-made products.

The Born-Again Patriots, who counted the National Rifle Association among their base, quickly rallied behind Breck Ammo, asserting that the only true gun was an American gun. Soon, Americans across the country were trading in their foreign-made guns for Brecks.

Breck leveraged this success to buy out all of the other American gun manufacturers. He cherry-picked their best guns, renamed them, and made them his own. The gun startup had become a monopoly.

While growing in influence, the Born-Again Patriots were still not the dominant force they are today. To win more elections, they needed more money. It was money that Breck was only too happy to provide.

Over the next twenty-five years, the Born-Again Patriot movement swelled into a tidal wave that wiped out opponents at the local, state, and federal levels. Breck never let them forget who had fueled their success.

Breck Ammo lobbied to flesh out Americans' rights under the Second Amendment. Politicians echoed the Breck line that the movement was about "self-defense" and providing "more freedom" to Americans.

Later, Breck's lobbying transformed into a push to make bigger guns "more accessible to consumers." In the crosshairs was the National Firearms Act, a law dating back to 1934 banning the sale of fully automatic "machine" guns. The Born-Again Patriots introduced a controversial amendment to the NFA to lift the ban.

Ten years ago, the legislation passed into law. Eight years ago, Breck Ammunition introduced a new gun to the market: an "easy-to-handle" assault rifle called the Yossarian. It is today the company's second-best-selling gun after the Breck 17 pistol.

Gun advocates like to point out that the number of shootings has not gone up since the release of the Yossarian. This is true, but what is rising is the death toll. This is because one sustained spray of the Yossarian can murder a whole crowd in less than a minute.

Today, the buzz on social media is that Breck Ammunition will announce a new gun on the Fourth of July. If *The New*

West must join the crowd of speculators, it will only be to predict that the true impact of the announcement will be seen not in tomorrow's headlines, but in the gun death statistics that will follow the weapon's release.

CHAPTER SIX

This Gun Is a Revolution!

Gerard Breck woke at precisely six in the morning. He silenced a vintage golden alarm clock and reached for his tablet. With a quick swipe, he opened his agenda. He had the schedule memorized but felt great comfort in seeing his day laid out in digital ink. In thirty minutes, he was to be in his office for a final meeting with Mr. Tom O'Brien, the gun designer, to secure an exclusive contract for the rifle, a fully automatic beauty pitched as "the hunter's machine gun." They would fly together to Liberty to announce the super-gun at the Breck Gun Show at precisely 10:00 a.m., with a demonstration for the media to follow. After this wrapped up at about noon, the company would open a booth to take pre-orders. By this point, he planned to be boarding his private airplane back home to Vegas for the Independence Day celebrations.

Gerard closed the tablet's black leather cover and placed it gently on his bed stand. Carefully, he ran his hand against the edge of the table to ensure no part of the device would hang off of the side. Then, he folded his blanket forward and stepped out of the bed, fully naked.

He turned to check the alarm clock. Three minutes after six.

That meant he had seven minutes to shower. He strode quickly into the master bathroom and declared, "Shower on!"

Hot water rained from the ceiling into a large and perfectly white bathtub, releasing a cloud of steam into the marble room. Gerard shivered slightly and stepped inside the shower. He strangled a near-empty bottle to pump crimson soap into a puffy white loofah, then methodically washed each part of his body, starting with his face and working his way down his spindly frame. He massaged medicated shampoo first into his thinning black hair, next into his neat-trimmed mustache, and finally into the closely cropped thatch below his waist. He repeated the process with an upside-down bottle of conditioner.

Squinting across the bathroom, Gerard saw that it was almost ten after six. He stood in the shower until the second hand struck twelve, and barked, "Shower off!"

In five minutes, he was dressed in a black suit with a gray shirt and red-striped tie. Stepping to the bedside table, he opened a drawer glowing from golden-wrapped breakfast bars. He chewed a bar by the window while contemplating the tall, black building across the street from his penthouse. Jutting up into the sky at a slight angle, the headquarters of Breck Ammunition was designed in the shape of a gun clip. Completed ten years ago, it was still the tallest building in downtown Vegas. It had taken Gerard nine long years to work his way to top. Today, he would show them all why he deserved to stay there.

*

He reached his office at half past six. His assistant, Elza Meller, was waiting for him by the door. She wore a short black skirt that he didn't much like. It showed off too much of her legs.

"Good morning, Gerard."

He leaned into her, bringing his coffee-stained teeth about level with Elza's eyes. "Is O'Brien here?"

The assistant gave an exaggerated sigh. "He has just rung to say he is running a bit behind schedule."

He winced. "That is *not* allowed."

She nodded. "I told him we had a very tight schedule today."

"Tardiness is not allowed on *any* day."

"I think he is only a few minutes —"

"Send him in the *second* he arrives."

Gerard pushed into his office and slammed the door in Elza's face. He stomped toward his black leather chair, careful to avert his eyes from the portrait of Albert Breck hanging behind the large oak desk. He stared at a clock over the entrance and tapped his fingers. Glancing at his gold Rolex, he confirmed that O'Brien was now two minutes late and counting. He pulled up his agenda to see if there was any room to give for this delay. It would have to come out of this meeting. He would have to secure the deal quickly.

There were murmurs outside: Elza's voice, and then a man's. At long last, the door opened.

"Mr. Breck," said the inventor, a small pudgy man with thick-rimmed glasses. "So sorry I'm late. The traffic —"

"Sit." Gerard directed O'Brien to a steel metal chair on the other side of the desk. "Have you looked over the contract? We haven't much time."

The man sat in the chair and began sifting through a brown accordion portfolio. "Yes, but there are just a few things I wished to clarify."

Gerard's face darkened as looked at his watch. What could not be clear? "You have ten minutes."

The inventor pulled a tattered piece of paper out of the portfolio and dropped it onto the table. Gerard winced at the crinkles along the edges.

"It's about the royalties," said the inventor. "It seems to indicate here that the percentage of sales you're offering is, well, zero."

Gerard tugged at his mustache. As evenly as he could manage, he replied, "What I am offering you is an immediate payment of fifty *million* dollars, and you get that before a single gun is sold."

The inventor looked stymied. "But, Mr. Breck, this gun is a revolution! You said so yourself! You'll get that money back on the first batch of orders alone!"

Gerard picked up a pen and began clicking it. O'Brien was a greedy bastard. How dare he make eleventh-hour demands like this? How dare he take advantage of Gerard Breck?

"Mr. Breck?" O'Brien prompted.

Gerard mumbled, "You know I wanted a deal done before the gun show."

O'Brien shrank in his seat. "It's not that, Mr. Breck. I want to sell it to you, believe me, I do, but I have a family to think of."

"Do you have a family or a village?"

O'Brien leaned forward. "Sorry? I didn't hear —"

Gerard shut his eyes and clenched his teeth.

The gun inventor grimaced. "Mr. Breck?"

Keeping his eyes shut, Gerard asked flatly, "Do you have a counter-proposal, O'Brien?"

The inventor's face lit up. He reached into the portfolio, took out another piece of paper and pushed it forward. Gerard sat down to read it. O'Brien wanted a whopping twenty-five percent of sales.

The CEO of Breck Ammunition looked at his watch. "I need time to think this over, but I think you will agree that time is not something we have. So, I will make you this deal: We will announce the new gun this morning *as scheduled*, under what we will call a 'draft agreement.' We will continue to negotiate the final terms of our contract, and the gun will not go on sale until we have them. Is that acceptable to you, O'Brien?"

The gun inventor looked suitably pleased.

*

Liberty's churchyard buzzed with anticipation for the general public to enter the Breck Gun Show. Rosa, who as a member of the media could enter early, saw killing machines everywhere she looked. Handguns, rifles, shotguns — even crossbows and medieval maces brought by antiques dealers. A mélange of heavy metal tunes, blaring from different locations, combined into one swampy muddle, while food stands on the edge of the yard smoked with dead meat.

She caught herself looking for the Wanderer. She knew he wouldn't be here, but she looked anyway.

She had been to a Breck Gun Show once before, but it was many years ago, when she and Jack were still small. She remembered holding a Lassiter revolver, feeling the weight in her hands and thinking that only a hero could wield it, as if the silver handgun was the sword in the stone. Dad ended up buying her a pink toy replica. It came with a roll of gunpowder packets that exploded when you pulled the trigger. Jack got one, too, except his had been bright green. They spent the rest of the evening shooting at each other, stopping only when the gunpowder strips had breathed their last fire.

"Are you the reporter from *Our Times*?"

"Hm?"

While Rosa's mind had wandered, the racks of ammunition and hunting jackets opened into a large grassy area with a stage and several rows of cold gray folding chairs. And now there was a beautiful model, a small-framed woman with aggressive makeup, standing in front of her.

"Yes, hi," the reporter stammered, extending her hand. "Rosa Veras. I'm covering for Stephen."

"I am Elza Meller, head of communications for Breck Ammunition," the woman said with a light eastern European accent. The flack presented a business card. "Mr. Breck and I were very sorry to hear that Stephen could not make it. Is he well?"

Rosa shrugged — she had never actually met the gun reporter, nor did she particularly want to. "Oh, you know Stephen …" She forced a chuckle. "I think he had another commitment."

"In any case, we are pleased that you are here to represent *Our Times*. The first row is reserved for journalists, so please have a seat, and we shall get going shortly."

Rosa forced a smile and made her way to the front. She

recognized a few of the other reporters, but they were absorbed in their screens. She made a point not to say hello. Not that she had time! As soon as she sat down, a trumpet announced the entrance of Gerard Breck. In a scramble, Rosa opened a new document and hit *RECORD*.

Breck strode onto the stage wearing a pressed black suit. There was a slight arch to his posture that gave him the appearance of a stray cat. The microphone squealed as he approached it, eliciting a murmur of discomfort from the audience. With an apologetic smile, he steadied the mic and spoke in a low voice — more than a whisper, but weirdly confidential in tone.

"Hello, my friends in the media. Thank you for coming out to the annual Fourth of July news conference at the Breck Ammo Traveling Gun Show! As you know, this is my first year as CEO of the company."

That's right, thought Rosa, scrawling *G's first as CEO* into her notes. Gerard's stepfather, Albert Breck, had died last year. She vaguely recalled there had been a question of whether Gerard or his brother would take control of the company, but she hadn't followed the story very closely.

"When Dr. Richard J. Gatling went to build a machine gun for America, he stated his goal simply," Gerard orated. "He said he wanted to make a gun that could be operated by one man but do the work of one hundred men, saving ninety-nine others for the country. Today, Breck Ammunition announces a modern, next-generation Gatling, and it can do the work of a hundred automatic rifles! It's coming just in time for Christmas — we call it the Breck 100X!"

He reached into the pedestal and procured a sleek black rifle with a scope. The other journalists applauded reverently as he held it high in the air.

Gerard's thin arm shook slightly and he had to bring the gun back down before continuing his remarks. Elza stepped onto the stage and took the gun from him to display it, beaming like a game-show girl.

Breck continued. "This is a fully automatic, extreme long-distance, super high–caliber rifle, featuring close to zero kickback. The gun can be set up at long distance and fire one thousand rounds per minute into the target with maximum precision. The Breck 100X shoots faster and more efficiently than the Yossarian assault rifle. And its digitally enhanced 100X scope provides computer-assisted long-distance shooting rivaling our own Montag hunting rifle."

Rosa gasped audibly while the other reporters cheered. Here it was — the second fully automatic gun to be released following the amendment to the National Firearms Act making them legal for consumers, and it was an absolute killing machine. Why would any normal person need a gun like this?

"One thousand RPM!" cheered one of the other reporters. "How long will that last you?"

"Each clip carries one hundred and sixty rounds, so you'll get nearly ten seconds on each pull. I can assure you that the clips are very quick to load, but you'll find that out for yourself in a few minutes. For, you see, we will be giving all of you a chance to try our newest hunting rifle today!"

There was a heavy mechanical *thunk-thunk-thunk* from

behind Breck. Rosa stood to get a view and saw a line of four black helicopters flying toward them from the red mountains in the distance. When the choppers were no more than fifty yards away, they shifted into a hover and slowly descended onto the pavement behind the stage. The wind from the spinning blades rustled Gerard Breck's pressed suit.

Over the mechanized din, Breck shouted, "We will provide more details, including pricing and availability, in precisely one hour! But first, we hunt!"

Elza herded all of the reporters toward a rack of flight headsets. When everyone was properly outfitted for the flight, the flack broke the journalists into pairs, sending each group into one of three helicopters. Elza left to join the fourth with Gerard and a small man Rosa had not noticed before. He looked familiar, but she couldn't quite place him.

"Come on in, then!" laughed a burly man with aviators, pulling Rosa inside the helicopter's fuselage. The chopper was loud, but the flight headset let her hear the man's directions clearly as he strapped her into a seat facing the front. Next, he helped another reporter — a gray-haired man with bushy eyebrows — into the seat opposite. The Breck employee closed the sliding door and sat next to the older journalist.

This was Rosa's first time in a helicopter, and she was surprised to find the interior to be as polished as a limousine. The seats had thick cushions of cream-colored leather and wide armrests with extra-large cup holders. They were set across from each other with two seats facing the cockpit and another two pointed to the back of the aircraft. There was so much room, you could probably stand comfortably between the seats.

"My name's Zeke," said the man in the aviators. His voice buzzed through the ears of Rosa's headset. "Our pilot today is Jo."

He pointed behind his head to a window looking into the cockpit. The pilot was a woman with short brown hair. Zeke tapped the window twice to attract her attention and twirled his finger in a circle. Jo acknowledged the signal with a thumbs-up and the engine's hum increased in volume.

As the helicopter ascended, the other reporter introduced himself as Ben Ho with *Good Gun Guide*. Rosa did her best to explain who she was and where Stephen was.

"Y'all are in for a treat today!" exclaimed Zeke. "We're goin' deer hunting!"

Rosa marveled at how small the cacti and even the great red rocks looked from so high up. After some time, they reached a clearing of mint-green brush. The convoy of helicopters spread out into a circle. Zeke removed his seatbelt, then motioned for Rosa and Ben to do the same. He pulled a long black case out from under his seat and opened it to reveal a shiny new Breck 100X.

"We've only got one of these beauties per chopper, so you guys are going to have to take turns."

Ben gestured to Rosa. "Ladies first."

After some hesitation, Rosa stood to take the gun. Zeke slid open the door of the aircraft and a gust of wind blew into the cabin. She nearly lost her balance and imagined herself falling headfirst into the jagged rocks below. But the big man caught her and helped her down into a prone position on the buzzing floor.

The gun felt light but solid, its stock hugging her shoulder tightly. She scooted toward the door and looked down at a smattering of brown smudges among the green.

"Those are mule deer," said Zeke. "With an average rifle, we'd have to fly much lower than this, but that's the beauty of the Breck 100X. Have a look through the scope."

At first, Rosa found it difficult to focus with the view sliding wildly about, but after several seconds her hands became accustomed to making slower, steadier movements. Finally, she found them — reddish-brown deer with dark foreheads, near-white faces, and almost comically large ears. The bucks had majestic horns and beautifully defined muscles.

"Before you try to kill those ugly beasts," cautioned Zeke, "click the button on the right side of the rifle. That will turn on the assisted aim."

She could tell Zeke wasn't a hunter. Rosa's dad had always taught her that the best hunters respected their prey. People like Zeke and Gerard Breck just liked to shoot things.

When she turned on the assisted aim, the deer became outlined in bright red and Rosa immediately discovered a sleeping doe she hadn't noticed on the first sweep. As she moved the green X over it, the gun suddenly vibrated.

"With the assist mode on," said Zeke, "you'll feel a short burst of force feedback to let you know you're on target. It'll buzz again if you move off target. You'll also notice a number in the corner of your display showing the number of rounds you have left. Should be a full hundred-sixty right now, but we've got plenty of extra clips when you need 'em."

Rosa brought the green *X* onto a buck. The gun buzzed approvingly at the deer munching on the sage.

She had hunted before, with Jack and Dad, but never like this. Back then, it was for a meal. What was the purpose to this hunt?

With a touch of impatience, Zeke urged, "Feel free to fire whenever you're ready."

She couldn't go through with it. At the last second, she moved the sight to the left, feeling the gun buzz in outrage, and fired at a boulder.

Rosa didn't feel a thing as an incredible volley of shots flew out of the gun. A second later, the great rock exploded into a plume of brown dust. She saw a flash of the buck running away into the forest, escaping. And then suddenly it burst in red and fell over, caught by a barrage of bullets sent from one of the other choppers.

Zeke whooped. "Happy Fourth of July!"

*

The air was thick with gunfire and the steady thump of helicopter blades. Elza watched Gerard attentively as he stepped closer to the open door, soaking in the mayhem below. Across from her sat a heavyset man with neon green racing sunglasses, holding a Breck 100X across his lap.

She didn't want to see any of it, so she had made up an excuse about vertigo and stayed planted in her seat. It wasn't that Elza had anything against hunting — she did work for America's gun company, after all. She just didn't share Gerard's passion for blowing up defenseless animals.

"A success," Gerard remarked quietly. "A *rousing* success."

O'Brien, perched against the opening with one hand pressed against the wall, tittered excitedly. "Amazing, aren't they? If only we could demonstrate the guns' durability — drop the guns from this height and show the reporters how well they can take the fall! We did tests from about this height — higher, I think. A few scratches but they still worked brilliantly —"

"I believe I may have a new deal for you, Mr. O'Brien," interrupted Gerard.

That was Elza's cue. With a knowing smile, she took a folded piece of paper from her purse and handed it to the surprised gun inventor.

"Just one page?" he inquired worriedly.

Gerard stepped closer. "Read it."

O'Brien took the paper and immediately paled. "But this isn't what we discussed. It's the same as before. No royalties at all."

"It's not the same. I've also removed the money I planned to pay you upfront. The new deal is simple: *you* sign over the gun to *me*."

Elza handed O'Brien a pen, trying her best to maintain a poker face.

The gun inventor made an awkward motion like he was hitting a fly with a feather. "You must be joking. Why would I agree to that?"

Gerard exchanged glances with the heavy in the Day-Glo shades, who immediately gave him the Breck 100X. He took the rifle and trained it on O'Brien. "How well does this gun work at point-blank range anyway? I know it's meant for longer distances."

The gun inventor's arms sprung into the air and he backed

slowly toward the opening of the aircraft. "What … what are you doing? You can't —"

"Given the caliber and firing rate, I'd imagine it would be quite painful, yes?"

O'Brien stopped himself at the edge of the door and looked back. The other choppers were moving on to a new location while theirs remained hovering in place. They were alone.

Gerard grinned. "I would advise you to sign the contract, Mr. O'Brien. Immediately."

Elza held out the ballpoint again, willing O'Brien to take it. This time he did. He scrawled his signature on the paper. The big man in aviators snatched it away.

Breck scowled as O'Brien continued to stare morosely at the gun. "Something on your mind?"

Some red appeared in O'Brien's cheeks as he exhaled bitterly, "Your stepfather would never have done something like this."

Elza sighed. She suddenly felt great pity for the foolish gun designer. She knew from experience that it was not wise to bring up Albert Breck around Gerard.

Gerard's eyes popped, but he did not raise his voice beyond its usual flat baritone. "My stepfather is dead. Don't you remember, O'Brien? You *were* at the funeral, yes? There was Dad, lying in his casket, big and fat as ever, coated in spray tan, with cold, dead fingers wrapped around a Pilgrim shotgun …"

"I'm sorry, Mr. Breck, I —"

"Yes, you were there, weren't you? I remember it well. Sitting in the back, smoking a stogie. When it was over, you patted me on the back. Then, you walked up to Al's real son, Errol. You shook my stepbrother's hand like …" He laughed. "Why, it was like you thought you'd be business partners!"

"Your brother would never treat me like this," replied O'Brien with anger rising in his voice.

"*Step*-brother," growled Gerard.

Elza knew that menacing tone. Touching Gerard's arm, she whispered into his ear, "Baby, it's over. He signed the contract. Take a deep breath …"

Gerard didn't acknowledge her. He just kept staring at the gun inventor. "Look, O'Brien, I feel badly. I mean, if you really want the gun back …"

He flung the rifle hard. O'Brien caught it, but the force pushed him back and over the ledge. The gun and its maker disappeared in an instant. Elza couldn't stop staring at the space where a man had stood just seconds before. A hand on her shoulder roused her finally from her stupor.

"Elza," Gerard said gently. "Would you please call someone to retrieve the gun? It doesn't have to be right away. Just whenever they can do it. I'd like to see if Mr. O'Brien was correct about the weapon's ability to withstand a fall."

CHAPTER SEVEN

Let's Round Up Some Bad Guys!

Ben Martin took a deep whiff of barbecue and released a nasal sigh of satisfaction. This ritual completed, he ripped the chicken meat from the bone with his front teeth. The brown sauce covered his lips, but he didn't mind the tang.

Discarding the clean white bone into the grass, the sheriff continued his slow roam around the churchyard. It was a real nice gun show. It had been a relatively small affair in previous years, but by virtue of this one happening on the Fourth of July, the town had pulled in a big crowd from all around the western states. If Mayor White had done one good thing his whole time in office, it was bringing the Breck Independence Day event to Liberty this year.

Ben paused at a stand to inspect the camouflage hunting equipment. The fabric had that new-gear freshness, and he almost would have bought it, except that he didn't really hunt much anymore, did he? And anyway, he had more than enough of these kind of supplies back at the police office.

"Oh man! Sweet!" chirped a young voice.

Ben smiled at the small boy turning over in his hands a Breck

Classic bolt-action rifle. It was a gorgeous gun with a warm maple body. The metalwork, too, had outstanding craftsmanship. Folks liked to say about that gun, "They don't make 'em like that anymore." Well, sir, apparently they still did.

Of course, the sheriff did have to laugh seeing the big gun in the boy's hands. It looked heavy enough to topple him! "You might need your daddy's help with a gun like that," he advised.

The father, who'd been inspecting various boxes of shells, turned to the sheriff and jested, "I'm just hoping he gives *me* one or two pulls!" The two adults guffawed loudly while the boy played with the trigger. Wiping happy tears from his eyes, Martin said his good-byes.

Around the corner, a hot mama in a bikini beckoned. The top barely covered the full surface area of her tanned breasts. She was leaning against a motorcycle and stroking a long Pilgrim shotgun. Martin stared and let his mouth hang a bit — just enough so she would understand he was paying her a compliment. God, it had been too long …

Out of the corner of his eye, he noticed two men looking his way. Dougie, one of Martin's former deputies and an old friend, was pointing in his direction. The other man, who Ben didn't recognize, pointed to confirm. With a collared shirt that looked recently starched, the man looked out of place next to Dougie, who sported a mullet, torn jeans, and a NASCAR wifebeater.

Ben Martin crossed his arms as the stranger jogged over to him. What had his deputy gotten him into now?

"Sheriff Martin?"

Ben rocked slightly. "That's me."

The newcomer's eyes lit up with pleasure and he extended his hand to shake. "It's an honor to meet you, sir. The name's Joe Lin."

Martin considered him skeptically. "You from around here?"

"Born and raised before it was even called Liberty."

Laughing, Martin released his arms from his chest. "That's what I like to hear. And what do you do?"

"I'm a firefighter — used to be paid, but we're all volunteers now, what with the cuts and all that. You know how it is."

"I certainly do. Well then, what can I do for you, Joe?"

Lin pointed skyward. "I read what you said about standing up to lawlessness."

"Huh." So Rosie had written her damned vigilante justice story and someone had actually read it. At least it sounded like she'd quoted him correctly. "What about it?"

"Well, you see …" Lin's voice cracked as he spoke. Hoarsely, he whispered, "Last summer, I lost … I lost —"

"You lost someone." Whenever anyone in Liberty began a sentence that way, they were talking about what happened at Walmart. Martin was tired of talking about what happened that day.

Lin's voice sped up. "I know you did everything you could, sheriff. I'm not here to bring all that up again. Like I said, I read your quote and I just … I just couldn't get it out of my head! I thought and thought about it, and then I had an idea. I came to see you today so I could tell you directly."

Martin invited him for a drink at the Coyote Tavern. It seemed like the right thing to do, and anyway, he was thirsty after all that salty barbecue.

Gently, Jack Veras dropped a hand over his son's arm and felt that Pablo was still warm. The wires and tubes connecting the seven-year-old to the life support system rustled with the slow rise and fall of the boy's chest. He looked as if he was sleeping, but the truth was Jack hadn't seen Pablo's beautiful brown eyes for more than a year.

Jack took a seat in the worn red chair that had become his second home. He ran a hand over his own long hair, checking that the rubber band was properly fastened around his ponytail. His boy's hair was also getting longer, but with a foreign shock of white.

"Hey, Pablito," he said. "Know what today is? The Fourth of July! Independence Day! You always loved the fireworks, remember? All those bright colors in the night sky. You'll never believe where half the town is celebrating, though. A gun show! *Loco*, right? It's like they've all forgotten."

Jack pulled off his backpack and unzipped the main pocket. After fishing around for a few seconds, he retrieved a colorful magazine depicting a superhero in neon-green sunglasses and a black cape. "I read it already," he confessed. "I mean, after that cliffhanger last issue with Eirnen Enemy, can you blame me? I won't say what happens, but I really think you'll dig it."

He added it to the pile of unread comics on Pablo's bedside table. It was the latest issue of *Spy-Boy*, a teenage superhero who fought crime with a mix of stealth and gadgetry. He was Pablo's favorite. Jack remembered loving the book, too, when he was growing up, but he'd stopped reading when he left for law school.

There was just no time, and anyway it didn't seem like the kind of thing a lawyer should be reading. Years later, when Pablo became fascinated by superheroes, Jack found himself picking up the bent issues from the floor of his son's bedroom and flipping through the pages. The stories reminded him why he'd gotten into law in the first place — to fight for justice and protect the people who couldn't protect themselves. These had not been the kind of cases he found upon opening a law practice in Liberty. Turned out, victims of serious crimes usually got their justice through armed confrontation or by signing a contract with a mercenary. That left Jack with the small remainder of disputes between people who didn't want to settle their differences with guns. Divorces, mainly. Well, depending on the couple.

"Oh man, I almost forgot to tell you!" With breathless energy, he told his son about the standoff in the church. "A selfless vigilante with a sense of justice! Pablito, he was a real-life superhero!"

The boy didn't respond.

"That's okay, I'll tell you about him again someday." Sighing deeply, he added, "I still haven't heard from your mom."

He hadn't seen Elaine since she packed up and left three weeks after Pablo entered the hospital. He'd hired someone to find her and was told she'd gone east and become involved with some group called the Rising Atlantic, but he'd never found out who they were. The investigator hadn't failed, exactly. He just never came back.

In a way, Jack didn't really want to know where she'd gone, anymore. Elaine had abandoned him ... abandoned them. But she was still Pablo's mother. It would be nice for her be around when their boy finally woke up.

If he ever woke up.

Jack took his glasses off and placed them on top of the stack of comics. With a thick inhalation of breath, he began to cry.

*

"I can't believe someone actually read that garbage," Dougie blurted as Martin brought three glasses of Bud to the table.

The sheriff flashed a reprimanding look that forced the former deputy's wiry arms into the air. With all his tattoos, Dougie almost looked like a Red Striper, but the sheriff knew he'd never join with that band of assholes. Dougie used to be his best deputy on the force, back when he still had a budget. Unemployed now, he still liked to tag along with Martin, particularly when there was beer involved.

The deputy backtracked quickly. "I don't mean what you said was garbage, Ben. I just meant that *New West* blog ... you know, in general like."

"Don't listen to him," Martin told Lin with a slurp of the yellow beer. "Still, I should probably set the record straight. Everything I told that reporter may be correct but — and I hate to say this — the situation just might be hopeless. I don't have the government's support to take on folks like the Wanderer. Those asshats in the legislature seem to think an individual's right to seek justice is more important than enforcing the law."

"That may be so," said Lin, "but see, that's what I came to talk to you about. I reckon there's truckloads of men who don't like it, either. I know I don't! Well, I say we get the whole lot together and form a militia, just like our founders said to do in the Second Amendment! You know what I'm saying? Let's round up some bad guys!"

"A militia?" repeated Ben Martin. He was skeptical.

Lin nodded. "We'll call it Martin's Militia. You'd lead, of course, being the sheriff and all. We'll be your eyes on the street. As soon as one of us sees trouble, we'll call it in and rally the troops and show those outlaws that the town of Liberty is under lawful protection!"

Some beer dribbled down Dougie's chin as he exploded in giggles. "Martin's Militia? Are you fucking serious? How are we going to get anyone —?"

"Shut up, Dougie!" Ben scolded. "Joe, I personally apologize for this nimrod. But while he may be rude, I have to say I do have some reservations of my own. You can't fight lawlessness with lawlessness, otherwise, we ain't no better than the Wanderer or the Red Stripe Gang. So if we're going to have a militia, it's got to be composed of good men who want to enforce the law. How the law used to be."

Lin nodded appreciatively. "Sounds reasonable enough. What do you propose?"

"I say we limit this thing to former police officers and maybe some of your firefighter friends, if you trust them to do the right thing. I reckon that will give us more than enough men."

"Well, sure, I wouldn't want it any other way. Anything else?"

"Just one thing, we still won't have a budget. You really think we'll get anyone to join this thing?"

Lin took a long sip of his Bud. "I do. It's just like you say, sheriff.

People are sick of lawlessness! They won't be doing this thing for the money. They'll be doing it to keep their families safe. This is a wonderful town we have. It's worth protecting."

Martin had to admit Joe Lin might be onto something. He'd had no luck with the mayor, and already a week had gone by without results from the bounty on the Wanderer.

"Martin's Militia," said the sheriff, savoring the words like hot peppers in a good chili. "I do like the sound of it."

CHAPTER EIGHT

Now Ain't that Romantic?

The Happy Gunfighter was starting to grow on Charlie, but he had to say that the silver stars taped to the walls didn't do shit to brighten the dank saloon. He didn't like the spray of glitter on the bar counter, either. It cheapened the place, and worse, it stuck to the pint glasses.

Charlie's ears pricked up as someone batted open the double doors of the saloon. He turned slightly on his barstool as the Wanderer moseyed over to his usual booth along one of the walls. The cowboy flipped his two guns out of their holsters and rested them on the table before settling into the cushion. He had on his standard outfit: gray Stetson, brown leather jacket, plaid button-down, blue jeans, and big black cowboy boots. It had been the same thing, same time, same place every day for the last week.

The bounty hunter smirked as a waitress with long dark hair and vibrant eyes arrived unrequested at the Wanderer's table with a pint of dark beer. It sure hadn't taken long for Freetown to figure out the man's usual.

Charlie noticed he wasn't the only man watching. A trio of rough-looking men on the opposite end of the bar were practically drooling over the waitress. By the way they dressed — red-and-white bandannas, black leather jackets, and tattoos — Charlie could tell they belonged to the Red Stripe Gang. That was reason enough to hate them. The Gang had been a constant headache back home. Vegas was no Red Stripe town certainly, but the Gang controlled most of the jobs and had kept his family poor.

He tapped the glass on his wrist to check for messages, breathing a sigh of relief when he found nothing new from El Tiburón. Well, even if there had been, it didn't matter. Tonight he was gonna finish the job.

The bounty hunter threw back the last of the margarita and threw several bills down onto the bar. He squawked upon seeing his hands coated with silver glitter.

*

The Wanderer watched the funny man at the bar dust off his hands and walk, scowling, out of the saloon. The gunman slapped his empty pint glass on the table and licked his chops. The waitress, Lola, came by right away to pick it up.

"Another?" she asked.

"Yeah."

He reckoned it was time to get on the train again, move on to someplace new. One more night, perhaps. He might as well stay for the fireworks.

Helen had loved fireworks.

The Wanderer breathed her name and a photo appeared on his eyepiece. Through the lens, it almost looked like she was sitting across from him in the booth, smiling that damned lovely smile.

"I dreamed about you again," he whispered to the ghost.

The nightmare went like this: Helen is sleeping, and he has his arm around her soft form. There's a noise downstairs. He grabs his Breck 17 and goes to look. The house still smells like lasagna when he finds the intruder and shoots him dead. Then there's another noise, behind him this time. He turns and fires ...

He'd risen in a cold sweat before the story could finish. He told himself it was just a dream. But it wasn't.

When the beer arrived, the Wanderer tipped his hat in thanks.

"Plans for tonight?" the waitress asked.

"Reckon I'll go to the meadow to see the fireworks."

"Sounds nice," she said, running her finger along the edge of the table.

"Thanks for the beer."

With a frown, Lola turned and nearly walked into a large man wearing a Harley-Davidson motorcycle jacket. He had a big, black beard and wore a red-and-white lined bandanna on his head. The Wanderer figured him for a member of the Red Stripe Gang.

"Easy, baby!" the gangster exclaimed. His voice was like gravel under the tires of a car. "Was just going to ask you if me and my buddies could get a taste of something."

He pointed to two men standing in the opposite corner of the bar. One of the men had a shaved head and a white singlet that showed off a spray of X marks running from his throat down to each arm. The other Red Striper was more compact, with arms and legs that looked like pipes. He was cleaning some kind of pistol, probably a Breck 17.

The Wanderer imagined the three gangsters sitting back on a

picnic blanket, pointing at the fireworks and holding hands. The picture made him laugh.

Noticing, the gangster growled, "What's so funny?"

The Wanderer pointed to his electronic eyepiece. "Oh nothin'. Just watchin' a rom-com."

*

Charlie passed a cart of white sheets and tiny bottles of shampoo outside Room 8 of the Freetown Motor Lodge. There was a sign on the door that read *DO NOT DISTURB*. Charlie tapped his wrist against the knob and went inside.

In the bathroom mirror, he stared himself down and shouted, "Tonight's the night! Tonight's the night!"

Turning to a small closet safe, Charlie keyed a code and procured a black case. Balancing it gingerly on the unmade bed, he lifted the latches and flipped open the top. He took in the sleek black handgun with a deep breath. Carefully, he screwed a scope and a silencer onto the Separatist, and loaded a magazine of bullets into the butt. He pulled up the pistol and made like he was about to fire. As he gripped the smart gun, his wristband glowed green.

Charlie could see it clearly. He'd find the Wanderer in the meadow where they were going to have the Fourth of July display. The sun would go down and the fireworks would begin. As everyone looked bright-eyed into the sky, Charlie would move through the crowd toward his target. The Wanderer would never see Charlie coming. Another firecracker would explode and the Wanderer would be dead.

That was all he had to do. Shoot the Wanderer, get the money, and move on to the next job.

Charlie dropped the gun on the white linen. As he did, the light on his wrist turned red and blinked off. He slipped on a burgundy track jacket, humming "America the Beautiful" as he admired himself in the mirror. Then he took the smart gun from the bed and slipped it into a custom-designed holster hidden inside his jacket.

Charlie sang, "*And crown thy good with brotherhood, from sea to shining sea!*"

When he opened the door to go outside, there was a maid standing in his way. "Done in there?" she asked. There was an edge to her voice that Charlie didn't appreciate.

Slapping the *DO NOT DISTURB* sign off the door, he replied, "Do what you gotta do."

When he got to State Street, he came upon a large throng of people carrying baskets, tote bags, and ice boxes. A sparkler whizzed by his face, and Charlie nearly fell backward.

"Sorry, mister!" the teenage perpetrator shouted back.

"Watch it!" He noticed his right hand shaking and stopped it with his left. Touching the gun inside his jacket for comfort, he joined the townspeople marching down the street.

The meadow was a big field on the north end of town, spotted here and there with saplings and sprays of colorful flowers. A large white gazebo sprang up from the ground at the far edge, where green grass ran up against the red desert. Inside the bandstand, children in a brass ensemble straightened music stands and blew spit out of their instruments. A group of fireflies joined them for the opening act.

Charlie leaned against a tree and scanned the area for the Wanderer. He was certain he would be here. For nearly a week, the rogue had been asking the locals about their strategies for seeing the fireworks. For whatever reason, the guy seemed to have a real hard-on for the Fourth of July. Personally, Charlie didn't get what the big deal was. What was there to celebrate?

When he finally spotted the Wanderer, he nearly burst out laughing. The gunman was on his knees, talking to a teary-eyed little girl. She appeared to be about ten, give or take a couple of years, and by herself. The Wanderer had a hand on her shoulder. She pointed away from the meadow to one of the dusty hills in the distance. Charlie pulled up his handgun and looked through the scope. In the sand were tire tracks from three motorbikes. Lowering the lens, he saw the Wanderer jogging back toward State Street.

"Where the hell do you think you're going?" the bounty hunter cried. For an explanation, he consulted his wristband, pulling up the social feed and localizing it for the meadow. In seconds, he had an answer. Several people in the area reported seeing a trio of strangers take a man from his daughter and force him onto the back of a motorcycle. Apparently, no one had tried to stop them.

There was a photo. It was blurry and not centered properly, but Charlie recognized the men immediately as the Red Stripers from the saloon.

Charlie let that last piece of information bounce around in his head. So the Wanderer was planning to take on the Red Stripe Gang, all on his lonesome. Only three of them, but still …

A laugh trickled ruefully from the bounty hunter's lips as the Wanderer hopped onto a parked motorbike and roared off in the direction the gangsters had gone. "That crazy son of a bitch!"

*

The Wanderer leaned forward into the handlebars of the stolen motorbike as it climbed the dusty red hill. The Red Striper who had taken the little girl's daddy couldn't have gone far, but he prayed he would make it in time.

For the life of him, he couldn't make sense of what she had told him. She'd come to see the fireworks with her pa. Three men wearing the colors of the Red Stripe Gang showed up on motorcycles, demanding that her daddy come with them. When he refused, the gangsters tied his hands together and forced him onto the back of one of the bikes. They drove him out into the desert up a big hill that had come to be known locally as Hangman's Last View.

The Wanderer had an idea of what might be waiting on the other side of the hill. What he couldn't figure out was why the Red Stripe Gang would care about this one man. They didn't kill people randomly, let alone string 'em up. He reckoned that girl's daddy must have riled up the Gang something fierce.

He spied a low bush of cactus just in time to pull left around it. But the move set the bike heading straight for a large red rock inclined forty-five degrees up over the peak of the hill. With no time to go around it, the Wanderer pulled up on the handlebars and lifted the front tire onto the boulder. Together, man and bike leaped into the air. For a split second, he took in the evening stars.

Then, as he pushed the bike down to complete the airborne arc, he saw the hanging tree and four men.

The bike landed with a thud, unleashing a sandstorm on the other side of the hill. The cloud of dust blinded the Wanderer but he was able to follow the gangsters' yells. When the exclamations grew loud and close, he swerved sideways and slammed on the brakes, setting off another wave of dust.

The Wanderer waited for the air to clear with his hands ready at his hip holsters. A flabby man with a bandana tied tightly over his mouth appeared through the cloud of dirt. The Gang members had tied the man's wrists and ankles and slung a noose over his head. The rest of the rope was swung over a thick branch jutting out sideways from a knotted tree, about ten feet up the trunk. The burly gangster from the bar in the Harley-Davidson jacket held the victim protectively like a shield, while the other two gangsters — the pipe-limbed crook and the man with the X tattoos — held the rope firmly on the other side. A strong pull could lynch the man in seconds.

The hogtied victim strangled out a wide-eyed exclamation.

"Let him go!" directed the Wanderer.

"Who the fuck are you?" yelled Pipes, letting go of the rope and waving his Breck 17 erratically.

Harley's eyes glinted with recognition. "You're the sissy from the saloon." A deep laugh erupted from his belly as he turned to enlighten his colleagues. "This is that wimp I was tellin' y'all about! The one who was watchin' some damn rom-com movie at the saloon!"

Pipes and Mr. X cackled gleefully, but stopped abruptly when the Wanderer laughed back. "Oh, there weren't no movie. I was just watchin' the three of you flirtin' with one another." That stopped their laughter, but the Wanderer kept going. He nodded at the knotted oak. "I reckon y'all found yourselves a mighty fine kissin' tree."

At that instant, there was a pop and an explosion in the sky. With a wide grin, the Wanderer stuck his thumb back at the spray of falling red light from the evening's first firecracker. "Now ain't *that* romantic?"

Pipes pointed his gun at the Wanderer's chest and looked to Harley for directions. Several more explosions lit up the sky. Faintly, in the background, the Wanderer could hear the brass band playing "The Star Spangled Banner."

Harley yelled over the commotion, "I think you best be getting back to town for the celebrations! This right here don't concern you!"

The Wanderer shook his head. "I'm afraid it does. I won't let you turn that little girl back there into an orphan."

Pipes gave his boss another look, raising his eyebrows in question. As Harley nodded, the Wanderer lifted his Lassiter revolver. When Pipes turned, the Wanderer fired.

The sky turned blue as the skinny gangster's plain white T-shirt turned beet red. Mr. X dropped the rope, letting it whip loose over the tree. Before the Red Striper could reach his gun, the Wanderer turned and fired a bullet through the ink cross on his throat. A quartet of trombones sang out in patriotic approval as Mr. X fell choking into the dirt.

Harley charged, carrying the bug-eyed victim in his arms like a battering ram. The Wanderer lined up a shot but, fearing that he might miss and hit the civilian, held his fire too long. The bound-and-gagged man flew from Harley's grip, and the Wanderer could do nothing to dodge. Taking the full impact of the victim's head in the ribs, he fell backward and dropped the Lassiter. The human missile fell heavily on top, pinning the gunman to the ground.

The Wanderer didn't need his smart lens to tell him that the girl's daddy was unconscious, a dead weight that couldn't easily be budged. But he had moved heavier loads before. Straining with all his might, the gunslinger pushed ... and pushed ... until finally, he managed to roll the other man off.

Harley lumbered forward. Sitting up, the Wanderer saw a chance to shoot the gangster with his Breck 17, but couldn't decide if he was ready to use the bad gun. Once more, hesitation got the best of him. The Red Striper tackled him like a football player, using his entire bulk to press him against the rocky sand.

"Hold still!" screamed Harley. He was trying to reach for a knife in his coat. The Wanderer twisted and bucked for all he was worth but the gangster was too strong and heavy.

As a blue firecracker reflected in the knife's mirror blade, he remembered kissing Helen on top of a picnic blanket on this day two years ago. She had looked so beautiful.

The dagger continued to hover inches away from his chest, but Harley was gaping at something in the distance. The distraction was behind the Wanderer and he couldn't see what it was, but he could hear the hum and scrape of an approaching motorcycle. Another firecracker went off. The gangster's mouth opened in a silent scream, like fresh bait on a fishing hook. Blood spluttered from Harley's forehead, and he collapsed in a sprawl on top of the Wanderer. Another dead weight, but this one was *really* dead.

Footsteps scuffed fast toward him. Someone grabbed dead Harley by the shoulders, pulling hard. The Wanderer pushed, and together they rolled the burly gangster onto his back.

*

Charlie watched the Wanderer tear a piece of cloth from the Red Striper's shirt and use the rag to wipe the blood off his own face. The gunman looked as though he could use a hot shower.

The bounty hunter tried on a puckish smile. Truth was, he didn't know how he was supposed to act in the circumstance. What do you say to a man after you save his life when what you'd meant to do was kill him? Charlie didn't like riddles.

The Wanderer picked up his Stetson from the ground, dusted it off, and replaced it carefully atop his wild brown hair. Charlie extended a hand, meaning for the Wanderer to shake it, but the gunman just said, "Nice to finally meet you, bounty hunter."

The statement knocked the wind out of Charlie better than any punch. So, the Wanderer had known! For how long?

"I appreciate the help, but get this straight — I don't like bounty hunters."

Charlie nodded slowly. "Because I was going to kill you or in gen —?"

"In general."

"Yeah, okay, man. Word. But, hey, for what it's worth, I ain't gonna kill you no more." He made a crossing motion with his hands to emphasize the point. "I mean, you seem all right, you know what I'm saying? And bounty hunting? Well, I think I'm just about done with *that* shit. Doesn't suit a man of my sophistication, you know? Besides, the way I see it, any man who's an enemy of the Red Stripers is a friend of mine!"

The Wanderer considered the three gangsters, following their lifeless stares up to the red-spattered sky. "Pretty night for fireworks."

Charlie laughed. "I like you, man! You got that dry sense of humor. Hey, tell you what: let me help you bring the guy in the rope suit back into town before his daughter runs off and gets into trouble. Least I can do, right?" Detecting an unsure look in the Wanderer's eyes, he pressed on. "Oh, and I know you like that sludgy dark beer. Well, when we finish this up, how about I buy you one? The name's Charlie, by the way."

"Heh." The Wanderer's eyes relaxed, and he gestured to the unconscious man. "Let's get him up, then."

*

The Wanderer reunited father and daughter and escorted the two of them back to their house in the Freetown suburbs. He let the bounty hunter tag along.

It was a messy home, but it was cozy, and the Wanderer could tell it was full of love. They sat around a wooden dining table, resting their drinks on magazines and torn envelopes. Three of the glasses contained whiskey; the fourth was filled to the brim with chocolate milk. The kid's drink belonged to a mousy little girl named Kitty. She was dressed for sleep but full of vigor, and a pair of thick red glasses magnified her rapt attention.

"You've been looking at me funny all night," said the Wanderer. "What do you want to know?"

"Are you the Wanderer?"

Charlie laughed. "He certainly is."

The Wanderer suggested, "Maybe you should go up to bed."

"She can stay," said her father, Tony Potobo, as he rubbed the red marks on his neck left by the rope noose.

Kitty beamed. "I've read about you, Wanderer, how you helped that girl in Liberty."

"You *read* about me?"

"There was a blog," explained Charlie. He meant the statement to be helpful but Kitty turned on him immediately.

"Who are *you* anyway?" she demanded.

The bounty hunter looked at the Wanderer for help.

"It don't matter who he is. He's just some punk kid who reckons he's a bounty hunter."

Kitty looked mad. "That's not a name."

Charlie laughed and told her his real name, but the girl still looked unsatisfied. "No, you need a cool name, like the Wanderer has."

As Charlie started to protest, the Wanderer burst out with a deep, booming laugh.

"Punk ... no," she continued undeterred. "Kid ... Hunter. Kid Hunter! That's a good name!"

"You know what?" mused Charlie. "That's actually pretty sick!" He lowered his voice and spoke like the narrator of a movie trailer. "Who's that cool stranger? It's Kid Hunter, and if looks could kill, you'd be dead already." He sat there grinning until the others' stares became too oppressive. "What?"

"That's not very good," said Kitty.

Tony guffawed and squeezed his little girl. "The Wanderer and Kid Hunter — gee, Kitty, you make these guys sound like a couple of Western heroes!"

"They are heroes! They rescued you!"

The Wanderer half smiled. "I don't know about that. I reckon Mr. Kills-With-Looks here didn't come to Freetown to save the day."

He had figured the kid for a bounty hunter from the day he stepped into the saloon. Charlie had been watching him for nearly a week. The Wanderer did some asking around and discovered that, yessiree, someone had put a bounty on his head. The job was posted not long after the shooting in Liberty, and this kid apparently was the one who'd taken it on. Well, he sure had a funny way of going about a kill.

"I never miss a chance to take down the Red Stripe Gang," Charlie answered. "Anyway, why did you come to Freetown, Wanderer?"

"Reckon I'm just here for the fireworks." He gulped the rest of his whiskey and pointed at the girl's father. "Look, I suppose that's about enough pleasantries. I want to know why the Red Stripe Gang was after you tonight."

Tony turned his glass on the table a few times before answering. "They ... they've threatened me before. Told me to stop making them."

"Making what?"

Kitty chimed in. "Daddy's a gun maker!"

Tony smiled modestly. "Not really. I just design them. People have to print them out themselves."

Charlie scrunched his eyes. "What do you mean, 'print them out'?"

The Wanderer grinned. "He's talking about 3-D printing. DIY gunmakin'. May I see?"

Tony excused himself to the garage. When he returned he was holding a plastic gun that was a ringer for a Breck 17. The Wanderer weighed it in his hands and whistled. "It fires well?"

"Just as you'd expect. I'm starting to work on a few enhancements that should make it better even than the stuff at Breck Ammunition."

It all made sense now. Printing your own gun wasn't illegal, technically, but the Wanderer knew for a fact the gun monopoly wouldn't like anything that might cut into its profits.

"So the Red Stripe Gang didn't want you selling your own guns?" asked Kid Hunter. "But why would they care about that? Did they want a cut of the action?

Tony said no. "They only ever told me to stop what I was doing. Delete the design, burn all records of it …"

The Wanderer waved the men to silence. "It's not the Red Stripe Gang who wants to destroy your design," he said, leaning back thoughtfully in his chair. "It's Gerard Breck."

CHAPTER NINE

Sensationalist Speculation!

Rosa had pulled an all-nighter writing the article about the Breck 100X for *Our Times*. It wasn't that she was slow, or that it was a complicated story. Something just kept stopping her from feeling satisfied. First, she tried writing it the way she knew her editor would want it. That was a piece of crap, so she tried writing it the way she wanted to write it. That felt good, but she knew Rebecca would hate it, so she started over again. On about the eighth version — and her fourth cup of coffee — Rosa sent in the article and called it a night.

Only it was already morning. So, she made a fifth cup of coffee and, with bleary eyes, opened *The New West* to check her traffic.

She sighed. A few hundred visitors in the past week. Not bad, but not great. The bland stories she wrote for *Our Times* usually got that many hits within an hour of publication.

Her phone rang. Rosa grimaced at the name on the caller ID.

"It's Rebecca," her editor confirmed when Rosa answered. "I don't understand your story."

The reporter felt her grip tighten around the cell phone. She took a deep breath and replied as cheerfully as she could manage.

"Hi, Rebecca. I'll pull up the article on my computer. Which part do you need me to clarify?"

The managing editor of *Our Times* emitted a small squawk. "I don't know where to start, quite frankly."

Rosa waited.

"I mean, there's your proposed lead: 'A new assault weapon announced by Breck Ammunition makes the statement that there is no such thing as overkill.'"

"Mm-hm?"

"Rosa, you do remember that Breck Ammunition owns *Our Times*?"

Rosa shook her head angrily. "I didn't realize my assignment was to write an ad. I thought I was supposed to report the news."

"News? This isn't news. This … drivel … is editorial! You're supposed to report the facts and only the facts. Leave it up to the reader to decide if the gun is overkill."

Rosa sighed. "I'll rewrite the lead."

"What if you just said, 'A new assault weapon announced by Breck Ammunition makes a statement,' and then just leave it at that?"

Teeth gritted, Rosa seethed, "I'll rewrite the lead."

"It's not just the lead. This entire recap of the hunt is overly gory, and you present it as if it's some kind of junket designed to bribe you into writing nice things about Breck Ammo!"

She nearly laughed. That's *exactly* what it was.

"In fact, I might just cut the hunt out of the story altogether. Just talk about the features of the gun and how the readers can make an order. In fact, I think you can also cut this whole section recapping how Gerard Breck took control of the company. That's irrelevant to the story."

Rosa's jaw dropped. "Irrelevant? This was his first gun show as CEO!"

Rebecca sighed deeply. "I just don't think it's worth mentioning. Cut it out of the story, rewrite the rest as discussed and send it back to me within the hour so we can post the article. We're already late on the story as it is. The gun blogs had this up last night and Breck Ammo is asking what happened to the national news article."

The phone beeped. Rosa stared in disbelief at the message on the screen: *Rebecca Song has ended the call.*

"Bitch!" she screamed into the phone.

Composing herself, Rosa turned to her computer. She made a copy of the document, renamed it *neutered gun show story* and began her edit.

Well, not quite yet. First, another cup of coffee was in order. She stood frowning over the machine as it dripped brown liquid into a glass pitcher. A flare of morning sunlight through the window provided momentary perspective. Get through this stupid *Our Times* story ... and then back to work on *The New West*.

She poured herself the coffee, added a splash of milk, and returned to her desk. It didn't take long to dumb down most of the copy to *Our Times* standards, but she hesitated to delete the part about Gerard Breck's takeover of Breck Ammunition.

He'd been in control of the company for less than a year, replacing his late stepfather, Albert, the company's founder. Nobody had expected Gerard's ascension; they figured Al's blood child, Errol, would take over the company. But something unexpected happened — Errol disappeared.

She studied a picture of Errol and realized she'd seen him many times before in *Our Times*. He was handsome, in a pampered rich kind of way. He had an expertly groomed brown mustache and beard, and he smiled as though he hadn't had to lift a finger his whole life. Perhaps the most notable thing about him were his eyes, piercing and green. There was a glamorous woman in his arms, too. She had stylish, shoulder-length blonde hair and wore a pink designer jacket. She had to be his wife.

He'd seemed to lead a pretty blessed life, so what happened? Rosa looked into that and found an obituary for Errol's wife dated right around the time of his disappearance. Some men had broken into the house — burglars, the article claimed — and one of them shot her. Errol had missed his wife's funeral. The Board of Breck Ammunition ordered a search, but nothing ever came of it. Officially, Errol was declared missing. A few days later, Gerard announced himself as the new CEO of Breck Ammunition.

The computer chimed with a new message.

Kittees4evaOMG:
@TheNewWest The Wanderer and Kid Hunter just saved my dad!

She read the message over a few times, trying to make sense it. Based on the user handle, it was either a little girl or some kind of amateur pornographer. Deciding it was more likely to be the former, she replied.

TheNewWest:

@Kittees4evaOMG Hi, there. Free to chat about it?

Kittees4evaOMG:

@TheNewWest Yea! Wat u want 2 kno?

Rosa opened a secure private chat and began to interview the girl. It didn't take long to realize that it was going to be one hell of a story for *The New West*. This was more than just another Wanderer sighting. He had showed up in Freetown and saved the life of a man involved in a 3-D gun printing business. This time, the Wanderer had teamed up with another vigilante, a new sensation apparently called "Kid Hunter," and together they'd stopped the execution, killing three members of the Red Stripe Gang. Perhaps most shocking of all, the Wanderer blamed the attempted hanging on the CEO of Breck Ammunition.

Her mind wandered back to the junket, and she remembered she still had to file a revised story to *Our Times*. She pulled up the document again, cut the remaining bits of controversy and sent it off to Rebecca. Whatever. She was over all that.

There was still something bothering her about the gun show. She remembered seeing a short, balding man get on the helicopter with Gerard Breck and his PR flack, but when they returned from the hunt, he wasn't there. She remembered now that she'd seen him during her research of the gun company. She checked back over her notes and found the picture again. She was almost sure he was Tom O'Brien, the gun designer who'd developed several of the weapons the company had released over the years. She'd planned to follow up on this later, but with the new information from Kitty …

Rosa searched *Tom O'Brien gun inventor* in the *Our Times* contact database. In seconds, she had O'Brien's home phone number. It rang a few times until a harried woman answered, "Tom? Is that you?"

"Uh, no, sorry … I'm actually looking for him. This is Rosa Veras. I'm a journalist." She didn't say from where.

The woman was O'Brien's wife, and she told Rosa that she hadn't seen her husband since he had left that morning to see Gerard Breck at his office. The two men flew together from Vegas to Liberty for the gun show. Tom sent her a selfie in the helicopter, but she hadn't heard from him since.

"I think I saw him get onto the helicopter," confessed Rosa, "but I didn't see him get off. I don't know what happened."

The line went silent.

"Mrs. O'Brien? Could you tell me why Tom went to see Mr. Breck this morning?" Rosa asked.

There was a sigh. "It was the contract for the new gun," Mrs. O'Brien said. "Tom hadn't signed it yet. That bastard Breck was trying to screw him out of the royalties. Tom said he was going to talk to him and make everything right."

Rosa thanked Mrs. O'Brien and said she would call back if she learned anything more. Opening a fresh document on her computer, the journalist's fingers whirred into motion.

When she finally came up for air, she exclaimed a string of profanities. The story was pretty damning. She should probably ask Breck Ammunition for comment.

Taking a deep breath, she picked up the phone and dialed the head of communications for Breck Ammo.

After two rings, a woman with an accent answered, "Breck Ammunition. This is Elza."

"Hi, Elza. This is Rosa from the press junket."

She bit her lip. Probably shouldn't have called it a junket. Luckily, the PR flack didn't seem to take offense.

"Oh, yes, Rosa! Have you put up your piece yet? We are looking forward to reading it."

It took Rosa a few seconds to remember which story she was talking about. "Oh, I just filed that. It should be up soon. That's not why I'm calling."

"Oh?"

"I'm actually working on another story." She pinched herself for the unsure way she spoke. Sound more confident! You're supposed to be a journalist!

Elza asked, "You're looking for comment?"

She told the PR flack the whole thing. Well, most of it. Mainly the part about Breck hiring the Red Stripe Gang to hang the guy with the 3-D printing operation.

There was a long silence on the other end of the line. When Elza finally spoke, her voice was cold and deadly. "This is a *joke*, right?"

Rosa felt like a mouse caught in a trap. "I ... um ... unfortunately it's not. I'm not saying I think your boss did that ... I'm just saying what someone else said ..."

All of the flack's former friendliness had vanished from her voice. "You mean what a nameless vigilante suggested, based on the hearsay of a ten-year-old girl. You are truly planning to print this?"

Rosa had to admit the evidence sounded pretty thin when Elza put it like that. "Well, that's why I'm asking you for comment, in order —"

"— to legitimize your story. Well, I'm sorry, Ms. Veras. We will not comment on sensationalist speculation! Off the record, I will tell you that your story is completely outrageous, and you would be very foolish indeed to publish it."

Rosa wondered if that was a threat. She decided not to clarify.

Elza continued. "You know, I believe that I will call your editor to learn what she thinks about this."

Rosa cursed inwardly. She was already on thin ice with Rebecca. Something like this could mean her job. She knew that was a possibility from the minute she came up with *The New West*, but she hadn't expected it to happen so soon. She'd barely gotten going. She needed more time.

"You don't have to do that ..." Rosa begged meekly. "Look, Elza, I'm sorry. I won't publish it in *Our Times*."

Another long pause. "Do you promise? I want to have your word, Rosa."

"You have it. I promise that I will not publish this in *Our Times*. But if you don't mind, I do have one other question. It's unrelated."

"What?"

"Was Tom O'Brien on your helicopter? I thought I saw him."

After a pause, Elza replied, "Yes, he was."

"Oh, because I didn't see him afterward." She added quickly, "I would have liked an interview."

"I am sorry we could not arrange that. Unfortunately, Mr. O'Brien ... had to jump off early."

BRECK CONNECTED TO RED STRIPE GANG

By New West Reporter

After Breck Ammunition unveiled its latest killing machine, the vigilante known as the Wanderer uncovered violent practices by CEO Gerard Breck to protect his company's monopoly.

The New West has learned that the Wanderer, who two weeks ago shot up a Catholic church in Liberty while seeking justice for an attempted murder, surfaced again in Freetown on the Fourth of July. This time, he stopped three members of the lawless Red Stripe Gang attempting to hang the father of a young girl.

The father, Tony Potobo, sold in the trade of 3-D printed guns, an emerging business that has placed increasing pressure on the revenue of America's dominant gun manufacturer, Breck Ammunition.

Evidence suggests that the Red Stripe Gang acted in the interests of Gerard Breck, who sought to put an end to Potobo's business. The hanging was to be a bold warning for anyone else who might try to compete with "Big Ammo."

Luckily for Potobo, the Wanderer was watching. Joined this time by an accomplice known as Kid Hunter, the Wanderer made quick work of the gangsters and reunited father with daughter.

"He was really nice," Potobo's girl, Kitty, said of the Wanderer. "Like, really serious, but also really nice. Kid Hunter was okay, too."

Kitty said she heard the Wanderer conclude that Gerard Breck and his company Breck Ammunition were behind the attempted hanging. We contacted Breck Ammunition for comment, but their spokesperson declined.

The Potobos fled their home in Freetown soon after the attack. The current locations of the Wanderer or Kid Hunter are unknown.

The events capped an explosive Independence Day celebration that began with Breck unveiling a rapid-fire hunting rifle — really a sniper rifle — at the company's annual gun show. Visiting journalists were treated by the company to helicopter rides during which they were asked to try out the super long–range guns on herds of mule deer.

The New West spotted the gun's inventor, Tom O'Brien, getting on Gerard Breck's helicopter for the shoot. Strangely, he has not been seen since.

O'Brien's wife said she has not seen or heard from her husband since he left their house that morning. She said he had gone to the Vegas headquarters of Breck Ammunition with an intention to change some of the terms in the contract for the sale of the Breck 100X.

The Breck Ammunition spokeswoman confirmed that O'Brien had been on the helicopter with herself and Breck during the time of the event. Asked to explain what happened to him, the Breck spokeswoman explained, "Mr. O'Brien had to jump off early."

CHAPTER TEN

This ... Blog ...

From atop his black leather throne, the CEO of Breck Ammunition gazed listlessly at two minions gesticulating wildly before him. They seemed to be trying to make a point, but so far, Gerard's main takeaway was that their gray suits were begging for a good tailor.

"What we need is a new paradigm for gun delivery," said one businessman.

"Agile gun delivery," finished the other, whose name Gerard also couldn't remember. "We come out with new models every couple of years, but with these print-at-home guns catching on, that's not going to be fast enough. We need more updates and a faster release cycle."

Gerard thought of the gun inventor falling from the chopper. "Do we ..." he said, stroking his mustache, ". . . have the R&D for that?"

"Oh, no need for extensive R&D," answered the first businessman, raising his eyebrows meaningfully. "The improvements won't be significant. By using clever naming and switching up the colors and build materials, I think we can keep the same functionality and still convince people we're releasing new guns. We'll even get collectors who want to have them all! Imagine, the Breck 17 S-series, featuring crocodile leather hand grips! Or gunmetal steel for the Breck 17 Classic! We'll add camouflage colors and call it the Breck 17 Stealth!"

The other marketer clapped his hands. "People will think we are advancing the shit out of guns!"

"Speeding up the cadence!" added the first.

"No more waterfall!"

"Agile!"

For the heck of it, Gerard did a quick spin in his chair. As he passed one hundred and eighty degrees, he caught a glimpse of his father's eyes looking down at him. He hated that mural, and yet he couldn't bring himself to get rid of it.

"Sir?" asked one of the employees upon the CEO's completion of the turn.

Gerard yawned. "Wait ... is this ... is this the same ... as that ... that, uh, good data thing?"

"Big data!" exclaimed one of the suits. "Yes ... and no! Going agile will integrate with big data *for sure*, but this is something else! Big data will let us predict who wants to buy a gun —"

"— before they even know they want it!" finished the second businessman.

The gun marketers high-fived. As they continued onto the next page of their presentation, Gerard's mind wandered back to his stepfather. Gerard had joined the Breck family at the age of nine when his divorced mother, Iris, married Al. Most boys that age resented the second husbands of their mothers, but Gerard was pleased to be joining the Brecks. His real father had left when he was just a baby, and he and his mom had been scraping along ever since. She never let him know what exactly she was doing to earn money, and Gerard knew enough not to ask.

When Al Breck met and fell in love with Iris, it was as if a beacon of light had shone down from Heaven. She wouldn't have to work anymore. He and his mother would have a future. And their savior was America's greatest gun inventor. Until, in one terrible instant, their fortunes changed.

He was sixteen and learning to drive on a permit. His mother was in the passenger seat of the Chrysler, telling him how well Errol was doing in his first year of business school. Gerard had lost it.

"You're supposed to be *my* mother!" he'd screamed while flooring the gas pedal. All he wanted was to scare her, to make a point. He didn't see the red light and was shooting right through it when something big slammed into the right side of the car. His last memory was a feeling of astonishment as the traffic revolved fast around him.

Gerard had awoken in the hospital with cuts and a broken arm. He'd asked for his mother but was told she never made it out of the car. An eighteen-wheeler had rammed into the Chrysler's rear wheel and passenger door, killing Iris Breck on impact and sending the sedan into a violent spin.

His stepfather had refused to visit Gerard in the hospital. It was only for the love of Iris that he'd put up with her troublesome son. Errol sent an e-card but never bothered coming home from college. When the hospital eventually released him, Gerard had no allies in the Breck household. Al called him a fuckup and sent him away to an out-of-state boarding school to finish his primary education.

That had hurt, but he'd ultimately decided that this cold knock of reality was good for him. He had spent his childhood letting Mom fight his battles. Without her, he would have to fight for himself. He would have to earn his stepfather's love on his own. It was either that or fall back to the hard existence from which he and his mother had risen.

And so Gerard had done as he was told and went to boarding school for two years. From a tiny shared dorm, he'd plotted his glorious return to Vegas. He would show Al Breck not only that he wasn't a fuckup, but that he was a true son to be proud of. He buckled down at school and stayed out of trouble. Gerard's grades improved, and by graduation, he was at the top of his class. Al didn't show up for the ceremony, but afterward rewarded him with a good job at Breck Ammunition back in Vegas. Gerard happily accepted, eager to show his stepfather that he was the right man to lead the company into the future.

"I'll never forgive you," the old man had told him over the phone, "but I promised your mother that there would always be a place for you here."

Gerard took it as a challenge. He was only eighteen and had never received any business education, but he went to work impassioned, learning the job on the fly. After several promotions and more than fifteen years of earnest work, he began to win back Al Breck's respect. His stepfather never told him this directly, but Gerard could tell from the way he looked at him.

Then the old bastard had to go and die. *Our Times* reported that it was lung cancer, an inevitable result of nearly sixty years of chain-smoking. It was true that he was sick, but Al Breck didn't wait for the cancer to kill him. In his hospital bed, the founder of America's gun company took his own life using his original prototype for the Breck 17.

Gerard had been devastated, but Elza told him it was an opportunity. There was a vacuum at the top of Breck Ammunition. Errol might be in line to become CEO, but he seemed disinterested in the responsibility. Gerard could take over the company and build his own legacy. He could still make his stepfather proud.

"So what do you think, Mr. Breck?"

Gerard glanced at the clock and saw that it was 7:59 p.m. "I think it's getting late. Leave me."

The enthusiasm faded from the marketers' faces, but they did as they were told.

Gerard pulled up his tablet as the clock struck eight. Time to read the daily report. It listed all the day's mentions of Gerard and Breck Ammunition. The references were ranked by popularity, which was based on the number of readers who had seen the article, how much time they spent on the article, and how many times the article had been shared. Gerard liked to read each headline with a sip of bourbon on ice.

Today's top headline, from a site he didn't recognize called *The New West*, proclaimed: *Breck Connected to the Red Stripe Gang.*

Whiskey spluttered forcefully from Gerard's lips. Some caught on the bottom of his mustache; the rest spattered across his tablet. Cursing, he grabbed a cloth and wiped the brown liquid from the screen. When the object was sufficiently smooth again, he tapped on the headline to read the story. An anonymous byline, he noted.

Laying the device carefully back down on the table, Breck pressed a button on his desk and seethed, "Elza, would you please come in here?"

Gerard thought about all the ways he might kill Elza. Throttle her neck maybe. Whack her skull with the tablet — no, he needed the tablet. He had several guns in the desk, but which was the right one? The Breck 17, or perhaps that was too ordinary? No, she deserved a better death than that.

Elza looked paler than usual when she walked into the room. "Elza," Gerard growled, "did you receive a call from a journalist earlier?"

"Rosa Veras," she said, trembling. "But she promised me that she would not print anything in *Our Times*."

He shook his head. "She didn't print it in *Our Times*. She printed it in something called *The New West*."

Elza looked pathetically down at the floor. "I know. I saw. And I am so sorry. She told me what she wanted to write, and I did my very best to discourage her."

Breck's eyebrows relaxed. There was something pretty about Elza when she struggled to keep afloat. It was how she had looked when he first met her years ago at the casino. Back then she was dealing cards — blackjack — at one of the high roller tables. She had lured him to her table with those Gypsy eyes. She was good at dealing cards, but he could tell she wanted so much more. He recognized this suffering as the same of his own. Desire for the American Dream was something they shared. And so he had

117

offered her a job with better hours and a lot better pay.

Taking a deep breath through his nostrils, he said calmly, "I am pleased you didn't comment on the Red Stripe Gang allegations. I am *not* pleased that you told her that O'Brien was in my helicopter. Or that he, I quote, 'had to jump off early.'"

"She spotted him. Lying would have created more suspicion."

"Hmm," he said, considering. "Perhaps."

She looked him directly in the eyes. "You will need to deal with Miss Veras."

Gerard drank in Elza's beguiling gaze. She had the eyes of Medusa.

"Yes," he said finally. He gulped down the rest of his whiskey and pointed to his glass. "Fetch me another bourbon, and then leave me. I need to think."

When Elza was gone, Gerard leaned back in his chair and closed his eyes. There were two problems he needed to figure out: the Wanderer and Rosa Veras. He already had a good idea of who the Wanderer was; Gerard would be ready for him if he came. The more immediate problem was Veras and her blog. She needed to be dealt with quickly, before she could cause any more damage.

He wondered what the reporter's angle was. Why was she trying to take it all away from him? A conspiracy? He tried to remember her. Besides Elza, she'd been the only woman at the media conference. Brown hair, or maybe black. A suspicious stare in a herd of smiles.

Gerard watched the share prices for Breck Ammunition tumble through the glass of his tablet. In the smudged reflection, he saw his father's disapproving eyes. They'd all wanted Errol to be the next CEO. His father, the damned board. But Errol had left. He'd never cared about the business anyway. They'd wanted him, but he hadn't wanted them. The board should've been happy when Errol left the picture. They should've been happy that Gerard was so ready, so eager to take over.

He took another gulp of the bourbon. What was the board going to say about this? The chairman, Corny Boone, didn't like him. Corny wanted him out.

No. He would fix this.

*

Rosa stared dumbfounded at the line chart displayed on her computer screen. That couldn't be right, could it? There was no way. No one had read the mission statement for *The New West* the day it was published. No one. Her first story on the Wanderer arriving in Liberty had gotten a couple hundred hits, which was nothing, then readers ignored her gun-show preview. But now this story about Breck Ammunition ... millions? Really?

The spike in traffic for the article had boosted visits to the other story about the Wanderer as well. And now her inbox was flooded with messages about possible Wanderer sightings around the country.

She looked worriedly at the black phone lying silently in wait on her desk. That PR flack — Elza or whatever her name was — she was going to call. She would have to, right?

Rosa reread her story. And then she reread it again. It made Breck Ammunition look bad. She had known it would make them look bad, but holy hell, it made them look really, really bad!

Maybe they wouldn't know she wrote it? She hadn't put her real name on the website and she was careful to set up an anonymous account for contacts.

"Yeah, but you quoted Elza, you idiot!" she berated herself aloud, realizing instantly how crazy she sounded.

Not only that, but she had written that she was part of the media junket. Rosa was the only one who could have written the story. The PR flack would have to be stupid not to make the connection. What had she been thinking? Not enough sleep? Too much confidence?

The phone rang. She peered at it through her fingers, let it ring for five seconds, ten …

"Hello?" she blurted into the mic.

"Rosa."

She felt a chill run through her entire body. It wasn't Elza. Much worse. "Hi, Rebecca."

"Did you write this filth?"

She could barely breathe. "Write what?"

There was a pause on the other end of the line. "This … *blog…*" She said the word like it was a curse.

She honestly wasn't sure whether she should continue to lie. Maybe Rebecca was bluffing and maybe it didn't matter. She was so toast.

The editor didn't wait for a response. "I just had a call with Breck Ammunition. They say you wrote this after promising not to publish it."

"I …" she managed. It was a struggle to speak. "Yes, that's true, but …" Maybe if she just apologized and promised to take down the article … ? No. She wasn't sorry. She had known from the start that *The New West* would ruffle some feathers. That was the whole point. She was a journalist. "I stand by the story."

Rebecca sighed. "Then I guess you're fired."

Before the line went dead, the editor issued one final remark. "God help you."

CHAPTER ELEVEN

The Wanderer and Kid Hunter!

Charlie was glad to see the Independence Day decorations cleaned up and thrown away at the Happy Gunfighter. All that remained was dust, grime, and bullet holes. The saloon's dim lighting and fermented odors suited him just fine, too. He'd spent the day cooped up in an overly clean motel room beating himself up for what he hadn't done and for not knowing what he was going to do next.

The problems hounded him still. He hadn't killed the Wanderer. He hadn't wanted to kill the Wanderer. It was the first time he'd ever taken a job and not completed it. Instead, Charlie had actually helped the Wanderer. And the worst part was now he wanted to keep helping the gunslinger.

He needed a drink.

"A beer," Charlie clarified for the man at the taps. "I don't care which one, so long as it's full strength and comes in a big fucking cup."

The barman pulled a pint glass from the ceiling and chose the IPA without hesitation.

Someone laughed gruffly behind him. "And here I reckoned

the would-be bounty hunter would be long gone by now."

Charlie didn't turn. He knew who it was. "Don't you have a train to catch?"

"Heh," the Wanderer replied.

The bartender wiped the suds off the side of the glass and placed it carefully on the counter. "Seven bucks."

Charlie stuck a thumb back to point at the Wanderer. "And a porter for my *sidekick* here." He cracked a smile at the Wanderer, a quick peek to see if he'd succeeded in getting a rise out of him. He hadn't.

They took the beers to the Wanderer's usual booth but it was occupied by a twenty-something geek on a white Apple laptop. The kid's glass was empty and looked as though it had been for some time.

Noticing the two gunmen, the geek jumped to his feet and yelped, "Wanderer!"

Very nicely, he volunteered his seat.

"Take your empty, too," the Wanderer commanded, pointing to the glass.

As they sat down, Charlie laughed. "He knew exactly who you were. Word spreads fast, don't it?"

"It's those damn articles."

Charlie cooed, "Guess you're famous now."

"I don't like it."

"Hey, I know what you could do to avoid attention!" He snapped his fingers to emphasize his point. "Stop shooting up towns!"

The Wanderer took a long sip of his beer and wiped the foam

from his lips. "Whoever's writing these stories is going to find himself in some fine trouble. Gerard Breck is dangerous. If Breck reads that last story — when he reads it — he'll make *The New West* and its author disappear."

Charlie knew he was right. One of his more recent jobs from El Tiburón had been for Breck Ammunition. One of the higher-ups, displeased with the company's direction, had threatened to leave and start his own rival gun company. Apparently he wasn't going to listen to reason.

Charlie hadn't minded that kill. The target was just another upper-class giant who'd spent his life pushing Charlie's friends and family down into the sewer.

"Why do you care about this writer?" he asked the Wanderer. "That'd be good news for you, wouldn't it? No more attention?"

The Wanderer looked at the table. "I've got to find this journalist before Breck does."

Charlie couldn't believe his ears! "Find the—?"

The Wanderer began to answer but his voice was smothered by a chanting sing-along to Neil Diamond's "Sweet Caroline."

The chorus cut off, and the other patrons resumed drinking.

"Kitty must have talked to the reporter," said the Wanderer, picking up from where he left off. "Maybe she'll know how to get in touch."

"*Kitty*? That's your plan? Man, that girl and her daddy are long gone!"

"I'll find them."

"For real?" Charlie cackled. "Man, don't waste your time! I'll get you what you want to know. Just give me a few minutes hacking time and I'll tell you the exact coordinates where *The New West* gets written. Provided, that is ..."

The Wanderer looked intrigued. "Provided what?"

"Provided you let me come with you." Charlie couldn't quite believe he said it and had to chase the request with a gulp of beer.

The other man raised his eyebrows. "Let you come with me? Just the other day you were trying to collect a damned *bounty* on me!"

"If I was still doing that, we wouldn't be talking. Actually, you wouldn't be doing much talking at all."

The Wanderer shook his head. "I don't work with bounty hunters."

"C'mon man. The Wanderer and Kid Hunter! Even you have got to admit that sounds dope as shit!"

"No."

He pulled up *The New West* on his wristband and ran an analysis on the blog. The Wanderer didn't say anything, just observed him working.

Charlie chuckled.

The gunman took the bait. "What?"

"The reporter is not a 'him.'"

The Wanderer put down his beer. "How'd you figured that out so quickly?"

"It's called skills, son!" Charlie exclaimed. Continuing to play with the device on his arm, he added, "Her name is Rosa Veras. And I know where to find her. But like I said, you have to let me come with you."

The Wanderer looked almost convinced, but Charlie could see

he still had reservations. The bounty hunter took a deep breath and said, "Look, man, I've made some choices. I know I have. But there's things you don't know about me. I come from Vegas, man, and not the glamorous parts. I had to survive — help my family survive — somehow, you know? The money I get, it's for my sister."

The Wanderer grunted in resignation. "Show me your gun."

He blinked. "My gun?"

"It's not a Breck model. I want to see it."

Charlie took the gun from his jacket and laid it on the table. The Wanderer carefully inspected each side. "This is a Canadian."

"I prefer Separatist, but yeah. How'd you know?"

The Wanderer didn't answer. "How close does it have to be to your wrist computer to fire?"

Charlie laughed. "I have to be holding it."

"Ain't you worried it might fail when you need it?"

"I guess I'm more worried about someone taking my gun and trying to use it."

The Wanderer smiled knowingly. "A few gun inventors have tried pitching smart guns to Breck Ammo. But the polling showed the American market wouldn't have it."

He placed the gun gently on the table and looked Charlie squarely in the eyes. "You've got a talent for tracking, I will admit. And you're not bad with a gun, either. But I meant what I said — I don't work with bounty hunters. If you're coming with me, you're going to have to give that all up. You so much as take *interest* in a hit job? Well, let's just say that'll be the end of Kid Hunter."

Frowning, Charlie looked down at his hands. "I'd like to walk away from it, man. I really would. But I've got a sister in Vegas to think of."

"What if I help you out with the money?"

"What?" He looked up in surprise. The Wanderer seemed to be serious. "Who are you?"

"That don't matter. All you need to know is I can help."

It wasn't too bad a deal. Truth was he didn't expect to get any more jobs from El Tiburón anyway, now that he'd let the Wanderer walk. What'd he have to lose?

Kid Hunter raised his ale. "To Kid Hunter and the Wanderer!"

"The Wanderer and Kid Hunter," corrected the gunman, clinking the glass with his porter.

CHAPTER TWELVE

Ain't Safe for You Here.

Steve the station manager looked up from a crossword puzzle as the silver locomotive burst through a red storm of dust. The first train of the morning screeched to a halt next to the trailer that served as Liberty Station. Two men strode down the metal stairs with bags on their backs. The first — an urban-looking fellow with a large shiny bracelet on his arm — well, he didn't recognize that kid. But the taller man in the Stetson? Now *he* looked familiar.

But why? Steve scratched his head. Who was he again? Not a resident of Liberty, that's for sure.

Whoever he was, the cowboy saw him looking and tipped his hat.

"Good morning!" Steve shouted to him. "Hey, I know you from somewhere, don't I? You been through here before?"

The two men approached the window of the trailer. The younger one whom Steve didn't know pointed to the more familiar one. "This here's the man they call the Wanderer."

Steve laughed. "Well, ain't that a peculiar name! And what do they call you, mister?"

"As a matter of fact, they call me Kid Hunter."

This name got an even bigger laugh. "Well, isn't that something? The Wanderer and Kid Hunter! Welcome to Liberty, boys. Hope you enjoy your stay."

"Won't be here long," said the Wanderer. "Mind telling me the time for the next train?"

"Sure thing! Where you headed?"

"It don't matter, particularly. We'll pay for the end of the line, either direction, and decide where to get off when we get there."

Steve couldn't believe his ears. "You know, you're the second man this month to ask me for that ticket."

The Wanderer cracked a smile.

"Well, looks like there's a train northwest in an hour and a half. Next train southeast is another hour after that."

"Then we'll take three tickets on the earlier one."

"You mean two?" asked Steve, looking over the pair's shoulders. He didn't see anyone else with them.

"Three," said Kid Hunter. "We're meeting someone."

The men paid in cash and went on their way.

*

Rosa reached up to turn off the lamp and discovered the sun had come up. She remembered slumping back into her sofa. She remembered the slouch becoming too low, and lifting her legs onto the cushion to stretch. She remembered thinking the lamp was too damn bright ...

Obviously, the coffee had finally given up on keeping her awake. After the firing from *Our Times*, she had stayed up late thinking about what to do. Her first thought had been to delete the article, but she realized that would be too little, too late. Even if she completely took down *The New West*, it wouldn't get her job back. Anyway, what about journalistic integrity? There was nothing wrong in seeking the truth and reporting on it.

Rosa moaned. She sure as hell didn't feel like she had slept.

She phoned her brother.

"Rosie …? What time is it?"

"The sun's out, Jack."

"That doesn't mean it's time to wake up."

"I got fired last night."

She could hear the rusted springs of his bed squeak as he sat up. "What?"

"I wrote some … bad things about Breck Ammunition on my blog."

"They fired you for that?"

"Breck Ammo owns *Our Times*, Jack. Of course they did."

"Yeah, okay, but still, I'm not sure if they can fire you for maintaining a personal blog."

"Why not? It's not like I told them about it."

"Yeah, I don't know. I'd really have to look at the case history, see if anything like this has happened before. If you want, I can come over in a bit, look things over with you. Maybe there's something we can do. It might not get your job back but at the very least, we might be able to give those guys some heartburn. That'd be fun, right?"

It always caught her off guard when Jack, her lazy brother, transformed into Jackson Veras, defense attorney. "That would be fun! You want me to make breakfast? I've got eggs, I think. How long does it take eggs to go bad? Well, there's at least cereal."

Jack yawned. "No, don't wait up. I might ... I might just catch a couple more zees ... and then I'll be right there, promise."

Ah, there was the little brother she knew and loved. "Okay, well, I'll be here. See you in a bit."

She put on another pot in her Mr. Coffee machine and darted over to her computer to again reread the story that had gotten her in so much trouble. She wasn't sure if it was the sleep or talking to Jack, but she suddenly felt proud of it again. It was good that she upset Breck Ammunition. Wasn't that the whole point? Wasn't that the test of success? If they hadn't noticed, if no one had read the article at all, wouldn't that have been the true disaster? The reality was that she was being punished for writing a good story in the so-called land of the free.

Gritting her teeth, Rosa closed the article and opened a fresh page.

*

With the town of Liberty sparkling on the horizon, the Wanderer and Kid Hunter took a sharp right into suburban sprawl. Soon they were surrounded by red-roofed ranchers and cute streets with names like Dandelion Lane and Snapdragon Terrace. The front yard of each home featured an attractive patch of prickly pear cactus.

The outward friendliness of the homes was misleading, but the only hint of the lie came from the red signs for security vendors sticking out of the grass in the front yards. At very least, this meant the family inside was doing twenty-four-hour surveillance of its property. But it could also indicate the presence of automatic cannons tucked snugly inside the gutters of the roof. In general, it was wise not to approach a house like this unless invited.

The Wanderer had seen this kind of neighborhood many times during his travels through the West. The development was charming old Liberty's cancerous growth, a tar-and-concrete appendage stretching miles to accommodate America's population explosion.

From the gunman's dry lips shot the breath of a laugh. Somewhere in this explosion of monotony was the writer of *The New West* — the foolish reporter burying herself into deeper trouble than she probably knew. In a way, he admired her courage. She had seen something wrong and took a stand against it. But even so, this Rosa Veras had chosen one hell of a thing to stand against. Breck Ammunition practically ran this godforsaken country — and a madman ran Breck Ammunition.

Kid Hunter had been singing a pop chorus slightly off-key but now cut it short to whisper, "Think we're getting some attention from the locals."

The Wanderer saw it, too. In the window of a rancher, a woman stared. Beneath a neighborhood watch sign, a boy pointed. "Just keep walking," the gunman advised his partner.

*

Rosa smiled, happy with herself and feeling courageous. She wasn't going to take down the article. She had decided. She was sticking to her guns, so to speak, and now her brother was going to help her find justice.

The doorbell rang. Perfect timing, but she hadn't expected Jack so soon. She looked at her watch and noticed an hour had flown by while she was writing. Her next, panicked thought was that she'd forgotten about the coffee. The auto-off function had broken about a year ago, so now the machine had to be turned off manually. She ran into the kitchen and flicked the switch, but she could smell that she'd burned it.

The doorbell rang again, followed by a pounding on the door.

"Shut up, Jack! One second!" She pulled the carafe off the hotplate and realized the plastic handle had melted. Cursing, she looked around frantically for a spot to put it down. In the end, she settled on the stainless-steel kitchen sink.

The knocking started up again as she reached the door. "I said knock it off, J—" The name turned into a gasp when instead of her brother she found two men standing on her porch.

The man on the right glanced at a tablet. "That's her," he confirmed.

"D-delivery?" said Rosa in a vain attempt to lighten the situation.

The men let fly an odorous burst of sour beer and cigarettes from their mouths. She looked over their shoulders and saw a pair of black motorcycles.

"We need you to come with us," said the ogre on the left. He wore a sleeveless leather vest. Tattooed to each arm was something like an American flag, but it was missing the blue square of stars.

She tried to sound indignant. "I'm not going anywhere until … until you tell me who you are."

It was a stalling tactic. She already knew they were members of the Red Stripe Gang, and their presence confirmed her story that the Gang was working for Gerard Breck. Odd how that failed to hearten her! She imagined herself tied to the back of one of the bikes and carried off into the desert toward a big tree and a long, thick piece of rope.

The gangster on the right grinned, displaying two rows of crooked teeth. "You sure are pretty. I think we're gonna enjoy this."

Rosa smiled politely. "Let me get something?"

Before they could respond, she slammed the door shut — nearly. She couldn't get the door closed! The wood splintered against one gangster's foot. Thinking fast, she gave one last push and then made for the kitchen. Thrown by the sudden lack of resistance, the gangsters stumbled violently into the house. Flag Tattoos fell onto the carpet, writhing from a twisted ankle. The other caught himself on a cabinet by the door, but Rosa was there with her Mr. Coffee pitcher and smashed it devastatingly against his skull. Rosa winced as some of the hot liquid splashed against her fingers, but most of it scalded the gangster's buzzed scalp. A shriek burst through his ruined teeth as the acidic brew soaked through bright red cuts made by the shards of glass.

Rosa froze in disbelief at the act of violence she had just committed. Flag Tattoos was starting to get up from the floor, but she was too sick with herself to try to stop him. She ran past him and through the cracked entrance of her home, barely seeing anything through the bright sun. Her eyes adjusted just enough to see the outlines of two more men drawing their guns. With a sob, she stopped in her tracks. There was nowhere left to run.

The gun boomed, but Rosa felt nothing. She spun around

toward her home and saw Flag Tattoos crumpled over her cactus patch and bleeding out onto the dirt. She turned to run but was caught by a pair of strong arms covered in leather.

"Whoa! Hold up!" directed their owner.

Freeing herself, she stepped back and froze in the green-eyed stare of her rescuer. He had a thin piece of glass over one eye and wore a Stetson. Immediately, she knew it was the Wanderer. But there was something else about his face … something familiar that she couldn't quite put her finger on.

"What am I, the invisible man?" chirped the other gunslinger, waving his palms frantically to get her attention. He had a lithe frame that countered his short stature. "Kid Hunter here! And this —"

"— is the Wanderer," she said, returning her gaze to the taller gunman. "And that's not all you are."

The Wanderer gazed narrowly at her. "How do you mean?"

Rosa took out her phone and typed a name into the search box. She held the device up for the two men to see. The screen displayed an image of Errol Breck, his green eyes shining warmly.

Those same eyes now widened with alarm as the Wanderer looked down at Rosa's phone, his former life staring him in the face.

*

Steve had been surprised that the men hadn't had a car nor had anyone picked them up. He was still pondering this when the phone rang. He fumbled with the device until it stopped, then chirped into the receiver, "Liberty Station. This is Steve speaking."

"It's Ben Martin."

"Sheriff! How nice to hear from you! The damnedest thing just happened. Couple fellows just stepped off the train and hoofed it into town. No car, no ride, nothing!"

"I'm sure that's mighty interesting, Steve, but I'm calling about another—"

"They had the most curious names, too," he went on. "One was called the Wanderer, and then there was this other fellow. Kid something. Kid Hondo?"

"Wait, stop. The *Wanderer*? Are you sure?"

"I think so. Or maybe it was the Wander Man. No … Wanderer, I'm sure of it. But I can't quite remember the other one's name now. King Huntsman, maybe?"

"When was this?" Martin demanded. "Where were they headed?"

"Couldn't have been more than a half hour ago. They didn't say where they were going. Just bought three tickets and walked off up the highway toward town. Guess they could have been headed to the suburbs, too, but they said they weren't staying long. They're just walking, though! I couldn't believe my —"

"Tickets? Didn't you say they got off the train?"

"Well, as I say, I reckon they don't plan to stay long. They bought tickets for the next train heading northwest, comes into the station in 'bout an hour, hour and a half—"

The phone clicked.

"Sheriff?"

Hearing no one, Steve hung up and slapped his knee. Must be something in the water today!

With a resigned sigh, the old man returned to his crossword puzzle. A minute into it, he snapped his fingers and declared, "Kid Hundred!"

*

After what felt like an eternity, the Wanderer finally cleared his throat and stammered, "No, I … don't know what you're talking about."

But Kid Hunter betrayed him immediately. Scratching the back of his head, he sized up his partner. "Well, I'll be damned — Errol Breck! Why didn't I pick that up earlier?"

Rosa winked at him. "Because you're a man."

"Come on, girl! You have to admit he looks different, all rugged and no 'stache!"

She was amused to see that the Wanderer had reddened several shades over the course of the exchange. "It doesn't matter who I am," he said, the cowboy way of speaking suddenly gone from his voice. "I've come here to help you."

She couldn't believe it. Didn't matter? Of course it mattered! The implications were enormous! Errol Breck had been assumed to be the next CEO of Breck Ammunition until he disappeared off the face of the map. She'd figured he'd either gone into hiding, or that he was dead and someone was covering it up. But this — roaming the west fighting injustice like a regular cowboy from the movies? It was a turn she'd never seen coming, and now she lashed into him with a pointed finger. "You listen to me, Wanderer! I'm in this mess because of your brother —"

"Stepbrother."

"Fine! Because of your *stepbrother*, Gerard! So please explain to me why I should trust another Breck to help me?"

The Wanderer opened his mouth but no sound came out.

She smiled victoriously, even though the truth was that he didn't have to convince her. She'd already decided to go with him. Her journalistic mind was whirring with story possibilities. A daring escape from the Red Stripe Gang! A conflict between the Breck brothers! Exclusive interviews with the Wanderer and Kid Hunter!

Desperate to contain her excitement, Rosa cast a casual glance to Kid Hunter. "I don't suppose you'll tell me *your* real name?"

"Ain't no secret," he replied winsomely. "It's Charlie. Charlie Johnson."

"I'd say that's about enough yammering," interjected the Wanderer, a faux-western twang returning to his voice. "We're getting you out of Liberty this instant. Ain't safe for you here."

When she asked where they would go, the Wanderer told her the train. It would be leaving soon and they would have to run. She offered her truck, but the sight of the old girl elicited a whistle from Kid Hunter.

"That is one *ugly* motherfucker," he said. "You're sure it'll run?"

She shrugged. "Hasn't failed me yet."

The Wanderer also shrugged. "As long as it gets us to the station."

Rosa gave him a look. "The station? Why don't we skip the train and just drive out of town?"

"Train's better. More anonymous."

Kid Hunter checked his watch. "There ain't gonna be time to

pack your stuff," he said apologetically. "We got to go right now."

"Gun?" asked the Wanderer.

"There's a hunting rifle in the truck. But my computer —" She looked back at her house. "I'm still logged into *The New West* — they could take it down —"

Kid Hunter swiped at his wristband and danced his fingertips against his palm. "I've just disabled the computer and erased your hard drive. We'll get you more secure equipment after we get you out." As an afterthought, he added, "Hope you didn't have anything important on there."

She was about to reply when a low moan rumbled from her front door. They all heard it.

"Someone else in there?" asked the Wanderer, reaching down to his hip holster.

"Um … yes," she replied. "But I don't think we need to worry about him."

*

The reporter gal had surprised him when she'd called him Errol. The Wanderer could tell right then that she was clever and had some serious fight in her. Still, he didn't expect to find himself so quickly in her crosshairs.

"The train is the fastest, most direct way out of town," he said defensively.

"No, this truck is," she declared. "Why would we stop to wait for a train? It doesn't make a lick of sense!"

He was starting to worry. Rosa was the one driving and it wouldn't be long before they would reach the station — and possibly fly past it. He wondered how difficult it would be to lean over and wrestle the wheel away. Probably quite difficult.

"It's not safe to take your truck," argued the Kid, riding somewhat awkwardly in the tight space between them. "Not just because it's a piece of shit, but because the Red Stripe Gang has seen it, and you can bet they'll be looking for it. Sorry, but we gotta ditch it fast."

Rosa laughed haughtily. "As if there won't be any people on the train to spot us!"

The Wanderer broke in. "I reckon the Gang won't strike in so public a place. They'll want to avoid attention, same as we do."

"I don't know if I believe that this band of idiots wants to avoid attention," she replied, breathing out a long sigh of resignation. "I will, however, give Charlie the point about recognizing the truck."

"Anyways," the Kid said with a wink, "can't you see ol' Wandy here has his heart set on the train? Just look at the way he's clutching those tickets."

He hadn't realized he was doing it and now shoved the papers back into his shirt pocket. Rosa laughed real big and loud. He wanted to snatch the Kid by the collar but settled for winning the argument against Rosa.

As they pulled into the parking lot at the train station, the Wanderer spied a police car in the parking lot with its lights flashing.

"That's Ben Martin," said Rosa. "But what does he —? Oh, right. He *hates* the Wanderer."

He gritted his teeth. "Stay in the truck. The Kid and I will handle it."

"Old friends?" asked Charlie.

The cowboy laughed. "I reckon he's the one who hired you to kill me."

"Whoa," said the bounty hunter. "Fucked-up!"

Rosa bristled. "You don't need to kill him."

The Wanderer checked the barrel of his silver revolver and clicked it back into place. "Yeah, well, the sheriff don't need to kill me, neither. But I'll try to keep that in mind."

As Rosa shifted gear into *PARK*, the police car emitted a short squeal of warning and two doors popped open. Martin stepped out of the driver's seat carrying a shotgun. "Wanderer!" the sheriff shouted, leveling the Pilgrim at the passenger door of Rosa's truck. "Come out with your hands up!"

The Wanderer popped out of the truck with his Lassiter pointed at the tin star on Martin's chest. "We're not planning to stay in Liberty, so why don't you drop the gun and let us get on the next train? We don't want any trouble."

Martin sneered. "Yeah, that's what you said last time, too. Right before you shot up my church."

"Now wait just a minute. I didn't fire a single shot in that church. That pig Jenkins fired, and I caught him outside to pay for his crimes."

Martin gave a look of disbelief. "And what about the law?"

"The world's changed, Martin. You keep thinkin' the way you do … well, it'll be your undoing someday."

Another man emerged from the police car and pointed a Breck 17 handgun at the Wanderer's head. He was a long-haired yokel and had a wad of tobacco stuck in his cheek. "Un-do what? Now

I don't know what in God's name that's supposed to mean, but I reckon you better shut the hell up and drop your —"

The deputy's concentration broke suddenly as Kid Hunter arrived at the Wanderer's side.

The Wanderer smirked. Seemed they had a standoff. He with his Lassiter on Martin, Martin with his Pilgrim on the Wanderer, Kid Hunter with his smart gun on the deputy, and the deputy —

"What's your name anyway?" the Wanderer asked.

"Fuck you!" the hick spat back.

Martin rolled his eyes. "Oh, that's just Dougie."

— and Dougie with his Breck 17 on Kid Hunter.

The Wanderer kept his eyes on Martin as a train horn sounded in the distance. Behind him, the door to Rosa's rusty truck squealed. Oh, God, hadn't he told her to stay in the truck?

Martin's eyes widened as he took in who it was. "*Rosie*? What are you doing with these men?"

Thanks to the distraction, the Wanderer knew he had a shot. But her request nagged at him. He didn't *need* to kill Martin. Before he could make up his mind as to what he needed to do, Rosa was standing straight right in the middle of the standoff. She was completely unarmed.

The *chug-a-chug* of the train grew louder.

Ben Martin growled. "Get out of the way, Rosie."

"Here's what's going to happen next," she said, commanding attention. "Everyone is going to put down their guns. When that train arrives, the three of us — that's me, the Wanderer, and Kid Hunter here — are getting on it. Meanwhile, Ben, you and Dougie are going to get back in that beat-up police car and head straight to my house."

Ben looked confused. "Your house?"

"A couple of men from the Red Stripe Gang are waiting for you. One's dead — and I bet the other one wishes he was after what I did to him. If you could please get them out of my house and lock the place up for me, I'd appreciate it. I really would."

Dougie ejected a wad of brown fluid from his lips. "We ain't goin' nowhere!"

Ben narrowed his eyes. "Dougie?"

"Yeah, boss?"

"Do as she says."

"What?"

"I *said*," seethed the sheriff, letting the Pilgrim fall to his side, "*do* as she *says*."

Dougie spat the rest of his chewing tobacco onto the parking lot and, dragging his feet, followed the sheriff back into the car.

"Wow," remarked the Kid, stretching the word until it was consumed by the noise of the passenger train rattling into Liberty Station. The locomotive's dented siding was black with soot, and there was a smell like burned rubber as it came to a shrieking stop.

The Wanderer stared at Rosa with disbelief. There was an assured smile on her lips.

"You boys can stop gawking at me and get your bags from the truck," she said. "We've got a train to catch."

CHAPTER THIRTEEN

Aw, Hell …

Touching her window, Rosa could feel the fire of the sun pressing against the dirt-streaked glass. A line of small vents on the ceiling wheezed cool breath, a commendable attempt by the train to head off the sun's charge. It was a battle she was sure the A/C used to win, but the man-made system had grown old and weary over the course of many decades fighting its eternal opponent.

She couldn't believe it was really Errol Breck sitting across from her in the four-seat arrangement. The Wanderer — it felt more correct to call him that — rode forward, having refused to ride the other way. Kid Hunter stationed himself by his partner's side near the aisle. Neither man talked. The Wanderer stared blankly out the window while the Kid absorbed himself in a pair of expensive red headphones.

She wished they *would* talk. Rosa had plenty of questions, but in spite of her best attempts to start an interview, the Wanderer had said little to nothing since they got on the train. He just kept staring out that infernal window. On her phone, she made note of this aloof behavior, along with his train seating requirements. She also wrote a description of the gold wedding band that he wore on his left hand. He was married — or had been anyway. From her research on the Brecks, she recalled that Errol had disappeared the same day the police found his wife, Helen, murdered in their house. Suspicious, but the corrupt Vegas Police Department dismissed Errol as a suspect early on, and the cut-and-paste journalists of *Our Times* never asked why.

Rosa studied Errol Breck's sorrowful eyes. She knew the Wanderer was a killer. Had Errol been capable of murder?

The train lurched, nearly sending Rosa's head into the window. It wasn't the first time, and she groaned bitterly. "This love of trains," she said to the Wanderer. "I don't get it."

"Heh," he replied.

*

Charlie hit *PAUSE* on his tunes and lifted his headphones. "So where are we going anyway? We getting off this train anytime soon?"

The Wanderer seemed annoyed by the question. "You'd know if you didn't have those damn headphones on."

As Kid Hunter winced, Rosa raised her eyebrows with interest and began to type something on her phone. "In fairness, you weren't saying much that Charlie could have heard."

The Wanderer glared at her device. "What's that you're doing?"

"Taking notes."

"What for?"

"My next article in *The New West*."

Charlie didn't get why, but that got the Wanderer super ticked off. The gunman swiped for the phone.

"Don't touch my phone!" she protested, pulling it away in the nick of time. "Are you crazy?"

The cowboy leaned in to Rosa's face and whispered sharply. "Listen to me. You're not going to write another article. You hear me? That's over."

She gasped. "I thought you were here to help me. What, you're on your brother's side, now?"

"*Step*-brother. And I reckon I am helping you! That blog of yours is going to get you killed."

She laughed. "I think that boat has sailed, don't you *reckon*?"

The Wanderer held up his palms in frustration.

Charlie had to laugh. He just had to. The two of them were acting like an old married couple.

"What's so funny?" snapped the Wanderer.

Charlie did his best to straighten his face. "Aw, it's nothing, man."

A small growl erupted from the other man's lips. He turned his face hard toward the window and disengaged from the others. Rosa's eyes fell back to the screen of her phone.

Charlie waved a hand in front of the reporter's eyes to get her attention. "If it helps, I'm happy to do an interview. You can feel free to snap some pics of my handsome mug, too, if you so desire."

Rosa's eyes lit up like she hit the jackpot. Charlie wasn't surprised, as he was used to having that kind of effect on the ladies. "Yes, that would be amaz—"

"He's not giving you an interview, either!" protested the Wanderer, turning back to face them.

Charlie grimaced. What was the big deal? He liked the idea of a little celebrity. The Wanderer seemed to think he had a leash on him. No one put this dawg on a leash.

"Well, Kid," Rosa said like it was no big deal, "we don't have to make you famous if your *boss* won't let you ..."

"He's not my boss!" He leaned forward and shoved a finger in the Wanderer's face. "I ain't no sidekick to you, and I ain't going to let you tell me what I can and can't do!"

He noticed Rosa making some more notes and yelped at her to stop.

"You listen real good, boys," she snapped. "I'll write *what* I want to write, *when* I want to write. That's how reporting works. Now if you boys give me an interview and say the right things, maybe you'll come out better in the final copy. How does *that* sound?"

*

Rosa tightened the cross of her arms and scowled bitterly out the window of the train. The Wanderer and Kid Hunter had responded to her protest by saying literally nothing — she looked at her pink plastic watch — for the last hour and forty-five minutes! The gunman kept his head turned to the window, while Charlie played a game on his wristband.

"Let's get off at the next station," said Rosa. "I'm tired of this train."

The Wanderer shook his head. "We should go farther. Increase the distance between us and the Gang."

"You say that like you know what you're talking about. But all you are, Mr. Breck, is a spoiled brat pretending to be a cowboy!"

The farmer's tan of the passenger behind him wrinkled as he

turned to see what the sudden ruckus was about. Rosa shot him a stern look that made him mind his own business real quick.

The Wanderer narrowed his eyes and pointed a finger gun at Rosa. "No, I'm the man who saved your life. I'm *still* saving your life."

Rosa laughed. Is *that* what he thought? "I don't need to be saved! I'm safe!"

He turned wearily to Charlie for backup, but the Kid was miles away, bouncing his head to the beat of his tunes. The gunman muttered something and looked out at the rolling desert.

"Look," she said, "maybe when we get to the next station, we should just part ways. I'll get off, and you boys can keep going to your hearts' content. I think it will be better for all of us, don't you?"

The Wanderer let a long breath of air escape through his nose. "If I agree to an interview," he said, "will you stay?"

Rosa tried not to show excitement, but her inner journalist was doing flips. She had him now.

*

Leaving the desert in its dust, the train bolted straight into a mountain range and began to climb. Soon they were surrounded by a scattering of dark emerald pine trees. The Wanderer watched with some amusement at the awed look on Rosa's face as she noticed the sudden greenery. It occurred to him that this just might be the farthest she'd ever been from Liberty.

A mustached conductor walking down the aisle distracted him from his musings. He looked a lot like Gerard.

"Why don't we start with a story about my stepbrother?" he asked Rosa.

She pulled out her phone to take notes. "Please."

"Okay, so when I was ... fifteen, I think, and Gerard was twelve, I heard him moaning about some smarty-pants at school named Arnold who was always upsetting the curve on exams. Gerard was never very good in school on account of never studying, and he was getting particularly anxious about an upcoming test on some book he hadn't bothered to read."

Kid Hunter laughed. "I know that feeling!"

"Two days later at recess, I found a bully beating another boy to a pulp. Turned out to be that smarty-pants Arnold who Gerard had been complaining about. I stopped the bully, but poor Arnold went to the hospital with a concussion, and he wasn't seen back in school again. Rumor had it his parents opted for homeschooling."

"Say what?"

He tried not to let the Kid's excitement derail the story. "Well, Gerard's big test came, and he ended up passing with a C+. The curve worked out for him real well without Arnold around. Gerard was pleased as punch, and that's when I started getting suspicious. I tracked down the bully, and sure enough, Gerard had paid him to do it!"

"That's fucked-up!"

"Says the bounty hunter," replied Rosa with some amusement. To Errol, she asked, "So what'd you do?"

"What any kid my age would do — I told my dad. He said it was wrong what Gerard did, but family takes care of family."

Rosa raised her eyebrows. She began to ask another question, but he cut her off. "That's all for now."

As he turned back to the view, he asked himself — as he did often — if it was a mistake to leave after what happened to Helen. If he'd stayed in Vegas and taken the CEO role at Breck Ammunition, there would have been none of that nonsense in Freetown. As for the reporter, well, he didn't know what he'd have done in Gerard's position, but he certainly wouldn't have tried to kill her. And, Jesus, there definitely wouldn't be any deals with the Red Stripe Gang!

*

A soft smacking of sneakers against carpet coming from the front of the car brought the Wanderer to his feet. Kid Hunter came pounding down the aisle without the beers he'd promised.

"We've got to get off this train!" cried the Kid, pulling down his large hiking pack from the overhead rack and throwing it over his back in one fluid motion. He scooped up his bright red headphones from the aisle seat and slapped them around his neck for safekeeping.

"What is it?" asked Rosa in alarm.

"The Gang's here!"

The Wanderer snatched his denim knapsack from under the seat and yanked the reporter onto her feet. As they fled single-file after the Kid, bumping through a jungle of ankles and hanging elbows, he heard Rosa shouting an apology to the other passengers. Personally, he wasn't worried about the other people on the train. In fact, he was glad it was so crowded. He reckoned even the Red Stripe Gang had some sense of morality and wouldn't dare fire their weapons without a clear shot on their targets.

"How many?" he yelled ahead to the Kid.

"Saw two in the café car — might be more!"

At the end of the compartment, Kid Hunter slapped a red button next to a glass door, and the door slid open. In the space between cars, the young mercenary paused to look out the exit, another metal sliding door with a slit window. The Wanderer had an inkling about what his partner was thinking and warned, "It's too soon."

With a short nod, the Kid continued into the next compartment. As the Wanderer neared the same passage, a lock clicked on his right and a steel hatch to the toilet popped open, blocking his and Rosa's path. He slapped the door shut with a quick motion of his wrist, pushing the person on the other side back into the bathroom with a yelp.

"Where are we going?" called Rosa. "There's an end to this train, you know!"

The Wanderer smiled. "It might be better I don't tell you yet."

"What's that supposed to mean?"

He was still formulating an answer as Kid Hunter came rushing into view at the end of the car. The Kid stopped again in the space between the compartments. The Wanderer stopped short in a last-ditch attempt to avoid a crash, but Rosa careened into his back and drove him forward into the bounty hunter. The three fell into a big heap on the ground.

Kid Hunter pulled himself out with a grunt. "Would you two stooges watch where you're going? Damn!"

"Why do you keep stopping?" snapped Rosa, picking herself

up off of the Wanderer's back. "And what's the plan, exactly? I knocked off some poor guy's reading glasses back there. I felt really bad!"

Kid Hunter opened the hatch to the outside. The rattling of train against track loudened to a pounding jackhammer. Pointing out at the fast-moving landscape of dry grass and pine needles, he shouted, "It's all in the tuck and roll!"

Connecting the dots, Rosa exploded in outrage. "Wait, what? Are all vigilantes this stupid? You can't actually jump from moving trains! That's just in the movies!"

"No, no, it'll work," asserted the Kid. "I've seen it done in … uh … just trust me, it'll work!"

The Wanderer looked back into the previous compartment. Incoming was a man with a bushy beard. He was holding a handgun — a Breck 17 from the looks of it. The Wanderer reached into his left holster.

"There's no time to argue," he said, aiming the silver Lassiter through the glass. "Rosa, watch the Kid carefully and do what he does. I'll be right behind you."

There was a sound of screeching metal and the three lurched toward the front of the train. The Wanderer caught himself on the glass door; in the same moment, the gangster reached and slapped the open-door button. The gunfighter could smell lunch, breakfast, and possibly last night's dinner in that Red Striper's beard. The Wanderer greeted him with a shot straight into the belly. The gangster groaned, and an awful stench rose from his bleeding gut. Keeping the Lassiter pointed down the compartment aisle, the Wanderer addressed the others. "There's more of 'em on their way. If we're going to jump, we've got to do it now!"

He received no argument. That seemed awfully suspicious, so the Wanderer stole a glance over his shoulder. He did a double take. The Kid and the reporter were gone. Stranger still, the ground outside had ceased moving.

"Aw, hell …"

Someone had stopped the train.

CHAPTER FOURTEEN

Cute.

Rosa did her best to keep up but Kid Hunter ran like a man on fire. She called, "Shouldn't we wait for the Wanderer?"

"He'll have to catch up!"

She stopped and panted heavily as the Kid disappeared into the trees. "Guess that makes two of us ..."

As Rosa rubbed her bare arms, she became aware of just how far north they had traveled. She was sure they hadn't left Arizona, but the rocky terrain and scattered pine trees of her current surroundings felt alien after spending most of her life in a dry environment of sand and cacti. Beyond the ponderosas, she could see brown mountains outlined by cold blue sky. She definitely hadn't packed for this. Actually, she hadn't packed at all, and now she was in the middle of the wilderness, actually running *away* from a train, the one thing that could bring her back to civilization.

A pistol cracked from the train. Two more gunshots followed in sequence. And then the terrifying chugging of an automatic — a Yossarian assault rifle. The sound of it knocked Rosa to her knees. She crumpled into a knot of limbs on the ground.

Kid Hunter burst out of the trees, running back toward her.

"The Wanderer's in trouble! We've got to help him!"

"I … I left my gun in my truck back in Liberty."

"Shit, you did, didn't you? Whatever — hide here. Just holler if you get in trouble. One of us will come running."

"Wait …"

It was too late. Charlie was already sprinting back toward the train. Rosa crawled to a spot behind a thick pine and reached for her phone, thinking she might calm down if she could just write some notes. With dismay, she noticed the phone's battery indicator blinking red.

The Yossarian blared, making Rosa drop her phone. She could die out here. She could actually be shot, and she would have no one but herself to blame. She could die because of what she wrote. Before, she had kidded herself into thinking she could just sit back and make observations. Instead, *The New West* had pulled her into the violent world she was writing about. She had made people angry before, but this was different. People actually wanted her dead, and not just anybody — America's biggest company and its worst gang of outlaws. Was writing the truth really worth putting her life on the line?

*

The seed of a joke tickled Kid Hunter's brain as he raced back toward the train. When Rosa said she didn't have a gun, it reminded him of how last time, she had stopped a fight without using a gun. He was sure there was a funny way to throw that back at her, but he couldn't quite figure it out.

A bullet whizzed by his head. He took the opportunity to duck behind a thick pine.

"Watch it," came a gruff voice on the left. The Wanderer was hiding behind a boulder a few yards away.

Kid Hunter returned a cheery shout. "I'm here!"

The gunman spat out a laugh. "And the whole gang knows it, too."

"Not for long."

Gripping his pistol with two hands, Kid Hunter bent out of cover and took a shot. He missed but at least got a lay of the land. The train was still stopped, and there seemed to be at least three gangsters hiding behind the trees closest to the tracks. There were a couple dead ones as well.

"The one on the left has got a Yossarian!" hissed the Wanderer.

That particular motherfucker was leaning out with the black assault rifle that very instant. Kid Hunter fell back behind the tree just as a spray of steel death thundered against the thick trunk. It was followed by an eerie quiet.

"Hey, Wanderer!" called one of the gangsters, the one in the middle with a Breck 17. "We just want the girl. Give her to us, and you can walk away from all this."

"Yeah," added the third Red Striper with a giggle. "You can *wander* on!"

Kid Hunter snickered — he couldn't help it — and the Wanderer scowled. Charlie whispered an apology, and made up for the transgression by sending a bullet straight through the joker's piehole.

The Yossarian replied with a steady barrage that kept the good guys trapped behind cover. Kid Hunter bit his lip. He'd gotten lucky taking down that one gangster, but two pistols against an assault rifle were still bad odds. The Wanderer looked cool and collected, but there was a dark look in his eyes, too. Like he didn't mind if he didn't make it. As if he was ready for death if it came to that.

Charlie thought of his sister panhandling for change back in Vegas. No way was he gonna die and leave her to fend for herself.

The Yossarian stopped and the Kid's ears rang. One of the gangsters yelled, "Hey, wait!"

Charlie rolled his eyes. "What do they want this time?"

The Wanderer shook his head. "He's not talking to us. Listen."

As the high-pitched ringing died, Kid Hunter heard the engine of the locomotive. He took a peek and saw the train sliding away and picking up speed. The gangster with the Yossarian tossed the rifle over his back and took chase, as if he thought he could catch up. He didn't get far before thunder cracked, and blood burst out the back of his skull. The Red Striper dropped to his knees and managed a dazed turn of the head before gravity took him completely. The Wanderer stood out in the open with his silver Lassiter gleaming in the sun.

The sound of the locomotive softened to a hum in the distance. Kid Hunter could hear the final gangster breathing heavily, panicked by loss of the train and his fellow men. Seeking a better angle, the Kid ran forward, taking cover behind another tree. He took the shot and nailed him.

Somewhere above, a bird sang out a sweet melody. Charlie relaxed his shoulders and the Wanderer patted him on the back. "C'mon, partner. We better find that reporter and get on our way.

It'll be dark before —"

Charlie startled as a woman's shriek shattered the quiet. What the hell was it now?

*

The Wanderer found Rosa deeper in the rocky wilderness, but she had company. Dead, rotting corpses in the middle of nowhere. They were a man and a woman, young backpackers on a camping trip. Something had torn the man's stomach open. The blood looked chunky and dry. The smell was repellent to everyone but the flies.

"Someone stole their stuff," said Kid Hunter, prodding the woman's body with a stick. "Out this deep, these folks should have supplies. But this is pretty gruesome for thieves."

The Wanderer tapped his eyeglass and scanned the remains. The lens highlighted several cuts and gashes across their anatomy, with a diagnosis for each. "Gunshot wounds on the both of them. Looks like a bear came along later and chewed on this fella."

Charlie gasped. "A bear?"

"There are bears in the mountains," confirmed Rosa, "but they're not monsters. Probably found the bodies, got curious —"

"And took a few bites," finished Charlie, raising his eyebrows. "Cute."

The Wanderer's eyepiece highlighted something else buried beneath a pile of brown pine needles. He bent down and dug out a blood-stained bullet. "This is a sniper round. Whoever did this, they shot from a distance, probably with a Montag."

"Oh, great!" the Kid groaned. "We're lost in the mountains with bears and snipers! This day just keeps getting better and better!"

"The bears will be just as afraid of you as you are of them," offered Rosa.

"And what about the snipers?"

"Just one sniper, I reckon," the Wanderer replied. "A lone wolf."

"Oh wow!" Charlie exclaimed sarcastically. "Now there's a wolf, too! I feel a whole lot better!"

The Wanderer dropped the bullet into a tangle of twigs. "Let's go. There's nothing we can do for these folks. I'll mark the coordinates and we'll tell someone in the next town where to find them."

"And how are we going to find the next town?" asked Rosa. "Shouldn't we head back to the tracks and follow them?"

He shook his head. "That's where the Gang will be looking for us." He pointed to his eyeglass. "According to my map, there's a small town called Founders Spring, maybe a couple day's walk to the west. Train doesn't go there, so maybe the Gang won't be looking for us."

Charlie's jaw dropped. "Wait, wait, wait! A couple days walk?"

"Give or take," shrugged the Wanderer.

"Which is it? *Give* or *take*?"

"Calm down," said Rosa. "You've got a hiking backpack. Haven't you ever used it for camping?"

The Kid grunted dismissively. "I've slept outside, all right, but I ain't never slept in the mountains. Anyway, it's not like I've got a tent in here — it's mostly stuff that needs to be charged. I don't see any outlets, do you?"

"Well, I've camped before," Rosa said proudly. "Not in the

mountains, but we should be fine. I mean, some extra clothes and a few sleeping bags would've been nice. It's already getting chilly, even though the sun's still out."

The Wanderer pulled on the strap of his denim knapsack. "I've got matches. We'll build a fire. Now, listen, I reckon we've got about two hours more until the sky gets too dark, so let's get away from the railroad and walk as far west as we can go. Then we can set up camp."

*

Dry twigs and needles crackled underfoot. Rosa, subconsciously grinding her teeth, scrunched her eyes in a futile effort to see through the orange beam of sunlight shining on her face. The pines provided occasional cover, but more often created a strobing effect that made the light more irritating.

"You know," she said, "none of this would have happened if we took my truck."

Charlie laughed, but the Wanderer took her complaint seriously. "There's less to worry about on a train. Usually. And at least we could talk, right?"

"You call that conversation? You staring at ghosts outside the window and him playing with his bracelet?"

"Wristband," corrected Charlie.

"Fine, then," said the Wanderer, adjusting his hat to better block the sun. "Hit me with a question."

She felt like a kid in a candy store. Where to start? "I guess there's the million-dollar question. Why did Errol Breck turn away from the company he was groomed to take charge of?"

Rather than answer, the Wanderer sniffed at the air and looked curiously down the trail. Rosa gritted her teeth, knowing she'd made a mistake. She'd come on too directly and too soon, violating one of the golden rules of interviewing: start with the easy questions, and strike with a hardball only when they're comfortable.

Kid Hunter suddenly came to a skidding halt. "Whoa, shit!"

Rosa squinted down the trail and startled at a ghostly figure creeping out of the trees. On closer inspection, it was a pale girl with wild red hair tied in two long braids. She wore Army sweatpants that looked one size too small and a gray hoodie that looked two sizes too big. Adorning the girl's feet were a pair of well-loved Ugg boots. She looked a few years older than Pablo, maybe eleven or twelve.

Rosa exchanged dumbfounded looks with the guys. They seemed fine with her making the first move. "Uh," she murmured, "hey there."

The girl backed away.

"Maybe she's scared of your weapons," Rosa whispered to the two men.

The Wanderer removed his gun belt and let it drop to the forest floor; Kid Hunter did the same.

The reporter took a few steps forward and crouched low to address the child. "Hey, don't be afraid."

The girl spun away and shook nervously. Rosa placed a hand gently on her back, but when the kid turned around again, she was holding a Breck 17 and wearing a smirk of supreme confidence.

"Wh-what are you —?" stammered Rosa, raising her hands

slowly into the air. It wasn't that she was scared — she was mortified! The girl couldn't be more than four feet tall.

"Bang!" yelled the child with a dramatic flourish of the semiautomatic. "Gimme all of your damn money and maybe I'll let you live!"

Rosa eyed her critically. Could this girl be the one who robbed the dead hikers? Could she have killed them? No, she was way too young.

The Wanderer spoke softly, clearly, and held his hands where the girl could see them. "We'd love to help you, darlin', but we're not carrying any cash."

The young thief's eyes flashed from Rosa to the gunman and back again. With a wrinkle of her freckled nose, she settled her attention elsewhere. Turning around, Rosa saw it was the blinking light on Charlie's wrist. "What's that bracelet do?" the child asked with a nod in the Kid's direction.

The bounty hunter looked genuinely upset. "Aw, c'mon, girl! It's a wristband!"

She rolled her eyes. "Whatever! Why's it blinking?"

"I don't know, man! I've got mail?"

The girl's eyes popped wide. "I want it. Gimme it."

"Oh, hell no!"

"Gimme it!" she screeched, shaking the gun.

The Wanderer smacked his partner lightly on the arm and nodded. With a deep sigh, Charlie unstrapped the device and stepped toward the girl. "Fine, but it's a little tricky to put on. If you hold out your wrist, I'll help you with the clasp."

The girl stared at him, appearing to measure his sincerity.

Finally, she extended her left arm, but she kept the semiautomatic in her other hand pointed at Charlie's chest. He brought the open bangle slowly to her wrist, snapped it shut and backed away with his hands in the air. Giddily, she admired the new toy like it was a candy bracelet.

Charlie sidestepped out of the gun's sights and whispered sharply, "Panic!"

The tween's eyes shot up but it was too late. The wristband throbbed and released a short electric zap. With a high shriek, the girl let go of her gun. Kid Hunter charged. A moment later, he had her arms pinned under his knees. The girl's cries were piercingly high. "Get offa me! Get offa me! Get offa me!"

Rosa darted forward and grabbed the girl's gun. She ejected the cartridge, which was full, and pulled the slide back to check for a bullet still in the chamber. She stuck the empty gun in one jeans pocket and the ammo in the other.

"Gimme my gun back! Get offa me!"

The Wanderer stood gravely over the squirming child and, in his most growly voice, directed her to shut the hell up.

She did. Rosa couldn't help but smile at how well that worked.

The gunman took a deep, contemplative breath. "You have a camp around here. Show it to us."

With a scowl she agreed, and Kid Hunter let her up. Muttering curses that were barely profane, the girl led them deeper into the woods. While the two outlaws stayed a few paces back, the reporter walked up close to the young thief, introducing herself as Rosie. "You're pretty brave," she said. "What's your name?"

The girl assessed her with brilliant green eyes. "Lindsay."

"It's nice to meet you on more civil terms."

"Yeah, I bet it is," said Lindsay, rolling her eyes. "Look, I'll take y'all back to my camp if you want, but my brother Jimmy's there, okay? I know I folded real easy, but you should know … compared to him? I'm sugar and spice and everything nice."

CHAPTER FIFTEEN

To New Friends!

Jimmy's back ached from hunching over the deadwood. He had the build of a football player — thick arms, thick legs, thick chest, thick neck — and a coat to match, bearing the logos of various NFL teams. But the jacket was stained with black soot, and his red hair had gotten too shaggy for sports.

He couldn't keep the damn match lighted. Every time he struck fire, a gust of wind would come and blow it out. After another failure, he roared, "Piece of shit!"

The mountains totally sucked. Once he made enough money out here, he was definitely moving back to Founders Spring. Or maybe Vegas. Yeah, in Vegas he could strike it really rich.

Well, he might not be able to light this fire, but at least they had loads of supplies: two tents and a pile of camping gear besides — sleeping bags, hiking packs, water bottles, cans of beans and countless packets of delicious Kraft Easy Mac — cheesy gold that never got old.

The crunch of a pinecone alerted Jimmy to someone's arrival. Couldn't be Lindsay. She walked with a lighter step. He reached for his Pilgrim shotgun, sprang up to his feet and aimed into the trees. "Whoever's in there better come the fuck out!"

"Don't shoot!" exclaimed a familiar voice, and Lindsay emerged with three adults he didn't recognize. The toughest one looked like a cowboy and was carrying a silver six-shooter. There was also a short but wiry guy wearing a bangle, and a sharp-eyed woman who looked as though she was dressed for an evening stroll.

"Linds?" screeched Jimmy. "Who the fuck ... ?"

"I'm really sorry," she whimpered.

Jimmy regarded his sister like a deflated football. Why did he have to get stuck with this little baby? All she ever did was slow him down.

"I found them about a half-mile away," she explained. "They took my gun and made me take them here. You can shoot them, if you wanna."

He nearly did, but froze when the weird cowboy pulled back the hammer of his Lassiter. "I wouldn't," he said gruffly.

Jimmy's face turned red. "Goddammit, Linds! Goddammit!"

"I'm sorry!" she whined. "I didn't have a choice."

"Now look here," said the cowboy. "We're not here to hurt you or steal from you."

Jimmy eyed him skeptically. "Yeah? Then why don't you piss off?"

"We'll go, but first I want to have a friendly conversation. Why don't you start by telling us about your operation here? You've got a mighty fine stash back there. So what's the game? Robbing campers?"

Jimmy didn't respond.

"We're not here to judge. I just want to know what you're planning to do with all that gear. Sell it back in town?"

"Fuck you."

The cowboy shot near Jimmy's foot, kicking up an explosion of dust. The teen panicked. "Wait, stop! Yes! We sell it in Founders Spring, okay? What's it to you?"

The woman asked, "Do you murder the owners, too?"

"What? No!"

The cowboy shook his head at her and continued, "How would you feel if we saved you the trip to town and bought some gear from you right here, right now?"

Lindsay interrupted. "You said you didn't have any cash!"

"No, but my smart lens"—he pointed to his eye—"still has a little juice left. I can transfer a payment to your bank account the instant we agree on a price."

Jimmy blinked a few times and smiled. After the payment cleared, he invited the nice strangers to stay for the night.

*

Rosa got the fire started on her first try. She felt herself chuckling as the five strangers sat around watching a pot of macaroni and bubbling water. The more they talked and joked, the less dangerous their hosts seemed. Jimmy and Lindsay didn't seem like murderers, though she still wouldn't have put it past Jimmy to steal from the dead. It still bothered her that he let his sister carry a gun, though. It was beyond irresponsible.

"How long have you been out here?" she asked.

"Forever," grumbled Lindsay.

Jimmy shook his head. He pulled a hot dog out of the fire and blew out a small fire caught on the end. "About a year."

Rosa crossed her arms. "So what happened?"

Jimmy glared. "None of your —"

"Jimmy got tired of our foster parents," Lindsay answered. Her brother looked pissed off, but she continued. "He made us drop out of school and run away."

"We *had* to," he said, emphasizing the statement with widened eyes. "There was no choice."

Rosa cast a withering look in his direction. "You know she's too young to be doing this."

"Am not!" protested Lindsay, rolling her eyes.

Jimmy held out his hands and said flatly, "Yeah. Look, I know."

As the night went on, Rosa found herself talking to Lindsay the most. The girl provided the best company. Kid Hunter kept getting distracted by the screen on his wrist, while the Wanderer just kept staring into the fire. Occasionally, the rogue gunman contributed a friendly "Is that so?" or "You don't say?" when Jimmy told him something, but that seemed to be the extent of his conversational abilities.

Lindsay softened as she talked about science class, Nerf guns, and Bugs Bunny. As the girl went on merrily about her Robin Hood adventures in the mountains, Rosa felt the ice of Jimmy's calculating eyes.

*

Errol wiped melted cheese off his face with a red bandanna, put down his plate, and leaned back contentedly on his elbows. The rest of the group also looked a strange sort of blissful, pleased with the processed food in the middle of the untamed wilderness. He hadn't eaten much of this so-called "Mac" before — it wasn't the kind of thing normally served to the heir of Breck Ammunition. Pretty tasty, though. It was a good meal and a good camp.

He hadn't done much camping as a kid. Dad had no interest in the outdoors; he would rather experience wilderness from the cozy confines of the Breck Estate's library. That was why most of the Breck guns were named after literary characters. A western novel by Zane Grey, passed from father to son on his fourteenth birthday, had sparked Errol's romance for the Lassiter six-shooter. Based on the old-fashioned Colt used by the hero, the Lassiter was not as quick as the semiautomatic Breck 17. But with its spinning chamber and shining steel exterior, the double-action revolver was the more elegant instrument. Played by the right musician, it was also the deadlier. He remembered lazy weekends spent shooting cans of Coca-Cola in the Breck Estate's backyard. Gerard rarely joined, preferring darker hobbies such as melting toy soldiers in the microwave, or peeling the wings off butterflies and observing their silent screams.

Errol sat up and stared into the bonfire. The ghost of Helen seemed to materialize in the flames, beckoning him with a bony finger. He wanted to join her. It was the fate he deserved.

Only the laughter of the little girl stirred him from his brooding. Lindsay was showing Rosa a card trick, surprising her with the result. He couldn't tell if the look on the reporter's face was real or exaggerated, but it seemed to please the child to no end.

Helen had wanted a girl.

He looked away from the fire and into the dark beyond. In a way, he was glad to be stuck here. These mountains provided the blessing of more time not to make a decision about Gerard. Obviously, he had to find a safe place for the reporter. It was the next part he wasn't so sure about. It hadn't really been that long since he'd left, but already his brother was out of control. Dad had been right about him. But on the flipside, he'd been wrong about Errol. The truth was neither of Al Breck's sons were fit to run that company.

"That nerd had it coming, though," finished Jimmy, who had apparently been telling a story. The teen looked funny in his football jacket, so far from civilization. He looked like a high school jock fallen upon hard times.

Errol forced a chuckle. "Is that so?"

*

Charlie cursed as his device's battery dropped to 29 percent. He was composing a message to his sister, Jane, to say that he was all right but might be incommunicado for a few days. He would send money home when he could. In the meantime, if anyone came by asking for him, she should just say he was away on a job.

He hoped she was all right. Even though she wasn't a kid anymore, he still felt responsible. He'd been away a long time and didn't know when he'd see her again. There was nothing but trouble waiting for him in Vegas. But he was still a better older brother than Jimmy, wasn't he?

The screen showed 23 percent battery — a six-point drop in only a few minutes of use. Charlie scowled. Why, with all the advances in technology, couldn't the damn scientists make a better battery? He got a couple days tops on a charge, and it always seemed to drain faster after hitting the halfway mark!

He shot off the message to Jane and put the damned thing to sleep.

*

Rosa was getting bored. Lindsay had gone into her tent to read a book, and now no one around the campfire was talking. She wanted to interview Errol, but knew it would be a bad idea with Jimmy around. No use staying up, so she faked a yawn and made a move to leave for bed.

"Wait," said Jimmy, stopping her with a wave of his hands. "Why don't we all have a quick drink first? I've got whiskey. You'll sleep better. Makes the night feel warmer."

Rosa tried to turn him down but Jimmy pressed on, and the others seemed keen. Finally, she gave in and sat back down.

"Great!" exclaimed Jimmy. He went into his tent and a few minutes later returned with four glasses of amber liquid. After carefully passing the drinks around, the young thief toasted, "To new friends!"

The men threw back the drinks while Rosa eyed the dirt-smudged glass critically. It could certainly do with a wash, but she needed the drink, so she followed the crowd and gulped it down.

She felt a bit wobbly when she stood but blamed it on getting up too fast. Certainly she hadn't had enough to be tipsy already.

Rosa had barely set up her tent when she noticed the Wanderer on his back by the fire, already fallen into deep slumber. Charlie was sleeping, too, having only managed to set up his tent in a lopsided, lean-to fashion. It provided cover but was far from finished.

"Hey, are you boys … all right?" Suddenly her head felt heavy. Like a dying woman straining to reach the mirage of an oasis, Rosa crawled into the tent and struggled into her sleeping bag.

Pablo tossed a tennis ball up into the air and caught it as he walked ahead toward the car. Rosa ran to catch up, but the seven-year-old boy's back kept sliding farther away. The ball went up. The ball went down. The ball went up. The ball hit the sidewalk, painting a long trail of red on the pavement.

Rosa broke out of the nightmare gasping for air. Distantly, she became aware of arguing voices, and light coming from a green tent. She knew something was wrong and tried to get up, but she felt too heavy to move.

CHAPTER SIXTEEN

So You Reckon You're a Real Reporter?

The sun had already soared high over the trees by the time Rosa came out of her tent. She could hear Kid Hunter snoring inside his tent, but the Wanderer was already up, stumbling a bit groggily around the shade of the campground. He didn't have his hat on, and his hair was crazy.

"What happened?" she called to him.

"We were drugged," was the grim response. He was holding a white plastic bottle of medicine. "Sleeping pills. They must be long gone by now."

"Were we robbed?"

He rubbed the stubble on his chin. "Oddly enough ... no, it doesn't seem so."

"Then why ... ?" She didn't finish the sentence. By her side she noticed a dirty envelope, scrawled with messy handwriting.

Hope u had a nice sleep. Now she's ur problem.

A fresh rush of wooziness overcame Rosa as she stepped out of the tent. She staggered drunkenly to the green tent on the other side of the dead fire. Through its polyester walls, she heard a heavy sob.

"Oh my God," gasped Rosa, tearing open the flap covering the entrance. She found Lindsay shaking in her sleeping bag. Her cheeks were stained with wet lines streaking from her eyes to the bottom of her chin.

"Jimmy's gone," the little girl cried. "Jimmy's gone."

*

Wet with dew and still cold from the night, the tent poles sent chills through Rosa's fingers. In a sudden burst of chivalry, the Wanderer offered to help, but she could do it herself and told him so. As it turned out, she ended up doing Charlie's in addition to her own. He'd barely even tried before loudly announcing his defeat. The Wanderer tried to assist, but it turned out he didn't know what he was doing, either. They were city boys through and through.

Lindsay handled her own tent quickly and efficiently, but afterward sat on the ground pouting beneath the gray hood of her sweatshirt. She spoke once, when the Wanderer asked if she knew the way to Founders Spring.

"There's a trail," she stated.

"Will you show us?"

With a heavy sigh, she rose to her feet and swung on her backpack. Without turning to check if anyone was ready, she set off into the pines.

Kid Hunter managed to keep pace with Lindsay, but Rosa and the Wanderer soon fell back. When she was certain Lindsay was out of earshot, Rosa asked him, "Should we have brought her with us? We've got dangerous men after us."

He took a long breath. "What choice do we have? We can't leave her out here."

"I'm worried about her. I think she's in denial about what happened. She either thinks Jimmy will come back for her, or that he's set a challenge for her and she just has to find him." Rosa knew neither were likely. "She's too young for a life like this. She's too young to be carrying a gun."

He shrugged. "I was shooting when I was her age."

"Okay, but you're a Breck. You probably had a gun in utero and shot your way out."

"Heh."

The path led up a hill and it soon became more difficult to walk. Rosa procured a rubber band from her pocket and began tying her jet-black hair into a ponytail. "What are we going to do with Lindsay," she said between heavy puffs, "when we get to town?"

It didn't sound as though Lindsay had anyone besides Jimmy. She had mentioned foster parents, but the way Jimmy had spoken about them made her think they weren't a good idea.

"We'll find a church," said the Wanderer. "They'll know what to do."

For some reason, the idea of just dropping her off like that, making it someone else's problem, didn't sit well. "And will you leave me with the church, too?"

He rolled his eyes. "If Founders Spring seems safe and it suits you, you can hide out wherever you want."

"For how long?"

"For as long as it takes."

She looked at him in disbelief. "And what'll you do? Catch a train to the next town?"

"The train doesn't go to Founders Spring."

She groaned. "Forget it."

He looked at her helplessly. It was a look she recognized from her brother. Jack … he probably was worried. She never told him she was leaving town. He'd probably showed up at her house and found it abandoned. If Ben Martin hadn't gotten there before him, there'd be a dead gangster in the front yard, and a horribly burned one still moaning inside.

She watched Lindsay stomp through the trees like she was having a tantrum. The girl with the gun, forced to live in the wilderness and steal from strangers. There were stories everywhere Rosa looked.

Part of her wanted to try to interview the Wanderer again, but she wasn't sure what would be the point. She'd gotten herself into enough trouble already. Even if she did interview him, she wasn't sure she had enough juice left in her phone to record it. She didn't trust her memory. What was she going to do? Scribble on a pinecone? She didn't even have a pen!

Just in case, she pulled out her phone to check its battery, but the damn thing wouldn't even power on. Not only would she not be able to use it for interviewing, but there was no way to call Jack.

"My eyeglass just died, too," commiserated the Wanderer. "Tried to wake it this morning but it was dead set on sleeping. Let's hope the girl knows where she's going."

His gaze stayed on her, and for a second, she thought he was going to say something.

"What?" she asked, unable to wait any longer.

He said, "So you reckon you're a *real* reporter?"

The familiar label made Rosa's eyes dart to the hot pink watch on her wrist. It was still working, naturally. The one good thing about a watch that wasn't smart was that it had a great battery life.

"A real reporter?" she replied, eyeing the rudimentary buttons on the watch's surface. "The truth is I don't know what I am anymore."

He studied her with confusion, as if she was some kind of gun without a handle.

She sighed morosely. "I thought I was better than other reporters because I was going to write the truth. I wasn't going to just write what the advertisers wanted. I wasn't going to have *any* advertising. I was just going to write about how things really were. But now — I mean, look at us. Lost in the woods with the Red Stripe Gang on our tails."

He nodded. "You've got guts. That's for sure."

When he looked away, Rosa tapped one of the buttons on the watch. A black circle appeared on the screen. The thing was recording! Despite herself, Rosa felt a familiar surge of excitement. It couldn't hurt to interview him. Even if she decided not to write *The New West* anymore.

"How about you answer one of my questions, now?"

"Heh," laughed the Wanderer. "What do you want to know?"

She certainly wasn't about to make the same mistake as yesterday and ask a question that would scare him off, so she started with a softball. "What's the deal with you and trains?"

He laughed, before proceeding to a variety of answers. He sprinkled each possible explanation with more awkward chuckles. She had never seen him so embarrassed. It was actually kind of cute. He offered a few fleeting memories of his childhood — a train set, a ride on an old-fashioned steam engine — as well as a few general remarks about the relaxing nature of riding the rails and how nice it was to look out the window. She didn't believe any of these reasons, though. Truth was she had him figured already. The Wanderer — Errol Breck — was running from something but couldn't decide where to go. On the train, he didn't have to. What he was running from was what she really wanted to know.

*

The trees glowed and suddenly gave way to azure sky as Rosa neared the edge of a cliff. Red giants loomed overhead, looking poised to crush them with sandstone fists. The sound of rushing water brought her eyes down hundreds of feet to a long river carving through the rocks. They had come to a canyon.

She looked on as Lindsay picked up a stone and tossed it hard over the edge. The rock met the water too many feet below with a faint yet emphatic *sploosh*!

"Yeah, yeah … I can beat that," challenged Kid Hunter.

He grabbed a small boulder with two hands and lifted it slowly over his head. With a grunt he pushed it into the air. Lindsay's eyes expanded as she followed the rock's heavy fall. The water burst as if struck by dynamite.

"Oh my God!" the girl exclaimed with pure delight. She pulled back her hood, revealing a brush fire of hair. "You must have just killed, like, I dunno, twenty fish!"

"That all?" replied Charlie with a pearly grin.

Rosa noticed the Wanderer chuckling and wondered if he had any kids. Figuring it would stir up memories of his dead wife, she decided to hold off on asking until she had won his trust.

"Hey, idiots!" shouted Lindsay, standing with Charlie by a dry and knotted tree. The petulant girl waved her hands like she was trying to get through to a pair of spaced-out drug users.

Rosa forced a smile but was sure it looked fake. "You have our attention!"

Lindsay told them about a dirt trail that wound down the canyon in a series of tight switchbacks, ending finally on one side of the river. "We can eat when we get down to the water. We'll follow the river through the canyon until sunset. Then we'll find a place to make camp for the night."

Rosa and Charlie both instinctively looked to the Wanderer.

He responded with a shrug. "She's the boss."

CHAPTER SEVENTEEN

Ain't You Just a Little Wanderer?

Kid Hunter trudged after Lindsay down the path into the floor of the canyon. She moved like a squirrel. He couldn't keep up, and the trail was too long to try. The pines had abandoned them and now there was no shade. Charlie could feel the midday sun through his burgundy track jacket, making him sweat. He tried taking the coat off, but then flies and mosquitos started attacking the flesh of his exposed arms. The bites hurt like hell, leaving him with tracks of itchy bumps. So he put his jacket back on and just suffered through the heat.

He was getting hungry, too, but then it occurred to him that the only snack food they were carrying was granola bars. There wasn't even a variety of flavors — just apple cinnamon. And the bars weren't even the moist, chewy ones; these were like crisp cardboard. They only made him thirsty, and there wasn't a whole lot of water to go around. Fucking hell. If he wasn't so hungry …

Lindsay paused and spun around with her hands on her hips. "You're so slow!"

"Naw, girl, I'm just saving my energy. In an hour, you're gonna fall over and I'll still be walking, slow and steady. Know what I'm sayin'?"

She grinned. "Yeah, we'll see."

When he caught up, she slowed her pace and walked by his side. "I like your secret names," she declared. "Wanderer, Kid Hunter … uh, Reporter Lady … I want a secret name!"

He raised his eyebrows. Seriously?

They resumed their walk down the path. Flourishing her hands like a magician, Lindsay announced, "I know! Call me … Lindsay."

"Uh," offered Charlie, narrowing his eyes, "isn't that your name already?"

"No, not Lindsay!" she corrected. "*Lindsay!*"

"Still not hearing the difference."

She rolled her eyes. "Like Lin, dash, zee."

"Wait, Lin … Z?"

She gave an exasperated nod.

"*Lin-Z!* All right, I get you!" burst Charlie with a deep laugh. "I have to say, though, that is a *really* dumb name."

She dismissed the criticism with a short breath. "Whatever."

"Plus," Charlie continued, undeterred, "if you ever ran into some British nob, they might call you Lin-zed. Ha! That's even worse!"

The expression on her face radiated pure rage. "Shut. Up."

He grinned so widely his gums showed.

"Anyway, this is America," Lindsay said. "When am I ever going to run into a British … what did you call him?"

Charlie waved it off. "Don't worry about it."

She didn't appear ready to back down. "Your name's stupid, too!" she burst. "I mean, what, do you hunt kids or something?"

"That's not —!" he cried out in alarm. Crestfallen, he mumbled, "Shit, that's a good point."

She smiled. "It's okay, I didn't think of it that way when I heard it the first time. Anyway, it's too late to change it now. You're already famous, right?"

Before he could reply, Lindsay skipped ahead, eyes fixed on the sky. Charlie wasn't sure what she was looking at. There weren't even any clouds. Even if there were clouds, why would anyone look at clouds? A flash of light from the woods on the opposite side of the canyon made him blink. He squinted into the trees but couldn't see anything. Probably nothing.

"So you're the sidekick, right?" she asked, pausing again to let him catch up.

He chuckled — what else could he do? "Naw, girl, the Wanderer and I are *partners*."

"I've *seen* the way you look at him."

He gasped. What was *that* supposed to mean?

She giggled. "I don't mean like he's your boyfriend. I just mean you look to him for the final word on things. It's okay! I'm a sidekick, too. Well, I mean I was ... before ..." Green eyes fell to worn boots.

Charlie nodded sympathetically. He knew who she was talking about. "You've got to leave all that behind."

"It's okay, really. Jimmy just likes to challenge me sometimes."

He shook his head. "He shouldn't have left you."

They stopped short as a small brown lizard bolted up from a rock in the path and skedaddled arm over arm into the bush.

Lindsay smiled like a tiny, sly angel. "Think I can have my gun back?"

Charlie laughed. He glanced back at the Wanderer and Rosa, chatting like an old married couple. "It's going to take some doing, I think. Rosa doesn't approve of you carrying."

"Yeah, she doesn't think I'm old enough. But I'm almost thirteen! I'm basically an adult! How old were you when you first had a gun?"

"Younger than you." Back in Vegas he had to carry … to protect his family and to get the things they needed.

"*See?*"

"But," he interjected, "I wish I hadn't needed it."

"But you did. Need it, I mean. And so do I. Have you ever shot anyone?"

"More than I like to admit. For money, mostly."

"I've shot some people …" She said it quietly while wringing her hands. "Well, I've shot at them. They didn't die, so I guess it doesn't count, right? Mostly, Jimmy and I would just, you know, wave our guns around, real threatening-like. Usually, people would just give us their stuff and run away like frightened bunnies. But I know how to shoot. I'm a good shot."

Charlie couldn't decide if she was trying to convince him that she was a lamb or a wolf. Instead, he told her about his wristband, and she watched with rapt attention as he ran through the features: smart gun control, apps for everything, the hacking interface … and then the battery blinked red, and the screen shut off.

"Shit!" he exclaimed. Then, realizing his audience, "Sorry. Shouldn't curse."

"Don't fucking apologize to me!" she returned. "That does suck, though. Can you still fire your gun if the brace — if the wristband's off?"

He pulled out the Separatist pistol and looked at it like it was a strange growth. "Well, shit."

"Where'd you get that piece of crap?"

"Canada."

She snorted a laugh. "Canada? Are you serious?"

Charlie slapped her on the back and sprinted ahead.

"Hey, what the hell was that?" she yelled after him.

"You're it, loser!" he shouted back.

Lindsay's stunned gape morphed into a gleeful grin. She took chase, gray hood flapping behind her.

*

"I'm not against guns."

The Wanderer smirked. He didn't believe Rosa for one second.

"No, really," she appealed. "When I was little, I used to go hunting with my brother and my dad, and I loved it. What I'm actually against is the *excess* of guns and the gun culture. Have you seen the Breck 100X? What regular person would need a gun that shoots that many bullets, that fast, over that long a distance? For that matter, what regular person would need any fully automatic rifle?"

A short laugh escaped through his nose. "Hey, America survived the Thompson, didn't it?"

Rosa gave him a look like he was wearing his left shoe on the right. "The *tommy gun*? Really? That's what you're going with? Okay, first of all, I don't think the Thompson had computer-assisted aiming as a feature —"

"I know the Breck 100X has more gadgetry — that's not what I mean. What I'm saying is … look, everyone was up in arms about machine guns back then, weren't they? But America survived another century, didn't it?"

"America *survived* the 1920s because it had functioning police, courts, and legislatures. Anyway, you know what the government *did*, right?"

The Wanderer let his silence answer.

"They *banned* machine guns. It was called the National Firearms Act. Maybe you heard of it? It's that law your dad got lifted so that his death company, no offense, could release the Yossarian assault rifle and make a profit."

Errol offered a long, impressed whistle. The reporter knew her history. He remembered his father's quest to change the law, but he'd never heard it phrased in quite those words. He had done his best to stay out of politics while his father was in charge of company. Above his paygrade, he liked to say. Also, he had always felt a little dirty about the amount of influence his dad had on public policy. Really, it'd been Gerard who'd wanted to get involved in those kinds of discussions, but Dad had been too stubborn to let him help.

"It's not just that, though," Rosa went on. "It's this American attitude that like, we have the *right* to just walk down the street carrying guns on our waist." She smacked her forehead. "It's like we're living in the Wild West all over again. It's like … when you leave the house, you're checking for your wallet, your keys, your phone, and your gun. Like these are equally essential things for the day ahead. And the kids — girls like Lindsay — they're the ones who get caught in the crossfire."

*

Charlie had to stop running at the floor of the canyon. Between heavy breaths, he panted, "Can we … can we put … this game … on hold … for … now?"

"What? That's stupid!" Lindsay looked outraged. "Either we keep playing, or I win."

The Kid spat a thick wad of mucus and watched it rust the copper dirt. "Fine. You win. Is it time to eat?"

"Not yet. I know a nice picnic spot a little way up ahead. Might take twenty minutes?"

He groaned. "Okay, well, I'm gonna rest here a minute and let the others catch up."

"Whatever." She turned back to the path, continuing full steam ahead.

Still gasping, Charlie turned to the river rapids carving through the red rocks. He put his backpack down while pulling a half-empty water bottle from the side. After a good, long swig, he tugged off his track jacket and tied it around his waist; bugs be damned. The cool air felt good against the film of sweat that had washed over his arms. He had just caught his breath when the Wanderer and Rosa came up behind him.

"She tired you out, huh?" asked the reporter.

"Naw," Charlie said. "I just thought I'd wait up for the slowpokes of the group. What's up, guys?"

The Wanderer looked secretly relieved to see him. "We're just finishing up my interview."

"Finishing up?" repeated Rosa with alarm. "We're just getting started!"

He shook his head no. "I reckon I better make sure the girl knows where she's going. Looks like you're up, Kid!"

As the Wanderer jogged away, Charlie let loose a high-pitched "Ha!"

Rosa held out her hands in consternation. "He literally just ran away from me."

"Well, he is known to wander."

She laughed.

"How about you interview *me* now? C'mon, girl, I just know you've been itchin' to get the scoop on handsome Kid Hunter."

She smiled at him. "All right, sugar."

He winked. "That's brown sugar to you."

She held up her hands. "Whoa there, stallion. How'd you meet the Wanderer?"

Charlie gave a look of mock outrage. "Is this about him or about me?"

"Okay fine. Where are you from?"

"Sin City. The mean streets of Las Vegas."

"What were you doing there?"

"This and that. Some might call me a mercenary. A mercenary with a kind heart. No, wait. How about ... a mercenary with a kind but *dangerous* heart."

Rosa frowned. "I don't think you understand how interviews work."

"Sure I do. I give you great quotes and you write 'em down."

The reporter sighed.

Kid Hunter grinned. Winning.

"You raise an interesting point, though. You seem pretty good-natured for a guy who shoots strangers for a living."

It was like a sucker punch to the gut. Charlie heard himself stammering incomprehensibly and it took some time before he was able to pull himself together. "That's what I used to do. And I did what I did for my sister. To keep her off the streets. So she could have a good life."

"A sister? Older or younger?"

"Younger. We used to be a team back in Vegas. Jane would charm the guy at 7-Eleven while I snatched the bread. You know, that kind of thing."

"So you were thieves."

"We were orphans."

"Like Lindsay and Jimmy."

He defensively waved his hand. "I'm nothing like Jimmy."

Rosa shrugged. "So, what? Stealing didn't pay?"

"Not those kinds of jobs. But then I started moving on to bigger things. I learned to hack, and began pulling off bigger jobs on my own. I guess that's how I attracted El Tiburón's notice. I'd never thought about using my skills for killing, but when I found out how much it would pay, and what that would mean for Jane, I couldn't say no."

"How did you learn to hack?"

He grinned proudly. "Self-taught. I always liked the planning of a theft more than the physical doing, so I got to thinking, maybe there's a way I can do this remotely. So, I … uh … got access to a pretty slick laptop, and I started learning the skills. I found a fairly powerful hacking community online. Got a lot of great pointers there."

"So you learned hacking to make theft easier. But then El Tiburón started using your skills to kill people. And this is the part I don't really get. I mean, you seem like a nice guy, Charlie. How did you put aside your conscience to accept a job and take a life?"

Kid Hunter frowned. "Hey, uh, I was just thinking ... do you mind not mentioning specifically that I worked for El Tiburón in whatever you end up writing? I'm in deep enough shit with that guy as is."

She nodded. "I don't have to specify."

"To your question," he said with a shrug, "I guess I tried not to think too much about my targets. I never found out anything personal about them. I didn't want to know who they were. They were always just targets. You know?"

Rosa smiled like she understood. He wondered how reporters remembered any of this shit later when they sat down to write. That girl must have a mind like a steel trap!

"You and Lindsay were pretty cute, running around up there," she said.

Charlie sighed with relief. It sounded like the interview was over. "She's an all right kid, I think. I guess she reminds me a little of Jane when she was young."

"Lindsay reminds you of your little sister. Interesting."

"Oh, shit!" he exclaimed. "I see what you did there. You know what, Rosa? You're pretty good at this journalism shit!"

*

When the Wanderer caught up with Lindsay, he didn't know what to say. The girl seemed to have a good memory of the trail. He had no doubt she knew where they were headed. He took comfort also in the fact that they were walking along a river, close to good water they could use for drinking and cooling off. Follow it long enough and it just might lead them back to civilization.

The Wanderer lifted his hat and wiped his brow. Talking to that reporter did his head in. Rosa made interviews feel like debates. What he'd do for a beer!

He heard Lindsay grumble and looked over. She was walking with a deeply serious pout and holding two finger guns by her hips.

"Hey, what are you —?" he asked.

"I'm the Wanderer," she growled. "Make my day."

"Hey!"

She started cracking up at how hilarious she thought she was, and then the Wanderer felt a deep laugh erupting from his own belly. Maybe it was the heat or the exhaustion, but soon they were bending over at the knees, nearly in tears. He took off his Stetson and slapped it playfully on Lindsay's head. The gray hat was too big and sank over her eyes, but she lifted her head back and balanced the front of the inside against her forehead.

"Well, now!" he exclaimed, playing up the Western twang. "Ain't you just a little Wanderer?"

A smile appeared on the girl's face, but it vanished as thunder echoed through the canyon. There was an explosion of dust a few yards from Lindsay's feet. The Wanderer recognized the sound as the report of a Montag sniper rifle. He shouted back to Rosa and the Kid to run for cover, while tugging Lindsay by the arm toward a red rock wall. She grabbed the Stetson off the ground and sprinted alongside him. Another crack of thunder hit, bursting against the stone just behind them.

He reckoned it was a miracle they still had their lives. He and Lindsay hadn't been moving that fast — a good sniper wouldn't have missed that first shot. Whoever was shooting at them wasn't a great shot and was probably drunk. He could still get lucky, though.

"Keep running!" he roared at the others.

A low opening in the rock appeared, just big enough to crawl into. The Wanderer pushed Lindsay inside and rolled in after her. It was a cave. It had a low ceiling but there was plenty of space for all of them. He watched as Rosa and Kid Hunter came running. Another blast. The mercenary howled but kept running. He dove into the cave, and Rosa crawled in after him.

The Kid's left bicep was bleeding.

"Are you shot?" cried Rosa.

He shook his head. "No — with that high-caliber shit he's firing? I'd be dead if he got a direct shot on me." He pointed to his arm. "He blew up a rock right next to me. Some of the shards must've scratched me."

She took a good look and breathed a sigh of relief. "It doesn't look serious."

"Okay, but it fucking hurts!"

A loud, wheezing breath turned the Wanderer's attention to

Lindsay. Her face was red, and she looked like she was having trouble breathing.

He reached into his denim knapsack and brought out a small metal box labeled Breck First Aid. The company had begun producing the kits about a decade ago, in response to the increasing frequency of gunshot wounds. Rosa took the kit and procured a roll of thick white cloth. As she wrapped it around the Kid's arm to stem the bleeding, the Wanderer went over to help Lindsay.

He smacked her in the back in an attempt to clear her lungs. "What happened? Are you all right?"

"Just … asthma," she whimpered. "I had an inhaler … in my … pocket … but it must have fallen out."

With trepidation, the Wanderer looked back out at the canyon. It wasn't safe to go back out there.

"Is it that blue thing?" Charlie asked. With his bandaged arm, he pointed to a shadow near the opening of the cave.

It was close enough to the entrance for the sniper to have a shot, but the Wanderer reckoned he'd have a second or two while the hunter took aim. He scuttled toward the object, picked it up and leaped back toward Lindsay. There was another crack of thunder and the spot where the inhaler had lain burst into a cloud of dirt. With a smirk, the Wanderer brought the inhaler to Lindsay. Gratefully, the wheezing girl took the medicine and brought it to her mouth for a puff.

Charlie exclaimed, "Fucking hell! Where's the shooter?"

The Wanderer shook his head. The echoes of the canyon had made it impossible to hear from where the gun was fired. Could be anywhere.

"Think it's the Gang?" asked Rosa.

"No," replied the Wanderer. "We lost them good, and anyway, sniping's not their style. I reckon it's our friend with the Montag — the same lone wolf who shot them hikers."

Rosa held her mouth in fright. "What are we going to do now? He'll get us as soon as we come out."

"I think there might be another way out of here," Lindsay interjected. She had crawled deeper into the cave and was pointing around the corner. "I think I see some light."

They crawled for several minutes until they reached it. The girl was right. It was an exit out the other side. The shooter wouldn't be able to get them without coming through the cave himself.

"And then what?" asked Rosa. "What's going to stop him from finding us again?"

"Nothing," said the Wanderer. "But if we head for higher ground, that Montag won't do him any good. If he still wants to get us, he'll have to be a little more personable."

CHAPTER EIGHTEEN

This Smells of Showboating!

Death was most obvious around the eyes, where the skin had darkened and begun to flake. The mouth hung slightly ajar, with yellow teeth cutting through chalky lips. A leather harness fit tightly around a shriveled chest and held the body upright, while a rope tied to the back kept it aloft. The rope connected to a butcher's hook on the ceiling designed to hang heavy slabs of refrigerated meat.

"Stage one!" blared a megaphone. A responding blast thundered against the body. The impact sent the corpse's bare feet back and up in an arc until they inched slightly above its skull. Gravity snapped the cadaver back down, and the feet arced forward until the soles could be seen. The human pendulum swung back and forth with decreasing energy until, finally, it settled into a breezy drift.

"Stage two! Keep it in the air!"

A drumroll of shots batted the body back up like a balloon.

The corpse vibrated under the rain of fire. Finally, unable to take any more, the thing separated at the waist as if it was slow-cooked brisket.

The gunfire ceased, filling the hangar with a heavy silence. Gerard Breck, looking splendid in a black pin-striped business suit, lowered his binoculars, pulled pink wads of foam from his ears, and discarded them on the cement floor. He was about a football field away from the corpse, standing alongside men wearing ear mufflers and white lab coats. Gerard watched with interest as they scrawled numbers and figures on their tablets.

He wet his lips as the test shooter came up from a prone position holding a Breck 100X rifle. "That was ... breathtaking."

Testing the guns had always been Gerard's favorite. It wasn't the firing of the guns that got him hard, but rather seeing what the guns could do to their targets. The varying effects of bullets on animal flesh was a particular delight. Changing the length of the gun barrel or the width of the bullet, for example, could mean the difference between a clean shot sunk into the meat or an explosion that sent the thing's innards spraying in all directions. Each was a beautiful sight in its own way.

One of the white coats came up to him and began to speak science. Gerard tuned him out, choosing instead to replay the scene of the levitating cadaver. In this version, however, it was his stepbrother on the line ... the so-called Wanderer. It was almost impressive, Errol's relentless knack for intruding in Gerard's affairs. Even after leaving Vegas in disgrace, it was like Errol couldn't help himself. Seriously, Gerard couldn't kill one pesky reporter without that moron interfering? How had he found her? How had he even *known* about her?

"Mr. Breck? Did you hear me?"

His eyes fell on Elza, who was wearing the stern, focused look that made her such an asset.

"We've got to get in the limo now," she stated, all business. "You're due in front of the board in less than twenty minutes."

*

Gerard didn't like to admit it, but there was actually one floor that sat above the office of the CEO. On the roof of the gun-clip skyscraper, the architect had added a clear glass bubble where boardroom meetings could be held. It was a beautiful space, with panoramic views across the city, but Gerard couldn't help but feel a sense of dread whenever he stepped off the elevator. No matter how prepared he felt going in, such meetings never went well.

As CEO, he was one of two executive directors on the board. The other was the CFO, Francis Cohn. Fran was an okay guy. Elza had recommended him for his ability to take all orders without question and fudge the balance sheet to meet business goals. Unfortunately, the four *non*-executive directors were real asshats. They'd been on the board since the dawn of time, and in the whole length of their existence had never said one nice thing to Gerard. In fact, it had only been with great reluctance that they had even allowed him to assume the position of CEO. They had wanted Errol then, and Gerard knew they still wanted Errol now. Well, Errol had missed his chance.

Chairman Cornelius "Corny" Boone, looking five years from the grave tops, tapped a stack of papers against the table, which was his usual way of calling for attention. "Mr. Breck, this new gun of yours —" he began, before falling into a coughing fit. The old man had to smack his own chest to loosen the phlegm.

Gerard's stepfather had been a longtime buddy of Boone's, and it was Al who had given him the nickname Corny. He used to joke that it doubled as a description. They had met as fraternity brothers in college, and after graduation, they became business partners. Al had always been the ideas man, which was why he got his name on the company, but Corny had provided the sales acumen that had driven Breck Ammunition to the top of the gun industry, eventually pushing out its competitors. Corny always said he never minded that Al stayed away from the finance side of things because he always held up his end of the bargain with great products that were easy to sell. Gerard had yet to receive the same sentiment.

"The Breck 100X?" Gerard offered. "I'm happy to report the advance orders are on fire already. In just a few days, we've hit our goal for the quarter!"

Sally Gomes, a frizzy-haired director sitting to Boone's right, broke in, "And how much, pray tell, will filling those orders cost the company?"

She didn't look happy. Gerard nudged his CFO to answer.

Fran spread out his papers on the table and began to search. "Ah, are you asking for a total figure or do you mean per gun?"

"That was rhetorical. I know the figures," snapped Gomes. "These super-guns of yours cost a *fortune* to build, and you're selling them for peanuts. You're going to be bleeding money on every sale."

"Ah," stammered Fran, "is that a question?"

Gerard intervened. "We're selling at a loss, yes, but we've modeled for that. The guns eat through an incredible amount of ammo, so the cost of the shells will cover the money we're giving up in … what was it, Fran? Three months?"

Anil Kumar interjected in his typically booming cry, "Aren't you assuming people will actually use this gun every day?"

Fran tried to answer. "We —"

"You're selling this as a hunting rifle, and it's absolutely gigantic! The average customer is going to use this gun once or twice a year and the rest of the time keep it on a rack. I must ask, does your modeling take that into account, Mr. Cohn?"

"Um, ah …"

Gerard looked helplessly at his occasional ally, the fourth non-executive board member, Joe Watts. Watts was even older than Boone and a narcoleptic. As usual, he was stuck in a state of deep slumber.

"You know, Mr. Breck," said Boone, recovered from his coughing fit, "there was a reason your stepfather did not try to reinvent the gun. He simply made more efficient arms. You, on the other hand, seem to think this company has something to prove."

Gerard scowled at the other board members. He wasn't going to stand for this. The Breck 100X was his baby, and it was glorious. Oh, if they could only see it in action. Then they'd understand.

"It's an amazing gun," he stated, holding up his hands to emphasize the point. "I was just at a test this morning and —"

"Yes, and about these tests," sneered Sally Gomes. "You are spending a lot of money. I understand you commissioned helicopters for a media demonstration? Who are you trying to impress? We have the market locked up. This smells of showboating!"

Gerard could feel his blood boiling. "Look, this is my gun and my company. People want the 100X, and you can be sure as fuck we're going to sell it to them." To emphasize this last point, he stabbed at the air with his finger.

"There's no need for this dirt-filled language!" shouted Kumar. "And tell us, Mr. Breck, what is this *New West* blog I have been hearing so much about? People are saying you have connections to the Red Stripe Gang! Is there any truth to this?"

Gerard gaped. "I … I'm handling the situation with that blogger. She's not reputable."

"Reputable or no, it's affecting the stock prices!" Kumar replied.

"I'm handling it! Now, can we wrap up this meeting?"

Boone laughed heartily. "You may be CEO, *Gerard*, but you are not the chairman. This meeting will not be adjourned until I say it is adjourned. Now let *me* tell *you* what's going to happen." The old man paused to clear his throat. "The way I see it, you have *three* options. One, you can increase the price of the 100X. Two, you can reduce the cost of the 100X. Or, three, you can halt production altogether."

Gerard managed to hold his composure. "We'll make a profit."

"I hope so, because in January, when you report your full-year financial earnings, you can expect we will be looking very closely at the numbers on this super-gun. If you cannot limit the losses, this board will be forced to look for new leadership."

Gerard heard his own heavy breathing. Through gritted teeth, he sneered, "Errol is gone. He isn't coming back."

Boone shook his head. "I didn't say a word about your brother, but now that you've brought him up, I know for a fact he wouldn't have approved this gun for production. He was just too smart for that."

Gerard felt his right hand tingle. He was clenching it so tightly it had turned white. Releasing it, he forced a smile. "Will that be all?"

*

Gerard sucked the whiskey off of his mustache and jingled the ice in his tumbler. He was sitting with his back to the desk, staring vacantly up at the portrait of Al Breck on the wall.

Before the car accident, his mother used to push him down to the pool to play with Errol. It usually happened when she wanted sex from his stepfather, which was often. Gerard hated it. The pool was rarely clean, and he didn't like having to swim through all the dry grass clippings and dead flies. If he really thought about it, the only thing he could really say he liked about the pool was playing with water guns.

Gerard smiled. He and Errol used to have epic water gun fights. Errol might have been the better shot, but Gerard was the master of escalation. He had an arsenal of water balloons and the best Super Soakers his parents' money could buy.

He remembered most fondly the big one he got on his tenth birthday. It was during the first year living in the estate after Mama's marriage to Al Breck. The old man had clearly wanted to make a good impression, so he'd gotten Gerard a mammoth Super Soaker that actually attached to two big water tanks he could wear as a backpack. It had produced an incredible burst of water. The thing could wipe out an entire ant colony in five seconds — Gerard had timed it.

However, the gun's shining moment had come the next summer, when eleven-year-old Gerard had spied fourteen-year-olds Errol and Helen eating ice cream by the pool. They'd been dangling their legs in the water and going on about the clouds or something similarly insipid. Gerard had strapped on the Super Soaker, come up behind them, and fired a stream of water into their backs so strongly, it sent the both of them straight into the pool. Fully clothed!

Errol had started yelling things at him from the water — really mean things. So Gerard had put the gun down, yelled "Cannonball!", and jumped. His kneecap had landed with a thud on Errol's head. Gerard's leg had stung like hell, but the next thing he knew, *he* was the one in trouble. Dad had grounded him for weeks. He'd spend hours up in his room, watching through binoculars as Errol and Helen stole kisses by that damn pool.

Dad always took Errol's side, even when his beloved Iris was still alive. When Gerard and his mother first joined the family, Al Breck had been kind to him. He learned later that this was only for the benefit of Al's wife. As soon as Iris died, all of the old man's love had dried up, and Gerard found himself the outcast of the Breck clan. Not even his old playmate Errol would have anything to do with him.

"Gerard, are you all right?"

He swiveled his executive leather chair around to face Elza. She looked worried, and he started to feel hard. "Those bunch of idiots on the board would seem to have some ill-placed concerns about the cost of the Breck 100X," he said. "They don't believe I can make a profit on it."

She licked her lips. "There are always doubters of great genius."

That perked him up. He beckoned her toward him. When she was close enough, he hooked his finger around the low neckline of her blouse and reeled her in. A moment later, he felt her cool hand dipping into his pants.

He loved the way she stroked his ego, even though really it was Elza who had been the inspiration to build such a magnificent gun. It was shortly after he took over as CEO. No matter what he did, Gerard couldn't shake the feeling that people thought he was just there to keep the Al Breck show running, or worse, to keep the executive seat warm until Errol returned. As usual, Elza had the solution — build a new gun, the most amazing gun anyone has ever seen, and create his own legacy. When he discovered O'Brien's prototype for what would become the Breck 100X, he knew he had found the means to finally set himself apart from his stepfather.

Elza pushed him back on the leather chair and straddled him. Delighted to find she wasn't wearing any underwear, he gasped, "I love you."

A few breathless minutes later, she said, "Feel better?"

He nodded. "But I was thinking about the board meeting. Fran wasn't very good. I think he's going to be a problem."

She smiled darkly as she slid off him. "I've already had Mr. Cohn dealt with."

He looked up at her, impressed. "You mean he's —?"

"We'll begin the search for a new CFO tomorrow."

CHAPTER NINETEEN

El Aspecto de los Muertos.

The sky looked huge and made the Wanderer feel small. But he didn't fear the sky.

The rogue gunman surveyed the snaking river from the edge of a rocky foothill. Although they had come to the highest point in the immediate area, the mountains still loomed overhead. It wasn't the most direct route to Founders Spring, but they needed to make camp for the night, and it was safer to be on high ground. They'd been easy targets for the lone wolf on the floor of the canyon. However, to get them up here, the sniper — or whoever else might be chasing them — would have to climb up and attack them at close quarters. And this time, the Wanderer would be ready.

He returned to the camp, where Rosa, Charlie, and Lindsay were busy warming their hands by the fire. The temperature always dropped at night, but it seemed to have downright plummeted at this high of an elevation. With the pines sparser up here as well, more of the wind got through to chill them, too. The Kid's sporty track jacket didn't seem to be cutting it, based on the way he was shivering. And Rosa was actually using her sleeping bag as a kind of blanket. Lindsay seemed the most comfortable, but she had her warm hoodie and what looked like a couple layers besides. Anyway, she had spent a lot more time out here in the wilderness.

"I'll tell you what," said Rosa. "You boys need a shave."

Reflexively, Errol felt the stubble that had formed on his chin.

"Yours is coming in gray, Breck," she added. "Makes you look plain old."

Charlie whooped. "She's right! You look about seventy, Wanderer."

He scowled. "I'm barely in my forties!"

Lindsay went all bug-eyed. "Forties! Holy hell, and you're still alive?"

The Wanderer changed the subject. "I reckon we should be able to make it to Founders Spring by tomorrow evening."

"Thank fuck," replied Charlie, slapping his neck and pulling off the juicy remains of a smashed mosquito. The bandage on his arm was brown with dried blood.

"Watch your language," snapped Rosa. She glanced protectively at Lindsay, who promptly rolled her eyes.

"God, it's like, I know the word *fuck*, okay?" the girl protested. "Fuck, fuck, fuck!"

Seeing that this was headed nowhere good, the Wanderer attempted once more to reset the conversation. "It's good to talk. Makes the night not seem so cold. Rosa, maybe if you have another question, I could —"

"What happened that made you leave Vegas? Why didn't you stay to take over the Breck company? When —"

"One question at a time, I said!"

Rosa grinned. "Okay. Why did you leave Vegas?"

They all looked at him. The Wanderer didn't want to tell the story, but he'd already agreed to answer, and now that they were all staring ...

"Helen and I — Helen was my wife — we were in bed when it happened. She was the one who heard the noise first. She woke me up, and then I heard it, too. Something downstairs was making a racket. Someone. She told me to lock the bedroom door and call security to deal with it, but I wouldn't listen. I used to keep my Breck 17 in the second drawer of the bedside table, so I grabbed that and went downstairs.

"I remember the ground floor still smelling like our lasagna dinner. And then I heard a sneeze from the kitchen. I moved as fast as I could. Some of our floorboards are creaky, so I did my best to avoid them. I think I surprised him pretty good when I burst into the kitchen with my Breck 17 drawn. He had on a ski mask but I could see the fear in his eyes and that gaping mouth. He was going through the refrigerator —"

"Was he fat?" asked Lindsay.

"A little, I reckon," said the Wanderer.

"Then what happened?"

He hesitated.

"Breck?" prodded Rosa.

"Sorry, I was just thinking how to tell it. Well, so I guess he saw me with my gun on him, and he just froze. I asked who he was, what he was doing in my house, but he just gave me this sloppy grin and licked a bit of tomato sauce off of one of his fingers. You know, from the lasagna. Like I said, he was a fat bastard. That's when someone grabbed me from behind."

Lindsay's eyes widened. "Who?"

"Another one — big and thick, like a heavyweight boxer. He squeezed my arms against my body, so that I didn't have a shot at anything but the floor. The fat one closed the refrigerator door and flashed his own Breck 17. He walked up real close and pointed it at my temple." The Wanderer held a finger gun to his head to demonstrate. "That's when I kicked the fat clown hard in the shin. It surprised the boxer, and he loosened his grip on my arm. I was still holding my gun, remember, so I pushed back my arm just enough to fire into his shoe."

"Oh, shit!" exclaimed Charlie, reaching for his toes. "That's fucked-up!"

"Cool!" added Lindsay.

"He screamed real loud and let go of me. I pulled myself free and fired a few more bullets into each burglar's head."

He noticed a skeptical look on Rosa's face. She didn't say anything, but still the Wanderer hesitated to continue.

"Then what happened?" said Lindsay, poking him with a twig. The girl's eyes glowed, completely riveted by the story.

"I ... heard someone behind me."

"*Another* burglar?" asked Lindsay.

The Wanderer blinked. "Right, so I spun around and fired. But it was ... it was too late. I found my wife. She was ... she was already ..."

He looked up at Rosa again and saw the former critical look in her expression had vanished. She smiled sympathetically, her eyes wide with understanding.

"Helen didn't have any last words," he said, his voice a low rumble. "She was alive one moment and gone the next."

"But you got him, right?" demanded Lindsay. "Your wife's killer?"

The Wanderer smiled weakly. "No. Not yet."

"But you're going to find him?"

Rosa interrupted, "Do you want to know why I started *The New West*?"

Errol nodded solemnly, happy she had saved him from having to explain anymore.

"It's for my nephew, Pablo. He's seven years old, and he's my brother's only child. A little more than a year ago, we were shopping for toys at Walmart. Something about the tennis balls caught Pablito's attention — I guess how bright and furry they look — so we bought him one of those cans they come in. We'd just made our purchase and were walking back to the car. It was a beautiful day, but of course my brother, Jack, and I were arguing about something. I don't even remember what. Pablo didn't mind. He was in his own world, tossing one of his new tennis balls up and down …

"I can still remember that heavy grinding — at first I thought it was a jackhammer. It wasn't just the sound. I felt it right in the core of me. But then the screaming … it came from all directions. I fell to the asphalt and crawled behind a green SUV. I thought maybe I'd been shot."

Lindsay looked alarmed. "Were you?"

"No, I looked and looked but didn't find any blood. Even so, I couldn't move. I didn't want to breathe for fear that he would see me ... I didn't even want to look. But then the gunfire subsided, and I did look. I saw a tennis ball rolling across the parking lot, leaving this crimson streak on the pavement. I didn't know what to make of it at first, but then suddenly I just knew. Jack knew it, too. He screamed like I've never heard him scream before. He was kneeling over Pablo ..."

The crackling fire filled the silence. The Wanderer watched a tear slide gently down Rosa's chin. He nearly choked up himself.

"The killer shot twenty-one people that day in Liberty before he was taken down," she said. "All but four of them died. Pablo was one of the survivors, but he hasn't been conscious since the shooting, and the doctors don't know if he'll ever wake up."

"I'm sorry," said the Wanderer. "Has your brother ... ?"

She shook her head. "Jack's ... it's not exactly denial, but we don't talk about it. We don't act like there's anything wrong. But sometimes one of us slips, and I see it in his eyes. My papa had a name for that look — *el aspecto de los muertos* — the look of the dead."

Rosa studied the gunman carefully. "It's in your eyes, too."

*

The Wanderer awoke with a start, and he cursed. He had volunteered to keep watch over the camp and hadn't meant to doze off, but the hike up the mountain had taken more energy from him than he had expected. For better or worse, Helen hadn't let him sleep long. Telling the others about what had happened — even if it wasn't completely accurate — meant he was still thinking about her when he fell asleep, and he ended up dreaming that whole terrible night all over again. This time, when he approached her body, Helen's eyes opened again and she moaned, "Why, Errol? Why?"

He rose to his feet and checked each of the tents. The Kid was snoring, so he didn't bother going inside. Poking his head into Lindsay's tent, he saw the girl sleeping peacefully. For some reason, he felt the most awkward checking on Rosa, but he managed to gather his courage and tipped the flap of her tent, too.

The reporter was gone.

"Shit." He shook his head. What was Rosa thinking, going off on her own? It was exactly this kind of naive behavior that had sent her on the run in the first place.

He'd have to go look for her now, of course. The Wanderer went back to Charlie's tent and whispered sharply through the flap. "Kid!"

Charlie emitted a weird noise that was something between a snort and a gurgle.

"Kid!"

He jolted upright into a sitting position. "Huh? What?"

"That fool reporter's gone off on a walk. I'm going to go after her but I need you to watch the camp while I'm gone," said the Wanderer.

The Kid reached to his side for a half-eaten bowl of leftover macaroni and cheese. "Yeah, okay, man. Go get her."

*

The wind whistled bleakly through cracks in the red walls lining the dirt path. The Wanderer walked alone, winding through the great rocks with only the moon to light his way. From somewhere in the distance, he heard the excited barking of coyotes.

He touched his left arm gently, remembering the way Helen used to pull him in close when they strolled together. The truth was she would've hated it out here. He always liked to joke that his wife had two favorite activities — shopping and brunch — and the big thing they had in common was air conditioning. Sometimes, Helen would join her friends for squash, but she'd confessed to him once that she only did it to keep up appearances.

A boulder big enough to climb materialized from the void, blocking the path several yards ahead. Something on top moved. Thinking it might be the lone wolf, the Wanderer reached for his Lassiter. But as he squinted into the inky darkness, he soon made out the silhouette of a reclining woman. She was resting back on her arms and gazing skyward. He kicked a few pebbles loose from the trail to get her attention. She turned sharply, breathing a sigh of relief when she recognized him.

He called, a bit annoyed, "What are you doing out here, Rosa?"

"Come on up, and I'll show you," she replied.

For whatever reason, he decided to make a show of it. He bolted down the trail and with a single push hoisted himself on top of the rock.

She rewarded the maneuver with slow applause, drawing it out to sarcastic effect. "Well, look at you."

"It's not safe to leave camp. What if the lone wolf comes back?"

"I can take care of myself."

"Did you even bring a gun?"

She shook her head. "All I had was Lindsay's ... and I left it back at the camp."

"Well, that's just plain —"

"Breck, would you shut up a second and listen to me! I said I wanted to show you something." She took a breath and pointed up at the night sky. "I've been taking in the stars. They're beautiful here, aren't they?"

When he looked, he wondered why he had never thought to do so before. "Looks like someone spilled milk all over the sky."

"Jesus," remarked the reporter, laughing. "You should be a poet."

He stroked his stubble. "Do you know any of the constellations?"

"Not a single one, but I don't mind."

He thought about that a while. "I reckon I'm the same."

For a long time, they sat in silence, tracing the heavenly objects from north to south.

"Ursa Major," he said.

She looked up to find the star pattern. "Oh, that's a good one. Where?"

"No, I mean, that's a constellation, ain't it?"

*

Lindsay lay in her sleeping bag with eyes wide open. She couldn't hear the Wanderer's footsteps anymore, and she'd seen the reporter lady leave the campsite nearly an hour ago. The Wanderer had woken up Charlie before he left, but Kid Hunter's time on watch hadn't lasted long. He was already snoring again. She had no idea where the Wanderer and Rosa had gone, but they'd left their stuff, so she figured they'd be back soon enough. She didn't have much time.

Popping on her soft gray hood, the great Lin-Z sprung out of the tent. A loud snort made her giggle, and she couldn't help but peer through the flap of Charlie's polyester shelter. He was on his back with a half-eaten bowl of mac and cheese resting on his belly. The pasta rose and fell with his breathing, which was loud and moist. On closer inspection, there was a sticky stream of drool oozing from his mouth. She grinned from ear to ear at how stupid he looked. She thought about taking a picture, but what with? Jimmy hadn't let her keep her phone. She considered tipping the macaroni into Charlie's mouth, or maybe pouring the sticky stuff all over his shirt.

"Focus, Lin-Z!" she whispered sharply, slapping herself lightly on the cheek. All that mattered was the gun.

She circled the campsite, doing a quick survey of the surrounding area, then popped into Rosa's tent. Falling onto her knees next to the reporter's big hiking backpack, the young thief's cheeks flushed with glee. This was just like Christmas!

*

"So how did you meet her?"

The Wanderer met Rosa's gaze and turned away just as quickly, twisting the gold wedding band on his finger. "Helen? I suppose I always knew her."

It wasn't much of a story. They'd grown up together, the children of magnates — he the heir to the gun monopoly and she the heiress to Big Oil. Their fathers were friends, so they were friends. Because they were the same age, they shared a private teacher. After class, they played. Helen had this one game where she'd chase Errol all around the yard, trying to plant a kiss on his cheek. He was too young to enjoy it at the time.

Gerard had always been jealous. It wasn't that he wanted Helen for himself; he just always wanted what Errol had. The object itself was irrelevant. Things only got worse when they grew into teenagers, and Errol and Helen began to explore beyond a chaste friendship. When the young lovers sought privacy and shut out Gerard, the stepbrother had turned mean.

"So the cowboy and the princess, huh?" Rosa summarized with a knowing grin. "Think I've seen that movie."

"Heh."

She put her hand on his and Errol felt the entire mood shift. She could flick off the sarcasm as quickly as she laid it on.

"I'm sorry about before, making you talk about what happened," she said. "It must have been so hard —"

"It was my gun that shot her." The air went out of him as quickly as the truth. He'd never told anyone that before. He'd felt the truth pushing against the inside of his lips all night, but he'd been too damn scared to let it out. Now he had confessed and to a reporter! What was he thinking? What a damned fool he was!

A hand fell softly on his shoulder. "I think I knew."

He recalled Rosa's skeptical look as he told the yarn about the burglars. "Some of the story was true. There *was* an intruder, but just one, and I shot him dead in the kitchen. There was no struggle, and there wasn't a second man, let alone a third."

Rosa squeezed his hand gently. "You heard a noise, so you turned and fired."

He closed his eyes, but it only made more vivid the image of blood bubbling from his wife's belly. He looked at Rosa instead. "I really did think there was another intruder. The one in the kitchen had a pistol, and so I thought ... then the bad gun fired and I saw Helen ... and she was just dead. I didn't ... there wasn't even a chance of getting her to the hospital."

"Is that why you left?"

He scowled sharply. "There was no place for me in Vegas, I didn't want the gun company, I had to start over."

Somewhere far away, a group of coyotes yapped and howled.

"I get it," Rosa said. "What you're doing, I mean. All the fights — protecting the innocents against the bad guys. You're trying to tip the scales of fate back in your favor. Well, I'd say you've already made yourself into a damn fine folk hero."

"Thanks."

"Hey, can I ask you something else?"

"Go ahead."

"Was the guy really pigging out on lasagna when you found him?"

The Wanderer laughed ruefully. "I might have embellished that part, slightly."

*

Charlie was dreaming about a yellow puppy with big brown eyes. It was his dog, a stray golden retriever he'd found in the streets of Vegas and took into his care. He'd called him Shadow.

He giggled. "Stop it, Shadow!"

The dog was making loud scarfing noises as it chewed some crumbs or something Charlie had left on his belly, and it tickled.

"C'mon, boy, I said stop it!" he exclaimed.

His eyes snapped open, revealing the dream for what it was, but the sound of eating continued and there was something big and warm on his belly. Peering down at his legs, Charlie saw furry ears and an enormous brown head dipping into a bowl. He yelped and the head lifted, revealing glowing eyes and a short black snout. Stuck between the animal's razor-sharp teeth was an orange-cheese sludge.

"Bear!" he yelped. The beast folded back its ears and emitted a low growl.

He couldn't tell how big it was, but it sure as hell was big enough. Pieces of an article about what to do during a bear attack raced through the Kid's mind. He remembered it being recommended to play dead, but also that this same tactic wouldn't put off a predatory black bear from his meal. Instead, with that kind of bear, you were supposed to do the opposite and fight back. Was this bear black or brown? It was too damn dark to tell!

A gunshot startled the bear. It sprang onto its hind legs, lifting the entire tent off the ground. Kid Hunter took the opportunity to roll out from under. He heard shouting and what sounded like banging pots and pans, but there was no time to investigate. Panting, he got up to his feet and made for the trail leading back down the mountain. He thought about climbing a tree, but then remembered that this was again the wrong thing to do for black bears, which were said to be excellent climbers. What a useless article! He kept running.

At the sound of gunfire, the Wanderer leaped off the rock and dogged it back to the campsite. He could hear Rosa's faint footfalls behind him. The lone wolf must have found them. Oh no. Charlie … Lindsay …

When he reached the camp, he couldn't explain what he found. It looked like a tornado had blown through, flipping Kid Hunter's tent on its side in the process. He discovered Lindsay awake and peering curiously down the trail they'd come up earlier. There was a gun in her hand — the gun Rosa had taken from her.

The Wanderer grabbed her by the arm and wrenched the pistol away. "Where is he?" he yelled. "What have you done?"

The girl carried a bemused expression on her face. "Oh, hi!"

"Where's the Kid?"

She giggled. "We had a furry visitor. Charlie screamed like a baby and ran off." She turned back to the path and yelled, "Hey, Charlie, you wuss, the bear's gone!"

He shushed her. "You trying to get the lone wolf's attention?"

She laughed. "You should've heard Charlie squeal. I think that boat has sailed."

The Wanderer followed the girl's long stare down the mountain trail.

"It's gone?" called a voice from the darkness. "Are you sure?"

"I'm sure!"

Rosa appeared. Her eyes latched instantly on Lindsay's gun. "You went into my tent?"

The Wanderer held her back. "Seems Ursa Major leaped down from the sky and gave Kid Hunter quite a scare. The Little

Wanderer here got her gun and scared him off."

"I didn't shoot him," Lindsay said, "but the gunshot got him out of Charlie's tent. Then I made a lot of noise, and the two of them ran off in different directions."

"Two?" gasped Rosa.

"The bear and Kid Hunter."

Something crackled. Something was coming back.

"Lindsay, get away from there!" cried Rosa.

The girl just rolled her eyes. "It's just the wuss returning."

Kid Hunter came out of the woods with a serious expression on his face. "Good evening," he said. "I'll just ... I'll just go fix my tent."

He flipped it and attempted to bend the frame back into shape. Occasionally he whimpered. He entered briefly and emerged holding a partially gnawed bowl that had once contained food. "Where can I ... ?" he started. "Where can I ... dispose of this? Safely?"

They spent the next hour removing any other open and leftover food that could conceivably attract another creature of the night. When they finished, Charlie volunteered to do one last check of the perimeter and stay up until morning to keep watch.

"No sleeping this time," chided the Wanderer.

"You kidding? I'll never sleep again!"

After the Kid left, Rosa addressed Lindsay about the gun. "You went through my bag?"

"But —!"

"I'm not finished, young lady! I will admit that it's a good thing you found the gun. Charlie's a bit of a drama queen, but — well,

217

I don't want to think about what could have happened. So ... we're going to let you keep the gun while we're still out here in the wilderness. For protection. That said, as soon as we get to town, you can bet I will take it away from you again."

"Yes!" burst the girl, unable to hide the excitement. She sheathed the pistol in the belly pocket of her hoodie sweatshirt and skipped giddily into her tent.

"She took that a bit too well," said Rosa to the Wanderer.

"I reckon girls will be girls."

She snorted. "What's that supposed to mean? Do you seriously just say things you think will sound good in that phony western accent?"

He shrugged. "Sorry, but I do believe it's my turn to ask a question."

She laughed real big. For once it felt great hearing it. "So, what do you want to know?"

He took a considered breath through his nose. "Just one thing. What's he like? Pablo."

"Oh, I think you'd like him," she said, a mischievous grin forming on her face. "He likes to dress up like a cowboy, too."

"Heh."

The reporter covered the gotcha smile with her hands and began to cry. Hesitating for only a second, the Wanderer pulled her close, letting her bury her head in the folds of his flannel shirt.

CHAPTER TWENTY

The Hero Never Dies, Right?

As the first pink rays of dawn warmed the summit, Lindsay peeked out of her tent and surveyed the campground. It was Kid Hunter's turn to watch the camp, but nature had called and he'd gone off to pee. Rosa's tent was still, while the Wanderer snoozed by the cold campfire with his Stetson dipped over his eyes.

The young thief who called herself Lin-Z emerged with a full backpack and a semiautomatic pistol. She pulled a gray hood over her bright red hair and made her way down the trail that led back down the hill.

Night had yet to entirely give up its hold. Occasional dots and lines of morning rays high up in the trees looked like strange apparitions jumping from one branch to another. At first, Lin-Z walked like a native, stepping softly around the needles and cones so as not to make a noise. But as she created more distance with the camp, she stepped more boldly, even taking pleasure in the noise she made with each skip and hop.

She was close. She had to be. Jimmy had clearly come through this way. He was as slow as a snail, so he couldn't be far ahead. She'd been tracking him for the whole journey while pretending to lead the way to Founders Spring. Well, it wasn't a total lie. She had brought the Wanderer and the others in the right direction, at least, and they could certainly find the rest of the way on their own. To be honest, she could have ditched them a while ago, but she'd needed to get her gun back. She had thought she'd have to steal it back, but last night's furry visitor had lent a helping paw and a convenient excuse.

Lin-Z grinned at the thought of the bear. She was glad she hadn't had to shoot the cute little guy. Okay, big guy. Whatever.

She did feel a little bit bad about not getting to say good-bye to Kid Hunter. He was actually kind of funny. The memory of him hightailing it out of the campsite made her giggle. He meant well anyway. She guessed they all did. Even the reporter lady who took her gun.

She snapped to attention at the sound of a moan and quick inhalation of breath. Instinctively, she dodged behind a tree. There was someone sleeping nearby. Realizing it could be Jimmy, she left her hiding spot to get a better look. Peering through brambles, Lin-Z found an extinguished campfire of black twigs and ash. There was a man sleeping with a scoped Montag rifle lying to his side. She could only see his back, but he was wearing a dirty white NFL jacket. Jimmy never took off that coat. Smiling mischievously, Lin-Z grabbed a stick from the forest floor and edged forward. With a small giggle, she poked him in the back. Jimmy flopped over to face her — and she saw it wasn't Jimmy at all. She noticed a black hole in the chest of the familiar coat, and a streak of dried blood.

With a short gasp, she pulled her handgun and aimed it at

the man's face. He had pink eyes and angry red facial hair. His breathing sounded difficult, sprinkled with little grunts and smacking lips.

"Lone wolf!" cried Lin-Z dramatically. "Where did you get that jacket?"

He displayed a facial expression several teeth short of a smile, and Lindsay instantly lost her brave front. As she ran, she heard the crack of a rifle. A single bullet whistled into the ground beside her feet, kicking up a burst of dust. Wide-eyed with terror, she struggled to control her breathing, but it just kept going in-out, in-out until she was wheezing from asthma.

"Okay," she gasped, trying to compose herself. "Okay."

The next bullet knocked her to the ground.

*

Errol's eyes snapped open at the echoing report of a distant rifle. When a second one came, he pushed himself to his feet and ran to the cliff to join Kid Hunter in gaping down at the land below.

Rosie burst out of her tent in a state of alarm. "Did you hear that?"

The Wanderer nodded grimly. "Sounded like a Montag. Wake up Lindsay. Could just be a hunter, but we ought to be prepared."

Kid Hunter gritted his teeth. "Think it's the lone wolf? Maybe he found a new target?"

The Wanderer narrowed his eyes. "It seems likely."

"Oh no," cried Rosie. She was standing outside Lindsay's tent. "She's gone."

He felt a chill run through his body. "Did she take anything with her?"

"The gun and her bag. I don't think she was planning to come back." She looked like she was about to explode with worry.

"How did she —?" Errol looked at Kid Hunter. "You were supposed to be watching! How did she get away, dammit?"

Charlie took a step back and stammered, "I ... I don't know. I was watching all night." He looked down at his hands for answers. "It must have been when I left to piss —"

"You left your guard?"

"Boys!" cried Rosa. "We're wasting time! We have to go find her!"

"You said she has a gun," he said to calm himself as much as he meant it to calm her, but the statement only served to make the reporter furious.

"You know what day it is, don't you? It's Saturday. Girls her age like to wake up early to watch cartoons! Not ... not to run off into the forest with a loaded gun!"

"I'm going for her!" shouted Charlie. He was already running down the trail.

*

Lindsay's sweatshirt was sticky with blood. She had managed to flip herself over to her back but she couldn't get up. Maybe if she just lied here long enough for the wound to heal — twenty minutes, an hour max — she'd be up on her feet again, good as new.

Getting shot had felt like an explosion emanating from the core of her body, but after that it didn't hurt much, really. That was good because it gave her time to think about what to do next.

Slowly, she became aware of crunching footsteps growing closer ... closer ...

She closed her eyes and gripped her handgun.

One foot smashed down into the pine needles by her left hip, followed by another on the right. She could smell the lone wolf's breath. It was like cigarettes and piss. With a sudden flick of her wrist, Lindsay flipped up her handgun. Over the blast she screamed, "For Jimmy!"

She expected him to holler but the lone wolf just gurgled. She opened her eyes in time to see his belly flop down on top of her. Lindsay started screaming. She couldn't get him off! She couldn't get up! And now, oh God, the sharp pain in her back! It had been there all along!

Lindsay screamed as loud as she could, praying that someone would hear her, that someone would come.

*

Kid Hunter ran harder when a third gunshot went off in the distance. It sounded different from the previous blast. It sounded like —

"That was Lindsay's gun," yelled the Wanderer from behind.

Charlie smiled. Then maybe she was still alive, still fighting.

Ahead he saw the top of a great boulder they'd had to scramble up earlier. He remembered it was a few feet taller than the Wanderer. He ran right to the edge and jumped straight down to the path below. He landed with a thud and nearly fell forward onto his hands.

"Careful!" Rosa called from behind him.

"I have to find her!" Charlie shouted back.

The Wanderer was right. It was his fault that Lindsay was gone. He'd done a poor job protecting her. He'd been no better an older brother to the girl than Jimmy.

Charlie kept running toward where he thought he'd heard the shot, but he couldn't find her anywhere. How much farther? Had he passed her somehow?

He was getting tired, had to stop to catch his breath. The others were still coming but he'd gotten pretty far ahead of them.

A girl's scream — quiet, distant, but unmistakable — turned his head forty-five degrees to the right.

"This way!" he hollered back to the others.

Lindsay yelled again. It was the sound of pain and desperation. Kid Hunter ran toward it.

*

"Lindsay!" someone called.

Frantic footsteps. The crushing weight of the lone wolf's corpse pulled away. Kid Hunter wearing a shocked look she'd never seen before. "You're going to be okay! I got you, girl."

Lindsay squinted at the bright blue sky beyond the pine needles and then over to Charlie's stubbly chin. She could see worry in the way his mouth fidgeted.

"I'm sorry!" she blurted. "I just … wanted to find Jimmy."

"I get it. He's family."

Rosa materialized through the haze. "Oh, God," murmured the reporter, kneeling over her. "I-I can put on a bandage, but she's going to need medical attention."

The Wanderer appeared over Rosa's shoulder. "Founders Spring isn't far," he said, pointing northwest. "Someone there will be able to help."

Hazily, Lindsay wondered where Charlie had gone. Eventually, she found him by the lone wolf's Montag. The sniper rifle rested innocently on the forest floor. Kid Hunter stared at the side of the barrel and muttered a few numbers.

"What ... what are you doing?" she asked.

"Memorizing the registration," he said. "189, 200, 756. Let's try to remember that."

"189, 200, 756," she repeated. "Why?"

"So we can figure out who this son of a bitch was."

Lindsay began to cry. "I can't ... I can't get up."

Rosa shook her head. "Guys ... I don't think she's going to be able to walk."

"It's okay, I've got her," said Charlie. He came over and lifted her into his arms. "Lucky for you, you're light as a feather."

Rosa shook her head. "What about your arm, Charlie? It hasn't had time to —"

"No, I'll carry her," he stated more affirmatively. "It will be slow, but I can do it."

"Then we'll split up," said the Wanderer. "Rosa and I will run ahead to get help in town, or maybe find someone on the way if we're lucky. When we find help, we'll come back and meet you on the trail halfway."

Before leaving, Errol took Lindsay's hand and spoke softly into her ear. "You're going to be okay. Just hang in there, Little Wanderer."

With Lindsay in his arms, Charlie followed the others back into the trees. Before long, his friends had disappeared into the shadows and he couldn't hear them anymore. There was just the sound of his own heavy footsteps.

"Charlie ..."

Glancing down, he was surprised to see all the fire gone from Lindsay's visage. It was like the girl in his arms had vanished, replaced by some wispy woodland spirit. "Don't talk," he said. "Save your energy."

"Is he ... is he dead?"

Charlie tried to smile. "Yeah, you got him real good."

"Oh."

He could see she was upset and changed tactic. "You did the right thing. He was a bad man."

Why didn't he stop her? Why didn't he get there in time?

"I killed him ..."

He remembered what she'd told him back in the canyon. "You've never killed anyone before. I've been there. We all have. It's hard."

"He killed Jimmy. I think he did anyway. He had his coat. There was a hole ... blood ..."

"You did the right thing."

There were tears forming in her eyes. Taking a life was never easy; you just got better at not thinking about it. Charlie could always do it when he knew next to nothing about the target, but as soon as he learned something — as soon as the target became a real person — he struggled. It was why he hadn't been able to kill the Wanderer, after all.

"Charlie?"

"Yeah?"

"Am I a hero?"

It struck him as a funny question and he laughed. "Well sure, I guess so. You are *Lin-Z*, right?"

Lindsay smiled weakly. "Charlie? The hero never dies, right?"

*

Trees, trees and more trees. To Rosa, the path seemed endless. Would they ever reach the town?

It was too soon to cry. She knew that, but Lindsay looked bad. The shot had missed her heart, but she was bleeding so much. She wasn't sure how long the girl could go on without a doctor. The Wanderer seemed to be thinking the same thing. He pushed one long leg straight out in front of the other as if he was some sort of machine.

In the rush to help Lindsay, they had abandoned all their supplies at the campground. There had been no time to go back and get anything. If they had to spend another night outside ...

Before she could finish the thought, a two-lane road appeared through the trees. Rosa stepped out onto the pavement and looked right toward a rusty old sign declaring the distance to Founders Spring: five miles. They could easily walk that distance and get to town well before sunset. But time was running out to help Lindsay.

The humming of an engine made Rosa yelp with joy. She turned around and watched the car appear mirage-like in the distance. Errol swung his arms wildly, while Rosa yelled as loud as she could yell. But the car didn't slow. She caught a brief glimpse of the driver's fearful eyes as the vehicle sped past them in the direction of salvation. She couldn't blame him. It was plain risky to pick up hitchhikers. If their roles were reversed, she wasn't sure she'd have stopped, either.

"There'll be another," said the Wanderer, but his typical confidence waned.

They walked down the road in the direction of town. The road was dusty and full of potholes, but it still felt easier to walk on compared to the mountain trail. A pang in her throat reminded Rosa she was thirsty. She hadn't thought about this for some time, but her body seemed to have picked up on the fact they were getting close to civilization and had lost its patience.

A low, mechanical growl developed behind them; it sounded angrier than the car. The Wanderer spun around and waved, but Rosa couldn't bear to look. This time, however, nothing passed her, and she heard the questioning voice of the driver. She turned to see Errol at the window of a silver pickup truck, his palms explaining what had happened. The driver popped open the passenger door.

*

"189, 200, 756," recited Kid Hunter, ignoring the numbness spreading through his arms. He carried Lindsay toward a bright spot between the trees, an escape from the shadows. It looked like some kind of clearing. As he moved closer, he saw it was a field of gray tree stumps and tall green grass. A place where lumberjacks once had been but had long since abandoned. As he moved among these round wooden tombstones, Charlie found himself suddenly turned around. Were they still going the right way?

"Okay, Lindsay, I'm … I'm just going to put you down for a minute while I have a look around. And then we'll get going again, all right?"

She didn't breathe a word.

"Oh no." He laid her on a fallen log. Her sweatshirt was soaked in blood and so were his arms. Desperately, he tried to think of what to do. He'd seen people do CPR on TV, but with the damage to her back, it didn't seem like a good idea to press on her chest.

She didn't breathe.

The hum of an engine and crackling of sticks alerted Charlie to a silver pickup coming up the trail. Before the truck could come to a complete stop, the passenger door flew open. Rosa and the Wanderer jumped out and raced toward him.

"They're here, girl! C'mon, you've got to hold on — they're here!"

She didn't.

CHAPTER TWENTY-ONE

A Militia!

Ben Martin squirmed in his seat. Church just didn't feel like church anymore. Yes, it still looked like one with its stained-glass windows and vaulted ceiling. But ever since that damn Wanderer came in here, the place just felt wrong. Like it had lost its … what was the word? Sanctity, maybe.

The preacher was going on about forgiveness, but Martin didn't see the point. That was the problem with Father James. The boy was just too damn naive. It wasn't his age, it was his lack of experience. He didn't know the world like Martin did. He wasn't there that terrible day at the Walmart. So what right did he have to preach forgiveness?

When the call had come in — "Shots fired" — the sheriff had been patrolling along the bleak highway of strip malls just east of the suburbs. He wasn't far from the store. Only a couple intersections, and he'd be there. Jaw clenched, he'd flicked on his siren and hit the gas pedal hard.

The terrified screams had told the sheriff he was in the right place. They'd risen — there'd been a sound like a snare drum — and they'd fallen. Martin had parked at a distance from the gunman, pulling his cruiser sideways so he'd have something to duck behind. He'd readied his Breck 17, and jumped out of the cruiser.

The shooter had worn a black trench coat. Martin remembered the lunatic turning, seeing him, aiming the Yossarian. But the sheriff had his shot lined up already and fired first.

For a moment, the scene had gone silent except for the sound of his own heavy breathing. Then came the moans of the dying. They were strewn across the ground like poisoned cockroaches — some on their backs, some on their bellies. Some he knew, some he didn't. Some were just plain too shot up to be recognized.

A man had cried out in anguish. Jackson Veras, crouched over his boy, willing him to live. Rosie had been there, too, looking too stunned to speak. Martin remembered telling them that ambulances were on their way and that everything would be all right as he made his way to the man who'd caused all this mayhem. The shooter hadn't moved a muscle when Martin turned over his body. The pale face greeting him hadn't belonged to anyone he knew, but he'd looked a lot younger than he had anticipated. Martin had checked him for Red Stripe Gang paraphernalia, didn't find any. He'd also checked his wallet, found a couple of bucks, and a student ID from a college a few towns over. That was it. Not even a death note explaining why. He was no one, and there was no reason. Just a kid, a gun, and seventeen dead.

The same thoughts ran through Martin's mind again and again: This kind of thing wasn't supposed to happen in America. How had this happened in America?

*

Father James frowned as he looked from one empty space to another between the parishioners in the pews. Church attendance had dropped sharply the week after the Wanderer's arrival in Liberty, and today it was even worse. He was giving a sermon on forgiveness, but wondered what good this lesson was with so few to hear it.

He closed his Bible and was about to dismiss what was left of the congregation when Ben Martin jumped out of his seat and strode purposely up the aisle.

"Sheriff?" gasped Father James.

"I just have a few words, if you'll let me."

"I don't think —" the preacher choked, but the fat sheriff had already begun to address the parishioners. Father James caught a sympathetic smile in the audience from Jack Veras.

"As you know," Martin said while adjusting his Army hat, "we had a psycho calling himself the Wanderer in our town a couple weeks ago. He showed up while we were all here and started firing his gun like a maniac. He killed a boy, one of Liberty's good sons —"

The crowd murmured some words of sympathy. Father James couldn't take it anymore and burst forward to take back the pulpit. "Now, Sheriff! Let us not forget what that 'good son' did to one of Liberty's good daughters!"

"Allegedly," spat Martin. He pushed the preacher aside and pulled back the people's attention with a raised finger and an exclamation: "I tried to get the Wanderer! I just couldn't do it alone. I went to our elected representative, Mayor Alex White himself, for assistance bringing that outlaw to justice, but all the government bureaucrat could do was shrug his highfalutin shoulders! But I tell you, men like the Wanderer are going to be the death of American society. It's already going to Hell. Before you know it, we're gonna be living among thieves, murderers, and cannibals!"

The crowd gasped.

"That's right — *cannibals!*"

Jack stood up like he was going to object. Martin must have seen him, too, because the pace of his diatribe quickened.

"As you well know, the Wanderer isn't the first thug with a gun who's shown up here in Liberty. About a year ago, we had a shooting over at the Walmart. You all remember. The gunman shot and killed nearly twenty people. I was just a block away when the shots started, but I couldn't get there in time. I took him down, but there were already so many dead, or dying, when I got there."

Jackson Veras paled and slumped in his pew.

"I'm sorry, Jack, to have brought that up," said Martin. "I know that day was especially hard for you. For your wife, Elaine. For your son, Pablo."

Father James frowned. Poor Jack. The recitation of each name looked like a stab in his heart.

Martin continued. "I don't mean to dwell on these two difficult days for Liberty — the shooting and the arrival of the Wanderer. The reason I'm addressing y'all here today is to tell you that I have a solution. Y'see, we may not have the budget for a police force, but by God we can still protect this town! The Second Amendment reads, and I repeat, 'A well regulated Militia, being necessary to the security of a free State, the right of the people to keep and bear Arms, shall not be infringed.' Hear that? A *militia*! And so, what I'm proposing is a volunteer group of good men to protect this town — Liberty's very own militia.

"Martin's Militia!" a man whooped from the pews. Father James followed the squeaky voice to Dougie, the sheriff's lapdog.

"Martin's Militia," affirmed Ben. "Now I should tell you that I won't take just anyone! I'm looking for policemen, former soldiers, people who remember the law and are willing to fight for it. This here is going to be a new beginning for all of us. It's got to be, and it's goin' to be. Maybe the government doesn't think we're worth the funding, but that doesn't mean we have to stop enforcing the law!"

There was a momentary hush, during which Father James saw a chance to win back the crowd. But a few claps quickly turned into a thundering applause. With a chill, the priest shrank behind his pulpit. Ben Martin looked back at him with a grin stretching ear to ear.

*

Jack added another comic book to Pablo's stack and sat in the chair beside the hospital bed. The comic's cover featured a red-cloaked superhero watching over a dark city. Emblazoned over his head in yellow was the title, *The Adventurer*.

"This issue isn't the best," Jack confessed. "It's kind of half an epilogue to the last one, and half setting up the next thing. Seems like there's some potential, but to be honest it didn't really make for a great read. I'm kind of thinking we should drop this series and just stick to *Spy-Boy*. What do you think?"

The machine keeping Pablo alive beeped in response.

Slapping his knee, Jack began to talk excitedly. "Oh man, Pablito, you'll never believe what that crazy Ben Martin said at church today. He says he's starting a militia, if you can believe that. What is this country coming to? The thing is, the other people at church, they seemed to eat it up. It's completely loco! I guess I've got a bad feeling about it."

Beep. Beep. Beep.

Jack's phone buzzed. He pulled the device out of his pocket and nearly yelped the caller's name. "Rosie?"

"Hey, Jack."

He couldn't believe his ears. He pressed the device harder against the side of his face and cupped his other hand against his ear. "Where are you? Are you all right?"

She began talking a mile a minute. She was with the Wanderer, they'd had to leave Liberty quickly, and she was sorry she hadn't told him where she was going. Gerard Breck and the Red Stripe Gang were after her, so she couldn't come home yet. "Some things have happened," she said. "I promise to tell you all about them when I see you again. But I'm all right. I'm just … planning my next move. I think I'm close to a really good story. For once in my life I feel like I'm going to make a difference, Jack. I'll call you again soon. I love you."

"Wait!" he cried as the phone disconnected. "Damn it, Rosie!"

When his sister had her mind on a job, she didn't give much time for anything else. But at least he knew now that she was safe. When he'd gone to her house Thursday to discuss her termination from *Our Times*, he'd found the door ajar and Ben Martin's car outside. The sheriff had told him that the Wanderer had taken her. The statement hadn't had the effect that Martin intended. Instead, Jack had breathed out a sigh of relief. For some reason, Jack firmly believed the Wanderer was a good man, someone who carried the same set of ethics as the heroes from the comic books. Rosie would be okay. He was sure of it.

The door opened, and Pablo's nurse popped in. The young, raven-haired woman wore powder-blue scrubs with a name tag that said *Mary*. When she saw Jack, a look of panic entered her eyes. "Oh, hello, Mr. Veras. I didn't know you were here —"

"It's fine. If you need to —"

"N-no, I can check on him later! You should definitely take your time."

Jack smiled warmly. "Thank you."

Mary moved to leave, but turned back at the door. "He's a tough kid, you know. We see a lot of cases like this, but Pablo … he's fighting hard."

Jack's eyes followed the nurse out the door. She was kind of cute. Not the way she looked — not that he had any complaints there — just the way she got all a-flutter. It was different from Elaine, who'd been always so sure about everything, even when she was wrong.

Everything about the way his wife had left was horrible. The split had happened right here in the hospital. Angrily whispering over their comatose son, she'd said he should've protected Pablo. Why hadn't he carried a gun? Why hadn't he stopped the shooter? Why had he frozen up and allowed the bullet to strike their son?

They'd been questions he'd often asked himself, but the more he thought about that day, the more the details seemed to blur. He remembered paying for the tennis gear ... popping the airtight can to let Pablo play with one of the balls ... laughing with Rosie as they walked back to the truck ...

And then ...

Oh God. His boy looked so still. The blood ...

He shook himself until the vision passed. He looked at his beautiful son, not dead but sleeping, and hugged him hard. He had to stop thinking about that day. It was too horrible. Too horrible. Pablito would recover. He had to.

Jack just needed to be patient.

CHAPTER TWENTY-TWO

So That's It?

Rosa sipped a cup of bitter coffee while watching cars splash water from small ponds in the road. The trucks created the biggest waves, occasionally drenching unwitting pedestrians on the sidewalk. One teenage boy made a valiant attempt to deflect the spray by bringing down his umbrella like a shield, but Rosa suspected he was unable to protect his socks, based on the awkward way in which he stepped afterward.

She was two coffees in, sitting at a window booth at a dirty old diner about a block away from the Old Inn at Founders Spring. She'd been making calls all morning. She couldn't track down any of Lindsay's family. At least she'd managed to find a small place for the burial and a preacher to officiate the ceremony. He wasn't available until tomorrow because, apparently, he had a dentist appointment, but the funeral home said they would let Lindsay stay another day. Anyway, it was probably for the best, given the weather.

She shook her head. *Let Lindsay stay?* As if the child could go anywhere.

The quiet rhythm of someone typing on a keyboard got her

thinking about *The New West*. She considered the blue pen and three sheets of Old Inn stationary on her table. The paper teased her with its blankness. She wanted — no, needed — to write about Lindsay.

Rosa turned back to the window. She thought she had decided to stop writing *The New West*. So far, all the damn blog had done was get her fired and nearly killed. There were still dangerous people out there who wanted her dead. If she stopped and hid out here in Founders Spring for a little while, maybe they would go away.

No, that wasn't an option. In this day and age, someone could find anybody if they tried hard enough. Kid Hunter could do it in seconds. The grim truth was that Gerard Breck had found her before, and he'd do it again.

Anyway, she'd need a new computer if she was going to post a new article. Or wait! Maybe the hotel had a business center. It would probably cost her a little bit, but she was a fast typist. It could work.

After another thoughtful sip of the rich coffee, she pulled the paper closer and picked up the pen.

Look, if she wanted to write, she might as well write. It's not like she *had* to post it.

As the journalist scrawled on the page, the coffee shop's bland guitar music faded into white noise. At the end of every paragraph, Rosa heard a voice in her head. It was a whisper that grew into a bold declaration: *Americans must read the story of Lindsay, the little girl with the gun.*

Well, Rosa only knew one publication that could tell it properly.

*

Charlie awoke to the stale smell of cold fries. It was raining. Every few moments, a gust of wind sprayed a blast of water against the window. He flicked on the lights, taking a few deep breaths as the hotel room revealed itself. Everything felt sore: his legs, his arms, and especially his bandaged wound. He got out of bed and checked his various devices, which were connected to each of the outlets around the room — the wristband next to the bed, the tablet by the desk, and the smart gun in the bathroom. Stomach rumbling, he turned to the hamburger sitting listlessly on his desk. Last night, he'd ordered two from room service and gobbled the first one down in less than a minute. He'd been unable to bring himself to eat the second, not because he was full, but because the first burger had tasted like a dead rat. Looking at it now, Charlie could see that the eight hours of rest had not served the sandwich well. He dropped it into the wastebasket.

He still felt tired. Even though the bed was comfortable, it'd been a struggle to turn off his mind and go to sleep. When he'd finally entered a dream, he found himself back in the endless forest with Lindsay in his arms and his feet stuck in some kind of swamp. He'd fallen into the muck and had to crawl forward on his knees. He remembered feeling certain there was something following them, something big and vicious …

A wolf.

He got them away from the wolf, but when he looked down, Lindsay was already dead.

Charlie splashed his face with water from the bathroom sink. The last part of the dream was true. Lindsay really was gone.

A loud pounding brought him to the door. It was the Wanderer. "I want to find out who that son of a bitch was."

Kid Hunter ushered him inside the room, hanging a *DO NOT DISTURB* tag on the door before closing it behind them. "I've already done a search on his gun registration. Unfortunately, it's registered to someone else."

"You mean he stole the Montag?"

"Or he faked the registration. Easy enough to do."

The Wanderer shook his head. "So that's it? We've got nothing?"

"I wouldn't say nothing," said Charlie. "We might not have the bastard's ID, but the registration does give me access to the gun's IP address. I can track where the gun's been and what other IP addresses it's communicated with. I might be able to piece together an ID based on that."

"Kid." The Wanderer's voice was grave. "You don't think he posted videos?"

A chill rushed through Charlie's body. The Montag came with a built-in camera that recorded about fifteen seconds before a kill and five seconds after, enough to show the shooter lining up the shot and the prey going down. Breck Ammo called the feature "Moments," and the idea was to share your best shots with your buddies. The gun manufacturer had sponsored a few websites where hunters could post their best shots and egg each other on. The sites only allowed videos of animal kills, but every now and then someone would try to post what was called a "murder take." The moderators tended to weed them out pretty quick. But there was another side to the Internet, a darker side, where one could post such videos for other sickos to consume.

Kid Hunter ran a search, praying to God it would come up empty. As the computer worked, he felt the Wanderer's hand on his shoulder.

"Kid … Charlie … I just want to say I'm sorry for what I said back at the camp. It's not your fault she ran off. You were on guard to keep the lone wolf out, not to keep Lindsay a prisoner. She wanted to get away, and none of us could have prevented that. She just waited for her moment and took it."

"Yeah. I know. Thanks, man. But I still wish I had stopped her."

One result. It was a murder-take website and the lone wolf's gun had sent videos to it. He had an anonymous profile. No name, no personal details, just a statistic:

Frags: 43

Below there was a list of videos. The most recent was dated July 8. Yesterday morning.

"Oh God," groaned Errol.

Calmly, Charlie unfolded a keyboard and began to type. "I'm taking it down," he said through gritted teeth. "I'm taking this whole sick website down."

Kid Hunter's fingers became a blur on the keyboard, moving faster and faster until …

*

… his fist exploded against the fat man's jaw. Kid Hunter ducked to dodge a punch from another drunk as the tub of lard staggered backward and fell into a wooden table. Someone came at the

Wanderer with a chair, but he jumped left and the chair came crashing down on another attacker rushing up from behind. Kid Hunter was still watching the fat man when another guy rammed into him from the side and snatched the Canadian gun from his holster. The drunk pointed the stolen weapon at Charlie's temple.

"Whatcha waiting for?" taunted the Kid. "Squeeze the trigger!"

With a grin, the drunk pulled, but nothing happened.

"And that, my wandering friend," shouted Charlie, swiping the pistol back with one hand and punching hard with the other, "is why I use a smart gun!"

The Wanderer grunted in acknowledgment. He had a chair leg in his hand and was brandishing it like a club. One of the other bar patrons put up his hands defensively.

The boom of a shotgun brought the brawl to a standstill. The bartender had a sawed-off Pilgrim in his pudgy hands. He leveled it first at Kid Hunter and then at the Wanderer. "It's over! Get out of my place and never come back!"

The partners put up their arms and exchanged amused looks. With a nod, they turned around and exited the saloon.

*

Errol felt a little wobbly as they shuffled past a watchful hotel employee waiting behind the reception desk.

"I bid you good night," he said to the clerk in what he thought was a sober-like fashion, but the salutation elicited snickers from his companion as they stepped on the elevator. Charlie's floor came up first, and Errol drawled another good night. The Kid tripped over the space between the elevator and the carpet but managed to catch himself at the last minute. Laughing, he waved at the closing door.

Errol swallowed hard when he reached his destination, and he had to hold the *OPEN DOOR* button to allow himself time to think. After nearly a minute, he hit the button for Rosie's floor. He was at her door before he realized. He raised a fist but didn't knock, and after a few seconds, he let the hand fall languidly to his side.

What was he thinking coming here? What did he think would happen? Mumbling a curse, Errol turned back down the hall. Tapping his eyepiece, he pulled up *The New West*. With some surprise, he discovered a new article. While he and Charlie had been out drinking, Rosie had been writing an obituary. The headline was "Ballad for a Little Wanderer."

He returned to his own room and read the whole thing from start to finish. After a second time through, Errol took off the lens and placed it gently on the bedside table. He closed his eyes, just thinking and breathing. He remembered how small Lindsay had looked in his Stetson, and a sob escaped his lips. He held a clenched fist to his mouth, failing to suppress the tears.

Tomorrow he was supposed to bury a little girl. The Wanderer wasn't sure he could go through with it.

BALLAD FOR A LITTLE WANDERER

By Rosa Veras

I knew a young girl who liked to carry a gun.

Her name was Lindsay. She was living in the woods up north with her older brother. They were poor and had no family, so they stole from hikers, campers, and other wanderers of the forest.

Lindsay died yesterday, shot in the back for sport. She was twelve years old.

I met Lindsay while on the run from the Red Stripe Gang, who, as I wrote in my last article, are working on behalf of Gerard Breck. The Wanderer and Kid Hunter had come to my rescue and offered to escort me to safety. Things got complicated, so we had to make a break for it into the woods.

The truth is that Lindsay tried to rob us. But the Wanderer and Kid Hunter were too smart for that. They tricked her into taking us back to her camp, where we met her brother and learned about their operation.

Then Lindsay's brother tricked us. We woke up and found him gone. He had abandoned his sister.

What else could we do? We invited Lindsay to join us. Anyway, she knew the forest. We quickly learned that she was much more than a thief. She was bold, she was brave, and she was funny. She was our guide, and I think she taught all of us a thing or two about the strength of a child.

But Lindsay left us far too soon. We woke up one morning and found her gone. The Wanderer told me she'd be okay. He said she was a "Little Wanderer."

We learned later that she had run off into the forest to look for her brother. All she found out there was death. A monster in the forest — a lone wolf sniper with a Montag hunting rifle — shot her in the back. Why? Because he found it fun. To him, shooting innocents was a sport.

Our Little Wanderer fought valiantly against this evil man. She shot the lone wolf straight through the gut. She killed him, but he'd already killed her. Kid Hunter found Lindsay before the end. She died in his arms. We tried so hard to save her, but it wasn't enough.

So this is the obituary of a little girl. I wish there was more I could tell you about Lindsay, but the truth is we barely got to know her. In the end, she left this reporter — all of us — with important questions:

How many more children like Lindsay are out there? Why must it be that living in the New West requires our children to carry guns?

CHAPTER TWENTY-THREE

I Ain't Nobody.

Kid Hunter pounded harder on the Wanderer's door. "Man, you in the shower or something? C'mon, the funeral's in less than an hour! We got to go!"

Somehow, calling it just plain "the funeral" was easier than specifying who the ceremony was for. Charlie shuddered. This was going to be a rough day. The aches in his arms still lingered, and he knew he wouldn't be through with the nightmares for a long time to come. He wondered how the others were coping. Probably not much better. Maybe gathering around a little grave would help them get through it. Then again, maybe talking about Lindsay would just make things hurt worse. Either way, he understood it was something they had to do.

"Look, man, I've got a hangover, too, but we're going to get through this together, all right?" Charlie held his ear up against the door to hear if he could detect any movement. With an exasperated groan, he'd stalked down the off-white hall to the elevator. He paused at the open door of another room, where a pretty young maid was busy stuffing linens into a metal cart with the faded green logo of the Old Inn. "Hey, girl, can you help me out a sec?"

She bit her lip, and he noticed her checking out his biceps. With a flash of his old, dependable sex eyes, Charlie explained, "My friend and I partied a bit late last night, and he's not answering the door. The thing is, we've got to get to a funeral. Do you think you could —?"

"Which room?" she replied at once. When they reached the Wanderer's room, though, she looked skeptical. "This one?"

"Yeah, would you mind opening it so I can go in and —?"

"I clean this room before. Customer check out already."

There was a boiling feeling in Charlie's stomach, like he sometimes got when he realized that he'd forgotten something important. "Naw, girl. That can't be right."

She slid her card through the lock and pulled the door open, releasing a soapy cocktail of Tide and Windex scents into the bounty hunter's nostrils. He stared in disbelief and didn't fall out of his daze until the elevator doors opened on the lobby, and Rosa marched up to him with hands firmly dug into her hips. He tried to smile, tried to make light of the situation, but he couldn't find a way. The reporter shook her head in disappointment and marched straight to the front desk. He watched her argue with the receptionist until a woman who looked like a manager appeared to call off the employee. She pulled a piece of paper out of a drawer and handed it across the desk. Rosa took the note, read it quickly, and sighed in disappointment.

Charlie approached the reporter cautiously. "I mean, he can't have gone far, right? He wouldn't miss this. He can't just —"

He cut himself off as Rosa held the note out for him to read: *Sorry, but I just couldn't stay. Rosie, you wrote a mighty fine obituary for Lindsay, and I hope you'll read it today. Kid, you'll be a hero if you keep fighting the good fight. Hope to cross paths again with the both of you someday.*

   Best of luck,
   Errol

*

"Heat's gettin' to you," the Wanderer mumbled to the cluster of flies bouncing around the empty bus depot. Drunk on sunlight, the dark insects careened around the room, crashing occasionally into the tall windows and the flat TV screen showing a daytime soap opera. Two bugs bumped into each other, then parted with an angry snap. One fly looped forward. When it landed on the brim of the Wanderer's Stetson, the bug ceased its nasal whine. He thought about brushing it off, but he liked the quiet.

He studied his ticket. He'd crinkled it without realizing it, and now shoved it deep into a jeans pocket to prevent further damage. The bus was due in twenty minutes, though he had his doubts. There was a reason he preferred the train. Buses might go to more towns, but he couldn't remember the last time he'd seen one show up on time.

The last time Errol had taken a bus was the day he'd left Vegas. It had left an hour later than scheduled, then proceeded to break down on the highway. The bus driver had called for assistance, but a posse of Red Stripers had showed up instead. Errol watched from his window as the gangsters forced the driver out of the bus and held a Breck 17 to his head.

Earlier that morning, Errol had shaved his trademark

250

mustache and beard so that he wouldn't be recognized as the son of Al Breck. He'd also bought a Stetson hat from a tourist trap near the bus station. It had reminded him of the heroes from his favorite Westerns, and as soon as he'd put it on, he'd started talking like them, too. All morning he'd felt as though he was wearing a silly disguise, but when he'd seen the four gangsters outside the window of his bus, something changed inside of him. He'd stood up from his seat not as Errol Breck, but as someone else entirely.

While the other passengers panicked, he strode forcefully down the aisle with the good gun in his left hand. One of the gangsters was on his way in, presumably to collect jewelry and other valuables from the bus. The Lassiter had fired, and the thug fell down the steps onto the pavement. The man who used to be Errol Breck leaped out before the other Red Stripers could react, pulled the trigger three more times, and it was over, just like that.

He remembered the stunned bus driver staring at him a long time, soaking in every detail of his face, but not recognizing Errol Breck.

"Wh-who are you?" the driver had whimpered.

"I ain't nobody," he'd said, hiding his true voice with the rough-riding twang of a Hollywood cowboy. Then the rogue gunman had hopped on one of the gangster's motorbikes and sped away. It had felt good saving these people, but Errol Breck was still far from redemption.

"The next bus will be thirty minutes late," droned a melancholy announcer over the loudspeaker, snapping Errol back to the present.

The Wanderer eyed the station entrance distrustfully. He stood up, sending the fly on his hat screaming away, and strode toward the window to peer out at the parking lot.

Empty. So no one had followed to come stop him. With a deep sigh, he returned to the same wooden bench where he'd sat before. A dusty fan hanging in one corner whined toward him, but he couldn't feel its breath. The Wanderer closed his eyes in hopes of meditating, but at that very moment, tinny pop music burst from a radio in the ticket booth. A bored-looking woman with a lined brown face fiddled with the controls, firing bursts of static and music into the Wanderer's ears until she found a local news station.

"— according to neighborhood watch. That said, they're tellin' us folks shouldn't panic yet. This kind of thing happens from time to time, and it usually ends real peaceful-like. The Red Stripers are probably just passin' through. Only reason we're getting an alert this time is because there's more of them than usual. About six bikes all together, spotted about five minutes ago heading toward the cemetery in Founders Spring —"

The Wanderer jumped to his feet. Stalking toward the exit, he pulled the ticket from his jeans pocket and dropped it on the floor.

*

Rosa averted her eyes as the first clump of soil landed with a *thunk* on Lindsay's coffin. The minister said a few words she didn't hear. She looked over at Charlie, saw the pain in his expression, and began to cry.

Another pile of dirt fell on the coffin.

She wanted to say that she couldn't believe the Wanderer had left, but the truth was it wasn't the first time Errol Breck had skipped a funeral. When things got too personal, the Wanderer ran. She had a bad feeling he might keep on running for the rest of his life.

"Do either of you want to say something?" the minister asked hopefully. He seemed desperate for someone else to speak. The funeral had been put together hastily, and she'd had to do a lot of convincing to get him to do the ceremony on such short notice.

Rosa pulled up the obituary on her phone. She wondered about Errol's note. Obviously he had read what she wrote, been touched by it. So why wasn't he here? Charlie had seemed to take Lindsay's death the hardest. After all, the girl had died in his arms. And yet, the young mercenary was still here to see her off. He hadn't run away.

As Rosa read aloud about Lindsay's bravery, she saw Kid Hunter smiling. But when she reiterated the tragic details of her death, his brave front crumbled, and he covered his eyes. She choked up a few times, too, but managed to keep her eyes fixed on the text and keep going.

She hadn't yet finished when the drum-brush rhythm of falling soil abruptly ended. The grave was not complete, but the digger had stopped filling it. Looking up, she followed his frozen stare to the parking lot. There were five motorcycles — no, six — and the Red Stripers were already headed their way. The gangster in the lead wore two bandannas on his face — a white one over the top of his head and a red one covering his mouth. Together, they formed a disguise that left only his burning eyes exposed. The rest of his body was cloaked in black.

The Kid gritted his teeth. "Who's Mr. Mask?"

Before Rosa could answer, the masked gangster lifted a Breck 17 and fired. She shut her eyes and screamed. Metal clanged against rock. When she peeked out at the scene, the digger's dead body filled the remaining few feet of Lindsay's grave.

With a yelp, the minister bolted in the opposite direction, hopping over a few gravestones and scrambling over a fence to make his escape. Out of the corner of her eye, she saw Charlie fingering his gun, but she reached out and held back his wrist. "There's too many," she told him.

Mr. Mask aimed his gun at Rosa and bellowed, "Thought you could run from us, huh?"

Rosa held up her hands. "I'm unarmed. We'll do whatever you want."

The masked man stared for a long time, before pointing his pistol at Kid Hunter. "Drop the gun ... and the bracelet."

Despite his clear frustration, Charlie did as he was told. The Red Striper gestured to two of his followers, big men with tattooed arms and bushy beards. They stepped forward while the remaining gangsters kept their guns on target. Rosa cried out as her wrists were wrenched hard behind her back and bound with a razor-sharp plastic tie. Kid Hunter yelled. The gangster nearest to him responded by slamming the butt of his gun against the mercenary's head. He slumped to the ground, limp and useless. The Red Striper took Charlie by the wrist and dragged him toward the bikes.

A gangster shoved Rosa from behind. She lurched forward. With her hands tied, she was unable to break her fall and crashed hard onto her face. As the Red Stripers cackled, blackness reached out to suffocate her. The reporter submitted to its cold embrace.

*

The Wanderer could see he was already too late as soon as his taxi reached the graveyard. Even so, he jumped out of the car and sprinted toward the plot of land marked for Lindsay. The gunman gaped with horror at the body resting atop the unfinished grave. The man was lying on his stomach. For a terrifying few seconds, he thought it was Kid Hunter. "Charlie!"

He knelt down and took the dead man's body in his hands, felt the stiffness of the corpse, and rolled it out of the grave. Upon seeing the face, he sighed with relief to see it wasn't his partner. Sweating, he picked up the shovel and filled the tomb the rest of the way with dirt.

"I'm sorry," he said to Lindsay's grave. "I'm so sorry."

The Wanderer didn't need his eyepiece to figure out what had happened. The Red Stripe Gang had found out Rosie was in Founders Spring, and they'd come to take her. Either the Gang had captured Kid Hunter as well, or the Kid had gone after her by himself.

Errol spiked his Stetson into the grass and bellowed at the heavens. He was stupid to leave them, stupid to think Rosie would be safe in this town. What had he been thinking? It was bad enough losing Lindsay. Now he had lost them all.

Well, he'd just have to find them.

As the gunman bent over to pick up his hat, a small black strap sticking out between the leaves of grass caught his attention.

Picking it up, he realized it was the Kid's wristband. A few feet away, he found Charlie's smart gun. So they had captured him, too. He tossed the gun into his knapsack and was about to do the same with the bracelet when he had a sudden inspiration. The Wanderer flicked on the band and waited for it to boot up. "C'mon, Kid," he muttered, "show me you're as smart as you think you are."

The device displayed a map with a blinking dot moving steadily west on a highway. Grinning, the Wanderer traced the road several miles west until his finger landed on a place called Union. Well, that finding sure wiped the smile off his face. He recognized that place — Union was a Red Stripe town. Shoving the wristband into a jeans pocket, he studied the cemetery's parking lot. The taxi was long gone, but there was one car: a mud-smeared pickup truck with spades and other tools for grave digging in the flatbed. The Wanderer turned to the dead man and searched his pockets. Sure enough, he had his keys on him.

Guilt pulled him back once more to Lindsay's gravestone. He removed his Stetson, revealing a matted haystack of hair. "Goodbye, Little Wanderer," he said, voice cracking just slightly at the end. He leaned forward and carefully placed his hat on top of the fresh grave.

The digger's key unlocked the black truck. Easing himself into the driver's seat, Errol took a few minutes to study the vehicle's controls. Tentatively, he slipped the key into the ignition and turned. The engine roared to life. He tried to shift the vehicle out of park, but the black lever wouldn't budge. Shaking his head in frustration, he looked around again at the labyrinth of levers spread around the vehicle. Closing his eyes, he thought back to a driving lesson with his father.

"Turn the key, press down the brake, and *then* shift into reverse," he recited in a low mumble.

He pressed the brake and got the truck out of park. Feeling a little glad that Rosie wasn't here to see this, he brought the truck slowly out of the space, took a deep breath, and shifted into drive.

CHAPTER TWENTY-FOUR

A Citizen's Arrest.

Ben Martin grabbed the burned waffle as it popped out of the toaster. It was too hot to handle, so he dropped it onto the dusty kitchen floor. He froze for a few seconds, considering what to do. The Liberty police station hadn't been cleaned since the mayor took away the department's funding and condemned the place. Oh, well, at least the dirt matched the burn. He picked up the waffle, plopped it on a Styrofoam plate, and brought the breakfast downstairs to the holding cells in the basement.

"Hate to be the one to tell you," Martin told the prisoner, "but we're clean out of butter. Syrup, too. Real shame."

The big man in the cage grunted. There were scars and a sweeping red rash splashed over his face where Rosie had struck him with her coffee pot.

"Figured you might not be in the mood for a cup of joe," laughed Martin as he slipped the plate through the steel bars of the cell.

The prisoner took the breakfast. "You ain't gonna keep me in here."

"Why's that?"

"You ain't got the authority. There ain't no law."

Martin preened. "In Liberty, I am the law."

"They'll come for me!"

"Who will? Oh, you mean your buddies in the Red Stripe Gang? You think they'll come for you, huh?" Ben Martin laughed a deep belly laugh. "You think they'll come for you after you failed a job catching a *girl*?"

The gangster crunched slowly on his waffle.

Ben Martin leaned forward. "Now you going to tell me yet why you were after Rosa Veras, or should I leave you down here another week?"

"Fuck you."

"Another few weeks, then?"

"Fuck you."

The sheriff spat on the ground. All this time, and he still hadn't gotten anything out of the prisoner. Maybe he'd lost his touch. Well, at least the piece of human waste was talking today. Ben Martin worried about Rosie. She was with that Wanderer, which meant she was still in danger. He hoped to God she'd return safely. He'd called a few other towns where he had friends and he thought the Wanderer might take her, but no one had seen either of them. He hoped someone would call back today. In the meantime, there were still answers to get from the prisoner.

"Why don't we start with something easy. Tell me about the Wanderer. What's your connection to him?"

The gangster looked confused. "The who?"

"The Wanderer. He's the one who shot your friend. And he shot a few of your other buddies in Freetown."

The gangster shrugged. "I don't know anything about that."

Martin grumbled. "How's that waffle anyway? Gritty at all?"

The prisoner didn't respond.

Ben Martin stood up. "Okay. Well, chew slowly. It's going to have to last you the rest of the day. I'll be back tomorrow morning."

He took the stairs back up to the ground floor, cursing as soon he was out of earshot. The gangster wasn't going to be cooperative, he could tell. But what the hell was he going to do about it? He'd have to let the thug go eventually, but he couldn't just free the bastard without getting something out of him, or at least punishing him for what he'd done to Rosie.

Ben's phone beeped. He had a message.

Armed outsider sighted on Main St. Engage?

The message came from Larry Wilkins, a friend of Joe Lin, and one of the new recruits to Martin's Militia. The sheriff thought about calling for more details but decided against it. He reckoned it would be a sign of good faith to trust his men's instinct. Also, the smell of that toaster waffle had made him kinda hungry.

Martin tapped out a brief reply in the affirmative.

*

Jack freed his hair from its rubber band dictatorship and leaned back against a tree in the park. It was a beautiful day in Liberty. Warm but not hot, partly cloudy skies. The green wasn't big — it could only really be considered a park in the urban sense — but it was still nice. There was a fountain, a bunch of trees and a well-watered lawn where kids like to run around and play tag.

It was great for people watching, actually. Jack observed a harried mother chasing an enthusiastic toddler around the playground. Then he watched a teenage couple lingering in the shade of a young tree, leaning in every few seconds for a chaste kiss, then checking around to see if anyone was looking. The boy pushed away the girl upon seeing that yes, another teenage boy in a baseball hat had seen them. He was sitting at one of the other park benches and laughing.

Chuckling to himself, Jack took off his glasses and wiped the round lenses with a white cleaning cloth from his pocket.

"Hey, man, get off me!"

Popping his frames back on, Jack saw that the yelling was coming from the kid in the hat. There were two men standing over him. One of them Jack recognized as Larry Wilkins, who'd been a football jock in his high school class. The other was Ryder Klein, a professional drunk. They both used to be policemen.

Klein wrapped one of his mitts around the arm of the squirming teen. Jack jumped to his feet and strode forcefully to the scene.

"What's going on here?" the attorney asked forcefully.

Klein regarded Jack like sour milk. "Get out of here. 'Tain't your concern."

"You gotta help me, mister!" yelled the teen. "These guys are trying to kidnap me!"

The defense attorney tried playing the high school connection. "Larry, c'mon. You know me. What's up?"

"Hey, Jack. S'all good, man! We're just making a citizen's arrest. You know?"

Jack laughed in disbelief. "A what?"

Klein looked annoyed. "You heard. A citizen's arrest."

"For what offense?"

"Now, now, easy there, Jack. We're just taking him in for questioning. We don't recognize this one from Liberty, so we're just gonna make sure he's all right, you know?"

"I *am* from Liberty!" the kid squealed. "And I got rights!"

"You do indeed," said Jack, placing a hand on the kid's shoulder. "What's your name, son?"

The boy looked at him skeptically, but relaxed in Jack's steady gaze. "It's Bert."

Jack turned to the other men. "I suggest the two of you leave Bert alone."

"We're taking him with us," insisted Wilkins. "We're under orders."

"Orders from who?"

"Sheriff Martin."

Jack laughed. "So he's got his militia going, has he?"

Wilkins grinned. "Martin's Militia! You should join up, Jack. We could use a man who understands the law."

Klein pulled a Breck 17, aiming it at the kid's temple. Bert whimpered, "Oh God, what are you doing, man?"

Responding to Wilkins, Jack said, "Yeah, it's pretty clear you could use someone like that."

Hoping to surprise Klein, Jack snapped a hand out to take the gun. But the ex-policeman whisked it away just in time. The miss set Jack off-balance, and he couldn't defend himself when Wilkins gave a hard shove against his stomach. The hit knocked the breath out of Jack, laying him flat on his back in the grass. Through strained breaths, he watched the two militia men take the kid by the arms and carry him off to a Jeep.

"Stop!" he yelled, scrambling to his feet.

It was too late. Wilkins revved the engine, and the Jeep roared down Main Street.

Panting, Jack dusted off the back of his jeans and sat down on the recently vacated bench. He shook his head with disappointment. Ben Martin had actually managed to collect some followers for his militia. They'd arrested a boy for looking suspicious. What would they do to him? And who would they go after next? He couldn't go after them alone. He'd need a strong ally to help rally the rest of the town to his side.

Jack took out his cellphone and dialed Father James.

*

When the tap at the door evolved into pounding, Ben Martin put down his Bud and yelled, "Dougie! Would ya get that, please?"

It seemed to take a lot of effort for the deputy to rise up off his ass. Dougie took a long swig of beer before stumbling out of the sheriff's office. Not long after, Ben heard a shout of protest and the slap of dress shoes against tile.

"Ben Martin!" cried a familiarly annoying voice.

"Why don't you come into my office?" the sheriff called out the door. Then in came Jackson Veras and Father James. The former looked angry while the latter just looked plain flustered.

"Next time, call first," said Martin.

"The boy, Bert," stated Jackson, slamming his palms against

the desk. "What have you done with him?"

Martin put his legs up on his desk and leaned back in the chair with the Bud. "Cool it, Jack. I ain't done nothin' wrong."

Dougie appeared in the doorway, panting like a scrawny greyhound after the race. "Sorry, Ben, they barged right in."

"It's okay. These boys just came to talk." The sheriff looked at the priest. "Ain't that right, Father?"

"That's right," Father James replied. "Sheriff, this militia you're trying to form is getting out of hand."

Martin slapped the Bud on the table and some of the beer fizzed out the top. "My militia is the only thing keeping Liberty safe! I explained this last week in your church, if you recall, and you had no objections then."

Jackson laughed curtly. "How does arresting innocent kids in the park keep anyone safe?"

"My men just brought in young Bert for questioning. You never can be too careful, you know. You are correct that he's innocent. We did a record check and discovered he belonged to a family in the suburbs. We let him go about an hour ago. He's probably home by now. You can check if you want."

Jackson took a step back, looking a bit unsure of himself. "You let him go?"

Martin brought his legs down from the desk and held out his hands in an exaggerated gesture, as if he was addressing an idiot. "Well, it wouldn't do any good keeping him here, would it? Seemed like the responsible thing to do."

Regaining his composure, Jackson growled, "The responsible thing would have been not to arrest him in the first place."

Father James nodded. "Yes, Sheriff. You must learn to trust in your fellow man."

That steamed Martin real good. "On the contrary, Father, I can list several passages in the Bible that says I shouldn't. Psalm 118, verse 8. 'It is better to trust in the Lord than to put confidence in man.'"

The young priest turned red. "I ... I ..."

"Jeremiah 17, verses 5 through 6. 'Cursed be the man that trusteth in man, and maketh flesh his arm, and whose heart departeth from the Lord. For he shall be like the heath in the desert, and shall not see when good cometh; but shall inhabit the parched places in the wilderness, in a salt land and not inhabited.'"

Ben Martin shook his head, completely disgusted with the minister. They should never have given the church to Father James. He was completely incompetent. "Shall I go on, *Father*? No? Then get the *fuck* out of my office and don't come back." He slapped his hand down on the desk. "Next time I won't be so *nice*."

He nodded at Dougie, and the deputy brought a Breck 17 to the back of Jackson's skull.

The defense attorney turned slowly and held up his hands. "What do you think you're doing, Ben?"

"It's not worth it, Jack," said Father James. "C'mon, we better go."

The triumphant sheriff returned to his beer.

CHAPTER TWENTY-FIVE

We Need to Talk.

No one cared for the interstate, and the highway didn't care much for riders. The Wanderer could barely make out the painted traffic lines, which had faded almost completely into the dusty black pavement. He thanked God the stolen pickup truck had semi-decent suspension, a critical feature for absorbing the bumps from cracks, potholes, and debris. He was also lucky that the road was straight, at least for the most part, and there wasn't much traffic. He still felt the tension in his shoulders, but it seemed to have eased slightly. What stress remained had more to do with where he was going than his mode of transportation.

The greenery outside the truck vanished, replaced suddenly by dead crimson. The familiar sight of open desert brought a slight smile to the Wanderer's face, but the good feeling dissipated when he heard the grunt of a mechanical wild boar. In the rearview mirror, he counted two motorcycles behind him — not the Red Stripers he was looking for, but Red Stripers all the same. The Wanderer glanced at the Lassiter on the passenger seat, but resisted the urge to grab the ebony-handled revolver. Chances were, the gangsters didn't know who he was or where he was going. It probably wouldn't do Rosie or the Kid much good to make trouble with the Gang before he even reached Union.

As the first bike screamed by, a pale leg caught the Wanderer's eyes. He followed the limb all the way up to a tight pair of black shorts. The woman was riding on the back of the hog with her skinny arms squeezed tight around the fat, leathery waist of a man in a beater. Neither of them wore helmets, but the female rider had a Pilgrim strapped to her bare back. Errol could just make out the red outline of a sunburn emanating from around the shotgun before the bike shot off over the horizon. Well, he guessed that was one way to get those red stripes.

A second motorcycle roared up, and, for a long while, the Red Striper rode closely on the Wanderer's tail. At last, the bike broke to the left and pulled alongside the driver-side window. The gangster stared daggers, and Errol wanted badly to swerve left and blast the asshole into the desert. Something splashed against the glass — a glob of spit, tinged brown with chewing tobacco. The Wanderer ignored the high-pitched laughter of the gangster and just waited patiently until the biker zoomed off after his buddies.

It might've been a different story if the window was open and the spit had come through. He reckoned that gangster owed his life to air conditioning.

*

A dusty blue sign welcomed the Wanderer to Union. In fact, someone had spray-painted a crude red-and-white striped flag over *Welcome*, but the gunman could still make out the word easily enough. He was still on a desolate part of Central Avenue, but on the horizon, he could see a cluster of shops comprising downtown. It didn't look like a far walk, so rather than continuing on wheels, he pulled off the road and into the parking lot of a diner.

It was weirdly quiet when he got out of the truck. Union was like a ghost town. He checked for the diner's hours and found a broken window instead. Through shattered glass, he saw a dark, dusty room with silverware and soda-fountain cups scattered across the floor. A spray of bullet holes on the wall behind the counter implied the story of the restaurant's closing. Something crashed, jerking the Wanderer's head toward the kitchen. All he caught was a streak of gray, but he reckoned a family of raccoons had made a den of the place.

He went back to the truck and took a red handkerchief from his bag, wrapping the bandanna around his head in the fashion of the Red Stripe Gang. Next, he strapped on his gun belt, checking that his Lassiter was loaded. Leaving his bag in the truck, the Wanderer crossed to the left side of the road and stalked into town. There wasn't a sidewalk, but that was okay since there wasn't any traffic. He passed several lifeless homes, though he thought he saw a curtain move in one, but he wasn't quick enough to confirm. Farther down the street, he found a pile of burned rubble where he presumed a house had stood. The houses to the left and right looked fine — maybe a little smoky on the sides facing the scrap heap — but he could see that the fire had been contained to the one property. Controlled and likely deliberate. He wondered what the Gang did to the people inside. And what would they do to his friends? Cursing himself, he pressed on, walking harder than before.

A loud clamor and the sour smell of beer lured him to a saloon called Smoky Joe's. The Wanderer adjusted his red bandana before pushing through the swinging doors. There were a ton of drinkers inside, considering it wasn't even six o'clock yet. He saw a lot of Breck 17 pistols, mostly in belt holsters, though one man had set his gun to rest right next to his beer.

A poker game in one corner of the room caught his attention because of how unnaturally quiet the players were. A Red Striper with an eye patch held most of the chips, and the rest of the party looked as solemn as if they were at an execution.

"New in town?" a gruff voice called from the bar. Brown sun spots stained the gangster's pink scalp, but he made up for the baldness with a bushy gray beard.

The Wanderer stepped over to reply. "Yeah, I came down from the north."

"Where about?"

After a small pause, he lied, "Montana."

The old gangster hooted. "Montana! Then you came a long way. The name's Erskine. Let me get you something to drink." He plucked a pint glass from a wooden rack hanging overhead, and leaned over the bar to fill it with beer. After a few seconds of overflow, he pushed the foaming lager into Errol's hand. The glass was warm and wet, and the Wanderer eyed the drink suspiciously.

"Cheers," said Erskine as they clinked glasses. "What'd you say your name was?"

"I didn't."

Erskine howled with laughter. "Then Montana it is."

The Wanderer took one sip of the beer and nearly choked on

it. Noticing his discomfort, Erskine howled with laughter. "The refrigeration's not working! You'll get used to it."

"Heh."

"So, you come down to get yourself a weapon, Montana?"

"How do you mean?"

Erskine's eyes widened in disbelief. "Don't you know? Got a big truck coming in tomorrow from Breck Ammo. I figured that's why you were here."

So Gerard had made another deal with the Red Stripe Gang. Concealing his outrage as best he could, the Wanderer replied, "Nah, just passing through."

"Well, a lot of our friends showed up in Union today, and there should be plenty more *mañana*. Stick around, and I reckon you'll score yourself a Yossarian, though you better watch your back if there ain't enough for everyone."

Errol rested the beer on the bar and wiped his mouth. "Is that so? We must be paying Breck a fortune."

The old gangster laughed. "Doubt it. Gerard Breck wants to keep us happy."

So that was it. Gerard's relationship with the Gang wasn't a one-off. His stupid brother was actually trading weapons to the Gang for their cooperation. Didn't he see? If the Red Stripers got enough guns, soon they'd be more than a gang — they'd be an army.

The Wanderer forced more of the beer down his throat. He was too thirsty not to try.

"Hey, *Montana*," said a man behind him, with audible amusement.

The Wanderer nearly blew his own cover when he saw who it was.

"Come on outside a minute?" said Kid Hunter with a wink. "We need to talk."

*

The Wanderer chuckled at a poster of a Muppet urging quiet.

"The Gang ain't much for reading," he observed. Besides the Kid and himself, there wasn't a soul in the entire two-floor library. There probably hadn't been since the day the Red Stripe Gang made Union its own.

"Lucky for us," replied Charlie, sitting at a round wooden table meant for study groups.

The Wanderer reached into his pocket for the Kid's wristband and dropped it under his partner's nose. Charlie's eyes lit up in ecstasy. He snatched up the device from the desk as if it were a hot dinner.

"I reckon you're happier to see that thing than you are to see me," said Errol, easing into a wooden chair across from him.

The Kid kept his eyes on the device and shrugged.

Errol exhaled sadly. "Is Rosie okay? Did she make it out, too?"

"Naw, man. They got her in the bank vault downtown."

The Wanderer asked the Kid to start from the beginning. Charlie described how a bunch of gangsters had showed up at the Founders Spring cemetery and knocked them out. When he awoke, he and Rosa were roped to motorcycles headed for Union. After arriving in town, the Gang locked them up in the vault at Second Union Bank.

"They said they was gonna keep us overnight," said Charlie. "From what I could make out, Gerard Breck's coming tomorrow—"

"For the gun trade."

"Oh, so you heard about that, too. Yeah, for the gun trade … and to collect Rosa."

"Have they hurt her?" asked Errol, gritting his teeth. The thought of Rosie abused was too much to bear, and all because of his stupidity.

"Not more than your average prisoner, I guess. She seemed all right before I left, but it's been a few hours. My bet is that they're saving her for the boss man."

"So how'd *you* get loose?"

Kid Hunter took a contemplative breath. "Well, we were in there together an hour, maybe two, and then the door opened and Mr. Mask came in to pull me out."

"Mr. Mask?" repeated the Wanderer, narrowing his eyes.

"That's just what I call him. I don't know his real name. He wears a red bandanna over his mouth and a white one over the top of his head. Oh, and black cotton from the neck down. Looks like some kind of fucked-up ninja."

The description was familiar. Charlie read the recognition on his face and asked, "You ever seen him before?"

The Wanderer grinned. "I reckon I'm the reason he looks that way. That is … me, a match, and a can of gasoline."

The Kid exclaimed, "That's fucked-up! Bet he deserved it, though."

The Wanderer raised his eyebrows. "That dog liked to start fires. I showed him reason not to. Didn't mean for him to live, but he was made of stronger stuff than I expected. He wrapped himself up like a regular mummy and slipped away. I sure as hell didn't think we'd cross paths again."

The Kid beamed.

"What?" the Wanderer asked.

"It's just … God damn, Wanderer, you are one sick motherfucker!"

Errol wasn't quite sure how to take that, but decided the Kid sounded more impressed than disgusted. "Enough about that. You still haven't told me *why* Mr. Mask let you go."

"Right." said Charlie with a sigh. "Well, the truth is, my old boss, El Tiburón, paid for my release. I guess Breck only wants Rosa anyway. But now El Tiburón wants me to come see him in Vegas. He thinks I owe him a favor, so now I'm in even deeper shit there. But, man, I didn't want to leave Rosa behind! So I figured I'd linger around here and try to come up with a plan to save her like the regular Prince Charming that I am. Then I ran into you!"

Charlie's excited expression took a sudden turn to the gloomy. "Where've you been, man? Thought you'd abandoned us."

Errol thought about all the things he wanted to tell Charlie — all the apologies — but in the end, all he could say was, "I know." He stood up and paced toward the window. Looking out at the ghost town, he added, "But I'm back now. And I reckon I've got a plan."

*

Kid Hunter watched the entrance to Smoky Joe's from a small alley across the street. He had to say Central Avenue looked off the chain tonight. It was all dressed up in Christmas lights, leftovers from last December before the Gang arrived. Maybe the red-and-white motif of the holiday suited them, or maybe they were just plain lazy, but the Red Stripers had never bothered to take down the solar-powered decorations from the trees.

It was late, and drunk gangsters had begun to trickle out of the bar to their motorcycles. Some were so wasted that they abandoned their motorcycles altogether, opting instead to walk back to their stolen homes. The ones who were even more sloshed got on their bikes anyway and sped away like maniacs.

The door to the saloon swung open, dropping Mr. Mask out onto the curb. A big man with an eye patch followed him out, shouting for attention. Charlie recognized him as the guy he'd seen taking everybody's money at poker. Owing to the Gang's lack of creativity, he was called Patch. Well, Patch had invited Charlie to join the game, but the Kid had been too smart for that.

Mr. Mask turned to face Patch. There was a slight lean in his stance and one of his hands hung low toward the holster on his waist.

"I ain't no cheater!" cried Patch. "I won that hand fair and square, and now you better pay up!"

Mr. Mask pulled a Breck 17 and aimed it at the other man, who withered like a poisoned weed and stuck up his arms to show he didn't want a duel. Mr. Mask didn't seem to want one, either, and shot him straight through the eye patch. The poker player collapsed onto the dirt like a rag doll.

"Anyone else want trouble?" Mr. Mask yelled at the door to Smoky Joe's.

No one did, so Mr. Mask put the gun away and stumbled down Central Avenue toward the center of town. That was Kid Hunter's cue.

*

The Christmas lights blinked. Mr. Mask stopped short and looked around curiously. Shaking his head, he continued on, but then the lights went out completely.

" ... the hell?" he asked in a low growl.

The lights snapped back on, but only the ones in front of him. He followed them toward downtown. The Christmas decorations cut power again at the next intersection, but to the right, on the perpendicular street, the lights in several abandoned shops came alive. He grabbed hold of his Breck 17 and shouted, "Who's there?"

No one answered, so he took the turn and tiptoed down the street, holding his gun with two hands in front of him. All the shop lights then went out, but somewhere a car radio began to play. Now he knew someone was messing with him. He took off at a trot with his pistol outstretched. "I'm gonna kill whoever the fuck is there if you don't show yourself!"

Mr. Mask stopped at a parked car buzzing from all the bass thumping out of it. When he peered inside, the automatic window rolled down and he nearly fell backward holding his ears. He ended up on the porch of a bookstore.

The car radio stopped, and a gruff voice from inside the shop greeted, "Good to see you again. Why don't you come on in? For old time's sake."

"Wanderer!" exclaimed the gangster. His skin tingled with the memory of fire and burning. Trembling slightly, Mr. Mask drew his Breck 17 and entered.

CHAPTER TWENTY-SIX

Rise and Shine.

The trucker lifted a mega-size coffee from an extra-large cup holder and brought it to his lips. The name *Rusty* was scrawled in black Sharpie on the Styrofoam side. The drink was only lukewarm, and he cursed himself for not ordering that self-heating mug from SkyMall. Maybe he could finally afford one after this job for Breck Ammo. He was nearly to Union — maybe another quarter of an hour to go, but he'd been driving since it was dark. He could hear the assault rifles in the big-box trailer rattling at every bump of the road.

Rusty had never done a job like this when Al Breck was still alive. He'd been driving thirty years for Breck Ammo, but this time his supervisor had asked him to bring a sixteen-wheeler full of Yossarian automatics into a Red Stripe town. Normally Rusty didn't ask questions, but he had to say, this job didn't make a lick of sense. Must be that stupid new CEO, Gerard Breck. They said he was Al's son, but guys who'd been around as long as Rusty knew that Gerard was a stepson and carried none of the old man's genes or his business smarts neither.

A loud thumping sound made him look up. In the sky, a

black helicopter flew at full tilt past the truck and out toward the horizon. Speak of the devil — that was the executive chopper. But what the hell was Gerard Breck doing out this far? Shit, that moron could have brought the truck himself!

When he looked back down, Rusty saw something in the road. No ... some damn *fool*, standing right smack in the middle of the highway! He pulled his horn, but the figure in the street just aped him with that infernal gesture the kids in the school buses always made. He was dressed in a burgundy track jacket, and there was some kind of bracelet gleaming on his wrist. Rusty honked again but the other guy's big grin remained. The truck slowed. Personally, Rusty would've liked to run the guy down, but his truck mostly drove itself and he couldn't override its safety behaviors. As much as he might've liked to.

"Obstruction in the road," reported the truck's rather sultry dashboard voice. Rusty liked the way she sounded, and the way she only gave pertinent information. Unlike his wife.

"Yeah, yeah, I see him, baby." With a deep groan, Rusty leaned out the window to give the asshole a good ripping. "Get out of the road, you damn fool!"

"Hey, now!" the weirdo called back. "The name's Kid Hunter! Can a brother get a ride?"

"What? No, a brother can't get no damn ride! What do you take me for, some kind of —!"

The fool pulled out a pistol. Rusty reached for his Breck 17 and opened the door, but the young fella moved quick and had his gun aimed at Rusty's chest before he could even lift his butt from the seat. The truck driver felt something hit his chest. It weren't no bullet, but it stung all the same. His eyes drooped and he felt himself drifting. On second thought, it felt kind of nice.

*

A metal groan drew Rosa's attention to the door of the vault, where a crescent of light expanded into a great round sun. For a few seconds, she couldn't see a thing through the glare, but as her eyes adjusted, she saw the shadowy outline of a tall man, and then the sharp face of Gerard Breck. He was wearing a tan summer suit with an obnoxious red bow tie. The shape of his waxed mustache matched the upward curve of his grin.

"Rise and shine," sneered the CEO of Breck Ammunition.

She nearly lunged, but stopped herself when three figures appeared behind him. She recognized his assistant, Elza, and the Red Striper whom Charlie had nicknamed Mr. Mask. The third was a man she hadn't met before, but he wore shades and an earpiece like a bodyguard.

Elza, who wore a tight blue dress and matching pumps, seemed pleased to see her. Rosa gave a vicious look in return.

Rosa checked her plastic watch, the only device she'd been allowed to keep inside the vault. Breck had arrived at 8:00 a.m. on the dot. Her stomach rumbled on cue with the realization that it was morning. She hadn't had a thing to eat since before the funeral. She didn't recall sleeping, either, though the time showed she must have, at least a little. She had aches in her neck and all the way down her side.

Gerard noticed her checking the time and said, "That's right, it's breakfast time." In a low growl to his flunkies, he added, "Bring her to the table."

The bodyguard took her by the arm and pulled her hard out of the vault.

Rosa couldn't help but ask Elza, "So this is your definition of public relations?"

The assistant laughed. "I would say we are well past good PR practices."

Mr. Mask held a Lassiter menacingly across his chest, daring Rosa to even try to escape, but she felt too tired to resist. Instead, heeding her reporter instincts, she made a move as though she was scratching an itch on her wrist while secretly clicking the *RECORD* button on her "smart" watch. The way she figured it, if she got free, she could use the tape for an article in *The New West*. And if they killed her, at least someone might find it and tell her story.

They brought Rosa into an office barely bigger than a cubicle and directed her into a metal chair with stained fabric cushions. The brother of Errol Breck sat across from her in a black-webbed throne behind a nameplate for Pete Johnson, Branch Manager. In a wide arcing sweep of the hand, Gerard knocked the triangular object off the table, along with a stapler and a stack of paper. A photo of a smiling woman and two kids making faces was next to go.

Dryly, he said, "I've never been much for family."

Rosa pushed back hard in her seat as he procured a jagged Army knife from the inside of his jacket. Elza held the reporter's chair in place.

"Every play five-finger fillet?" asked Gerard, splaying the fingers of his other hand on the table. He brought the blade of the knife slowly down into the table between his thumb and index finger, up again, and down between the index and middle fingers. Rosa stared, transfixed, as he continued the game methodically all the way to the end of his hand and then back to where he started. Gerard smiled. "Not bad, eh?"

He did it faster, still managing to miss his digits with the knife. When he finished the cycle, she asked, "What do you want?"

He stared. "You know what I want. I want you to stop writing malicious things about me and Breck Ammunition."

"Okay," she replied flatly. "I'll stop."

Laughing, Gerard played another round of five fingers, completing it even faster than before. This time she noticed a scar near the bend of his middle finger. "You know this game isn't as easy as it looks. And as my assistant indicated earlier, I'm afraid we're past the point of negotiation."

"Wh-what does that mean?"

"It m-m-m-means," he said, making fun of her stammer, "*give me your hand.*"

When she didn't make a move, the bodyguard grabbed her wrist and pushed her palm down on the table. Gerard lifted the blade over the reporter's hand.

"Wait, please ..." managed Rosa, trying desperately to push her fingers as far apart as they would go—and convince herself that would make any difference.

"Hey, I got a joke!" announced Gerard. "What do you call a writer who can't tell the truth?"

He brought the knife down between Rosa's thumb and index finger, and then up and down slowly between the rest of her fingers.

When she didn't reply, Elza asked, "What?"

"A *journalist*," he answered, completing the knife-play chain in reverse. When only Elza smirked, Gerard said, "Well, maybe that one needs a little work. Whatever. So anyway, how about a little faster this time?"

"That's enough!" shouted Mr. Mask, suddenly aiming his silver six-shooter at Gerard's head. "Stop or I'll shoot!"

Peripherally, Rosa saw the bodyguard reaching for his gun. Mr. Mask swiveled slightly. She shut her eyes as the Lassiter went off. When she looked up, Mr. Mask had his gun trained on Gerard again.

All of Gerard froze except for his eyes, which slid up sideways to get a look at the Lassiter in the Red Striper's left hand. "Errol?" he groaned.

Rosa gaped at Mr. Mask, seeing for the first time the sorrowful eyes of the Wanderer. Elza ran away from him, passing Rosa, but the reporter stretched out her leg and tripped the PR flack. Elza cried out again as her head hit the triangular nameplate for Pete Johnson. The blow immediately knocked her unconscious.

The Wanderer pounded a fist on the table and leaned into his brother with the Lassiter. "Damn it, Gerard, what is all this? Kidnapping journalists? Gun trades with the Red Stripe Gang? Are you *trying* to run the company into the ground, or are you *really* this incompetent?"

The CEO stood his ground. "Is there a third option?"

"Gerard!"

"I'll have you know the Gang are paying customers, and they're helping to keep this company afloat —"

"What, by wiping out the competition? You asked them to knock off a gun maker in Freetown!"

"Gun maker? Errol, I would think you'd know better than to call a 3-D printing garage operation like that gun making."

"You hired gangsters to hang a man!"

"That's just business," said Gerard, waving it off like it was nothing.

"Business? Dad *never* did business that way."

Gerard licked his mustache. "Dad's dead."

The Wanderer gave a look of exasperation. "Remember that man you nearly hanged? Did you know he had a daughter?"

Gerard shrugged his shoulders. "From what I hear, little girls are made of pretty tough stuff these days. Maybe she'll be another *Li'l Wanderer*, if you see what I'm saying."

The Wanderer snapped forward like a snake. His right hand snatched Gerard by the collar, while his left pressed the Lassiter against Gerard's forehead.

"Sorry, sorry!" gasped Gerard. "I admit that was a low blow."

The Wanderer tightened his grip into a chokehold. "Don't you ever bring up Lindsay again!"

Rosa touched Errol's arm and he seemed to relax. He'd looked close to pulling the trigger, but the reporter didn't want to see anyone else shot, even after everything Gerard had done to her.

Errol let go of his stepbrother's collar, but kept the gun close by his head.

"Better leave quick," advised the sociopathic CEO, curling his lips upward. "The Red Stripes just received a nice little delivery, from what I hear."

The rogue gunman winked. "From what I hear, your delivery truck got a little lost coming to Union."

Gerard darkened. "What do you mean?"

Rosa wondered the same.

"Let's just say the Gang's not going to be too happy when they finally find you and your assistant in the bank vault."

The Wanderer swung back his Lassiter and whipped the steel barrel hard into Gerard's temple.

*

The door of the bank vault shut with a satisfying heavy click, locking the unconscious Gerard and Elza inside.

"Errol," said Rosie, standing behind him.

As he turned, she caught him between her arms and sprang onto her toes to kiss him. An explosion of warmth coursed through his body. Gradually, he brought his arms down her back. She felt warm and alive.

There was a look of mischief in her eyes as she pulled away. He didn't know what to say.

"Well, don't just stare blankly at me," she said with a laugh. "We have to go, right?"

He led the way to the door and they exited onto the street, where a black sedan with tinted glass was idling. The window came down, revealing Kid Hunter behind the wheel. "What were you guys doing in there? We've gotta get the hell out of here!"

They jogged over and got in. Rosa took a seat next to Charlie in the front, while the Wanderer opted for the back. He reckoned it was a better spot to be if they encountered any trouble from the

Red Stripe Gang.

"I'm still mad, you know," said Rosie, turning around in her seat to address the Wanderer.

"I know," he said gruffly.

Kid Hunter, who apparently failed to detect the romantic undercurrent in her voice, burst, "Me, too!"

"Uh-huh." He was still thinking about his stepbrother. It felt good sticking him in the bank vault, but it wasn't a permanent solution. The Gang would check up on him sooner or later, and they'd let him loose. Even if they were steamed about the gun trade, Gerard was still CEO of Breck Ammunition. He could be mighty persuasive to the types of greedy individuals who took to the Red Stripe Gang.

"Oh shit," murmured the Kid.

The car had just pulled up to a street festival of Red Stripe Gangsters, and most of the them were looking their way.

"Reverse!" the reporter cried.

"Maybe they won't bother us," reasoned Charlie. "I mean, they let me go. I'm a free man. And the Wanderer looks like Mr. Mask."

"But Rosie looks like the journalist who should be in a bank vault," Errol responded. "We'd better get out of here and fast."

A few of the Red Stripers drew semiautomatics and marched toward the car.

"You don't have to tell me twice," remarked the Kid.

"Reverse!" Rosie yelled again.

"Okay, so maybe you do." He started to back up and jammed on the gas. When he had enough speed, he swung the steering wheel sharply to the right and dropped the transmission into drive. The momentum of the car swung it around in a 180-degree turn. A few bullets whizzed by the car, and then another popped into the back bumper. The Kid slammed the gas pedal again.

The Wanderer watched out the back window. As the car picked up speed, he saw some of the Red Stripers retreat to their motorcycles.

"It's okay," said the Wanderer. "We can get out of Union this way, too. We'll just have to head south instead of north."

Kid Hunter took a deep breath. "So, was that it?"

"How do you mean?"

Rosie laughed. "I think he means — you call that an apology?"

"I —"

"You abandoned us!" she yelled. "You skipped Lindsay's funeral!"

"I went back to pay my respects —"

"— after you *abandoned* us and *skipped* Lindsay's funeral!"

One motorcycle appeared behind them, and then another. Then three more. Four men and one woman. The Wanderer rolled down his window and leaned out with his Lassiter. His arm shook as he attempted to line up a shot, but a reticule in his eyeglass helped him stay on target. It beeped, and he fired. The gangster on the left slumped over and his bike went sliding off Central Avenue into the sidewalk. Errol fell back into the car as one of the other gangsters aimed a Breck 17.

"Well?" Rosie asked expectantly.

"Can't this wait?" The Wanderer leaned back out the window and shot another bullet. It missed, but threw the intended target off so bad that he leaned too hard and fell off his bike. That left three more on their tail. Squinting, he recognized one of the three men as Erskine from the bar. The old man knew how to ride!

The Wanderer fell back into the car seat as Kid Hunter took a hard right onto a twisting highway ramp, taking the turn as fast as possible without sending the sedan into the guardrail. The wheels squealed in protest, but just managed to hang on until they reached the highway proper.

"Look," said Errol, "I shouldn't have left. I know that. It's just … what I do. It's what I always do."

Rosie's expression softened. "So why did you come back this time?"

He thought about it but couldn't come up with a good explanation. "I had to."

The back window exploded, raining glass down on the Wanderer's back. The shards cut, but at least the bullet missed its target, ending its journey somewhere inside the radio.

"And here I was gonna play some tunes," said the Kid. "Probably something bittersweet, given the mood in here."

The Wanderer leaned over the backseat and took three more shots through the space where the rear window used to be. That left one slug in the barrel. It was enough. One gangster swerved off into a guardrail, which stopped the bike but launched the rider off into the grass. The female Red Striper hit the brakes, but when her bike finally came to a stop, so did she, and she slumped forward in the vehicle. Erskine attempted to retreat, however the sudden U-turn on the three-lane highway sent him on a path directly in the way of an oncoming sports car. He hollered pretty loud for an old man.

Errol relaxed in his seat and began to peel Mr. Mask's bandannas from his face. "So I guess what I'm saying is … I'm sorry."

"S'all good, man," replied the Kid. "Right, Rosa?"

She shrugged. "I was happy you came for us."

"So where we headed next, Wandy?"

Errol winced at the nickname, but decided it was best not to make any more trouble for himself. "I reckon it's time I head back to Vegas. It ain't right what Gerard did to you, Rosa. He could have killed you! He was *goin'* to kill you!"

The Wanderer shook his head with disgust — not only at Gerard for the murder he'd nearly committed, but at himself for the murder he almost failed to prevent.

He continued. "It ain't right what he did to the gun printer in Freetown, either. Or killing that inventor, O'Brien. I reckon this gun trade with the Red Stripe Gang is just the last straw in a big haystack of reasons to go back to Vegas. My stepbrother ain't fit to run Breck Ammo … and maybe I ought to. The truth is I've been too damn chicken to go back, but I reckon what scares me more right now is what could happen if I don't."

The others remained silent, and the Wanderer wondered if they'd soon be parting ways. Well, if the apology wasn't enough, at least he'd saved their lives one last time.

The Kid spoke first. "I might as well come with you. Seems I got a date in Vegas with El Tiburón … and I figure you could probably use a little backup."

Rosa chuckled inscrutably. "Have to admit, she said, the pitch of her voice rising, "sounds like a story I shouldn't miss!"

"Heh," laughed the Wanderer, struggling to keep his expression serious. "I reckon I know better now than to try and stop you."

*

Rusty woke up with his head pounding. He could use his cup of joe, even if it was stale and cold, but he couldn't reach it because his hands were tied behind his back. He was still in the semi's driver's seat, but his truck was driving itself. Glancing at the onboard navigation system, he saw that the truck had set Breck Ammo's main distribution point in Vegas as its destination. Judging by the distance traveled, he'd been out for two, maybe three hours.

There was a note, scrawled in black ink on a Breck-branded sticky note:

Hey man,
Sorry I tranked you.
Your pal,
Kid Hunter

A low rumbling laugh erupted from the truck driver's belly. So the guns never made it to Union. He hadn't done his job. Oh well — not his problem!

Rusty closed his eyes. "Good girl," he told the truck, falling back into a dream.

CHAPTER TWENTY-SEVEN

You and What Army?

Ben Martin crouched behind the passenger side of his Ford Police Interceptor with a Pilgrim pump-action shotgun resting between his thighs. Beneath his Army trucker hat, he wore sports shades with reflective green lenses. Dougie sat next to him with his back against the hot car and his legs stretched out on the asphalt. Thick sweat matted the party section of his mullet against the back of his neck. He was carrying a Breck 17 handgun.

Martin peeked over the top of the Interceptor at the bright red drive-through window of the Wells Fargo bank. Ducking again, the sheriff brought a handheld radio to his lips and clicked the *PUSH-TO-TALK* button. "How's the front looking?"

Static.

"We got four guns trained on the entrance," Joe Lin then radioed back. "They're not getting out this way."

Static. Pop! "Who's with you?"

Static.

"Got Larry, Alyssa, and Rico."

Static. Pop!

"Okay, good. Dougie and me are positioned by the teller

window. In a second I'm gonna give them a scare. Should send 'em running to you."

Static.

"Roger."

Static. Pop!

"And Joe, tell the others I want these bastards alive."

This was important. He wanted to make an example of them. Martin put down the walkie-talkie and stood up with the butt of the Pilgrim rested against his shoulder. He fired at the drive-through window, smashing in the glass. A woman inside screamed. Martin figured it was the teller.

"Keep down!" he yelled.

A man in a black ski mask appeared in the window with a Breck 17. Martin pressed up against his vehicle and trained the Pilgrim at the man's heart. "I wouldn't," the sheriff warned.

The bank robber hesitated.

The reports had indicated there was one more bandit inside. He'd have to tread carefully. "The name's Ben Martin — Sheriff Ben Martin — and you're under arrest. How about you drop the gun on the road right here, and I meet you and your buddy out front?"

Martin was excited. It was like a feeling from the past, long forgotten, had woken up again. The thrill of the chase. He knew the adrenaline would soon be followed by the ultimate satisfaction that came with a successful arrest.

"You and what army?" sneered the robber.

The deputy popped up with his semiautomatic. "That's my cue, right, Ben?"

Martin cringed. Dougie sure was a dum-dum, sometimes. The bandit looked unimpressed until a volley of shots rang out from the other side of the building. Jolted by the noise, the robber turned from the window to look back inside the bank. He called out to someone, presumably the other robber, and received a muffled moan in reply.

"Hey!" the sheriff shouted to get his attention.

The bandit turned shakily. "I-I think he's shot. Oh God, they said this town didn't have law enforcement."

"This town is under the protection of Martin's Militia. Now throw out your damn gun. Based on his bitchin', it sounds like your pal is still alive. If you surrender now, maybe we can help him keep livin'."

Dougie tapped the sheriff on the shoulder and gave a look of consternation. "Why would we do that?"

Martin exhaled sharply in frustration. That idiot could sure run his mouth. "Would you shut the hell up for a minute?"

The robber looked back and forth between Ben and the inside of the bank. Finally, he tossed the Breck 17 out the window, and the gun skidded under the police car. Ben Martin caught it with his foot on the other side. He radioed Joe to let him know the standoff was at an end. The criminals were coming out.

*

The blank boxes on the page stubbornly refused to fill themselves in. Steve the station manager held a palm tightly against his forehead, straining to come up with an answer. He clutched a pencil in his other hand, absentmindedly tapping the eraser end on the table to the beat of "God Bless America." A dusty wire fan blasted machine wind through what was left of his hair, then turned away. This repeated every few seconds, with each gust reminding Steve that he still had not come up with the solution.

Ten down, ten down … why was it always ten down?

Steve counted through the eleven spaces and mumbled the hint. "This deadly creature carries a musical instrument." He rapped the fingers of his other hand against the table. Harp fish? No, not enough letters. Whistling duck? No, too many. And besides, it didn't work with three or six across.

The station manager gazed out the ticket window as the red-and-white gates rang out in warning. What started as the drum roll of a marching band grew louder until it was more like thunder, and great boxes of rusted green, blue, and maroon shot from right to left over the rails. On a few he caught the logo for Breck Ammunition, but he failed to recognize most of the other symbols. With a final blast of horn, the colorful parade disappeared into the bleak desert.

"What was I doing again?" Steve asked the fan. As he pondered the question, he noticed the pencil and crossword puzzle lying on the table and figured he might as well work on that.

Steve stroked his chin thoughtfully. Ten down, ten down … why was it always ten down?

A tap at the counter broke Steve's concentration. Realizing it was a customer, he slapped shut the orange book of crosswords and let go of the pencil. The pencil rolled back off the desk and dropped softly onto the worn carpet. Steve strained to reach it.

The tap again, this time followed by a stern voice. "Hey,

grandpa, I haven't got all day, okay?"

Abandoning the pencil, Steve looked up with his best smile. The man across from him had an irritated look on his face, but what caught Steve's attention the most was the silver six-shooter the man had left on the counter with the barrel facing into the ticket window. "Wh-where you headed?" he stammered.

"Liberty police station," the man said.

Steve scratched his head. Another puzzle. "I reckon you don't need a train to go there."

The man laughed. "I *know* that. I mean I need directions."

Looking him over, Steve had a sudden bout of déjà vu. The slim man wore a Stetson and a plaid shirt. That, combined with the Lassiter on the table …" Hey, I remember you. The Wander Man, right?"

Steve spotted another guy smoking by a pair of black motorcycles in the parking lot. He was surprised he hadn't heard them come into the lot, but figured they must have arrived while that loud marching band was coming through.

The Wander Man waved his hand in front of Steve's eyes. "Did you hear me, old man? I asked you a question."

Steve pointed over his shoulder. "Say! Is that Kid Hondo over there? You boys sure are a sight for sore eyes!"

The Wander Man responded with a narrowing of the eyes. "I don't have time for games, old man. Okay? The police station. Where is it?"

Steve clapped his hands together and provided enthusiastic turn-by-turn directions, recounting the exact number of traffic lights before each turn and excitedly describing a few shops along the way. The Wander Man turned away before Steve could finish listing the pies available at Betsy's Diner.

"Well, I'm sure you'll find one you like. I've yet to have a bad pie from there, I'll tell you that."

When the Wander Man was halfway down the walk to his bike, Steve snapped his fingers. "I'll just call the sheriff, let him know you're coming."

The fingers on the Wander Man's right hand, hanging languidly by his hip, coiled around the handle of the Lassiter. "I'd rather you didn't."

The flat delivery sent a chill down Steve's spine. Or maybe that was just the breeze from the fan. Either way, he was worried. What if Sheriff Martin didn't want to see this Wander Man? A picture came through the fog like a remembered dream. The sheriff and the deputy, caught in a standoff with the Wander Man and Kid Hondo. He'd seen the whole drama from the station window. How could he have forgotten?

Well, he was sure of one thing. Martin would want to know about this Wander Man asking for directions. The station manager reached for the phone. "I really think I should. Will only take a second."

"Yes," hissed the gunman, "only a second."

There was something reptilian about the Wander Man's eyes as he whipped his gun arm around. With a gasp, Steve realized he had the answer to ten down. "Rattlesnake!"

The Lassiter flared, the glass of the ticket window shattered, and Steve's whole world went black.

*

It was only two lawbreakers, so Ben Martin and Dougie took the men in the sheriff's car while the other militiamen headed for the saloon. Martin promised to buy 'em all a round in an hour's time. Turned out Alyssa Carey had struck an artery when she'd shot the second robber. He died spraying out his insides in the car. The other one, the one they'd faced off with in the back of the bank, started bawling.

"Fuck, let's just toss him out," said Dougie.

Martin smirked. "Which one?"

That got Dougie laughing real loud. "Good one, Ben. That's a real good one."

The sheriff made a U-turn and drove a few miles out into the desert. He turned on a dusty service road. When the land looked sufficiently empty and the town of Liberty was out of view, Martin stopped the car. The sheriff and deputy got out and looked around.

"This'll do, I reckon," said Martin, popping open the back door. Ignoring the cries of the other criminal, they pulled his partner's corpse out onto the red sand. The body landed with a pleasing *thunk*.

Dougie pointed up at a black vulture circling the cloudless sky. "They always seem to know, don't they?"

*

Upon returning to the station, two militiamen brought the surviving robber down the stairs to the holding cells. He was still covered with his friend's blood. Martin put him in the cage across from the Red Striper with the burned face. The gangster, looking slightly gaunter than before, whimpered slightly as Martin locked in the new prisoner.

The sheriff frowned. That was two cells filled. If the other bandit hadn't died, the place would be full, and the next prisoners to come in would have to share cells with the ones already here. This jail wasn't designed to be permanent — just a place to hold criminals until they could be transferred to state prison. Martin would have to come up with something, and soon.

Dougie's voice, calling his name from upstairs, pulled Martin out of his head. "Ben! Get up here quick!"

The deputy was standing by the window facing the parking lot. There were two motorcycles parked across the handicap spots, and a gangster leaning against a tree smoking a cigarette. They hadn't been there earlier. Before Martin could speak, the front door swung open and a second Red Striper entered the station.

"Anyone home?" the stranger boomed.

Dougie reached for his Breck 17, but Martin called him off with a wave of the hand. "Let's see what they want first," the sheriff ordered.

The gangster brought a cigarette down from his lips and stubbed it out on the surface of the dusty reception desk. "You Martin?"

He looked cleaner than your average Red Striper. Not nearly as bulky, either. He wore a pair of regular-fitting, dark-washed blue jeans and a red flannel shirt with rhinestone buttons. Something about his appearance struck Martin as familiar, but the sheriff couldn't place it. "That's Sheriff to you."

The gangster chuckled like it was a joke. "Okay, *Sheriff*. And what should I call your boyfriend?"

"Deputy," spat Dougie, wearing the bristled expression of a dog around unfamiliar house guests.

Again, the gangster snickered. "The name's Slim. I'm with the Red Stripe Gang. You killed one of my men. The other one's here, and I want him back."

Killed one of their men? What was he … "Now wait one second. Tweren't us who killed your man. It was that no-good Wanderer."

"The Wanderer," Slim repeated flatly. If he cared, he didn't show it. "You know, this town of yours — what's it called?"

"Liberty."

"That's right. Liberty. On my way in here, I was looking around at all the nice houses and thinking to myself, 'This must be a mighty fine place to live.' I told that to my man outside, and he reckoned I was right. So now the both of us are thinking, maybe we'll move here. And maybe we'll tell our friends, and maybe they'll move here, too. Imagine that, Sheriff? You and me. Neighbors!"

"Now you listen here," Martin replied sternly, "your men tried to kill one of my people. A good woman from my town. I can't just let you waltz in here and —"

A Lassiter seemed to materialize in Slim's hand. The silver revolver fired and a spray of warm liquid struck Ben Martin across the right side of his face. Feeling no pain, the sheriff lowered his head like a bull and charged forward. He tackled the gangster before he could shoot again, sending both him and Slim crashing to the dirty tile floor. Martin pinned the gangster with his knees and wrestled the Lassiter out of the man's hand. When he looked at the man's face again, he saw the Wanderer.

"You!" he cried. The sheriff lifted the Lassiter high over his head and made to swing it. The Wanderer gasped an apology, but the sheriff was like a train that couldn't be stopped. The steel pistol swung down devastatingly into the gunman's face. Once, twice, three times …

Martin held up once the other man passed out. He reckoned another blow might be fatal. He checked himself for bullet wounds. When he didn't find any, he looked over his shoulder and saw Dougie. There was blood oozing out of his head, forming a crimson pool on the tile. With a groan of effort, Martin pushed himself onto his feet and took a closer look. Dougie was dead, no doubt about it. Martin took off his Army hat and held it over his heart for a moment of silence. He went to put the hat over Dougie's contorted face but his hand kept shaking and he dropped it into the puddle of blood.

"Shit!" screamed Martin. "Shit! Shit! Shit!"

"Slim?"

The other Red Striper had arrived. He had a Breck 17 in his belt, while Martin found himself yet again unarmed. For a while, the two men stared at each other, refusing to budge from their positions. Then, miraculously it seemed, the Red Striper bolted. Martin went to the window and watched the gangster get on his bike and zoom away from the station. With a sigh of relief, the sheriff snatched his phone and called Joe Lin.

"The Gang?" repeated Lin with a tremor.

"Get everyone you can together and bring 'em over here right away."

Hanging up, Martin stepped back toward the unconscious

Slim. It was funny how much he looked like the Wanderer. Martin was sure now he wasn't, though. The Wanderer and the Red Stripe Gang mixed like oil and water. Grabbing the gangster's ankles, Martin dragged the body toward the stairwell. At the edge, Martin gave a push and Slim tumbled the rest of the way down on his own. He heard the gangster's head bounce against a few of the steps, but it didn't appear to crack.

"Oh my God!" gasped someone down below.

Martin reckoned it was the attempted bank robber. "Shut the hell up, or it's you next!"

When he reached the basement himself, he was dismayed to find that Dougie's murderer had survived the fall. He opened the last available cage and dragged the bastard inside. He locked the door, but it didn't feel like enough, so he spat at the still body through the iron bars.

The basement was full of scum, and the scum kept coming. These lawless freaks needed to be punished, made into an example. Yet what was he doing? Feeding them? Giving them water? What good did that do anyone?

"Why don't you just kill us, too?" bawled the bank robber.

There was a glint in Ben Martin's eye as he smiled. "Better get some sleep," he said. "Sun up tomorrow, you get your wish. We're having us an old-fashioned execution."

Martin headed back up the stairs to wait for his militia. The station stunk with death, so he went outside and stood by the front entrance. Reaching into his pocket, he pulled out a crumpled tissue and wiped some of the blood off his face. A ghastly squeal and heavy flutter of wings snapped the sheriff's attention to the gangster's motorcycle in the parking lot. Perched on its handlebars was a large black bird with a bald head. As the vulture gave Martin a sidelong stare, he echoed the words of his late deputy. "They always seem to know."

CHAPTER TWENTY-EIGHT

This Is Madness!

The morning was still dark as Jackson Veras sped down Main Street in a blue Chevrolet sedan. He'd been rudely awakened by a phone call from Father James just after four in the morning. One of his parishioners, a member of Martin's Militia, had just informed the priest there was going to be a public execution in the town park at the crack of dawn. There were three men — a bank robber and two Red Stripers — who'd be killed. Ben Martin, this parishioner said, had gone mad.

There was no one at the park yet, so Jack turned the car around and drove to the police headquarters. The lot was full of flatbed trucks and SUVs, and the station glowed yellow with light. Jack parked somewhere near the back. Opening the dash, he pulled out a Breck 17 handgun and stuffed it in his pocket. He didn't usually carry, and not even Rosie knew he had a gun. He'd bought it after the shooting at the Walmart.

Jack jogged up to front entrance, passing a large white police van used for transferring convicts. The station door was open so he let himself in.

The station was buzzing like the old days. Men and women

were rushing around in police uniforms, creating a white noise of chatter. He was surprised how many there were. Jack thought Martin had collected maybe five or six hicks from the town, but here there had to be twenty, maybe more.

"I thought I told you to call first," came the familiar drawl of Ben Martin. The sheriff flashed a half smile, blackened by a wad of chewing tobacco. Jack noticed a blood stain on his shirt.

"Is it true, Ben?" he asked. "An execution?"

Martin looked at his watch. "We're just starting to call everyone up and let them know to come down to the park, if they want to see."

"You can't just kill these prisoners of yours!"

Jack felt the heat of many eyes and realized a crowd was beginning to form to listen to the exchange.

Martin looked at him like he was joking. "Don't you see, Jack? These lawless folk need to be made an example of. Otherwise they're just gonna keep on comin'. This execution is just the start of a return to civilization!"

Just the start? It was true. Martin had gone mad. Well, Jack still had to try to reason with him. "You talk about the law as if you're bringing it back. But according to the law, these men deserve a fair trial."

Martin scowled and for a long moment held his head in hands. When he peered up at the lawyer again, there was a dark look to his eyes. "It's too late for a trial."

Years of lawyering had taught Jack that when one argument failed, it was time to try another. "From what I'm told, you've got two members of the Red Stripe Gang. Have you thought about what happens when you kill them? You think the Gang is just going to let that go?"

"I ain't worried, if that's what you mean. I can take care of myself."

"It's not you I'm worried about, Ben. It's the whole town that could pay the price!"

"Martin's Militia will protect Liberty."

It was clear the man wasn't going to listen, and Jack had run out of arguments. "Then I'm going to have to stop you," he said, reaching into his pocket. Unfamiliar with the gun, he struggled to bring it out quickly. There were at least ten handguns on him before he could finish the threat.

Ben Martin laughed. "That's pretty stupid, son! Bringing a loaded gun into a police station! Oh, my lord!"

"This isn't a police station," said Jack, gritting his teeth, "and you're not police."

The sheriff walked up real close, so close that Jack could almost taste the tobacco on his breath. Martin bared his incisors and squirted something black and wet onto Jack's glasses. The lawyer lunged for the sheriff's neck, but someone strong tugged him back by the ponytail, making Jack wince with pain. More of Martin's Militia pushed him down to the floor on his stomach, pulled back his arms, and shackled his wrists.

Stuck like a pig on the barbecue spit, Jack hollered, "You going to kill me, too?"

Martin crouched down to look him in the face. "No. You're not worth the trouble, and frankly, I like Rosie too much to kill her only brother. But I am afraid you will miss out on today's festivities."

"Today's murder, you mean."

Clicking his tongue in pity, Martin stood up and gestured to two members of his militia. "Lock him up."

A man and woman who Jack recognized as former police officers Elroy Wolfe and Alyssa Carey lifted him up to his feet and pushed him toward the stairs. Twisting his head back, Jack roared, "So you finally get to throw another Veras in jail! Huh, Martin?"

The sheriff marched up to Jack, grabbed him by the scruff of the neck, and growled, "You know very well how I tried to be there for you and Rosie after your pa went to prison."

Jack laughed absurdly. "Is that right? You were there for us? Then where were you when my boy got shot?"

The sheriff turned red. "I ... I stopped the shooter!"

Through angry tears, Jack screamed, "You were too late! Why weren't you there sooner, Ben? Why did you allow a monster like that to come into our town?"

"No, that's not —! I've done everything I —"

Something inside the sheriff's head seemed to snap. Jack caught just a glimpse of Martin's fat fist flying toward him before everything went black.

*

The sun shot rays of red from its hiding position, crouched beneath the dark hills overlooking Liberty. Father James ran hard down Main Street toward the park. He could already see the crowd of people. Ben Martin was looking down on them from his perch on some kind of crate.

The Catholic priest shivered. He was losing his flock. Oh, God, maybe they were already lost.

"— no room for lawlessness in Liberty!" Martin's voice boomed.

Father James fought his way through the crowd. At first, they resisted, but the wall broke when the people saw it was their preacher coming.

"Stop!" he cried out to Martin.

The sheriff cut off his speech and peered down at the priest. Without his usual Army hat, Martin's unkempt hair came up in two tufts like horns. Father James looked around wildly for the prisoners. Was he too late? No, there they were sitting on the ground, bundled in rope. He gasped — each of the three men was tied to the back bumper of a truck — one to a Ford pickup, another to a Chevy SUV and a third to a Jeep. The engines were running.

"Come to hear their last words, Father?" asked Martin.

"This is madness!" Father James turned to face the audience. "People of Liberty, please don't listen to this mad man! This is not God's way! He teaches *forgiveness*. Thou shalt not kill —"

*

The gun blast gave way to a collective gasp of horror among the gathering. Ben kept his Breck 17 trained on the body of Father James, who now lay sprawled out on the grass.

"He's ... he's dead," stammered Joe Lin.

Ben Martin leveled Joe a cold stare and holstered his gun. "Then we can continue." There were still murmurs of conversation among the gathered, so he said it louder. "*Then* we can *continue*!"

When there was silence at last, the leader of Martin's Militia turned toward the condemned men and gave the signal. The trucks took off for the desert, leaving streaks of red between the tracks of their tires.

*

The conclusion of the execution left the militia frothing for more Western justice. Ben Martin reckoned he knew just where to find it.

There were seven of them with him: Larry Wilkins, Elroy Wolfe, Deon Douglas, Ryder Klein, Alyssa Carey, "Mad" May Mackenzie, and Rico Velasquez. They pulled up onto the well-watered front lawn of the mayor's mansion in four trucks, including the three from the execution. They came out of the vehicles carrying a few different guns — mostly Breck 17 pistols, but Martin brought his Pilgrim, and Mad May rolled up with a Yossarian automatic.

Joe Lin would have come too, but he'd excused himself because he thought someone should return to the police station to watch Jackson. Martin agreed it was a good idea. Lin seemed like a good man. Martin was thinking about making him his new deputy.

The door swung open before the sheriff had made it halfway up the walk. Onto the porch stepped the butler in his dark brown suit. "You can't park there!" the butler shouted, waving the brush end of a broom in the air. "What is the meaning of this?"

There was a blast and a high whistle as a bullet ricocheted off the porch. The butler yelped and ran back inside, slamming the door behind him.

Annoyed, Martin swiveled around. "Who did that?"

Eyes turned toward Ryder Klein, and the sheriff stopped the inquisition as Klein looked guilty as hell. "Dammit, don't fire until you get my say so!" Martin ordered.

There was a gunshot. Klein screamed out in agony.

"Sniper on the roof!" yelled Mad May, unloading a volley of automatic fire at the top of the building. Martin looked up in time to see a man in black security garb fall two stories onto the lawn.

Klein was still screaming. He was lying on the ground now, shirt soaked with blood, as useless as an injured horse.

"For God's sake," said Martin, "would someone please put him out of his misery?"

May aimed her Yossarian.

"No, no!" yelled Klein.

There was a short burst of fire followed by relieved silence. With a puff of impatience, Martin trotted up to the door and knocked. "Now listen here! I apologize for my man back there, but you're going to have to let us in. I told them not to fire anymore. I just want the mayor."

There was no answer. Martin tried rattling the door but found it locked tight.

"Fine," he said flatly. "Have it your way."

He took a few steps back and leveled the Pilgrim at the keyhole. It took only a couple trigger pulls for the door to swing open on its own accord. Martin stepped inside and smiled smugly back at the portrait of Thomas Jefferson hanging over the foyer. It was quiet. The butler had gone into hiding. Maybe the mayor, too.

"Stop!" yelled a guard, coming down the stairs with a Breck 17.

Martin fired the Pilgrim. The guard fell forward, rolling down the final six steps in a crumpled heap. The sheriff tapped him with the barrel of the shotgun to make sure he was dead. He was.

Martin's Militia piled through the entrance behind him, but they all still managed to stand comfortably in the foyer. The sheriff directed the women to secure the ground floor while he took the other four men upstairs to look for Mayor White.

About halfway up the steps, Martin had to stop to take a few wheezing breaths. "Damn stairs," he muttered. "I remember you now."

At the top, there was a long hallway with many doors. Martin directed his men to spread out and check each one, while he headed directly for the room where he had met White previously.

In the study, the big TV was on with a live feed of the Arizona state legislature. Martin saw the webcam's light was off and took a few cautious steps inside.

"What — what do you want?" a small voice cried from the mayor's desk.

Ben Martin pointed his Pilgrim directly in front of him and did a quick sidestep around the table. He found White cowering on the other side, covering his bald head with trembling hands.

The mayor peeked up at him. "Sheriff? There're some men outside — I heard a gunshot. Are you here to help?"

"I am."

White sighed gratefully. "I can't tell you how much of a relief it is to —"

The Pilgrim went off in Ben Martin's hands. With a cry, Mayor Alex White fell backward onto the blue carpet. He wouldn't shut up so Martin shot him again. In silence at last, Martin watched a dark red circle expand slowly from the edge of the politician's American flag pin.

The other militiamen rushed into the room. Martin turned to them with a wide grin and declared, "The mansion's ours!"

He stepped toward the room's east-facing window, pulled open the blinds, and looked out upon Liberty. Something in the lower half of his vision caught his eye. It was someone running away from the house in full business attire. The butler had cleared the lawn and was making a dash for the desert. Martin was just about to say something to his men when he heard a long grinding blast downstairs. The butler fell flat on his stomach with arms and legs spread out in all directions. From the second floor, he looked to Martin just like a squashed cockroach.

*

Jack couldn't believe his ears. Not only had the execution gone off as planned, but now Father James was dead and Ben Martin had set out after the mayor.

So said Joe Lin, firefighter turned jailer. He was a man who Jack couldn't quite figure out. He'd been one of Ben Martin's first recruits for the militia, but yet here he was confessing to Jack how uncomfortable the priest's death had made him feel. Jack wanted to tell him he should have thought of that before joining up with Martin, but it didn't seem like the smartest play given that Lin was the one holding him in jail below the Liberty police station.

It was difficult to wrap his head around the simple fact that Father James was dead. They'd known each other since they were kids. They were never great friends, but as schoolmates they'd often chatted about tests, teachers, and of course, Jack's sister. Jim and Rosie had been pretty serious in high school. The priest, who wasn't a priest then but wanted to be, told Jack about his plans before he told Rosie. Maybe he thought Jack could convince her to be the one to end the relationship. As if Jack could ever convince his sister of anything!

"This is all my fault, you know," continued Lin. "The militia was my idea. I convinced Martin to start it up."

The confession startled Jack. All he could say was, "Why?"

"I was at the Walmart with my wife. She was pregnant and we were going shopping for baby things. We were just coming out of the car to go inside when … when …"

"I know," Jack replied gently. "I was there, too. I lost my son."

Tears burst from Lin's eyes. "This isn't what I wanted!"

"Then let me out, Joe. You don't want Martin to kill me, too, do you? You know he will. It's just a matter of time."

Lin scratched his head. "I reckon you'll be all right. He just wanted to hold you so you wouldn't interfere earlier. He'll let you go when he gets back."

"Yeah, maybe. But, I mean, if you think so, why can't you just let me go now? The execution's over, right?"

Lin glanced at the ring of keys lying on a desk on the other side of the room. "I don't know. I think I should wait for Ben to get back."

Jack rubbed his face in exasperation. "My son — he's in a coma at the hospital. I need to go make sure he's all right. You need to let me go."

Lin took a step in the direction of the keys, but then walked past the desk and up the stairs. "I'm sorry, Jack. I ... I probably shouldn't be talking to you."

WANDERER BREAKS UP BRECK GUN TRADE WITH GANG

By Rosa Veras

The Wanderer and Kid Hunter on Tuesday intercepted a Breck Ammunition truck bringing Yossarian assault rifles to Union, a Red Stripe town, as part of a trade organized by Gerard Breck for protection services from the Red Stripe Gang.

Now the Wanderer has said he will come to Breck Ammo headquarters in Vegas to put an end to the CEO's reign and his unholy alliance with the nation's worst criminals.

If there is an unofficial capital to the New West, it has to be Las Vegas. It started out as "Sin City," and things only got worse from there.

As laws loosened across the country, the scum of Vegas tightened their control of this city of casinos, strip clubs, and debauchery. The place has become a safe harbor for industry giants like Breck Ammunition to do as they please, and for organized crime to take care of business without fear of indictment.

There are still police in Vegas. When public money stopped funding their paychecks, the corporate giants and the mafia stepped in. Unlike towns like Liberty, where the de-funding of law enforcement has wiped out formal law enforcement, the corrupt cops of Vegas have managed not only to survive, but to thrive like rats.

It would be an understatement to say this deregulation had an impact on the police's priorities. In reaction to these changes, the city's booming tourism industry has not shrunk so much as it has degenerated. Gone are the families of four and tech conference registrants; in their place are lowlifes looking for the kind of wealth, sex, and power they can't buy back home.

This is why Vegas is one of the few places in America that was not renamed during the Born-Again Patriot movement. Vegas has always been synonymous with unchecked freedom.

What happens in Vegas, stays in Vegas.

CHAPTER TWENTY-NINE

It's Not Your House.

Rosa gazed with morbid interest out the car window at the parade of leather-clad women and tattoo-splashed thugs walking under the fluorescent streets of Vegas. She was sitting in the back of a limousine with Errol and Charlie. The driver had been Errol's chauffer from long before the Wanderer even existed. He was a stocky, gray-haired man named José, who insisted he was loyal to only one Breck brother — "Al's good boy."

The reporter never had any reason or desire to come to this candy-coated urban hellhole before. The Wanderer and Kid Hunter appeared unconcerned, but she couldn't help but watch for potential threats.

She once heard a story about a woman from Liberty named Betty who had been driving here when a man in a puffy jacket stepped out in the middle of the street. Betty had braked hard to avoid hitting him, but when she'd stopped, he'd had a Yossarian automatic rifle pointed at her windshield. Betty had ducked and floored the gas pedal as the first spray of bullets shattered the glass. She'd slammed the car into the shooter, killing him instantly. A crowd of merrymakers stopped to see what had happened, but the big casinos never shut down for a second. And why would they? This was all just part of the show.

The limo stopped outside tall, turquoise gates with the name *Breck* inscribed in gold across the middle. The doors parted, and Rosa found herself unable to look away from the great mansion within. The Breck Estate was an adobe-red palace in the style of an old-fashioned Mexican governor's mansion, glowing brightly under the beams of carefully placed spot lighting. The two-floor building seemed to stretch endlessly in either direction. Despite Errol's long absence, the lawn and garden surrounding the building appeared to be in good health, as if it'd never occurred to the servants that their master was gone at all. As the car pulled up to the front entrance, she asked, "You're sure your stepbrother didn't move in?"

"Gerard moved out a long time ago to a penthouse above the Strip," Errol replied. "He hated it here, couldn't wait to get out."

José got out of the limo first and opened each of the back doors to let the others out. The Wanderer paused in front of the door to the mansion, as if he wanted to size it up before entering. Finally, he brought forward a key but seemed to have trouble with it, rattling it against the lock.

"You all right?" Rosa asked him.

He took a deep breath and unlocked the door. "Fine."

*

Errol wanted to tell Rosie it wasn't Gerard he was worried about, but the ghost of Helen. He hadn't been back to the house since that horrible night, and it still didn't feel right setting foot here again.

316

Kid Hunter hooted as they stepped inside. The grand entrance featured a tall ceiling and a redwood spiral staircase. "I think I'm gonna like living here!"

Living? "You can stay for a few days until we get things sorted out," the Wanderer insisted.

Charlie laughed. "I'm just fucking with you, man. I know we can't stay forever." He paused a beat. "Or *do* I?"

Errol pointed to the stairs and gave directions to the guest rooms. When they'd gone, he took a deep breath and stepped quietly toward the kitchen. He paused briefly in front of a watercolor of the desert landscape, but his eyes crept down to the floor. The stain in the carpet was gone, but he still felt Helen's presence. His legs weakened, and he had to brace himself against the gilded frame of the painting to keep from falling.

"Hey, careful. I always liked that piece," came a syrupy voice from the kitchen.

Errol turned sharply and caught a tall man with a black mustache standing in the entrance.

"Welcome home, brother," said Gerard.

Errol didn't want to alert the others, so he spoke as forcefully as he could manage without raising his voice. "How *dare* you break into my house?"

"It's not your house. It's Dad's house. And I didn't break in. I still have a key. Anyway, it's not like you've been around."

He ushered Errol into the tiled room and pulled out a wooden chair. The Brecks sat across from each other at the solid oak table where, a lifetime ago, they had shared pancakes. The Wanderer glanced at a steel block of knives resting on the slate counter behind his stepbrother's back. As far as he could tell, Gerard had come to the estate by himself, and a quick scan using his smart lens revealed he wasn't armed. No reason to get out the Lassiter just yet.

"What are you doing here, Gerard?"

"It's great to see you, too," said Gerard, stroking his black mustache. "We didn't really get to talk in Union, did we?"

"I reckon I wasn't in the mood for conversation."

"You 'reckon.' There you go again with that cowboy talk. I believe you may have read one too many of Dad's Western books when we were growing up." Gerard motioned to his eye and screwed up his face as if to indicate the presence of a gross pimple. "Hey, would you mind taking off the eyepiece? I know those things are supposed to glow red when they're recording, but I'd feel a lot better if I knew for sure no one else was watching."

Errol slipped the glass off of his face, made a show of clicking the power switch, and slipped the gadget into the front pocket of his flannel shirt. He then said, "I didn't know you'd be here, but maybe I'm glad. You're why I came back."

Gerard smiled. "Oh yeah? Missed your bro?"

Errol maintained his serious expression. "It's like I said in Union. I've got misgivings … about how you're running the company."

"Oh! The company's just great. We have a new gun coming out. I call it the Breck 100X. Incredible thing. You must try it! It's got this amazing—"

"Shut up. I'm here to shut you down."

Gerard didn't even blink. With a lick of his lips, he taunted, "I know why you ran from home."

"What do you know?"

"I know that you shot poor, poor Helen."

Speechless, Errol fell back into his chair. How? The reports of his wife's death in the paper had blamed the house intruder. No one had ever tried to cast the blame in another direction.

"I know, I know. You want to know how I figured that one out. But of course I knew, and so did the police. They aren't stupid! They're just corrupt." Gerard described how the police had removed the bullet from Helen's skull and quickly determined it had come from Errol's Breck 17. "Why do you think no one ever came after you? I paid them off." He held out his palms like he was waiting for a thank-you.

"You helped me," said Errol. "Why?"

Gerard shrugged. "I figured it would be better for the family and for Breck Ammunition if we didn't have a murder scandal hanging over our heads. Don't you *reckon*?"

"But wouldn't it have been easier for you to take the company?"

"Easy, maybe, but what you don't understand — what you've never understood — is that I wanted to *earn* the right to lead this company. But damn it, you always take away my opportunities! Do you remember when we were kids, and Dad used to take us to the baseball diamond to play? Just the three of us, Dad pitching, one of us up to bat, one of us in the outfield. You were always so much better at hitting than me, and I could see it in the way Dad looked at you that he knew it, too. You'd smash his pitches out of the park, but me, I could barely put down a bunt. He was proud of you and ashamed of me.

"One day though, when Dad was pitching and I was up to bat, something just clicked for me. He threw a pitch right over the plate. I reached back and swung — *crack*!" Gerard jumped up to his feet and held his hands high in the air. "The ball went sailing into the outfield! Back! Back!"

Gerard leaned over the table and scowled. "And then you just had to *fucking* leap and catch it." He shook his head angrily. "So, of course, Dad, he runs over to you and starts cheering, 'What a catch! What a catch!' I finally do something right, and you *still* got all the applause!"

Errol leaned back in his chair and crossed his arms. "I remember that day. I seem to recall you chasing me around with a baseball bat afterward."

Gerard's anger flicked to mirth in an instant. "Did I? Good!"

"So what's your point, exactly?"

"I wanted to earn the right to lead this company, and I was prepared to fight you for it. But then you just went and left! I'm only in charge of this company because they had no choice, because of *you*! So the fucking board has doubted me from the start. They think I'm not fit for this job. But I'll show them. The Breck 100X is going to be a success and then they'll see I was always meant to lead this company!"

"You've run out of time, Gerard. You've managed the company terribly. You're making deals with the Red Stripe Gang! Well, I reckon I'm back to fix your mistakes."

"No, I don't think you're going to do anything." Gerard sat back down, leaned over the table, and served up a Cheshire grin. "See, Errol, I might have paid off the cops to get them off your case, but

I can just as easily bribe them to reopen Helen's file."

Errol frowned. Blackmail. So that was his stepbrother's game.

"Don't worry, I'm not a bad guy. As long as you're willing to recognize me as the CEO of the company, you can stay right here in Dad's mansion. Hell, I'll even see my way past the thing with that bitch blogger. She can stay, too, provided she stops publishing that damn yellow rag. I'll leave you two lovers alone and you can have a lot of sex or whatever." Gerard turned to leave. "Just do the company one favor, okay? Try not to shoot her."

The Wanderer pulled the Lassiter out of his belt and aimed it Gerard's head. "Actually, I was thinking about shooting *you*."

Gerard laughed. "You wouldn't murder your own brother, would you? Besides, I may have asked *you* not to record this conversation, but that doesn't mean I'm not. You know how I've always liked to watch."

The Wanderer lowered his gun.

"By the way," Gerard added, "I'd threaten the bounty hunter, too, but it sounds like he's got bigger problems already. Word has it that El Tiburón himself wants his head!" He wriggled his fingers ominously. "Ooh … *El Tiburón!*"

*

As soon as Kid Hunter learned that Gerard had been in the house, he went to work checking the entire property for bugs. So that they could talk, the Wanderer showed them the laundry room in the basement, which was one place where Errol said he was sure there were no CCTV cameras.

"How long is this going to take?" whispered Rosa as she leaned against a silver washing machine.

Kid Hunter knocked on his tablet like a magician. "Done!"

He swiped quickly through the results on the screen. Sure enough, the Breck Estate's surveillance system was broadcasting footage to Breck Ammo HQ.

"Turn off the broadcast," directed the Wanderer.

The mercenary shook his head. "Not that simple. We don't want Gerard to know that *we* know that *he* —"

"Movies made you this way, didn't they?" interrupted Rosa, rolling her eyes.

Ignoring her, Charlie went to work reprogramming the cameras to broadcast a looping stream of old footage. It wasn't perfect since they weren't actually in any of it, but it was at least a temporary fix, and if Gerard's goons were dumb enough, they might not even notice.

The Wanderer described Gerard's demands. Errol was to support him as CEO of Breck Ammunition, and Rosa was to stop writing *The New West*.

"How's he going to stop us?" asked Rosa.

"Blackmail," said the Wanderer, staring accusingly at his Breck 17. "He ... knows what I did ... with the bad gun."

"Wait, what do you mean?" said Charlie. He'd noticed that the Wanderer never used the Breck 17 but assumed it was some kind of superstition.

Errol looked at Rosa, who sent back a supportive smile. "Back in the woods, when we were camping around the fire and I told you what happened to Helen, I wasn't completely honest. The truth is it weren't no burglar who shot her. It was me."

Rosa quickly came to the Wanderer's defense. "It was an accident. Errol thought she was an intruder."

"Shit, man ... that's heavy." Charlie let out a deep breath. "That must have been hard to come back from."

He could see from the Wanderer's expression that he wasn't back. Not really.

Charlie shook his head. "Well, you don't have to defend your past around me, Wanderer. I know where your heart is, and frankly I've done some things myself that I'm ashamed of."

"Thanks, Kid."

Charlie rubbed his hand thoughtfully against the smooth arm of the easy chair. "So Breck said he'd tell. Is that it?"

"That's the long and short of it. He says he'll tell the cops the truth if we make any more moves against him."

Rosa laughed. She couldn't help herself. "The cops? What do they care about the truth? Or the law, for that matter?"

"They care about money," said Errol, "and Gerard has lots of it."

"You have money, too," she pointed out.

"But Gerard has something more important than money. He runs Breck Ammunition, and Breck Ammunition supplies the police with guns and ammo."

Kid Hunter shrugged. "All right, so what if we kill him?"

Rosa scowled at the idea, but the Wanderer just laughed. "Did you know I nearly shot him dead when we were kids? I mean ... it was an accident."

The reporter raised her eyebrows. "Gun deaths often are."

"What happened?" asked Charlie, ignoring the wisecrack.

"It was back when Dad was first teaching us how to shoot. We were at a shooting range practicing with the Breck 17. It was the end of our lesson — time to unload our guns. So I ejected the magazine and handed the gun back to my Dad. I had the barrel facing Gerard. Well, I must have had my finger too close to the trigger because suddenly the gun went off. The bullet only clipped Gerard on the arm, but a few inches to the left and I would have struck him square in the chest. He would have died in an instant. So there was Gerard, writhing on the floor, wailing about his arm. Dad started screaming at me about how I forgot to check the chamber for a bullet after I ejected the clip. I couldn't speak. I was so ashamed at what I'd done."

Errol's expression turned grim. "Lately, I've been wondering what might have happened if Gerard had died then."

"That's neither here nor there," replied Rosa, shaking her head. "Assassinating Gerard Breck now isn't going to get you the company back."

Errol nodded. "You're probably right."

For a long time, they sat in sepulchral silence. Charlie couldn't take it anymore. "So what, we give in to that lunatic's demands?"

The Wanderer shook his head. "No. We'll figure out another way."

Rosa looked up in surprise. "Even if you have to reveal the truth?"

"I reckon it's about time I faced up to it. Just have to decide the right way."

"So we get in front of the story!" she exclaimed. "Errol, I've got an idea! Let me tell your story."

The men looked at her. Errol beat Charlie to asking what she meant.

"Before Gerard can go to the police, I'll tell your story in *The New West*. We'll spoil his threat and get the American people on your side!"

"Heh," he said. "You really think that will work?"

"Errol, I've been getting hundreds of thousands of hits on my articles about you. Not only that, but a lot of people are writing in. They think the Wanderer is a true American hero!"

It sounded pretty good to Charlie, but his partner took this all in without a flicker of emotion.

"Will they still think the Wanderer is a hero when they learn what I did?" asked Errol.

"I do. Charlie does."

Kid Hunter offered a thumbs-up.

The Wanderer still looked uncertain.

"All we have to do," said Rosa, holding out her hands like the scales of Lady Justice, "is put the truth against the context of you roaming the West saving lives. We'll let the people decide whether you're a good man or not."

The Wanderer stroked the long stubble on his chin. "I reckon that might work, but we'd have to act fast. The police could still arrest me as long as Gerard's in charge of the company. My original plan was to go to the board and convince them to vote to have me replace Gerard as CEO. We'll have to time this article to come out just before the vote." He sighed. "I don't know. Kid, what do you think?"

Charlie grinned, "I think you're going to need someone to watch your back."

CHAPTER THIRTY

A Job is a Job.

The Wanderer entered a Greco-Roman paradise of olive trees, painted urns, and marble columns. Clashing with the classical ambience were neon-lit slot machines that dinged loudly over the groans of the clientele.

He consulted a map on his smart lens to guide him through the labyrinth of the Olympia casino. After following the winding trail for nearly ten minutes, Errol found Cornelius Boone in a small conference room used for breakout business sessions.

The casino's owner and Breck Ammunition's board chairman bided his time in one of eight chairs around a circular wooden table. He wore a pink collared shirt with ivory snaps and sleeves rolled up to the elbows. A bolo tie featuring a bald eagle on turquoise tightened the old man's collar. Behind him, a nude Aphrodite gazed hungrily, as if she might pounce out of the mural.

Boone sprang to his feet at the sight of Errol, beaming as if the gunman had come in carrying a full plate of Texas barbecue. They pumped hands, then Boone followed up with an even stronger hug. "Well if it isn't Errol Breck! What a fine sight you make on a Thursday morning!"

"It's been a long time, Corny," said Errol as the two men sat across from each other. "I ... I wanted to apologize for skipping town."

The board chairman shook himself as if trying to wake from a nightmare. "I'm sorry to say it, Errol, but it's been hell. Your stepbrother is an enormous idiot and his new gun is an expensive catastrophe! He's going to ruin the business and destroy everything your father worked for."

Errol nodded gravely. "Did you know he's giving guns to the Red Stripe Gang in exchange for favors?"

Boone paled, which was a feat for such an old, white man. "We saw the reports in *The New West*, but Gerard denied —"

Errol's eyes darkened. "Gerard is a liar."

The chairman took a long, acknowledging breath through his nostrils, and looked hard at the Wanderer. "I trust you're here to rectify the situation?"

Errol dropped his elbows on the table and clasped his fingers. "I'm ready to take over the company, if you'll have me."

Boone's giddy expression made it clear that he'd been waiting to boot Gerard out on his ass for quite a long time. "You'll have my vote, and I have no doubt the rest of the board will agree."

Errol smiled. He didn't think it would be this easy, but apparently Gerard had done most of the convincing for him already. "What do we need to do to make it happen?"

"I'll call the board together for a meeting tomorrow. I'll have to invite Gerard, of course, as he's an executive director, but we won't explain the purpose of the meeting — or that we have a guest of honor — until he arrives."

Errol raised his eyebrows. He wondered how Gerard would react when he discovered the world crashing around him. Probably not well.

"I'd recommend carrying protection, just in case things go sour," Errol warned. "Gerard knows I'm in town. He already thinks I might try something like this, and he's resorting to blackmail to keep me from going through with it."

Boone flashed his pearly whites, followed by a Lassiter. "You know me, Errol. I keep myself well protected. But I'll let the rest of the board know to be on their toes. But what's this about blackmail? Nothing bad, I hope?"

He shrugged his shoulders. "It's … about how my wife died … and why I left. I'm dealing with it. We're going to preempt Gerard with a full reveal in *The New West* blog tomorrow. I hope it won't change your mind about me, but if it does, I'll gladly hand the company over to someone else. So long as Gerard doesn't get to keep it."

Boone laughed. "Oh, you don't have to worry about that, my boy. I don't know if there's anything that could convince me to leave the company with that fool."

*

Gerard put down the phone and poured himself another glass of whiskey. The board had scheduled an emergency meeting for the next day. That was highly unusual.

There was a smudge on his tablet. He opened the top drawer of his oak desk and took out a microfiber cloth folded into fours. He opened it carefully and rubbed it against the glass. When he finished, he folded it neatly back the way it was, placed it in the corner of the drawer, and closed the desk. Then he downed the whiskey in one swig and poured himself another.

Gerard tensed up. He'd heard a whisper.

"Gerry," it said.

Gerard spun around in his chair and looked up, aghast, at the portrait of Al Breck.

"This is no good, Gerry. No good at all."

The CEO swung the chair back to the desk, grabbed his drink, and spun back to the painting. The eyes of Al Breck watched him. There was something disapproving in the old man's visage.

"I'm not doing anything wrong! I'm making all the right decisions! I'm building Breck Ammunition's next great gun!"

"The board doesn't think so," said the ghost. "What will they do if you don't make a profit?"

"I'm going to make a profit!" screamed Gerard, slamming the glass tumbler on the table. He hated that the apparition had asked that. Always doubting him!

"What about your debt to the Red Stripe Gang?" Al asked.

"I'm taking care of that!"

"You're lucky they let you out of Union."

"The Gang *needs* me."

The ghost didn't reply. For a while, Gerard just stared into the eyes of the portrait.

"If only Errol …" whispered the ghost.

Gerard clenched the whiskey glass so hard, it looked like it might shatter in his hands. "If only Errol *what*?"

The ghost said nothing.

"I get it! You think that Errol would know what to do! You think that he would run the company better than me. Is that it? So what are you saying? Do you suggest I go find him and beg him to come help me? Is that what you suggest? 'Oh, please, brother dear, I just can't do anything without *you*!'"

The ghost said nothing, but Gerard was already on his feet and yelling. "I don't need Errol! He's not better than me! And you're not supposed to take his side!"

It happened before he even realized what he was doing. He was holding the glass, and then his hand came forward, and the glass — well, it must have slipped. There was a heavy crash as it smashed against the portrait of Al Breck, embedding splinters of glass in the canvas.

Gerard looked with horror at his shaking hands. He hadn't been this angry since the day of the car accident. He'd been so careful to watch his temper.

The paint began to run on the portrait of Albert Breck.

"Dad!" Gerard cried, grabbing the microfiber cloth from his desk and dashing over to the painting. He kicked away the broken glass and ice cubes on the floor, climbed onto the bookshelf and reached up to press the cloth against his stepfather's head. But it only seemed to make things worse.

*

"Daddy, I'm so sorry. I didn't know what I was doing! I'm sorry! I'm so sorry, Daddy, I'm so sorry —"

Elza shook her head at the live security camera footage of Gerard collapsing onto his knees and sobbing like a baby. She had it streaming on her computer, which was located only a few feet from the entrance to his office.

She leaned back luxuriantly in her chair, a comfortable, webbed thing made of black plastic mesh. She felt a little bad — maybe. Gerard was the one who had recognized her talent, given her a real job. She had been dealing cards at the casino for the high rollers when a man in a sharp black suit and carefully trimmed mustache had sat down by himself to play. He didn't introduce himself, but she knew exactly who he was.

"You're the most gorgeous thing I've seen all night," Gerard had said after several rounds. "Why are you working here?"

Playing up her exotic way of speaking, she had replied, "What is it that they say? A job is a job."

He had asked about her accent and why she had come to America. She'd made up something about looking for streets paved with gold. The funny thing was that Breck was terrible at blackjack and kept losing money. Even so, he'd continued to spend. He'd said it was so she wouldn't get in trouble for talking to a customer. Finally, Gerard had told her his name. He'd said that he had a senior role at America's gun company, and that he wanted her to be his assistant. And just like that, her destiny had revealed itself.

Gerard had never asked her to dress provocatively; she'd understood the need to look good for clients. She'd suggested that he dominate her in public and she encouraged the leers of potential business partners. It was all part of the show, and together they were brilliant. Their rise to the top office at Breck Ammunition was inevitable. Errol had never had a chance.

Elza stroked her forehead, felt the deep scar left by that bitch Rosa Veras in Union. It was not long after meeting the reporter that things had begun to unravel. Veras had exposed their dealings with the Red Stripe Gang, and now that coward Errol had resurfaced and wanted to save the company from Gerard. Elza knew it would not be not long before the board would welcome the prodigal son with open arms. Gerard was done for, and where would that leave things for her? She was not willing to let Errol throw out years of careful planning.

She allowed herself a deep breath. It was okay. She accepted it. She'd gambled on one horse for too long. Gerard had taken her far, but now it was time to cut her losses.

CHAPTER THIRTY-ONE

Very, Very Lucky.

The bouncer at Wild West Casino refused to let Errol come in wearing a smart lens. The Wanderer responded by showing him his Lassiter, and soon they agreed on a compromise. He wouldn't wear the eyeglass, but he could keep it in his pocket. This was under the condition that if the cameras caught him putting it back on — or even so much as taking it out — he would be kicked out immediately.

"I guess I should've told you," Kid Hunter said over the din of slot machine bells that came rushing to greet them as soon as they stepped inside. "For real, did you think you could wear that in? You ever been in a casino before?"

Errol shrugged. "Never really saw the point."

Rosie laughed. "What kind of cowboy are you?"

"A rich one."

"Trust me," advised Kid Hunter, "if you're going to cheat, there are subtler ways."

The policy made sense, but removing the eyeglass made Errol feel even more naked. Rosie, God bless her, wouldn't let them leave the house until both men had shaved the fuzz off their faces.

That wasn't so bad, but then she'd demanded that he change his clothes, too. So here he was, wearing a chocolate suit and a crisp, powder-blue shirt that was unbuttoned at the collar. At least she'd let him keep his grey Stetson.

The Wanderer thought he smelled a farm animal, but couldn't locate it in the artificial desert that was the Wild West Casino. There were cacti everywhere and the floor was dusty like a dirt road. A lot of the restaurants and stores inside had names beginning with "Ye Olde." The buxom waitresses were all dressed as cowgirls. The casino piped in music from old Westerns. Currently, it was the whistling theme from *The Good, the Bad and the Ugly*.

"All they need is the cow shit," Errol commented dryly.

The others seemed amused. Errol had to say, though, that the constant ringing of bells and blaring of electronic melodies from the gambling machines somewhat undermined the theme. The clientele was also typical Vegas. A smattering of slick twenty-somethings in expensive suits or tight-fitting dresses surrounded the craps tables, while the slot machines were dominated by ladies who looked as though they'd taken a few too many turns at the buffet.

It had been the Kid's idea to go out for the night, a last chance to let off some steam before the board vote to oust Gerard. Things were bound to change after that. Errol hoped it would be peaceful, but deep down he knew his stepbrother would not bow out easily. Also, if he did manage to win back the company, Errol would have new responsibilities, and he wasn't sure how much he'd see Rosie and Kid Hunter anymore.

The trio headed straight to the blackjack tables. It was the one game they all felt more or less confident playing. To get there, they crossed an artificial moat onto a life-size replica of an old riverboat with four giant paddle wheels spinning in place on the back. It had three floors of card games. Kid Hunter made a move for the stairs where the casino kept the high-stakes tables, but Rosie, fine woman that she was, redirected the group to a twenty-dollar dealer instead. Errol was pleased to find at least one person in the group worried about where his money went.

He found himself stealing glances at Rosie. He'd let her borrow one of Helen's dresses, and she fit it well. It was a white thing that offered an eye-catching contrast to the reporter's deeply tanned skin. He had been thinking a lot about that kiss back in Union. They hadn't talked about it at all since it happened.

The blackjack dealer was a middle-aged Chinese-American, but the casino had him dressed as the ludicrous stereotype of a Mexican, complete with a bright pink poncho and giant sombrero. As Errol and the others settled into their seats, one of the cowgirl waitresses took drink orders — one of the few things in the casino that didn't cost a penny.

Errol drew a seven of diamonds and three of hearts the first hand, while the dealer had a jack of hearts. The Wanderer tapped the table and got a queen of hearts. With a smirk of confidence, he waved over the cards to stand at twenty points. Rosie followed with a seventeen — respectable. Laughing victoriously, Kid Hunter presented twenty-one.

The dealer turned over the queen of clubs, and Errol and Rosie groaned. That added up to twenty, which beat Rosie's hand and pushed Errol's, meaning he hadn't won nor lost.

On the next hand, Errol drew a nine of clubs and a three of diamonds, adding up to twelve. The dealer had a three of spades. A bit annoyed after the results of the last round, the Wanderer tried doubling down, but the next card to come up was a king and he busted.

"Ooh, sorry, man," commiserated Charlie.

Rosie hit a few times and ended up with nineteen. Kid Hunter got twenty-one again.

"Very lucky," said the dealer, who flipped out cards until he had eighteen.

"All right!" exclaimed Rosie.

The Wanderer finally won on his next hand, but Rosie busted. When Charlie won his third straight hand with twenty-one, the dealer looked up at the ceiling and said, "Very, very lucky."

"How you doing that?" the reporter asked.

Kid Hunter smiled at her. "I'll never tell."

A pair of heavies stepped up behind Charlie and tapped him on the shoulder. "Sir? I'm afraid we're going to have to ask you to leave."

Errol stood up. "Hey, that's my friend. What's going on here?"

"I'm sorry, sir, but your friend here appears to be breaking casino policies."

"By winning?"

"By cheating."

Kid Hunter waved Errol off. "It's okay, man. I'm feeling tired anyway. Maybe I'll just get a hamburger then call it an early night. You guys have fun!" He turned to the bouncers and handed them his recently won chips. "Here, you can have them back. I'm going."

The bouncers seemed fine with this and let him go. When he was gone, Rosie commented, "An early night? It was his idea to go out, wasn't it?"

"Hmm," responded the Wanderer, watching his partner fade into the crowd of gamblers. The Kid wasn't stupid. Something about the whole thing seemed off. A waitress carrying a margarita and a frosty bottle of dark Mexican beer interrupted his chain of thought. Well, they could still have fun without Charlie, couldn't they?

*

Charlie didn't go for a hamburger. He got in a cab and directed it off the Vegas Strip to a gentleman's club called Roxy Rox. He took a seat at the bar and ordered a whiskey with ginger ale. Liquid courage.

Roxy Rox was a dive, even for a strip club. It wasn't a place for amateurs out on a bachelor's party. Tonight's entertainers were dripping with sweat, and the male customers were practically lapping it up with their hanging tongues. The music throbbed a steady bass pulse, and the glass on the disco balls looked like it had yellowed a few shades over the last few decades. Yeah, the girls looked hot, but also pretty fresh off the boat. They'd be here only as long as it took them to get out.

Charlie stuck a machine in his ear and dialed a number on his wristband. Someone picked up but didn't say anything.

"It's Charlie. I'm back in Vegas. Roxy Rox. I'll be at the bar."

He knew from experience that business with El Tiburón couldn't wait. If he didn't deal with it now ... well, he didn't even want to think about what could happen. The tricky thing had been not involving Rosa or the Wanderer. They were chronic helpers, especially the Wanderer, and would have come looking for him if he'd gone out by himself and didn't come back for hours. But going out with them and pretending to call it an early night? He should change his name to Kid Genius.

"Can I get you another?" asked a woman with an eastern European accent.

He glanced at his empty whiskey, and then at the hottie who had spoken. She looked like a runway model. Sure, he usually liked to have a little more to hold on to, but the girl had an alluring face and a damn fine figure.

It occurred to him he was in a strip club, so it wasn't really remarkable that there was a hot girl chatting him up. She wasn't offering to buy him a drink. She was just a waitress asking him if he wanted to order one, and maybe a lap dance, too. That wasn't why he was here. "I don't have time for anything," he was sad to inform her. "Someone's meeting me soon."

The woman sidled up next to him, close enough for him to smell her exotic perfume, and took a seat on the barstool next to him. "At least buy *me* a drink then?"

Charlie covered his gaping mouth in embarrassment. Strippers didn't ask you to buy them drinks. They didn't even accept drinks if you bought one. He'd tried.

"I'm sorry, I thought you were — I mean — of course I'll get you a drink, baby! What do you like?"

"Cosmo," she said, "and you thought that I worked here. This is okay. I am not offended. I used to work here."

He imagined her writhing on a pole, that red silk dress slipping off …

"Well," he said in an attempt to snap himself out of it, "I guess I'm not surprised."

"Why? Do I seem promiscuous to you?"

He gasped. "Wait, wait, that's not what I — I just meant you've got the body for — I mean you're a fine-looking woman! You know."

She smiled. "I make you nervous. How cute."

"I ain't nervous!" he declared a bit too loudly. He pointed dramatically at the ceiling. "No one, and I mean no one, makes Kid Hunter nervous."

Summoned by his airborne finger, a bartender came by to take their order. He asked for a cosmopolitan and another whiskey on the rocks, even though he hadn't planned to have another himself. More liquid courage.

"You call yourself Kid Hunter," the woman said, rolling the name around her tongue. "Are you a stripper, too?"

He grinned. "Only when the mood is right."

Laughing, she extended a dainty hand. "I'm Miranda."

"Charlie. So, I take it you found your way out of this dump?"

"I never planned to stay. I arrived in this country poor. At first, I had to take whatever job I could get. Exotic dancing was easy to break into but *so hard* to keep up."

Miranda leaned forward, giving Charlie a salivating glimpse down her front.

"On some nights I would meet a nice guy, say … a young man out for his bachelor's party. He would be too shy to even touch me. I could stand clients like that. It was cute. It was the regulars who were trouble — the career gamblers and the Red Stripers. Those men are not real men."

The drinks arrived, and Charlie took a long sip.

"The benefit of this line of work is that, if you are good, you make connections," she said.

"Oh yeah, I've heard good things about those stripper networking meet-ups."

Miranda laughed and smacked him lightly on the arm. "You kid, but it is true. I made connections, which I used to get a job at the Olympia Casino as a blackjack dealer. I was good at this job, too. The cards flew in and out of my hands like a magic trick, and I had a sharp eye for spotting cheaters. After only a month, the boss moved me up from the cheap tables to the high rollers."

Charlie was about to say something clever when he noticed a scar on her forehead. She'd obviously tried to cover it with makeup, but when the light struck her face the right way it was visible. She saw him looking and turned away blushing.

"What happened?" he asked, all of the previous humor drained from his voice.

"Oh ... my boss. He —" She pointed to his whiskey. "He threw a glass at me."

Charlie was appalled. "He what? Who is he?"

"It does not matter."

He thought about the selfless way in which the Wanderer helped people he barely knew, fighting because it was the right thing to do. He put his hand on Miranda's shoulder. "It does matter. I can help you. Just tell me his name."

She bent over and kissed him on the lips. When she began to move away, he pulled her back for more.

"Well, well, Charlie! Caught yourself a real fine fish tonight!"

The newcomer flashed a mouthful of teeth filed into sharp points. It was Cochise, the top dog of El Tiburón. He wore a muscle shirt and jeans, and kept his black hair short and spiky.

Charlie let go of Miranda. "Sorry, baby, but I've got to go with this friendly fellow for a little while. It won't take long. You planning to stay a while?"

She licked her lips. "Depends how quick you are."

"I'm only quick when I want to be, baby. With girls like you? I like to take my time."

Cochise squeezed the Kid's arm. He looked absolutely disgusted. "You are testing my patience."

"Oh shit, I'm sorry," said Charlie, accenting the apology with a high-pitched laugh. "I'm sorry you had to see how a *real man* does it."

The hit man's wolflike eyes cut away at his confidence. Cochise seethed, "Enjoy it while you can."

*

Rosa perceived a glorious blur of lights as she ran down the Strip with Errol in close pursuit. Blackjack had been good. She'd broken even. With all the free-and-oh-so-refreshing margaritas, that was a win in her book. She wondered why she'd ever thought this place was so dangerous. Maybe there was a seedy underbelly somewhere, but here on the Strip, all she saw was life, fun, and music.

A blast of brass called her toward a club with a green neon sign blinking *Salsa! Salsa!* Without asking, she pulled Errol by the wrist.

"What are we doing?" he asked with a tipsy smile.

"Why, dancing, of course!"

The trumpets gave a royal welcome as they entered the warm club. Red and yellow lights washed over a mob of couples doing the salsa. The band bobbed with the music, lost in a sea of bliss. She felt her heart adjust to the tempo of the spicy beat.

Errol looked unsure. "Do you know how to dance?"

She smiled. "My mother taught me when I was little. But I've never been to a place like this. C'mon, it's easy!"

Soon they were in the thick of the dance floor doing the two-step. Errol leaned into her ear and whispered, "I have a secret talent."

She gave him a puzzled look as he shifted his hands, swung a leg back, and performed an expert turn. On the return, he held up his hand and moved her to mirror the move.

"You can salsa!" she exclaimed, feeling warm in the cheeks as they joined palms and continued the dance. "Since when?"

"I took classes with …"

He cut off the sentence, but she knew who he was going to say. Frowning slightly, she said, "I'm having a lot of fun tonight, Errol."

He stepped forward and they locked eyes. "I'm glad you came home with me."

She couldn't believe how well he cleaned up. Beneath all that stubble, it turned out Errol had smooth skin and a square jaw. She thought the chocolate suit was a nice change from all the flannel and dusty jeans, too. Something kept eating at her though. Before they'd all gone out, Errol had said this might be the last night they'd have for any fun. Tomorrow, they would make their move against Gerard, and nothing would be the same afterward.

She asked him the question rattling around her brain. "You're going to kill him, aren't you?"

As she stepped forward, Errol stepped back. "If I have to."

He stepped forward. and she stepped back. She reminded herself that Gerard was a bad man. He'd tried to kill her. The Wanderer *should* kill him. But how could she reconcile this against the peace she was trying to achieve in *The New West*?

*

A left hook crashed hard into the side of Kid Hunter's head. He was tied to a metal chair by his arms and legs in a small, dark room. There was a sheet of black glass in front of him, but he couldn't see through it. His only company was Cochise, and he didn't much care for the kind of company that Cochise provided.

Kid Hunter quipped, "Funny, I thought you'd be right-handed, being a right-hand man and all."

A right hook struck Charlie across the cheek.

"Yep," he coughed. "Definitely a lefty."

Truth was, he was just happy Cochise hadn't hit him on his upper arm, which was still sore from the lone wolf attack in the mountains. It was healing up, and he didn't want to risk opening up the wound again and ruining another of his good shirts.

He had to believe the punishment couldn't go on much longer. They had kept him here a while now, though he wasn't sure how long. First, they'd left him alone with his thoughts for what felt like hours, then Cochise had come in and started punching the shit out of him. He hoped that hot girl at the club would wait for him.

Cochise reached back for another punch, but the voice of God stopped him. "Enough."

The voice came from all directions and the sound was low and garbled, most likely sent through a filter. Kid Hunter stared at the black glass, behind which he guessed El Tiburón was sitting. He couldn't say he was surprised. He'd never seen El Tiburón before, never even heard his voice on the phone. They usually communicated by text. Charlie knew a few other bounty hunters who had done jobs for El Tiburón. None of them had ever met him, either.

Cochise relaxed and began to massage one of his own palms. No one spoke, so Charlie took the initiative. "Look, man, let's just cut to the chase. You're pissed because I didn't kill the Wanderer."

El Tiburón laughed, which through the voice filter sounded halfway between a hyena and an electric can opener. "I don't care about the Wanderer. This is about you not doing what I asked. You see, the success of my operation depends on my people doing the jobs I have hired them to do. If we get jobs and do not finish them, people will stop giving us jobs. Do you understand?"

"I get that, I get that. And that's why I'm resigning. I failed, right? So I won't do another job."

There was a deathly silence followed by a crackle of static. "That is … not exactly how things work around here. When our bounty hunters fail, you see, they do not *live* to do another job."

*

On the next rotation, Errol let go of Rosie's hands, and another man caught her. He was a slimy fellow with a Hawaiian shirt and slicked-back blond hair. He carried what looked like a Breck 17 semiautomatic in his hip holster. Errol was surprised to see Rosie take the exchange in step.

"Hey!" yelled the Wanderer, now standing by himself in the middle of the dance floor. Either the jerk didn't hear him or had chosen to ignore him, so he grabbed him by the shoulder. "Hey, Slick!"

"Hands off, I just want a quick turn with the *señorita*," the other man said.

Errol looked helplessly at Rosie, who shrugged back at him. To his annoyance, she didn't seem to mind.

"All right," growled Errol, pointing to the bar. "I'm gonna get a drink."

Someone bumped into him on the way off the dance floor, and he yelled for them to get out of the way. People were giving him funny looks now, but he pushed them aside and made it out.

"Beer — darkest one you've got," Errol instructed the bartender. He had to shout to be heard over the brass band. Instead of getting the beer, the bartender spoke back. The Wanderer leaned over the bar, asking him to repeat it.

"I said we don't got anything dark," the bartender said.

"Well then, what've you got?"

"Corona, Coors, Bud, and Miller Light."

Fucking hell. "Corona, then, and it better have a lime in it!"

The Wanderer took the beer to a railing that overlooked the

dance floor. He took a swig and wiped his mouth. Even with the lime, the beer still tasted like piss — citrus piss. He let the bottle drop to his side and stared at the mob. Part of him had hoped Rosie would make an excuse and join him at the bar, but she was still out there dancing with Slick. He tried watching the band — a big outfit featuring two trumpets, a trombone, bass guitarist, drummer, and three singers. But he couldn't focus. The cry of the horns, which had felt so welcoming on the way into the club, now sounded like a discordant mess. The Wanderer guzzled the rest of the Corona and slapped the empty onto a nearby table.

He cut and weaved through the dancers much more quickly than he had on his way to the bar. He grabbed Slick by the shoulder and pulled him away from his dance partner. "Think you've had long enough."

Slick's face turned red as he smacked the Wanderer's arm. "I told you to keep your hands off me!"

"And I say you've had long enough!" Errol swung back his fist and smashed it into the dead center of Slick's ugly mug. The dancers nearby spread out to give them space. Cursing, Slick wiped the blood off his nose. Errol saw the other man reach for his hip holster, but he got his Lassiter out quicker. "If that's how you want to play it," growled the Wanderer. "Why don't we take this outside?"

Slick gave a macho nod and headed toward an emergency exit in the back. Errol started to follow, but Rosie stopped him with a forceful hand on his chest.

"What do you think you doing?"

"Protecting your honor."

"Protecting my ..." Reproachfully, she placed her hands on her hips. "Looks to me like you're protecting your own damn honor!"

Slick stepped through the exit, probably figuring he was right behind him. Errol looked down at the Lassiter in his left hand. He always called it the good gun, but how was he planning to use it? Go outside and have a duel with a stranger? Slick wasn't like the other men he shot — what had his crime been?

He holstered the revolver, but the other dancers maintained their distance. "You're right. I'm sorry, Rosie."

She nodded slowly with crossed arms.

He held out his hands in defeat. "Do you want to dance some more?"

Rosie looked wistfully at the other couples and sighed. "I think we better go back. Charlie could probably use the company anyway."

*

"Whoa, whoa, whoa!" exclaimed Charlie. "Okay, how about this. I *don't* resign. Instead, I'll be all like, 'No, no, I'm sorry! Please let me keep my job!' But then, what you do, is you just go ahead and fire me anyway! Real cold, you know? Then I still get to walk out, but you get to tell everyone how awful I am, and how satisfying it felt to give me the ax! And I'll never even ask you for a reference! In fact, if my next employer calls you up, you get to tell them how terrible I am!"

The voice of El Tiburón groaned mechanically. "Cochise ... would you please?"

With a coyote grin, Cochise clasped his hands together into a ball, swung back, and slammed his hands devastatingly into Kid Hunter's belly. The force of the blow knocked him over backward and the metal chair clanged against the hard ground. Charlie tried sucking in oxygen but found he couldn't breathe.

"If you are done with the joking, perhaps we can make a deal," said El Tiburón. "While I should kill you, you have always been one of my best men. In job after job, you have done the work swiftly and discretely. This fuckup, to be fair, is your first fuckup."

Charlie could feel himself regaining his breath. Slowly, the oxygen was getting in again. Cochise leaned over and pulled him back up with the chair.

El Tiburón continued. "I can also understand your desire to leave this life behind. You are not the first mercenary to feel burned out, you know. Even Cochise goes on vacation."

The spiky-haired thug looked slightly miffed to be mentioned in this light but held his tongue.

Charlie narrowed his eyes. "I don't want a *vacation*. I want *out*."

"You will take some time off. How about … six months? And then, if you still feel the same way, you can resign. But I do not think you will."

Charlie didn't believe it would be so easy, but the suspension would at least give him a little time to figure things out. Still, something didn't smell right. "So, you're just going to let me go?"

"Yes, with a catch. You may have your break, but no matter what you decide, I will need one more job. You failed your last job. This means you owe me a success."

He had to smile. Figured. "Even if that was all right with me, I don't have the time right now for —"

"I don't *have* this job for you yet. But one day, I will. And when I do, you will take it. You will do this job for me, and then you may go to Disney World."

"Sounds fun, I admit, but what if I don't agree to these terms?"

"You die."

"Right! That makes sense! Okay, I agree."

El Tiburón directed Cochise to untie him. The thug brought him to the exit and gave him a push out into a dark alley.

"Hey, man, can you give me a ride back to the club?"

Cochise pulled the door shut and was gone. Charlie heard a woman's scream a few blocks away, followed by the crack of a rifle. With a sigh, he pulled up his wristband and called for a cab.

*

A river of headlights surged by Rosa and Errol on the Strip, but none of them were the limousine. She thought the desert was supposed to cool at night, but the city of Vegas seemed to trap the heat. A drunk woman staggering down the sidewalk brushed shoulders with her, spilled some of her cocktail on the concrete, and squawked in outrage. As always, the Wanderer leaped to Rosa's protection, and the gal moved on.

Rosa was anxious to write her article on him and move onto something else. She wasn't happy with how little she'd managed to write for *The New West* over the last week. Yes, she had a perfectly good excuse, but the readers didn't know that. The blog might be getting a lot of traffic at the moment, but so do Internet memes. If she didn't keep writing fresh content, the audience would vanish and move on. They would forget about her.

Errol was staring regretfully at something on her dress. Glancing down, she noticed that some of the drink had reached her and left an orange stain on the smooth white fabric. However, this didn't bother her. Maybe because she knew the dress wasn't hers; it belonged to a ghost. The truth was she'd felt weird all night wearing it and couldn't wait to change.

She felt weighted down by Errol's beseeching eyes, wanting something from her but not getting it. It was something she needed to talk to him about.

*

Charlie hadn't really thought Miranda would wait for him, but he saw her almost as soon as he entered Roxy Rox. She'd had a few more drinks, obviously, because when she saw him she went off like a firecracker, jumping into his arms and kissing him hard on the mouth.

"It's good to see you, too," he said.

Into his ear, she whispered, "Let's go back to my place."

She was all over him in the taxi. The cabbie seemed annoyed, but it didn't bother Charlie one bit. When they reached their destination, Miranda led Charlie into a large mirrored elevator that he was astounded to find opened directly inside of her pad. She had a penthouse fitted out with a leather sofa, mahogany bookshelves, and a giant television. This girl was just full of surprises.

"You said you used to work as a stripper?" he asked as she handed him a glass of champagne.

"You could say I am living the American dream."

"Cheers to that." They clinked glasses. "But what I was really getting at was —"

"I know what it is you are getting at," she said, downing the champagne in one gulp. She took him by the arm and led him to the bedroom.

*

When the sex was over, Elza pulled up the silk sheet and let it fall airily over their naked bodies. She smiled at the satisfaction on Charlie's lips.

"Damn, girl," he said.

He was cute, this one. "What is it they say? You are not so bad yourself. But you know, we forgot to turn off the lights."

The bounty hunter's soft brown eyes settled on her own. "Maybe I like seeing you."

Of course, he did not see Elza, really. He saw a pretty and helpless girl named Miranda, who needed to be saved. Elza did not need saving.

"Did I hurt you?" she asked.

"I can handle it, baby," Charlie replied.

"No, I mean because of your arm."

He looked at the bandages dismissively. "Oh, that's barely anything. Anyway, I've been numbing it pretty good. If you bumped it, I didn't feel a thing."

As she cuddled up to him and brought her head closer, she felt him tense up. "What is it?" she asked.

"You never told me who your boss was." He stroked the scar on her forehead. "The one who did this to you."

"It does not matter."

His face grew serious. "Please, Miranda. I want to know."

She sighed. It was time. "It was Gerard Breck."

His jaw dropped. "Like Breck Ammunition, Gerard Breck?"

"Yes."

Charlie sat up straight and pushed himself off the bed. He started pacing around the room, looking desperately for something on the ground.

"What are you doing?" she asked.

"Looking for my pants," he said, pausing to look at her. "Why didn't you tell me it was Gerard Breck? Fuck!"

"What does it matter who he is? He hurt me, Charlie. He threw a glass at my face. I was bleeding all over the carpet!" The image appeared to freeze him in his tracks, so she continued. "I don't remember much after that. I fell … and when I awoke, he was gone."

He looked upset. "You don't understand. I'm … friends with Gerard's brother."

Elza produced her best look of confusion. "Errol? But he has been gone for —"

"He's back. We're going to — shit, I shouldn't be telling you any of this. I've got to go."

Elza slithered out of the sheets, flipping herself so that she was lying naked on her stomach with her face toward Charlie at the foot of the bed. She reached gently for his lithe thighs and looked him directly in the eyes.

"I …" he said, swallowing as she lifted the hand farther up his leg.

"Is Errol going to kill his brother?" she whispered.

"I don't know. He's going to the board tomorrow to force a vote and — damn that feels good — take back the company."

"And will they let him?"

"The board's already on his side. Gerard doesn't know about it."

She pulled her hand away. "You know Errol shot his wife, yes?"

He gasped. "Yeah, but he said it was an accident."

"Not entirely. He was set up."

"What do you mean? Gerard?"

She nodded. "Errol was in line to get the company after Al Breck died. The board was not going to even consider Gerard. His only choice was to eliminate Errol from the equation. So he hired a hit man to break into the Breck Estate and kill him. It was supposed to look like a house burglary."

"But Errol killed the hit man first —"

"And his wife, also."

Charlie covered his mouth with his hand.

"There is a saying in this country that the ends are more important than the means, yes? Helen was not meant to die. But when she died, Errol abandoned the company and left town. The board had no choice but to make his stepbrother the CEO."

"How do you know this?"

"When you work for a man like Gerard Breck, you learn things. And he has never been good at keeping secrets."

Charlie started pulling his pants on again. "I've got to go tell Errol."

Elza pushed herself up off her stomach and sat up on her knees so that he could see the full front of her body. "It is late, Charlie. Stay with me. You can tell him in the morning."

He froze in his tracks. Charlie's hands loosened and he dropped his clothing back on the floor.

"Yeah," he said, drawing toward her. "I guess it can wait 'til morning."

She pulled him on top of her and nibbled his neck. When she could tell he couldn't take any more of this, she whispered into his ear, "Will you kill him for me? Gerard, I mean."

He looked at her gravely. "I think I'm going to have to."

She reached down and pulled him in.

CHAPTER THIRTY-TWO

The Truth?

The Wanderer watched as Kid Hunter pressed a paper bag into the security camera. "Anyone home?" came his voice over the intercom. The bounty hunter was standing outside the front gate. "I've got bagels!"

"Look who the cat dragged in," said Errol, pressing a button to open the gate.

On his way to Rosie, he stopped at a hallway mirror, an antique oval with gilded edges that had been with his family for generations. He had on a fresh, blue plaid shirt and was happy to see some stubble returning to his chin. Errol patted down a cowlick in his dusty brown hair before moving on.

He found the reporter in the kitchen, attempting to find ingredients that could conceivably be turned into breakfast. He knew it was no easy task. He hadn't lived in the Breck Estate for many months, they hadn't made a trip to the grocery store, and Errol hadn't gotten around to letting the help know he'd moved back in. "I reckon you can give up. The Kid's back, and it looks like he's brought breakfast."

Rosa sighed with relief and commenced a new task of closing

all the cabinet doors she'd opened during her search. "I did find some coffee at least," she said, pointing at the percolating filter. "So, there's that."

"Mm-hmm," he said. "Smells real nice."

They took seats across from each other at the wooden table, the same one where he'd argued with Gerard the previous day. Rosie was back in comfortable clothes — jeans and a green Nike T-shirt — but the way the cloth fell over her breasts still caught Errol's eye. He took a deep breath and said what he wanted to say. "Rosie, I'm real sorry for last night ..."

"We never talked about what happened in Union. You came to save me, and I ... I don't know. You're a handsome man, Errol, and you've got a heart of gold. You've become one of my best friends, but ... I don't think it can be any more than that."

He felt a hard lump forming in the back of his throat, preventing him from making a case for himself.

She continued. "It's just ... you believe in that Lassiter of yours, and well, as hokey as it sounds, I believe in peace. I want to keep fighting for peace. I want to keep writing *The New West*. Anyway, when you take back Breck Ammo, how's it going to look if we're —? And then there's Helen. She still haunts you, doesn't she?"

She was right, but he'd be lying if he said it didn't hurt. "I've been thinking about how I almost went out and shot that man last night. For so long I've been thinking of my semiautomatic as the bad gun because it's the one that shot Helen. But last night I nearly shot a man with the Lassiter just because I was jealous."

He unstrapped his gun belt and placed it on the table. "Maybe there is no good gun, Rosie. Maybe there's just me."

She smiled warmly. "You're a good man, Errol. I've always known it. That's why I've been writing about you in my blog — so everyone else can see what I see."

He took a deep breath. "That reminds me, there's something else I've been thinking about."

She laughed. "Sounds like you've been thinking quite a lot."

"When this is all over, I want to help you expand *The New West*."

She raised her eyebrows. "How do you mean?"

"You know my family owns *Our Times*, right? Well, I know they fired you, but how would you feel going back to work as the editor-in-chief? You could still write, but you'd also have people to give assignments."

She appeared speechless at the offer. He couldn't tell if that was a yes or no, and so he asked her.

"I … I need to think about it."

He was perplexed. What was there to think about?

*

She found it difficult to explain why she couldn't just go ahead and accept the offer. It was an amazing offer. There was so much she could do with the budget of a national newspaper. In addition, she would get the chance to reform *Our Times* and maybe turn it into something respectable, something better for the American readers. She guessed the hurdle was how the newspaper could be run independently if its principle source of funding was America's gun company. No matter how much editorial control Errol gave her, in the end it would still be Breck Ammunition writing her paychecks.

Errol waved his hand dismissively. "You could write what you want. I'd keep out of your way."

She frowned. Were good intentions enough? "I don't know. Just give me a little time?"

He shrugged. "Well, no reason to get too excited anyway. We still have to deal with my stepbrother."

"Or you *could* get excited," suggested Charlie, strutting into the room, "because Kid Hunter is back and he's got bagels!" The Kid poured a dozen of the savory beauties from the brown bag onto the table, and spread several packets of cream cheese over the table as if they were playing cards.

The sleight of hand failed to keep Rosa from noticing the bruising on Charlie's cheek. "What happened to you?"

The Kid paused like he was unsure how to answer that.

"I reckon it's not that hard a question," prodded Errol.

Eventually, Charlie answered, "I needed to go sort out things with El Tiburón."

Errol glared. "You went alone?"

It looked like Charlie had taken more than a few hard punches to the face. "El Tiburón did this to you?" Rosa asked.

Charlie explained. "El Tiburón was the one who asked me to kill the Wanderer. I never completed the job, obviously, and I want out of the mercenary life. So I went to see him to, uh, clear the air."

"And did you?" asked Rosa in disbelief.

"Yup," he said. "Totes."

She wasn't convinced. "Why did it take all night?"

A sneaky grin popped onto the Kid Hunter's face. "Well, I also kind of met someone."

Rosa guffawed. "Only in Vegas can you get beat up by a mob boss and score with some bimbo on the same night. Who is she?"

Charlie looked hurt. "She's not a bimbo. As a matter of fact, through the miracle of coincidence, she gave us a great lead. See, she works for Gerard Breck."

The revelation sucked all the oxygen out of the room until, in unison, Rosa and Errol exclaimed, "Elza?"

"Who? What? No! Her name is Miranda. She doesn't work for him anymore — Gerard hit her pretty hard with a glass. He left a scar —"

"On her forehead?" Rosa completed for him.

Kid Hunter shut up.

"And was she thin and pretty? And did she have an accent?"

Charlie cringed. "How do you know all this?"

Rosa exploded, "Because you got *screwed* by Elza! She's the bitch who got me fired from *Our Times*, and then helped Gerard nearly cut off my fingers!"

"But the scar …" Charlie replied shakily.

"*Gerard* didn't do that to her," said Rosa, holding her forehead in exasperation. "*I* did back in Union. That's from when she was trying to run away from us, and I tripped her!"

"You?" yelped Kid Hunter. "Oh … shit."

She took a deep breath. "Did you tell her anything?"

"Uh, well …"

"Charlie!"

"Look, I might have told her our whole plan, but —"

She nearly smacked him. Kid Hunter appeared to anticipate this and held up his hands defensively. "Look, maybe she lied about her name and how she got the scar, but I still really don't think she's on Gerard's side."

Rosa rolled her eyes and stood up to leave. "Well, my article is ready to go. I better publish immediately. If we're lucky, it won't be too late."

She lingered in the room as Errol, who had been absorbing the exchange with cold fury, suddenly spoke up to berate his partner. "Kid, what do you mean you don't think she's working with Gerard? Because of one night of bliss?"

"No, no! Because, because ... she told me the truth about Helen."

Errol paled. "The truth?"

"Man, I'm sorry to be the one to tell you, but Gerard set you up! That wasn't no burglar who invaded your house. He was a hit man! Your stepbrother hired him to kill you so he could have the company. If he hadn't sent him —!"

"Helen might still be alive," finished Errol. His expression turned to stone and he seemed to pale several shades.

Rosa looked at him with worry. It sounded plausible, even if it had come from Elza.

"Errol ..." she said, touching his hand.

But Errol was gone. There was something different about his eyes, something cold as ice, and the reporter knew what he planned to do. There was no doubt now. No matter what happened at the board meeting, the Wanderer was going to kill Gerard Breck.

CHAPTER THIRTY-THREE

Riders!

Ben Martin woke up in a canopy bed designed in the colonial style of the first American presidents. He searched the bedside table on the left for a clock. Not finding one there, he checked the other side of the king-size mattress and happened upon a fancy digital tablet with the time: 11:30 a.m. That was a lot later than expected. He had tossed and turned for most of the night, which he reckoned was a combination of sleeping in an unfamiliar place and the aftermath of nearly two days of drunken celebration. Must have finally gotten some real sleep a little after sunrise.

Stepping into the hallway, Martin nearly collided with Elroy Wolfe. He used to be an officer on the Liberty police force and was about ten years Martin's junior.

"Good morning, Sheriff!" Wolfe greeted brightly. "We're all up on the roof. Why don't you grab a beer and join us?"

Martin confessed that was one order he didn't mind taking from a subordinate. He went downstairs for a couple cans of Bud, then huffed his way up to the roof of the mayor's mansion. The other six militiamen were stretched out in blue directors' chairs and white beach recliners. It was a hot, clear day, and they had a glorious panorama view of the town of Liberty surrounded by red mountains.

Martin cracked open one of the Buds and eased himself into one of the empty plastic beds. Maybe he was still a little tired. It felt good to lie back in the sun. He sipped his beer and listened to the others chirp about the militia's progress toward restoring Liberty to its former glory.

He reckoned he could declare himself mayor now that White was dead. He'd turn the militia into a real police force, using his own taxes to pay for it. There'd be law again, and no one would be allowed to come in and make trouble. Not even the Wanderer!

Martin drained the rest of his beer and tossed it behind him. "We should invite Joe over," he said to the group. "He's been stuck at the station with that dumb lawyer since … what's today again?"

"Friday," someone answered.

"Friday? Shit, I reckon he's been there since Wednesday!"

As he laughed about that with the others, Martin realized he needed a piss, but he couldn't bear the thought of all those stairs. Rather than put himself through all that again, the sheriff stood up and strolled over to the ledge of the roof facing into Liberty. With his back to the militiamen, he unzipped his fly and arced a sparkling yellow stream onto the lawn two stories below. As he was finishing up, he noticed what looked like a line of ants parading south from the desert and down the big road that led into the town center.

"Oh my God," whimpered Alyssa Carey from behind him. She was up and staring into the town, too.

Martin didn't get it. He looked blankly from Carey to the view and back again. She turned to address the rest of the lounging militiamen. "The Red Stripe Gang are here! They've … they've brought an army!"

Beers splattered onto the floor. Yelling war cries, the men and women of Martin's Militia raced to the stairs.

*

Between thick bars of steel, Jack watched Joe Lin's head dip and jerk upright. The situation reminded him of a Looney Tunes cartoon in which Elmer Fudd fell asleep with a big ring of keys around his belt. The imprisoned Bugs Bunny then stretched his arm several feet out of his cage to steal them. Unfortunately for Jack, he didn't have quite the same reach or flexibility as a cartoon rabbit.

He scratched the stubble that had formed on his face after two days of captivity. Sweat darkened the armpits of his checkered short-sleeve button-down, and there was a definite odor emanating from his feet. But there was nowhere in the jail to shower, nor did he have a change of clothes. He was lucky to have a toilet, but even that wasn't private. Lin had come and gone a few times, but Ben Martin had never shown up, and Lin was unwilling to release Jack without the sheriff's permission.

A sharp squeal of static woke the sleeping guard. "Joe! Come in, Joe!"

The static-filled message came from a radio on the desk. Lin bolted toward it and answered, "Ben, is that you?"

Static. Pop! "The Red Stripe Gang is coming! Round up anyone left in town and tell 'em to bring their guns!"

"Roger," said Lin. But as he dropped the radio, he looked at a loss for what to do.

Jack pressed his head against the bars. "Joe, if the Gang is coming, you've got to warn the whole town!"

Lin flashed a worried expression. "The Gang? But that means … I brought them here. It's my fault! Oh God, now I've failed everyone!"

"Listen to me, Joe! You can still help. They used to do atomic bomb tests in the desert not far from here. There should be a switch somewhere upstairs to turn on the —"

"Nuclear evacuation siren!" exclaimed Lin, suddenly emboldened. "And I know how to send wireless alerts to people's phones!"

Jack nodded encouragingly. Funny how he'd forgotten about the modern warning system, which allowed emergency services to send alerts to any wireless device in a designated location. Of course Joe would know that. After all, he'd been a firefighter before this mess had happened.

When Lin was nearly at the stairs, Jack called frantically, "Wait! Before you go, you've got to let me out of here! I have to find my little boy!"

Lin picked up the keys and stared uncertainly at the metal objects clutched between his fingers.

"Please, Joe! Don't make me beg!"

Jack didn't need to. It was clear from the militiaman's drooping shoulders that he would relent. Lin tossed the chain in Jack's direction and ran up the stairs. The keys fell on the floor a couple feet short of the cell, but maybe it was close enough. Heart racing,

Jack fell to his knees and reached through the bars. When he couldn't get it, he howled for Lin to return. All he received in return was the wail of the nuclear evacuation siren, low at first and then rising into a terrible metal scream. Now Lin would never hear him.

Jack's phone beeped from across the jail. That would be the emergency alert. Now he had two warnings to get the hell out of Liberty, yet here he was, trapped in a cage. What would the Red Stripe Gang do when they discovered him down here? He didn't want to know. But what the hell could he do?

Unless …

He lowered himself all the way to the floor and got onto his right side. With the better angle, his arm stretched farther through the bars, and his middle finger touched the edge of one of the keys. Ignoring the sweat pouring down his brow, he dragged the chain toward him.

*

Ben Martin absorbed the panicked faces of oncoming traffic swerving around either side of his Chevy. Many of the vehicles had pieces of furniture strapped to their tops or piled in their flat beds. Martin's black SUV and the other three trucks belonging to his militia seemed to be the only ones traveling into Liberty. He was the farthest back in the line and couldn't see much of the town over the tops of the other trucks, but one thing he did catch was the bell tower on top of town hall catching fire.

"Did you see that?" cried Larry Wilkins, who was riding next to him in the passenger seat. "Oh dear lord!"

There was a break in the traffic and the three trucks in front of him fanned out so that they were side by side and taking up the entire width of road. Ben Martin trailed behind them, creating a formation that looked like the bottom half of a plus sign. There was a Jeep on each wing with a red Ford pickup truck between them. Ben Martin slowed as the others flashed their brake lights.

Now completely stopped, the sheriff couldn't see beyond the trucks to learn what was holding them up. He was thinking more evacuees until Mad May leaned out of the Jeep Wrangler on the left side with a Yossarian in her muscular arms. He could also see Velasquez's hand hanging out the driver window of the Ford with a Breck 17.

"What are they doing?" Martin asked Wilkins. The other man stared blankly, so he got on the radio and asked the question directly. "What are you doing?"

Static. Pop.

"Here they come." said a man's voice. Velasquez, based on the accent.

Martin clicked his radio. "Who?"

"Riders!" The militiaman's voice cut out. "— coming up the road to — there must be at least six —"

A thunderstorm of bullets sprayed into the Ford. In horror, Martin watched the head of Velasquez flop to the side like someone had cut the strings. Mad May returned fire from the left wing, but a bullet clipped her through the exposed frame of the Jeep.

The pop of the passenger door roused Martin from his trance. Wilkins was going to try to make a run for it. The sheriff grabbed his arm, trying to pull him back, but the unnerved militiaman ripped himself free and bolted for the mountains. A cackling Red Striper trailed Wilkins out into the desert, kicking up a storm of dust behind his black motorcycle. The gangster pulled alongside the militiaman, grabbed him by the collar, and dragged him along the ground.

Ben Martin didn't wait for the gunshot. Cranking the steering wheel left and planting his boot on the gas pedal, he forced the SUV into a squealing turn and sped off-road, into the desert. With bullets slapping the back of the truck and the passenger door flapping in the wind, Martin sped away from the gangsters and his fellow militiamen. A couple of motorcycles took chase after him but appeared slowed by the uneven ground. In his rearview mirror, Martin saw the pickup truck explode in a massive fireball that knocked his friends' Jeeps onto their sides.

EXCLUSIVE: THE TRUE IDENTITY OF THE WANDERER!

By Rosa Veras

The Wanderer is Errol Breck, son of Albert Breck, the late founder and CEO of Breck Ammunition.

Errol is Al's oldest son and was in line to take over the company following his father's death. However, when Errol shot his wife during a home invasion, he left Las Vegas to wander the country on a mission of redemption.

Errol told *The New West* that the death of his wife was an accident.

"I didn't mean to kill her," he said. "I really did think there was another intruder. The one in the kitchen had a gun, and so I thought ... but then I saw Helen ... and she was just dead. There wasn't even a chance of getting her to the hospital."

He fled the scene. The police attributed the death of Helen Breck to murder by house burglars and declared Errol missing.

"There was no place for me in Vegas," he said. "I didn't want the gun company. I had to start over."

Leaving behind the life he knew, Errol turned himself into the rogue gunman in the Stetson hat we now know as the Wanderer. In the months following the death of his wife, he has wandered the New West helping others find justice.

Now the Wanderer's journey has brought him back to Vegas. Errol Breck told *The New West* that he intends to take back his father's gun company. He pledged to fix the mistakes made by his stepbrother Gerard and make serious reforms to how Breck Ammunition does business.

"I want to keep guns out of the hands of the Red Stripe Gang and other criminals," he said. "I aim to convince the Board of Breck Ammunition that they should oust my stepbrother and vote me in as the new CEO."

He added, "I don't expect anyone to forgive me for what I've done, but I hope you will support me."

CHAPTER THIRTY-FOUR

You've Still Got a Brother.

Rosa took a deep breath as the article went live. She was sitting next to the Wanderer in a room in the Breck Estate that used to serve as Errol's personal office.

"It's good," he said. "It'll work."

She believed that he approved, but he didn't sound happy. "What's wrong?"

Slowly, the Wanderer removed the Stetson from his head and put it in his lap.

"I've known Gerard since I was twelve," said Errol. "I ... wonder if I could have prevented all this if I'd acted differently to him growing up."

Rosa shook her head. "From what you told me about him before, he's always been a bad seed."

"He never had a father. His real one left when he was little. He wanted my dad to love him, but it never was enough. And then, after the accident —"

"The accident?"

"It was a car accident. He was with his mother. Gerard was driving. Something happened. Gerard went speeding through a red light and a big truck slammed into them. His mother — my dad's second wife, Iris — died instantly. And Dad never really forgave Gerard."

"God," breathed Rosa.

"Can you blame him? Gerard killed his *wife*." The life drained from Errol's face as he added, "I guess I have more in common with my dad than I thought."

She didn't know what to say to that, so she put her arm around his shoulder instead. He turned to her, eyes wide with regret.

"I should've visited Gerard in the hospital or at least have come home for Iris's funeral. It's just … I was in my freshman year of college and was caught up in that whole world. I didn't think I had time to come back. I guess I kept thinking I'd see Gerard on my next visit home, but then Dad sent him away to a boarding school to finish his primary education. I didn't end up seeing him again until we were both done with school and had jobs within Breck Ammo. Even then, it was always business. I married Helen, and got caught up in my life with her. More than fifteen years went by during which I barely saw Gerard at all. I didn't have any time for my screwed-up stepbrother. We didn't really talk again until Dad's funeral. And when we did, I could hear so much resentment in his voice. He knew I was in line to take over the company, and he didn't think I deserved it."

Errol scowled deeply and shook his head. "I should have seen this coming."

Rosa placed a hand gently on his shoulder. "You can't blame yourself for the things Gerard has done, Errol. It doesn't matter how hard his life was. The only destiny you can control is your own."

He picked the Stetson up from his lap, nodded, and put it back on his head. "I should get ready."

Rosa got the feeling he wasn't talking about figuring out what to wear to the board meeting. As he stood up to leave, she said, "Maybe you won't have to fight him. Maybe there's still a chance to have a relationship with him."

In a low rumble, the Wanderer replied, "I reckon it's too late for that."

*

The Breck Estate's largest room was a garage completely devoid of vehicles. Al Breck had used it as a workshop and it was here that he had developed the concepts for many of his guns. The cars he'd kept outside.

After his funeral, however, dust had covered the once grand workshop. Errol had never gotten around to cleaning it up. All the tools were just where his father had left them.

Sitting at a large workbench, the Wanderer flipped open the latches of a beat-up wooden case and peered warmly inside at an array of brushes and rods. The cleaning kit had been a birthday present from his father. To the right, Errol placed glass bottles of Breck No. 12 solvent, Breck lubricating oil, and Brand-X lemon oil. Each was about a quarter full and the labels had begun to peel off. In front of the bottles, the Wanderer's silver Lassiter rested on a worn black pad.

All this time he'd spent blaming himself for Helen's death, and yet it had been Gerard the whole time. Why did his stepbrother hate him so? Why couldn't he ever let him be happy? Gerard had been gunning for him since the day he moved into the mansion with his mother, but this time he'd truly crossed the line.

The Wanderer double-checked the cylinders and barrel for any bullets still inside. Finding none, he dipped a bore brush into the cleaning solvent, then pushed it through the front of the barrel until it came out the back. He pulled it back and repeated the motion several times. Next, he took a cleaning patch from the kit and attached it to a rod. He dipped this into the solvent, feeding it through the barrel, then following it with two dry ones. He repeated this process several times also. When the barrel was clean, he went to work repeating these steps in each of the chambers on the cylinder.

And to think, just yesterday, Gerard had sat right across from him at the table, looked him square in the eyes, and threatened to tell the world that Errol Breck was responsible for Helen's death. The liar!

He took a copper toothbrush and cleaned around the muzzle and the rear cylinder opening of the long-barreled revolver. With another dip of the toothbrush, he went to work brushing the cylinder on the outside and the ends, followed by the extractor rod. He cocked back the hammer and brushed around that area, too.

"I'm going to kill him," he muttered under his breath.

The Wanderer reassembled the gun, picked up a clean cloth, and dripped some of the gun lubricant onto it. With this he wiped the silver exterior of the gun. After drying off the excess oil, he used a Breck-branded silicone gun cloth to polish the steel. Feeling quite calmed by this cleaning of the Lassiter, he drew out the process longer than perhaps was needed. Breathing the lingering smell of solvent in through his nose, the Wanderer smiled with satisfaction.

"I'm going to kill him," he said louder.

Finishing with the steel, he applied lemon oil to another rag and wiped that over the ebony handle, restoring the wood's dark glow. As he rested the gun back on the pad to let it soak in, Errol heard the dancing footsteps of Kid Hunter come into the garage.

"Whoa!" gasped Charlie, spinning to take in the full size of the garage. "You've got a dope setup in here!"

He smiled slightly. "It belonged to my father. Feel free to use it if you need to maintain your gun. Or do you have to send yours back to Canada for reprogramming?"

"Shut up, man. It's a good gun, and Canada ain't so bad, either." He dropped a friendly hand on Errol's shoulder. "Getting ready?"

The Wanderer didn't answer.

"Well, I'll leave you to it, but I just came in here to say … look, I'm not one for flowery speeches, and I know you really ain't one for 'em, either, so I'll try and make this short. I want to thank you for giving me a chance back in Freetown. I know you didn't want to, but you did."

The Wanderer smiled. "I reckon I saw something in you. And I was right. You done good, Kid."

"Thanks man, but I just wish there was some way to pay you back."

"Why don't you pay it forward, instead?"

Charlie nodded. He made to leave, but turned back with a look of embarrassment. "Don't tell Rosa about our little talk, all right?

You know how she is."

"Heh."

"Oh, and just one other thing I wanted to say."

"Say it."

"Gerard is family. He sure ain't good family, but still, it can't be easy for you."

Errol didn't know how to respond, but he nodded to show he was listening.

"Well, I just wanted you to know that no matter what happens with Gerard ... you've still got a brother."

"Thanks, Charlie ... brother." Errol stood up and held out a hand to shake.

Charlie pulled him in for a quick hug and slap on the back, then moseyed over to the door. "All right, bro, I'll leave you to it. I'd better get ready, too."

The Wanderer finished drying the ebony handle of the Lassiter, and then reached down the workbench for the next gun to be cleaned. It was the bad gun, but he knew it could be good again.

*

Gerard breathed loudly through his nostrils as Elza told him about Errol's plan to oust him from the company. When she was finished, he shut his eyes and shifted into a state of frozen introspection. He felt Elza's hand fall on his shoulder, but he shook it off.

"Get me the police," he said in a level baritone. "Now."

The assistant dialed and handed him the phone. Calmly, Gerard explained to the chief of police why Errol Breck needed to be arrested immediately. However, the chief sounded disengaged.

He kept saying, "Uh-huh, uh-huh," without committing to any action.

Gerard was confused. "You are going to arrest him, right?"

"No," said the chief of police.

"What?"

He felt himself tense up as the cop told him that he wouldn't reopen the case on Helen Breck, that he wouldn't take down Errol for what he'd done.

"What is it you want?" he seethed. "Money? More guns?"

"It's over, Gerard," said the chief.

"It's not over!" Breck screamed into the receiver, unable to contain the anger any longer. "I'll take all your guns away! From the entire fucking police force! Then what will you do?"

The chief just laughed. "To be honest, I'm not worried. You're not going to be CEO for long."

Gerard tossed the phone across the room and turned his anger upon Elza. "Why won't they fucking listen to me?"

She was swiping up vertically on the screen of a tablet. "Because America has turned against you," she said with annoying certainty in her voice.

He snatched the device from her. It was a social media feed of mentions by people on the Internet about Breck Ammunition.

CalvinCool:
Gerard Breck is dangerous. No more deals with Red Stripe Gang! #ErrolBreck4CEO

BigFat Stan:
Hahahaha! Jarrard Breck just got screwed by @TheNewWest!

HeartStar911:
Errol, we love you and forgive you!

SpyBoyRoOlz:
The Wanderer should TOTALLY be in charge of Breck Ammo. #ForReal

RhondaSweets:
Breck Ammo better kick out Gerard ASAP. #ErrolBreck4CEO

He staggered. "What … but how did he…?"

"Many of the posts link to an article on *The New West*."

He pressed the link, opening an article with the headline, *Exclusive: The True Identity of the Wanderer!* The story read like his own death sentence. At the end of every paragraph, Gerard muttered, "I'm going to kill him." The statement grew louder and more certain each time he said it.

"Yes," Elza said, drawing closer. "It is the only way."

He smelled hyacinth on Elza's skin, and a strange calm passed over him like a warm blanket. "How long do we have before the board meeting?"

CHAPTER THIRTY-FIVE

The World's Changed.

The parking lot of the police station looked clear, but Jack smelled smoke. In the valleys of the nuclear evacuation siren, he could hear a roar of motorcycles from Main Street a few blocks away. Something from that direction exploded, and the noise of it brought Jack down into a protective crouch.

Gathering his courage, he got up and ran for the back of the parking lot where he'd left his blue Chevy. When he got there, he cried out, "You have got to be kidding me!"

All four of the tires were completely flat. That bastard Martin must have shot them out sometime after locking him up.

Okay, so maybe he could steal something. Not usually a legal thing to do, but this was an emergency. Whirling around, he was surprised to find a police car labeled *Sheriff* parked close to the station. Martin must have taken another vehicle to the mayor's! Jack made a mad dash for the Ford Interceptor and pulled on the door handle. Jack cheered when it responded with a click, but held his nose when he smelled the stench of death inside. Peering into the back, he saw the seats were stained with dried blood. The red stuff had been baking in the sun for who knows how long.

It was repulsive, and now he understood why the sheriff had taken a different vehicle to the mayor's mansion. Jack was about to search for another option when he caught a couple of Red Stripers in his peripheral vision. They were pulling into the lot on motorcycles. He dove back into the car, shutting the door before they saw him. Willing himself to breathe, he searched the glove compartment and both of the sun visors, but couldn't find a key to start the car.

Something sharp in his front pocket was pressing into him, but he ignored the pain and continued to think. In the movies, a person in this situation would usually bust his hand through the dashboard, or maybe go outside and look for some colored wires under the front hood. But he couldn't remember *exactly* what they did to start the car, and a lot of that was probably made up anyway.

As the Red Stripers drew closer, Jack ducked his head down. It still didn't look as though they'd seen him, and suddenly he realized they couldn't because most of the windows were shaded black. To see him, they'd have to actually go around front and look through the windshield. And maybe they would, but it at least gave him more time to find a way to start the car.

"Think, dammit, think!"

The pointy thing in his pocket was still stabbing his leg, so he reached in and pulled everything out. When the key chain from the station came up in his hands, he nearly whooped. Jack flicked through the keys and found one with a Ford logo.

The key slipped neatly into the ignition, but Jack waited to turn the car on. The gangsters had parked their bikes and were now walking casually by the sheriff's car. He held his breath until they reached the top of the stairs to the police station and disappeared inside. Exhaling, he turned the key.

He pulled out of the lot, opening all of the windows for sweet fresh air on the way out. He got on a backroads route to the hospital. He didn't see any Red Stripers, but the road was still jammed with people evacuating town. He was about to unleash a fury of profanity when the driver in front of him stuck his hand out the window and waved him to pass. He couldn't figure it out until he looked around him and realized what kind of car he was in.

With a nod to a figure of Jesus stuck to the dash, Jack flicked on the police siren and lights, then pulled into the oncoming lane. There was no one there. The evacuees were maintaining a ridiculous level of order despite the crisis. Jack pulled up to the guy who'd waved him past and shouted out the window, "Wait a few seconds and then move into this lane. Make sure the other people follow. Everyone will get out a lot faster!"

Soon, Jack had the Ford police car speeding along at more than one hundred miles per hour with a trail of cars not far behind.

*

The town of Liberty shrank into a smoky smudge in Ben Martin's rearview mirror. The Red Stripers had long ago disappeared in the SUV's dusty wake, and the sheriff was sure he had lost them.

He'd barely had a breath when something caught onto the bottom of the Chevy, and the truck started dragging it. When Martin looked into the mirror to see if he could spot it, there were three bloodied corpses hanging off the back. Screaming, the sheriff slammed the brakes.

He turned off the truck, but the engine continued to tick from heat exhaustion. Martin pushed open the door and jumped out.

When he didn't find any bodies behind the truck, he checked underneath and found the prickly arm of a cactus lodged in the undercarriage. Cursing, Martin decided to let the truck cool down for a while before proceeding any farther. He shooed a lizard off of a flat red rock and sat down.

Those beers hadn't done him any good, and now he was thirsty. Oh well, if he could just get to the next town, he'd be all right. He almost got up to look for his Army cap in the truck, but a sudden recollection of the hat soaking up his deputy's blood kept him seated.

A harsh croak turned his attention to a black vulture perched maybe thirty feet away in the brush. The creature had blood on its beak, but whatever it was eating was well hidden by the vegetation. Martin had a raw feeling that it was the corpse of the bank robber whom he and Dougie had left. But that was crazy. That spot was far from here, wasn't it?

He got up to have a look. When he was nearly halfway there, something in the brush reached up and grabbed him. The sharp pain sent a shock wave up his leg and in a flash of white light he thought he saw Father James wearing the disapproving look that was frozen on his face when he died.

"No!" cried Martin.

Stumbling to a clear spot of desert sand, he saw what had bit him was still there — a fuzzy mass of jumping cholla, a tubular cactus in a fur coat of sticky needles. That was a relief anyway. He thought it might have been a rattler. Carefully, he grabbed a dry twig and used it to push the spiny segment off his ankle. When he was done, he glanced back at the vulture and caught its red eyes staring back. Only now the bird's bald head belonged to the mayor.

Martin reached for the Breck 17 in his hip holster and fired, but he missed wide. The bird took off into the sky.

Shaking, Martin returned to the truck with the words of the Wanderer echoing through his head like a curse: "The world's changed, Martin. You keep thinking the way you do, and it'll be your undoing someday."

He was right. Martin had thought himself protector, but what he'd actually done was lay a bloody red carpet into his hometown. Now, Liberty was going to be a Red Stripe town.

And so there it was — the Wanderer had killed him, after all.

No. Martin had killed himself.

Calmly, the sheriff opened the door of the SUV and pulled his Pilgrim off the seat. With his back against the door, he held the barrel of the shotgun firmly against his throat and slipped his thumb through the trigger guard. Gazing skyward, he noticed the familiar dark shape of a vulture circling the sun.

*

A pair of armed guards in black uniforms stopped Jack at the hospital entrance. They were thick-chested men armed with Yossarian assault rifles. Well, that was certainly new. He'd never seen these guys before in his life.

He didn't wait for them to approach. He rolled down a window and shouted, "My son is in there. I need to see him!"

Astonishingly, that seemed to be enough. They waved him through.

"Good luck, officer," one of the guards said as he passed.

Jack smiled. So it wasn't the decency of human beings he had to thank after all. They just thought he was a cop.

Besides the increased presence of security, he was surprised to find the hospital operating normally. There was no evacuation here, seemingly no panic at all. Jack pulled up to the front, parked his car in the drop-off space, and rushed inside. He didn't bother to sign in at reception, just ran straight to the elevator.

When the doors opened, he recognized Pablo's nurse talking to a doctor.

"Mr. Veras!" exclaimed Mary.

"I'm here to take Pablo! I have to get him out of here!"

He tried to rush by her, but she stood in his way. "Slow down. You can't just —"

"The Red Stripe Gang is taking over Liberty. It's not safe for him to be here. It's not safe for any of us to stay! We have to leave immediately!"

A security guard took notice and joined Mary in blocking Jack's path to his son. The guard was a short woman with an angry demeanor. "Sir, you have to calm down right now!"

Mary smiled apologetically for the intrusion. "We're aware of the situation in Liberty, Mr. Veras. But you need to stop and think about what you're doing. Pablo is in no condition to be moved, certainly not without a medical vehicle."

"We've secured the hospital," added the security guard.

"What, you mean those guys standing by the road? You think that's enough to —"

"Yes, them. And we have snipers on the roof. You can be sure this place is now a fortress. The Gang's not getting in here without a fight. And frankly, we don't expect them to try. They wouldn't know what to do with a hospital."

Jack's shoulders drooped as he realized they were right. This was the safest place for Pablo. He was risking his son's life if he tried to move him. But he couldn't abandon his son. Not like Elaine did.

No, there was no choice at all. He would have to stay in Liberty.

Mary seemed to understand without him saying. "I'm afraid we don't have room for guests to stay here, but you can stay with him a little while. Just until things calm down out there."

She looked cautiously to the guard for approval.

"Just until things calm down out there," repeated the guard with a stern look of warning.

Jack nodded gratefully. "Yes, I understand."

The guard plucked a radio from her belt and walked away. Mary stepped aside to let Jack through, but he lingered to say thanks.

"Of course, Mr. Veras."

"It's Jack," he said, holding the nurse's gaze just long enough to make her blush.

Putting on a smile, Jack went to see his boy.

CHAPTER THIRTY-SIX

Make Sure He's Dead.

The view from the Breck skyscraper revealed the true urban madness of Vegas. Here was a city of fools trapped in the barren desert, spitting toward the sun through oversized fountains. Even the boardroom would be a greenhouse if not for the air conditioning being pumped into the room twenty-four hours a day. The glass bubble extended from the edge of the skyscraper where the Wanderer stood to about the midsection of the building. On the other side, there was a large, flat area where a helicopter could land, but today the pad was empty.

The Wanderer looked out over his city, waiting for something to happen. It was high noon, and Gerard was a no-show.

"You might think you have a nice view up there, but I'll tell you what, man," buzzed a voice in his ear, "there are some *fine* ladies out today! Damn fine!"

Irrationally, the Wanderer peered down at the park, as if he thought he might spot Kid Hunter among the dots of colors crawling around the green. He was down there, but by virtue of the Wanderer's eyepiece, he had an eye in the boardroom. It was the Kid's own idea, and the Wanderer agreed it was safer than having him up here, just in case Gerard were to try something. He trusted that Kid Hunter was an expert enough hacker to help him from far away if he needed it. But this was a dispute between stepbrothers, and the Wanderer hoped to keep it that way.

"I thought you had a lady now," the Wanderer whispered so the board members wouldn't hear him talking.

The Kid laughed. "Doesn't mean I can't look. Wait, does it?"

The Wanderer gazed from face to face around the room. The board members did not appear bothered by his stepbrother's tardiness. Corny Boone was demonstrating his golf stance to Anil Kumar, while Sally Gomes played a game on her phone, and Joe Watts snoozed peacefully in his chair. The Wanderer circled the table until he was clear on the other side of the boardroom, looking out at the helipad. Gerard was nearly fifteen minutes late, now. Where was he?

"In any case," continued Charlie, "I don't think that particular relationship is going to work out."

A sudden high-pitched smash whirled the Wanderer around on the balls of his feet. A rainstorm of broken glass filled his vision while the chug of a distant automatic weapon boxed his ears. He ducked under the table at the same moment as the glass wall behind him fell away. Then the ceiling shattered and came down, too. The Wanderer shielded his face with his Stetson, but a few broken shards bounced off the floor and stuck painfully into the legs of his jeans.

Everything went quiet. While reaching to remove one of the glass daggers, he spied Corny and Kumar lying dead on the floor. With the fallen glass, it looked as though they were covered in ice.

He could also see the legs of Gomes and Watts — they were still sitting in their chairs.

Kid Hunter yelled, "Wanderer! You all right? What happened?"

Errol crawled carefully out from under the table, making sure he didn't cut his hands. Lifting his head just inches over the table, he peeked in the direction of the gunfire, half-expecting to see Gerard with a Yossarian. Instead, he saw Gomes holding her phone but missing her head. A few seats away, Watts seemed to maintain a peaceful slumber, only now he was frosted with glass and riddled with bullets.

"Incoming!" screamed Kid Hunter.

The Wanderer ducked as more bullets flew over his head. "Where? Did you see the shooter?"

"Didn't you see the helicopter? Must be a Montag to shoot at that distance, though there'd have to be about fifteen of them to get that many shots in!"

"It's not a Montag," said the Wanderer, grimacing in realization. He leaped into a forward roll as the next barrage of bullets cut the heavy wood table in half.

*

Kid Hunter put down the screen showing the Wanderer's point of view and began typing frantically on another tablet. A crowd of people had assembled not far from his park bench, but they were too busy bending their necks back to pay him much attention. They'd been coming ever since glass started raining down from the black, clip-shaped skyscraper.

"Too far away," the Wanderer huffed in his ear. "I'll never reach him with either of my guns."

"I'm on it, I'm on it!" shouted Kid Hunter. "Just shut up a second and be safe!"

The thumping chopper increased gradually in volume.

"He's circling around now," reported the Wanderer. "Still too far for me to get a shot."

Kid Hunter whooped as a wireframe image of the helicopter popped onto his screen.

"What happened?"

He grinned. "Sit tight, Wandy. I got this bastard."

*

The green crosshair seemed almost to move on its own as Gerard scanned the broken boardroom through the sights of his Breck 100X. Saliva dribbled down his chin as the automatic rifle throbbed, ready to fire another 160 rounds in less than ten seconds.

Just as he was about to squeeze the trigger, the helicopter swiveled, and the gun pulsed to signify he had moved off-target. Annoyed, Gerard took aim again but felt suddenly off-balance. Lifting his eye from the long-range sight, he noticed the city streets slowly filling up the view out the open door of the aircraft. With sudden panic, he lunged for one of the safety bars to keep from falling, which made him lose hold of the super-gun. Gerard watched, horrified, as gravity dragged the Breck 100X out the open door. The helicopter righted itself the instant after the gun fell.

Gerard stormed toward the cockpit. Into the mic of his headset, he screamed at the pilot, "What the fuck do you think you doing?"

Spinning around in his chair, the Breck employee stammered, "I d-didn't do anything! It's m-moving on its own! I don't have c-control!"

"How is that possible?"

"I don't know! Someone must have hacked into it. But our security —"

"Kid Hunter." Gerard sighed heavily. "Well, I lost my gun. So give me yours."

Nodding more times than seemed necessary, the pilot took a Breck 17 from his shoulder holster and held it out.

Flipping the gun into his right hand, Gerard said, "You know, I guess if someone else is flying this chopper, I don't need you anymore."

He fired into the pilot's chest, then took a few steps back as the dying man fell forward from his chair. There was a satisfying static pop in his ears as the microphone piece of his headset slammed into the floor.

Gerard felt a little better after that and moseyed back into the passenger area to sit down. Whipping out his phone, Gerard tapped out a quick message to Elza.

Going to be home late. Don't wait up.

*

The Wanderer felt a hot breeze against his face as he followed the path of the helicopter. With the boardroom reduced to broken concrete, splintered wood and jagged glass teeth, he'd moved onto the relatively clean helipad to stand waiting.

"Sure this is what you want?" asked Kid Hunter.

"It is."

"Bringing him to you now."

The Wanderer added, "Do me a favor and don't land on me."

The Kid laughed. "Don't worry, I know just where to drop that bastard."

The Wanderer held his hands up by his two hip holsters and shook out his hands. The helicopter flew straight toward him, turning sideways when it reached the opposite side of the roof. Through the aircraft's open doorway, he could see his stepbrother sitting passively. To the Wanderer's amusement, he appeared to be wearing a three-piece suit. Gerard always was a flashy dresser.

Gerard tore off his headset and stepped cautiously to the edge of the helicopter. He held up his hands and shouted something, but Errol couldn't make out a word with the helicopter still going. Figuring it was something about not shooting until he got down, the Wanderer lifted up his hands to show he wouldn't shoot. In the end, the exchange of signs didn't matter. The helicopter tipped, dumping Gerard into the rubble.

Kid Hunter cackled over the radio.

"Heh," replied the Wanderer. "Now send it away."

"Roger that!"

The helicopter floated off the roof, descending out of sight. While Gerard struggled to his feet, the sun hid behind the clouds and the day turned dark. A gust of wind sent a piece of loose insulation rolling through the wide space in between them.

When Gerard had closed the gap enough for conversation, the

Wanderer said, "I tried to do this the right way, you know."

"The right way?" repeated Gerard in disbelief. "You mean going behind my back to curry favor with the board?"

The Wanderer scanned Gerard with his eyeglass, detecting a Breck 17 in the pocket of his suit jacket. "It was the only option you left me."

Gerard mimicked Errol, slurring the sentence in the whiny voice of a child. "It-was-the-only-option-you-left-me!" He leveled his tone to its usual calm baritone. "You've never treated me with any respect, Errol. You're worse than Dad."

The Wanderer ignored him. "You're a murderer, Gerard. You just killed four good people."

"I'm sorry?" Gerard asked incredulously. "Are we talking about those asshats on the board?"

"And they're not the first ones. You killed O'Brien to steal his gun design. You tried to kill Rosie because of a few articles she wrote. You actually made a deal with the Red Stripe Gang to wipe out the competition! And you know what else I found out recently? You —"

"Would you shut up already? You are so *boring* when you string more than two sentences together. If you're asking me to duel, I accept! It will be just like old times. With the Super Soakers, remember?"

An image returned to Errol of the play fights around the pool. When things inevitably turned sour, his stepmother Iris would get Dad to pull the brothers apart. Dad would always take Errol's side while Iris took her son's.

"Gerard ... before we do this ... I want you to know that I'm sorry I didn't come home when your mom died. I know you didn't mean to kill her."

"You're sorry?" All of the humor went out of Gerard's face. "No, Errol, I'm sorry. It's … it's too late for you to be my brother."

The sun burst through the clouds behind Gerard. In the sudden flash of light, Errol shielded his eyes with his dominant left hand. Gerard reached into his coat.

The Wanderer's right hand fell to the bad gun, the Breck 17.

*

On the tablet screen, Kid Hunter watched Errol and Gerard Breck line up their shots. He heard two shots, and then the view through the Wanderer's eyeglass jerked violently and fell to the ground.

"Errol!" he screamed, not caring if anyone in the surrounding crowd heard him.

The brutal clouds mocked Charlie through the digital view. He could not see the Wanderer; only what the Wanderer was looking at. He couldn't tell if he was still alive.

A familiar cowboy hat dipped into view and Charlie saw the Wanderer peering down at him. There was a deep cut in his right cheek where a bullet had scraped off a chunk of flesh. The impact must have knocked the lens off the Wanderer's face.

"Dude!" cried Charlie. "You nearly gave me a heart attack!"

"I'm all right, Kid."

"Did you get him?"

A hand reached down and scooped up the image, returning it to its former location six feet above the ground. Squinting at the picture, Charlie could just make out the fallen body of a man in a nice suit.

*

The Wanderer wrapped a white handkerchief around the lower part of his face to contain the bleeding. He directed the Kid, "Find someone to clean up this mess, would you?"

"All right, but do me a favor?" Kid Hunter paused on the other end of the line. "Make sure he's dead."

The Wanderer tapped the side of the lens to switch off communications, and walked toward the still body of his stepbrother. He wanted to be alone for this next part.

Kneeling down to inspect the body, he discovered that his shot from his Breck 17 had clipped Gerard cleanly through the chest, turning his crisp white shirt crimson beneath the black vest and suit jacket. He was still holding a pistol in his right hand. The Wanderer kicked it away, but turned back sharply when he heard a moan.

"Errol …" Gerard's cough sounded thick with blood. "I see you weren't playing."

The Wanderer crouched over his stepbrother and stared into his laughing eyes. "I ain't been playing since you killed Helen."

Gerard looked puzzled. ". . . Helen?"

"I know you put a hit on me that night. You wanted me dead, but Helen got caught in the crossfire."

"No, I …"

Now Errol was mad. "So you're going to continue to lie until the bitter end? Is that how it's going to be?"

On that question, Gerard thought a bit too hard for the Wanderer's liking. "What? What is it?"

"It was …" With a sharp exhalation of breath, he gasped, ". . .

hell ..." Then his head drooped sideways.

Finding no pulse, Errol got up and strode numbly to the edge of the building. He was still carrying the Breck 17. Now he paused to study the plastic semiautomatic. The bad gun. Even if his stepbrother was responsible for sending a hit man to Errol's house, he still wasn't the one who had pulled the trigger on Helen.

A GUN TO KEEP US SAFE

An editorial by Rosa Veras

Sometimes it feels like America is spinning in an opposite direction from the planet Earth.

Gun control laws, including everything from limits to outright bans, are present in every other civilized country in the world. They have been for years, and the data shows these places have far fewer gun deaths. Leaders of these countries look at America and are aghast, not only at the high death rate, but at our unwillingness to do anything about it.

No matter. In America, we don't care what the rest of the world thinks.

The Born-Again Patriots asked for our isolation. America was tired of foreign products. So we shut down international trade and made guns for ourselves alone. America was tired of diplomacy and fighting other country's wars. So we called back our diplomats and gave our troops' weapons to the American public.

Now America is a self-made island that thinks itself safe from the outside world. But what about the rot from within? What about the Red Stripe Gang and other gun-toting psychopaths who continue to do harm and kill our loved ones?

"Don't worry!" Albert Breck told us. "Here's a gun to keep you safe."

For so long, we have fought fire with fire. But change could be on the horizon. There is a new king of guns in America. Errol Breck — the man who fought injustice as the Wanderer — is not his father, and he is definitely not his stepbrother. It may be too late for the government to reduce gun violence in this country, but perhaps there are still actions that can be taken by the gun monopoly. It will be up to Errol Breck to take them when he sits down in his Vegas throne room.

Will he? *The New West* will watch closely.

CHAPTER THIRTY-SEVEN

Battle Scars.

Peering into the mirror, Errol snapped an eyeglass into place above the bandage on his right cheek. The doctor had stitched up the wound, and it didn't hurt much anymore, but he knew the damage to his face would remain long after he healed. It would forever be a reminder of all the ugliness that had defined the Breck family.

He adjusted a white Stetson atop his head. His face was freshly shaved, and he had on a clean blue shirt with rhinestone snaps. He picked up his Lassiter from the dresser but hesitated to slip it into the holster, considering the gun like a favorite shirt that no longer fit. He opened the cylinder and dropped the silver revolver's six bullets into the palm of his right hand, then gently tucked gun and ammo into the top drawer.

José met him on the front drive and pulled open the door of the Breck family limousine. A bouquet of yellow wildflowers waited expectantly on the backseat. Helen's favorite.

*

The streets of Vegas didn't look much different from when

Charlie was just a kid on the wrong side of the tracks. He kept his wits about him as he meandered through his old neighborhood, passing a pawn shop offering cash for gold, a store offering cash for checks, and a Dollar Express offering junk for cash. He lingered by a condemned casino themed after the circus, remembering the bad years when he had to live inside those striped walls with his family. It wasn't so bad, actually. Derelict, maybe, but at least they had shelter. Startling at the peeling white face of a clown, painted on what used to be the grand entrance, Charlie hurried onward.

A tall, gaunt man on the other side of the street stared. Charlie recognized him as a skilled grifter from his childhood. He was a lot older now, but he used to be a master at conning wealthy folk into giving him money. The problem was that he was even better at losing money. Charlie shouted hello, but the grifter just kept staring, showing no sign that he remembered him.

Turning down a familiar alley, he saw a burned heap of a newspaper and other trash, the remnants of a campfire. It smelled of piss. Not far ahead, a group of children played beneath the dusty black stairs of a fire escape. They watched him closely as he approached. One, a small boy of about eight years old, saw Kid Hunter's wristband and pointed.

"How much for that?" the boy asked.

"It's not for sale," Charlie replied.

A girl who looked the oldest of the group stepped forward with a Breck 17 in her hand. "Then give it to us."

She reminded him a little of Lindsay, and a little of his sister, Jane, too. He used to be part of a gang just like this, sticking up strangers and taking their possessions. It was how you survived here. Kid Hunter laughed as he suddenly recognized her as the cute little girl on his block who liked to draw pictures of pop singers and movie stars. He remembered when she was just a baby.

"Hey there, Mona," he said, "what's Teresa gonna say when she finds out you shot me and stole my favorite wristband?"

Surprised by the mention of her mama, the girl lowered her gun. "Who are you?"

"They call me Kid Hunter. I used to live around here."

The eyes of the little boy who first accosted him lit up like Christmas. "You're Kid Hunter? Like, Kid Hunter and the Wanderer?"

He grinned, particularly pleased at the order of the names. "You got that right, my man."

"Kid Hunter … *here*?" another boy about the same age exclaimed.

With a grand bow, the Kid responded, "At your service, ladies and gentlemen."

"Charlie," said Mona, smiling as a memory clicked into place. "Here to visit your sis?"

He said yes, but then again, maybe a visit would be too short. These were good kids, these dreamers and survivors, who happened to have been brought up in poverty to a violent life. Like Lindsay, like Jane, and like him. But maybe it didn't have to be this way. Maybe he could give them a second chance, like the Wanderer gave him. Errol hadn't wanted Charlie's thanks; he'd just wanted him to pay it forward.

"What's with your arm?"

Kid Hunter followed the end of her small index finger to his own bulging T-shirt sleeve. "Aw, you know, that's just muscle, girl."

Mona raised her eyebrows. "Just working out on one side these days?"

He laughed and pulled the sleeve up so she could see the blood-stained bandages beneath. "Battle scars."

The arm still felt a little sore when he moved it, but the wound was healing up nicely.

"Charlie!" cried a familiar voice from a window up above. It was Jane, looking like a real grown-up. "You gonna stay down there all day and play games with the little ones?"

He addressed the kids like little soldiers. "Well, men, women, I'm afraid Kid Hunter's got to run. But don't worry, I'll be around!" He grinned. "Maybe I'll teach you a thing or two about how to be awesome."

*

THE NEW WEST, proclaimed the website header in big block letters. Rosa smiled warmly at the blank document on the screen. It felt good to be back at the keyboard, on her own terms, in her own place, with no one telling her what she could or couldn't write. She had no regrets about turning down Errol's offer to be the editor-in-chief of Our Times. It had been tempting, but she knew she would never feel independent if she had to rely on the money of Breck Ammunition. It didn't matter who was running the company.

Rosa jumped when something smacked against the other side of the wall. It was followed by a muffled argument between a man and woman. Rosa pulled on her headphones to play some music.

So this wasn't exactly her own place. It was a motel about twenty miles outside the hubbub of Vegas. The walls were paper thin, and this was hardly the first time she'd been interrupted by her neighbors. She couldn't decide if she preferred them fighting or having bombastic sex.

Rosa's phone flashed with a message from Jack. It was a picture of the Church of Santa Maria with one key difference: there was a massive Red Stripe flag hanging on the flagpole between the two bell towers. It was still difficult to believe — Liberty, a Red Stripe town. But the craziest thing was that Jack planned to stay there. She couldn't persuade him otherwise. There was just no arguing that he shouldn't stay close to his boy. He made his case as Jackson Veras, star attorney. Well, she could never win against *that* Jack.

The picture was a reminder that she couldn't go home. But she knew she couldn't stay with Errol, either. She was a vagrant. Perhaps this was just how the life of a *New West* journalist was lived. She'd figure something out, but first she needed to write another article or two about Errol taking control of Breck Ammunition. She had interviewed him yesterday before hitting the road. She already knew her lead would be about how he planned to cancel the commercial release of the Breck 100X. It was a baby step, but it was important. It showed that under Errol Breck, America's favorite gun company might just have a conscience.

The journalist sifted through a pile of records on Gerard's activities during his short tenure as CEO. It wasn't hard to convince Errol to give them to her; she just had to explain how it would show why his stepbrother was unfit to lead. One document caught her eye immediately — Gerard's last will and testament. The bastard didn't seem to have a friend in the world, let alone an heir, so she wondered what would happen to all his wealth.

Finding the relevant section, Rosa gasped when she saw who stood to inherit everything. "Elza?" A few seconds later, the reporter added to the outburst, "*Wife?*"

She buried her head in her hands and began to think. If Elza was married to Gerard, why had she slept with Charlie? No, first, when did Elza marry Gerard?

She checked through the documents and found a form with the couple's hasty signatures. Gerard and Elza had married not long after Errol had left Vegas, and they'd done it at a small, local chapel known for officiating impulse marriages.

It was suspicious, but then again, Elza didn't kill Gerard. So unless she *knew* he was going to die, she couldn't have ... wait! Maybe that was why she went to Charlie. It was from Elza that the Kid learned Gerard was responsible for the death of Helen Breck. When he passed that information on to the Wanderer, it made Errol want to kill his stepbrother. Then, Elza told Gerard about Errol's plan to oust Gerard, which, in turn, had made Gerard show up to the board meeting with guns blazing.

Rosa stared out the window without seeing what was on the other side. What was she saying? Elza slept with Charlie just so she could set up a duel between Errol and Gerard? So that she could get Gerard's money? That sounded way more complicated than it needed to be.

She typed out all these thoughts in an attempt to pull them together into one cohesive timeline, then sat back and read over everything, digesting the information. Something still wasn't clicking. If it was just Gerard's money that Elza wanted, why had she stood by while he spent absurd amounts of money building the Breck 100X and making deals with the Red Stripe Gang? Why had she let him tear the business apart from the inside? It was almost like … she wanted him to.

Rosa snapped to the screen and began searching for information on Elza Meller. But she couldn't find anything on her before her time leading communications for Breck Ammunition. Well, of course there wasn't anything. Elza had probably made up her name, just like when she had told Charlie her name was …

On a whim, the reporter searched for:

Miranda Meller AND guns.

The browser spit back:

Do you mean, Miranda Zeller?

Heart pounding, Rosa went along with the suggestion.

She gasped at the results. Miranda Zeller was a direct descendant of the owner of what used to be the world's top gun company. The European company had been the world's leading gun manufacturer until Breck Ammunition pushed it out of the world's biggest gun market — America.

So it was revenge. Elza wanted Gerard to ruin Breck Ammunition. Things got tricky when Errol came back to save the company, so Elza set up a situation where the stepbrothers would want to kill each other. It would have been easier for Elza if Gerard had won the duel. Things would have gone back to normal; Gerard would have gone back to destroying the business. But the Wanderer had prevailed.

That meant Elza had only one move left.

Biting her lip, the reporter snatched up her phone and dialed Errol. She had to warn him before it was too late.

The call went straight to voicemail.

*

Gravel crunched gently underfoot as Errol trod through the cemetery. The grass looked unnatural among all this death, growing green on a great hill in the middle of an arid desert. Technically, he was still in Vegas, but one had to drive far to rest in peace. He had been here before to bury his father. Once was enough, or so he had reckoned.

He knew the way to Helen's grave almost instinctively. Even though he'd never come to see her in person, he had practiced this walk a million times in his mind. The marble monolith floating into view looked different than he had imagined — not as big, not as bright. Holding the yellow bouquet tightly, he read the epitaph:

Here lies Helen Breck,
beloved wife, treasured daughter.
Violence took her life,
but now in death, peace will find her.

Gently, Errol laid the flowers on his wife's grave.

As he stood up again, the Wanderer's eyeglass lit up in warning.

"Hello, Elza," he said without turning around. The vision in the glass wavered to display the view behind him.

In the glass, he saw her stop short, apparently taken aback by his notice. She wore a tight black dress and tall black boots, and carried a Breck 17 semiautomatic. "How … ?"

"I've got the Kid with me, and he's got you in the sights of his Montag. Personally, I'm unarmed, so why don't you throw that gun of yours over to me, and we can talk like civilized folk?"

She didn't move. Errol turned around to face her, making sure not to make any sudden movements. She looked uncertain, shaken up. He glanced up at the trees over her shoulder and said, "Kid —"

"Wait!" she cried. She pressed a button on the hand grip to eject the magazine, and threw the gun at his feet.

He picked it up for inspection. "I know about your marriage to Gerard. You think that if you kill me, you'll inherit the company."

Elza sneered. "Not at all! I've *never* wanted to own Breck Ammunition."

"But …" he stammered. "Then why … ?"

"All I've ever wanted, Errol, is to ruin the Brecks' business. Just like your father ruined *ours*."

His eyes widened as he made the connection. "Your accent …"

She smiled coldly, but Errol's thoughts had already moved elsewhere. Gerard's last words, denying any involvement in Helen's death, rang chillingly in his ears: "It was …"

"… Elza," Errol finished. He stared her hard in the eyes. "You claimed that Gerard sent the hit man to my house. But it was *you* who sent them."

"Gerard was a terrible businessman, and I knew I could control him. So I put him in a position to take over the company. Your wife's death was … a mistake … but I could not complain about the results."

He gritted his teeth. "Until I came back."

She shrugged. "It does not matter. Gerard wasted a fortune on the Breck 100X, and now he is dead. The board is dead. Do you not see, Errol? You are the last Breck, and your company is broken, hanging by a thread."

"I'll fix it."

She crossed her arms in defiance. Looking off to the side and speaking flatly, she said, "And you will begin by asking your partner to shoot me?"

He narrowed his eyes. "No. You're going to take the next train out of Vegas, just like I did. Only — and you listen good to this — you will *never* come back here."

A smirk turned into an absentminded chuckle as Elza searched the trees. "Kid Hunter, he is not even really here, yes? You are unarmed, and you have no backup. You bluffed to get me to drop the gun."

Errol didn't respond, just kept his grim expression as she leaned over and reached into one of her boots. Naturally, she had another gun attached to her ankle, this one a small, snub-nosed Zeller revolver. She leveled it at his chest. "You see, Errol? I am calling your bluff. I get to finish the job, after all. I get to finish the Brecks!"

Errol raised the semiautomatic in response.

It was the gun that she had given up just a minute before, and she looked at him like he'd lost his marbles. "That gun's empty! Did you not see me —?"

He fired and Elza's gun hand exploded in crimson. Screaming, she dropped the Zeller and fell to one knee. Sprinting over, the Wanderer scooped up the little pistol and stacked it between his palms on top of the Breck 17.

"You forgot to check if there was still a round in the chamber after you ejected the magazine," he declared over the woman's wounded cries. "There was."

She moaned, clutching her wounded hand tenderly. "Why not shoot me dead?"

"Heh," he laughed, pausing momentarily to look back at the monument for his wife. "The truth is, I don't blame you for Helen. I want to. Hell, I want to blame anyone or any*thing* for what happened. But I've come to understand that it's on me. There's nothing I can do, nor no one I can shoot, that's going to change the fact that *I* fired the gun that killed my wife."

A cool breeze burst forth from the monument, rustling the fresh grass around the tombstones. The wind carried the gunman away from a whimpering Elza, through black iron gates to a skyline view of the city at the dead heart of the New West.

Errol Breck understood where he needed to be. It was time, at long last, for the Wanderer to come home.

* * *

About the Author

Adam Bender is an award-winning journalist and author of speculative fiction that explores modern-day societal fears with a mix of action and romance.

In addition to *The Wanderer and the New West*, Adam is the author of two dystopian sci-fi novels about government surveillance: *We, The Watched* and *Divided We Fall*. Adam adapted the first book into a screenplay and has written several short stories.

In his day job as a journalist, Adam has covered politics and technology for Communications Daily and Computerworld Australia. He has won multiple investigative reporting awards from the Society of Professional Journalists and the Specialized Information Publishers Association for his telecom and internet news coverage.

Despite how this all might appear, Adam is generally a rather modest and amiable fellow. He lives in Philadelphia with his wife Mallika, and he'd be happy to have a craft beer with you at the next Phillies game. Check out Adam's blog at WatchAdam. blog and follow him on Twitter (@WatchAdam), Facebook (facebook.com/wethewatched) and Goodreads.

WE, THE WATCHED:
A novel by Adam Bender

Break through the government propaganda and avoid surveillance cameras in the novel acclaimed by *Kirkus Reviews* as "a page-turner of the highest order" and a "deeply allegorical and powerfully thought-provoking dystopian must-read."

Told from the first-person perspective of an amnesiac, *We, The Watched* places the reader in the shoes of Seven as he struggles to go unnoticed in a surveillance society.

Seven enters a dystopia where the government conducts mass surveillance and keeps a Watched list of its own citizens. The Church has become as powerful as the State, and people who resist are called Heretics and face execution. Seven's amnesia gives him a blank-slate perspective that helps him see through the propaganda, and he soon gets involved with a group of rebels called the Underground. But this same perceptive power could get him into trouble with the government police force known as the Guard.

For more information, visit the official website at *WeTheWatched.com*.

DIVIDED WE FALL:
A novel by Adam Bender

The war has come home. The mission has failed. Agent Eve Parker just wants Jon back.

Eve must arrest her fiancé after he loses his memory and becomes a revolutionary named Seven in a fight against the government. However, when she learns more about the President's plan to broaden citizen surveillance, she begins to question just who is right.

Divided We Fall, a sequel to *We, The Watched*, takes place in a dystopia where the government conducts mass surveillance and keeps a Watched list of its own citizens. The Church has become as powerful as the State, and people who resist are called Heretics and face execution.

"Bender's sequel is a worthy delivery on the promise of his riveting debut," said *Kirkus Reviews*. A novel about a scheming president offers an excellent read for those who love thrillers or 21st-century history."

The critically acclaimed novel was a *Library Journal SELF-e* selection. Amazon and *Publishers Weekly* honored the manuscript as a quarter-finalist in the *Amazon Breakthrough Novel Awards*.